Agnes Limerick,

Free and Independent

JAMES McKEAN WOOD

ISBN 978-0-9896724-1-2

www.agneslimerick.com

This novel is a work of creative fiction. With the exception of noted historical figures and places, any resemblance of the dramatized characters to individuals, living or deceased, is coincidental.

Published by Middle River Press

Oakland Park, Florida

middleriverpress.com

First Printing—Printed in the USA

Agnes Limerick,
Free and Independent

JAMES MCKEAN WOOD

2013

MIDDLE
RIVER
PRESS

TO R. F. Z.

AND GREAT TEACHERS EVERYWHERE ...

1

AGNES JUST COULDN'T MAKE UP HER MIND. Yes, she loved Beethoven's piano sonatas, but didn't feel up to the efficient *Waldstein* or the untamed *Appassionata*. Not today, the worst Thanksgiving since—since that year. So she settled on *Les Adieux*, the final sonata Mr. Larney had taught her.

She put her fingers to the worn-smooth ivories of Granny's Steinway and felt the usual vibrations as the keys met the hammers and the hammers met the strings. Fingers, keys, hammers, and strings—the magic quartet. Beethoven's lilting tones warmed her ears and echoed off the dark-paneled walls in Mama's parlor. The tangy sweetness of her mother's simmering cranberries made its way to Agnes's nostrils. So how could Mama not forget, with such beauty as Beethoven and chutney, what a horrible delinquent she'd been—

The sound of crashing crystal jolted the piano's reverie. It sounded like the collapse of a Philadelphia greenhouse. And then she heard Mama, followed by Granny.

"Mary, Mother of God!"

"Horse manure!"

Agnes darted into the kitchen, and once her eyes adjusted to the brightness—walls, cabinets, and tiled floors, all white—she saw what had happened. Mama stood in front of the sink, a round mass of distress surrounded by a jagged maze of broken crystal. Granny sat at the corner table, her face as flaming as her hair.

"Oh, poo," Granny said, her high cheekbones as prominent as the Irish brogue that spiked her words even after sixty years in America. "Your mother slipped and the Waterford vegetable bowl went kaput. Go fetch the broom, princess. Siobhan, stay where you are."

"Not Daddy's Waterford," Agnes moaned. They'd been saving that oval bowl for when she got married. But life was falling apart, and it might be years until she found someone she actually wanted to marry.

"Saints preserve us, this holiday has my hands tied in knots," Mama said, turning her head around, her eyes like wet glass and her lower lip trembling. "No different than when the influenza took your father twelve years ago today."

Agnes sighed. She'd known Mama would mention it. No matter that Granny had decreed, "No morbid talk, Siobhan. It will ruin the appetite."

Agnes grabbed the broom in the pantry but averted her eyes from the empty shelves as she swept. What a meager dinner: a scrawny runt of a turkey in the oven an hour, a vegetable casserole, a pot of potatoes, Mama's chutney. Four dishes when in years past it had been countless bowls of piping hot vegetables, generous platters of turkey, abundant vegetable garnishes, mashed potatoes, sweet potatoes, even oyster stuffing. And today they'd count only Patrick and Uncle Collin as guests rather than the multitudes of Dohertys and Limericks who'd always come. Not even Aunt Lucy, who'd remain at St. Monica's praying with the nuns. Yes, 1930 was limping to an excruciating end.

As if reading Agnes's mind, Mama began to cry. Her mother's soft tears stirred even quieter rumblings in the back of Agnes's throat, but she didn't want to cry, at least not on Thanksgiving.

"Mama, please," Agnes said. "It's only glass. We've got other bowls."

"We can't afford to replace it. And all this work to prepare an elegant meal ..."

"I'm sorry. This wouldn't have happened if I'd been in here helping."

"Twaddle," Granny said. "Don't blame your pretty red head about the crystal. After you clean up, go back to the parlor and play some more piano."

"But not that music," Mama said, drying her eyes, "as sad as waving good-bye to an empty train."

"Don't pout, Siobhan," Granny said. "With your cheeks, it makes you look like a chipmunk."

Les Adieux did indeed play as a sad good-bye, and they hardly needed more of those. After fifty-six thriving years in Philadelphia, Limerick's Bricklayers had closed its doors six months ago when Uncle Daniel defaulted on loans he took before the crash. He jumped out the window a week later and broke his neck. They told the bishop he fell, so Uncle Collin was permitted to read a Catholic funeral Mass for him.

Thank heavens for the piano. Their red-bricked manse at 6th and Pine Streets seemed covered in a gloom heavier than Mama's red-velvet draperies, a gloom not even Granny's staccato belches could pierce—nor the furor over Agnes's latest brouhaha. But they'd all agreed to put hostilities aside for Thanksgiving.

"The music's sad only at the beginning, Mama," Agnes said. "It brightens up as soon as I get beyond the introduction."

"Never mind the piano. I need your help in here. Let me remind you, missy, Uncle Collin hasn't forgotten about your thoughtless behavior. He'll be talking to you after dinner about the secretary's job at St. Monica's —"

Racer barreled into the kitchen. "No, Siobhan," Granny said, "Agnes must walk the dog. Otherwise, we'll have a golden retriever with bloody paws. Do you want that on your oak floors? Siobhan, finish up dinner yourself."

Agnes's heart contracted from remembering when Racer had cut his puppy paws years ago on a vase of Daddy's that klutzy she had broken. After they'd rushed the dog to the veterinarian, her brother had laughed it off, saying no harm had been done. The recollection made Agnes clench her jaw, but she breathed deeply and relaxed her face.

"Mama, when does Uncle Collin meet Patrick's train?"

"Two-thirty. And shall I be asking your grandmother to help with dinner, an old woman who just buried her second son?" Mama made a sign of the cross. "Poor Daniel, gone to join my Martin in the graveyard."

Granny's mouth popped wide open, and her eyebrows rushed together. No wonder. Granny would rather swallow ink than hear anyone call her an old woman, especially her daughter-in-law.

"If there's any old woman in this room, Siobhan Limerick, it is you," Granny said. "Mind you, don't be talking about the dead today. Let there be no question of it, it's a festive Thanksgiving we're to be having. It's what you do in this world, keep trudging along, is what I say. You do what you have to do … And pumpkin, you've got to walk Racer. Now, young lady."

Agnes glanced in the hallway mirror — yes, pretty enough for twenty. She buttoned her tartan plaid tweed coat. She squeezed her hands into gloves, along with her "killer thumbs" as Mr. Larney called them. But they weren't really that large, at least compared to her monster hands. Maybe she'd even out one day and become as stout as Mama, but without her apple cheeks. Yes, she'd gotten Mama's circle mouth, but her high cheekbones had come straight from Daddy.

Forty degrees and sunny greeted her and Racer as they trotted down the broad steps onto Old City's sidewalk. She squinted in the glare. She wouldn't have cover from the oaks and elms whose golden leaves had fallen weeks ago, but she didn't want to go back for a hat. Besides, she liked the cold air on her face, and her alabaster skin wouldn't burn or freckle in fall's sun.

They reached Washington Square and Agnes felt the vast emptiness of the approaching winter. The square's trees had lost their leaves, so she could see all the way to Independence Hall. Racer spotted a squirrel munching acorns on the ground, and he galloped ahead as the squirrel darted up a tree. Agnes nearly lost her balance. Why'd she worn her best shoes? There was no money for new ones. But as always, she'd wanted to wear her best for Uncle Collin. Her heart ached at how she'd disappointed him. He'd surely box her ears at dinner.

No traffic stopped her when she crossed Broad Street, looking up toward City Hall and William Penn's statue, and down toward the Bellevue-Stratford, the Academy of Music, and South Philadelphia, never more sparkling. An old man sat on the stoop of the white-marbled Girard Bank, his yellow toenails poking out from shoes matching a corduroy jacket pockmarked with thistles. His fedora sat face up on the sidewalk with a variety of shiny seashells inside. Brown circles and purple veins framed his eyes. He gestured to Agnes, please buy.

She didn't have even a few pennies, so she averted her eyes and picked up the pace. But her curious dog lagged behind.

"Don't dawdle, Racer."

Agnes knew she'd have to get some kind of work, but what? The prospect of working in a rectory bored her, and her family knew she wanted something different. So why'd they act as if she'd shot President Hoover? All she'd done was skip the interview Uncle Collin had arranged so she could attend Leopold Stokowski's lecture at the Academy. But they treated it like the Valentine's Day Massacre.

Oh, how she'd rather work in a music store, play the piano, balance books in a business — yes, that appealed to her most of all. She loved math and excelled in arithmetic, algebra, even the calculus at St. Patrick's. When Sister Kathryn James had reported to the principal — who also happened to be Uncle Collin — that Agnes was the only girl ever to master differential equations and derivatives, her uncle had snorted, "No well-raised girl should ever admit to such a thing."

Agnes had apologized for her vulgar display of mathematics. But she had to admit she loved working with numbers and equations. Surely somewhere there'd be jobs for girls who were smart with numbers, even if Mama and Uncle Collin didn't think it was ladylike.

She adored Uncle Collin. After all, he'd steered them through those grim first years after Daddy died, holding Agnes while she cried at the funeral, managing Mama's finances, tutoring Patrick in math, even climbing a ladder to fix their roof. But she didn't want to work in his — or any other — rectory. She could imagine the duties — taking dictation, writing letters to errant boys' mothers, mailing bingo invitations, serving tea and scones to blue-haired gossips. And most demeaning, cleaning up the floor when little girls and boys threw up.

Before she knew it, they'd walked all the way up to Rittenhouse Square. She scanned the square's majestic oaks, the blue sky shining through leafless branches, all framed by a sidewalk bounded by Walnut and Locust Streets in one direction, 18th and 19th Streets in the other. She stood on the far east side next to the Curtis Institute's gray stone façade. Last week she'd dreamed that Artur Schnabel collapsed during an Academy performance of Mozart's Piano Concerto No. 24. "Might anyone finish?" the conductor called out. Agnes had darted up to the stage and overwhelmed the audience with her brilliance.

It'd been difficult enough giving up piano lessons with Mr. Larney after finishing school at St. Patrick's. Mr. Larney had assured her she'd be accepted at Curtis because of her talent. Mama had put aside money, and the school had even begun waiving tuition for students in '28. But no, Limerick's Bricklayers had to fail and now she had to work. Dreams of Curtis and being taught by Leopold Stokowski would have to wait.

Sighing, she turned away from Curtis and crossed 18th Street into the square and up the diagonal path to the central fountain. She released Racer from his lead and watched him sniff dried-up rhododendrons. She sighed again when she eyed Longacre's Music and Instruments up 19th Street. Even browsing for music would have to wait. She always bought when she browsed, but she had no money today.

Agnes knew Mama wouldn't have cut back on expenses unless necessary. Her heart ached for her mother, cleaning her own floors for the first time in thirty years. Since Limerick's failed, Mama had fired the servants and cut back on everything from firewood to milk. Agnes wondered if her father could've prescribed a cure for their predicament had he survived Spanish influenza. After all, he'd had the wisdom to set up a bond trust for her, but that wouldn't mature until '34.

"Come, Racer, we've been dawdling too long. Time for home."

Patrick and Uncle Collin would be there and well into their rummy game. She took a different path this time past the brownstone at 10th and Clinton where Granny and Grandpa had settled after coming over from Ireland. Mr. Larney now lived in that same third-floor apartment. Oh, how she missed laughing at the melodramatic wave of his arms when he corrected her mistakes — and his broad smile when she perfected a difficult sonata.

Agnes entered the back door into their kitchen, refreshed from the cold air. She put aside thoughts of piano lessons and savored the usual scent of roasted turkey, the room warmed by the flames of Mama's gas stove, the dark drapes, and the oak table where Mama and Granny sat now, Granny with a glass of sherry. Her mother's legs were crossed, and she was tapping her index finger on her cheek. Mama looked so tense. She should have been drinking the sherry, not Granny.

Granny smiled and nodded at Mama. "You can stop your fussing, Siobhan. The green-eyed princess of Old City is come back to us."

"Nearly two hours you've been gone, Agnes Mary. I thought someone had kidnapped my baby." Mama walked to the counter and began mashing potatoes, with far greater force than needed.

"Oh, Mama, we walked all the way up to Rittenhouse Square. The sky was crystal clear, and the sun cast such a glow on the red-bricked buildings, all orange and blue." She hung her coat on the rack near the back door and commanded Racer to sit. She removed his lead and grabbed a cloth to wipe off his dirty paws.

"I let Racer run all around the park. Granny, I walked by the old place at 10th and Clinton."

"It's younger than you I was, my lass, when there we lived," Granny said. "More than ten years in those three cramped rooms until I had my seventh baby and your grandfather snatched up this place."

Agnes marveled at her grandmother, her petite frame more upright than any woman half her age might expect — or any woman who'd borne half as many children. She still wore black for Grandpa Andrew but dyed her hair red even with eighty only a year away. Why shouldn't she have a little fun, Granny would insist, since precious few pleasures remained for wrinkled old witches like her.

"And how's the fancy Mr. Larney?" Granny said.

Agnes looked up to her mother before answering. Mama always bridled at Mr. Larney, but never made her reasons clear, just mumbled that men should drink whiskey, play poker, and smoke cigars, not attend the theater, vaudeville, and lectures. Agnes knew that if Daddy hadn't insisted she take lessons from the bow-tied bon vivant, Mama would've made her quit.

"He's in Pittsburgh visiting a friend for Thanksgiving. Some of his students have dropped out, he tells me, because their parents can't afford to pay. 'Alas, that's life,' he said. Did I tell you he wants me to do a recital, Mama?"

Mama stopped mashing potatoes, and her shoulders drooped. "About ten times. We'll worry about piano recitals later. A paying job is what concerns me now."

Agnes couldn't see her mother's face, but nonetheless she sensed her round cheeks turning red. And she recognized the tinny shake in her voice. It crept all too frequently into their conversations these days.

Agnes finished wiping the dog's paws and stood up. "Now, Racer, are we a good boy? Here's a cookie for the best dog ever." Agnes reached for a cracker from the plate near her grandmother just as Mama turned and faced her.

"A human cracker, no less. Did you wipe down that dog's paws? I don't want him soiling my clean floors."

"I just finished, Mama. Okay, Racer, off you go."

The dog bolted out of the kitchen, into the hallway, past the stairs, and into the parlor. "Uncle Collin must be in the parlor," Agnes said, and her heart went thud. She'd have to face him.

"Not five minutes in the house, he and your brother started a game. Today is continental rummy. Collin must be winning, to judge from Patrick's bellowing."

But it could wait a few more minutes. Agnes sat down at the table next to her grandmother and rubbed her hands together. "We're going to have lots of snow this winter, I can smell it."

Granny rubbed Agnes's hands in her own. "Mercy, child, it's cold as a witch's titty you are. Have some sherry." She pointed to her glass, still full. "This will warm you up."

"Daughter, don't you be drinking sherry," Mama said, going back to mashing the potatoes. "You will lose your balance. Now run into the parlor and say hello to your uncle like a good little girl. And Patrick too. You haven't seen your brother since last Christmas."

Granny shook her head. "Siobhan, you leave her be. I'm enjoying her company."

Agnes never knew when sparks between Mama and Granny would fly. From the day Granny moved in, only a month after Daddy died, they'd bickered over nearly everything—Mama's recipe for corned beef cabbage, where to place Granny's volumes of Dickens, whether Uncle Collin would sit at the head of the table, Patrick's decision to move to Washington rather than go into the family business—but mostly about Agnes.

Mama sighed. "Very well. Agnes, help me in here. Grate the cheese, and we'll melt it with cream and salt so it can go on the vegetables."

"That sounds yummy, Mama." Agnes's stomach grumbled for the snack it expected this time of day, but she resisted munching on the cheese. They barely had enough for the five of them.

"Siobhan, where is the crudité? It had better not be in the icebox."

"Mother Limerick, no one calls them iceboxes. They're refrigerators. You know that perfectly well. It's been ten years since we got ours."

"I'll never get used to that funny word. What about you, Agnes, what do you think of these *freddy readies*? All these new machines, bah!"

"I like machines, Granny," she said, grating cheese. "You do too. I hear you listening to Al Jolson and Fanny Brice on the victrola, and that's a machine."

"No, sweetheart, that's music. This refrige—this refrigerator is a machine."

"But it's a new day. Automobiles, trains, zeppelins, and airplanes flying in the sky! Someday when I'm rich and famous, I want to fly an airplane." Just like Amelia Earhart, free to do as she pleased.

Finished with the potatoes, Mama threw the ladle into the sink and faced Agnes. "That's not something a young lady would do."

"Why the hell not, Siobhan? My granddaughter can do anything she puts her mind to, can't she now?" Granny's narrow face cast a bright smile at Agnes.

"Mama, what does being a lady have to do with this? I don't think flying an airplane or driving a car is something only for men. It's a new decade, the 1930s."

"And it's off to a roaring start, I see. You're such a silly child with your modern ideas. When you grow up and raise a family, you'll understand woman's lot. Airplanes and zeppelins, indeed."

Agnes finished grating the cheese. "Aren't you the one who wants me working?"

"As a secretary, daughter, or as a governess. The families in Chestnut Hill, they all want to take on respectable Irish governesses. But you want to ask at all the wrong places — banks, accounting firms, construction firms."

After melting the cheese, Mama removed the turkey from the oven. The vegetables, the mashed potatoes, and the orange-cranberry mold rested on the far counter.

"But I love working with numbers, and I don't want to be a governess to bratty Episcopalians." She cringed at picking up toys for screaming children, cleaning up vomit from expensive Oriental rugs while society matrons played bridge and boasted how their rich husbands had stolen money from the indigent.

"My dear, that's not for you to say. Why are you so fascinated by ciphering? Young girls aren't supposed to be good with math."

"Poppycock," Granny trumpeted. "Any woman who raises children ought to be good with numbers. I raised nine, didn't I? Everything I did was counting." She threw back her head and laughed.

"Good point, Granny," Agnes said, but seeing her mother's eyebrows rise, added, "I'll take the side dishes into the dining room. We can alert the men."

"Ask your uncle to inspect the turkey for carving."

Granny walked to the sink. "No. Patrick should carve the turkey. He's still head of the Limerick family, whether he lives in Philadelphia or Washington. Or Timbuktu."

"Annie Kate Limerick," Mama said, turning around, "I wish you'd keep your opinions to yourself. As long as my brother is here, he carves the turkey."

The two women faced each other, just feet apart — Granny's posture so erect, she looked like a five-foot-tall pencil, and Mama, so stooped at the shoulders, she looked like she carried the state of Pennsylvania on her back. Why did they disagree so much? Maybe because they'd each managed this household alone at times, neither could share the job. Or, maybe it stemmed from some biological need to protect the nest. Whatever the case might be, Agnes hoped she'd never have to live with a mother-in-law ... or a daughter-in-law.

"That's your choice, Siobhan, but you're getting my opinion whether you want it or not. Give these children responsibility, or they'll never grow up. Watch this one here. She'll surprise us, so many ideas, so many new ways of thinking."

"'These children,' Mother Limerick? I thought we weren't supposed to treat them like children. Let's get these plates on the table. Collin can inspect the turkey in the dining room."

At last, she'd have to face Uncle Collin, the moment of judgment and those pesky butterflies in her stomach. What alternative did she have? She couldn't dodge her uncle for the rest of her life.

Agnes carried the cranberries and the vegetable bowl out of the kitchen. Granny followed with the mashed potatoes, and Mama brought the turkey platter. "Look what we have," Agnes broadcast to the men beyond.

Thank heavens the dining room was the largest in the house. She could remain on one side of the broad walnut table far away from Uncle Collin's wagging index finger on the other side. Maybe she could hide behind Mama's crystal chandelier, tall candlesticks, and Granny's centerpiece. As the women set the food down, the men came in — Patrick with a frown, Uncle Collin with a grin.

Agnes turned and faced her uncle. But he didn't come over to kiss her on the forehead, as she'd expected. He nodded at her and walked over to his chair. She directed her eyes at her brother, who nearly tripped on the Oriental rug when he walked to his chair. What an oaf for a thirty-year-old man, she thought, looking at his big chin, big mouth, big nose, big hands, and big feet that always bumped into Mama's furniture and doorways. Agnes laughed. "I think I know who lost the annual Thanksgiving game."

"I took five of the seven hands and won twenty cents," Uncle Collin said in an agreeable tone that surprised Agnes. He boasted as if he were a boy of seven rather than the thunder-wielding priest of St. Patrick's.

"I don't mind," Patrick said. "Uncle Collin, I don't know how you do it. You always win."

"The luck of the Irish, my lad," Uncle Collin said. Despite his voice, Agnes detected an angry shade of pink in Uncle Collin's complexion. His eyebrows seemed even more sharp than usual, and his thick cheeks appeared a little more solid—not the happy, soft face that usually greeted her at holiday dinners.

Granny sniffed. "The boy's just as Irish as you, Collin Doherty."

The conversation shifted to Mama's dinner display, and Agnes felt relief that her uncle said nothing about her recent behavior. So Agnes played her part too. They stood behind their chairs waiting for Mama to take her seat.

Despite their recent austerity, Mama had taken care to set the table with the finest from Grandpa Andrew's success in the 1880s—Granny's Wedgewood, silverware, trays, and serving dishes monogrammed with sloping Ls, crystal goblets for water, glasses for wine, eight tall candlesticks, a fall centerpiece of gourds, cobs, and red-leaved branches Granny had collected from the trees behind Independence Hall.

The small turkey, waiting for Uncle Collin's carving, looked ridiculous sitting all by itself on the large silver platter, not even a bowl of gravy to keep it company. Opposite the turkey were the mashed potatoes and vegetables with Agnes's cheese sauce, the cranberry chutney in the middle.

By tradition, Mama sat at the end closest to the kitchen, while Uncle Collin sat opposite in Daddy's old spot. Agnes sat on her mother's left with Granny directly across. Patrick snatched up the seat between Agnes and their uncle. Three dejected chairs stood empty at the far corner. Perhaps next year there'd be enough money to invite the others.

"Patrick, dear, you know perfectly well Agnes always sits there," Mama said, lighting the candles rather than turning on the chandelier. "She's left-handed, you know. If you switch, she might not spill things so easily."

Her brother rolled his eyes. "Twenty years old and still writes with her left hand. What did they ever teach you at St. Patrick's, Agnes?"

"As you well know, we could never get this little devil to write right," Uncle Collin said. "Two years I personally tutored her, and she would not budge."

"She's always been a disobedient child, this one," Mama said, "never more so than now. Always has to be different."

Agnes rolled her eyes at being demoted from young adult to unmanageable toddler. She felt just like when Mama told people the first things she noticed at Agnes's birth were orange hair and long piano fingers. It made her sound like an alien. Those twin pigtails Mama made her wear for years hadn't helped, either. At least, Mama now allowed her a single ponytail.

"Mama, you're embarrassing me. You know I can't write with my right hand. And I'm perfectly happy sitting where I am."

Uncle Collin gave her his first smile. Perhaps he'd forgive her? And Granny winked at Agnes. "That's all right, pumpkin," she said. "We all love you, left or right."

"Collin, would you be saying the blessing?" Mama said once they were settled. She patted Agnes's folded hands. Uncle Collin was deep in conversation with Patrick but raised a finger. They held hands and bowed. Uncle Collin recited his prayer in a slow rhythm.

"Oh, heavenly Father, maker of all things seen and unseen,
We thank thee for the bounties on our table . . ."

Agnes felt a great sense of peace listening to her uncle's bass. When she was younger, church had been an opportunity to spend time with her father, who was otherwise busy with patients, rounds at the hospital, and visiting neighbors too ill to leave their beds. At church, he'd carry her on his shoulders, laugh at people's stares, chase her in the courtyard, play hide-and-seek between the pews. Even now, she could feel the stubble under his chin, see his spectacles' wires on the sides of his temples, and smell tobacco on his tweed jacket. And since Daddy had died, she'd come to associate church with her uncle. When he recited Mass, gave a homily about fairness to the poor, or said prayers at meals, everything in the crazy world seemed to make sense again. His resonant voice always seemed to restore peace, harmony, and love to their table.

They crossed themselves at the end of the blessing. Patrick passed the chutney to Agnes, who loved the sweet taste of the cranberries, oranges, and lemon rinds. She took a large portion and passed it to her mother.

Everyone began talking. "But Collin, what's your view on excusing children from the homily? Doesn't it set a bad example?" Mama's voice rose over Granny's staccato chattering to Patrick about the rummy game. Agnes migrated between conversations, darting her head back and forth as if watching two games of verbal tennis. She didn't want to grab Uncle Collin's attention, so she remained as silent as the turkey he was carving.

As the others quieted down, Mama and Uncle Collin continued debating recent changes to the religious education of children and the proper way to rear loyal Catholics. Uncle Collin believed religious education could not substitute for daily Mass. To him, only mass offered the unique gift of grace to good Catholics.

"Uncle Collin," Agnes said, winking at Granny during a lull in the conversation. "Would you pass the mashed potatoes, pretty please? I'm over here on Mama's *left*."

"Of course, child, and don't be impertinent. Mind you, don't eat all of the potatoes," he said over a mouthful of turkey and mashed potatoes. "There might be less this year, but we can share what we do have."

Agnes couldn't resist. "I didn't mean to be impertinent, I'm just hungry and felt *left* out."

Granny laughed, her emerald eyes sparkling. "That's my Agnes, speaking up for herself."

Uncle Collin harrumphed. "Annie Kate, our Agnes would do well to speak less for herself. Look at the trouble she's made. The child has committed a grave sin. No, several of them. I cannot think what might have possessed her—"

Mama knocked her knuckles on the table three times. "Not at the dinner table, Collin, we agreed."

"Forgive me, sister." His brows rushed together after a quick look at Agnes. "I insist we clear the air."

Double drats. Why'd she have to fan the flame with cute little puns? Uncle Collin's thunderbolt hit Agnes squarely in the forehead, the roster of deadly sins she'd committed by skipping an interview for the music lecture. Greed and envy, lust and gluttony, but the worst of it—pride.

"You disappoint me, Agnes Mary, putting your desires ahead of the needs of others," he said with a penetrating stare. "On no account may you indulge yourself when the rest of us are making sacrifices. Am I understood?"

Agnes was thankful Patrick's six-foot frame sat between her and Uncle Collin. But Uncle Collin wouldn't let her out of jail for free. "Answer me, young lady."

She looked at her uncle and felt his disappointment seep into her body. Everything inside her slowed down, so she said the only thing she knew would rid herself of that leaden feeling. "Yes, Uncle Collin, I apologize."

"Good. Saturday morning, you will come to St. Patrick's to say your rosary and mop the school floors. It's time you settled down to earn a living."

He shoveled in a spoonful of brussels sprouts and washed them down with red wine. "By the grace of God, I've persuaded Father John Paul to give you a second chance at St. Monica's. On Tuesday, I will personally escort you there."

"You know I don't want to be someone's secretary, Uncle Collin. I want to work in a music store. Or, could you help me with the bishop at St. Paul's? They need a bookkeeper, and I'd like that too."

Granny clucked like a bird. "Collin, it's a good point the lass is making. The dear girl loves music and numbers. Pumpkin, remember this. Do the thing you love best and all good things shall follow. I got your grandfather out of the fields of Ireland, I made this house what it is today, I raised my brood of nine, and look at me now. Red hair at eighty."

Mama joined the fray. "That's red dye. Anyone can do that. But Agnes, there's something unladylike in balancing books. It's one thing to do it at home, dear, but you cannot do it in public, and most certainly not with the bishop. You might consider the convent like Aunt Lucy. A woman can find no better way to obtain a state of grace ..."

Agnes knew why Mama trailed off. She'd always insisted that Agnes, the only girl in her generation of Doherty cousins, must marry and have children.

Uncle Collin sallied forth in the wake of his sister's momentum. "Quite right, Siobhan, the bishop would not like it, so St. Monica's it will be. Agnes, do I have your consent."

"All right, Uncle Collin," Agnes replied, and then *sotto voce* to her grandmother, "but I'll tell him I can't type, so I won't get the job."

Uncle Collin frowned. "We'll have none of that. You type faster than anyone. For shame, it's a poor attitude you're showing when you're in the doghouse."

An awkward silence descended on the otherwise gabby gathering. They made polite conversation about neighbors, but that fizzled after only a few minutes. Granny broke through the silence. "Siobhan, all things considered, it's a fine Thanksgiving meal you've prepared."

Agnes looked at Uncle Collin, feeling a wave of guilt at his downcast eyes and dour expression. Why did she always relent when he looked unhappy with her? It felt like a magician's hypnosis. But she couldn't bring herself to disappoint him after everything he'd done for them.

"Uncle Collin, I'm sorry. Please forgive me. I'll do this job at St. Monica's."

"Ah, that's my favorite niece."

Agnes let out a little giggle. "But Uncle Collin, I'm your only niece."

He threw back his head and laughed, then winked at her. "Be that as it may, you're my favorite. I'll make you a promise. You work hard at this job, and if you still want something different after six months, I'll consider it. But you must promise me you'll give this your best effort and stick with it. You change your mind at the drop of a hat."

"Yes, Uncle Collin." Agnes didn't care for his last remark, but her heart jumped at a new thought. "Besides, I can always play the piano when I get home. I can take lessons again with the money I earn."

"Agnes, we're depending on your income," her mother said, rolling her eyes. "This is an expensive house to run. Remember, our income's dropped by half just in the last year alone, and it will get even worse next year."

Agnes groaned. No matter how hard she tried, someone always put up a brick wall. She loved her mother and worshiped her uncle, but there were times she felt like Don Quixote fighting windmills—useless, and with no chance of getting what she wanted.

"Hard times can't last forever. I want to take lessons from Mr. Larney again. There are still a number of pieces I want to learn, like the final three Beethoven sonatas."

"Not *want*, daughter, *would like* is more ladylike."

Granny saved Agnes. "Want or would like, it's a clean plate Agnes has, and that means it's time for music. All this talk of jobs and money is giving me gas. Agnes, let's have something cheery on the piano. You brought a smile to my Martin better than anyone, and that's a blessing to remember about my firstborn."

Agnes's heart melted at the mention of her father's name, especially from Granny. She could see him escorting Granny down Pine Street, his posture always straight in his mother's presence.

Her mother frowned. "I need to clear the dishes. Collin, you're dripping cheese sauce. Would you and Patrick like some sherry? We won't be having dessert for some time. Perhaps we can sit in the parlor and listen to Agnes."

"No sherry for any of us, Siobhan, but piano music, yes," Uncle Collin said.

With the sound of chairs sliding backward and plates being collected, everyone except Mama shifted to the parlor. Granny sat in the chair next to the Steinway grand she'd bought for Agnes ten years ago, six feet of rich maple. Uncle Collin settled into one of the high-backed chairs across from the piano and lit a cigar. The earthy smell reminded Agnes of burned leaves in fall. Her father had always smoked in this room.

Patrick stood behind the other chair as far away from the piano as he could get. Agnes knew he was planning his escape. She wanted to stick her tongue out at her brother. He never paid any attention to her playing on his rare visits to Philadelphia.

The sounds of running water and clanking dishes came from the kitchen as Agnes started into Beethoven's *Pathetique*. The dark chords of the C minor introduction filled the house. But in the quiet pause before the allegro, the sound of Mama's shoes approaching on creaking floors broke through the music.

"Daughter, we asked for something cheerful," she said in the doorway.

Agnes sighed, but got a better idea. Who could complain about Schubert's E-flat Impromptu? Her fingers flew up and down the keyboard like the summer hummingbirds circling Granny's bird feeders out back. Music could shift her mood, and this one took her back to when she and Daddy played hide-and-seek. She'd played it in her head many nights as she tried to fall asleep, its rapid scales chasing toward the dawn.

The three gave her a rousing applause. She started into the slow movement of Beethoven's *Pathetique*. Agnes loved this sonata and might have forgone the dark first movement out of deference to Mama. But under no circumstance would she omit the second and its beautiful melody. She didn't intend to continue after finishing the Beethoven, but Uncle Collin implored her. So she played the final movement of the *Pathetique*, a lively rondo unlike the somber first movement and longing second. It moved like lightning.

"What a gift you have," her uncle praised her. "I haven't heard you play since last year. Your progress is inspiring. One day you will make a husband very, very happy with your music."

"*If* she gets married, Uncle Collin," Patrick said. "Agnes, who was that suitor from the boys' school? Tommy something-or-other?"

Agnes fumed. Her brother never let her get away with anything. "Tommy Callahan was only a friend."

"That's not what I remember Uncle Collin telling me."

"Sometimes you can be really trying, Patrick. When I marry, it will be for true love and for no other reason."

"If you have the luck of God on your side," Uncle Collin said. "For the most part, love comes after marriage. People are lucky just to meet someone they like when they marry, then fall in love afterward. The best marriages are arranged by the parents — with their priest's consent, of course. It's the grace of God and the holiness of marriage that bring true love to a man and his wife."

"But how will I know when he's the right boy, Uncle Collin?" And how would her uncle know? He'd never been married.

"My opinion," interrupted Granny. A pink glow and a gentle smile came to her face. "In your heart, you will know. When I met Andrew Limerick back in the old country, I was but a lass of fourteen. It's true love we experienced and long before we were married. I would've married your grandfather with or without my parents' consent."

Collin's mouth popped open. "Woman, mind your tongue in front of the girl. You can't mean to suggest ..."

"Poppycock, Collin Doherty." Granny turned her attention back to Agnes. "Love opened a whole new world for us, Agnes. Patrick, you listen up too, for you're bound to marry a lass not quite so foolish as that simpleton you followed to Washington."

Granny paused, which Agnes knew signaled a story about the old country. "We were as poor as dirt in Ireland, but love came to us all. I'll give your uncle what he said. Yes, it's more common to love your husband after you marry. But you'll achieve a state of grace unknown to most poor fools if you take your marriage vows in the presence of love."

Uncle Collin gave Granny a stern look, but she returned it like a bludgeon. Agnes knew her uncle disliked being contradicted, especially by Granny. But Uncle Collin soldiered on. Having settled the question of her job, Agnes supposed, he'd focus on her matrimonial prospects.

"Ah, my dears, you're women, and you have queer notions about romance. You'll learn, Agnes. God always has his own ideas for us, and we must follow. Life doesn't always go the way we plan."

"No, Uncle Collin." Agnes turned back to the piano for some Debussy. "I suppose it doesn't."

2

AGNES'S JOB AT ST. MONICA'S CERTAINLY DIDN'T GO as Uncle Collin planned. She worked for the requisite six months as parish secretary to Father John Paul, only to endure the huffy disapproval of the nuns and tortured boredom of typing up the monsignor's homilies. Buckets of pleading tears failed to convince Uncle Collin she needed the change. But when Father John Paul caught her reading Descartes's *Geometry* in the confessional when she should've been inventorying clerical robes, Uncle Collin threw up his arms and admitted she needed a different outlet for her "cute little talent with numbers"—at least, one that didn't have her reading banned works by heretics.

"Make the next one work, Agnes, or you'll have to go back to St. Monica's," Uncle Collin said. But Agnes knew Father John Paul was only too eager to get rid of her when he talked to his brother, Mr. Smith, the managing partner at the architectural firm, Smith and Weisskopf. He interviewed Agnes for the position of junior bookkeeper.

"Young lady, our bookkeeper has resigned to have a baby," the pucker-lipped fiftyish bachelor with the pencil neck said. "Times being what they are, we have a hundred applicants. Would you add this long column of figures for me?"

She tallied the numbers in her head and spit back the correct answer fifteen seconds later. There'd been carryover, odds, evens, primes, even a few three-digit numbers.

"Mercy me," Mr. Smith said, his neck getting even thinner and his eyes bulging out. "No one, not even a man, has ever done that without paper."

He looked her up and down. "Do you plan on getting married?"

Agnes wondered what marriage had to do with the job, but she just had to have it. Working at St. Monica's had turned her weeks into monotonous days of mindless servitude brightened only by weekends of books and piano music. She knew she'd find this job more challenging, not to mention a lot more fun.

She manufactured a polite laugh. "I don't even have a suitor. Mr. Smith, I have to help my family. We've had such a hard time this year, and I need to work a good, long spell, several years at least, before I even consider marriage."

"Child, that's commendable. Anyone who can add that row of numbers in her head has the job. I'll talk to John Paul. You start Monday."

He hiccoughed a little smile. "It's a relief to meet a young lady who wants to work rather than get married. Some people around here believe every girl should be married by twenty, so mind you, don't tell Mrs. Weisskopf. She'll have a fit."

On Agnes's first day, the peripatetic gray-haired Mrs. Weisskopf chose Agnes's matrimonial prospects as her next project. Would she like to meet this architect or that draughtsman, she needled Agnes.

"It's what she does with all the new girls," Mr. Weisskopf said. "Don't tell Mr. Smith. He'll have a fit over the *mischegoss*."

Notwithstanding the pencil-thin Mr. Smith on one side of the matrimony question and Mrs. Weisskopf on the other, Agnes learned the rules of her job in only a few days. The administrative staff worked in the middle of the 3rd floor offices of the firm's Locust and 20th Streets building, surrounded by two design studios for the architects. The group consisted of three other women—Mrs. Findlay, the middle-aged supervisor with pointy glasses and a receding chin; Mrs. Levine, Mr. Weisskopf's secretary and sister-in-law; and Mrs. Rosamilia, Mr. Smith's secretary. Mr. Smith kept a close eye on the ladies from the vantage of his *pince-nez* and the unobstructed view from his office.

The firm had bustled in its heyday from nine o'clock when the architects arrived until long after the administrative staff had left. Night owls all, most of them young bachelors, many architects remained until evening—a happy hunting ground for a pretty young girl like Agnes, Mrs. Weisskopf said. She blushed and looked askance at Mr. Smith's office.

But all was not well at Smith and Weisskopf, Mrs. Weisskopf whispered. The architects worked long hours these days because they'd applied for projects with President Hoover's Reconstruction Finance Corporation, itself a reaction to the deepening economic crisis (so Agnes read in the *Inquirer*). The firm needed to win at least a few of the projects, or the staff would have to be cut. Mrs. Weisskopf voiced doubt about the prospects. But Mr. Smith and Mr. Weisskopf always smiled whenever they passed Agnes's desk, so she surmised the interfering lady was wrong.

On her second day, Mr. Smith's secretary told her, "You call me Cristina, and I'll call you Agnes." She immediately liked the twenty-four-year old Mrs. Rosamilia—Cristina, she meant—who advised her to butter up Mr. Smith, whose constant need for tidy desks agitated Agnes in a way that reminded her of Sister Kathryn James. Cristina rattled off the architects' abridged biographies like a librarian and filled her in on the latest gossip, this architect wooing that secretary, this married man chasing after that flit. This last was news to Agnes. She had no idea adults carried on like that.

Cristina lived just eight blocks from Agnes with her husband, Angelo, and her parents, the Cassatas, at Christian and 6th. Mr. and Mrs. Cassata operated a market in the epicenter of Philadelphia's noisy Italian community. They enjoyed good food and laughing around the kitchen table every evening with plenty of wine, Cristina added *sotto voce*. Scandalous.

Cristina had a hearty, tall figure with a bigger bosom and wider hips than Agnes. With wavy brown hair and eyes, and a deep olive complexion, she had eyebrows so thick that she looked like a man, and she wore thick black glasses for reading. She had a lantern jaw and a high-bridged Roman nose, so unlike Agnes's up-turned and short nose. Cristina told Agnes she inherited her looks from her Sicilian mother and her height from her father, whom she described as a *lombardi* of pink skin, blue eyes, and white hair.

With those eyebrows and glasses she might have been homely, but her personality gave her magnetic beauty even more affecting than her gold necklaces, bracelets, and earrings. Cristina had a throaty voice she attributed to Pall Malls. This jarred Agnes; she knew no women who smoked. She made fun of Mr. Smith's neatness ("that old maid") and Mrs. Weisskopf's gossiping ("such a *ficcanaso*"), but it was clear Cristina liked them both. How different from home! Agnes never could poke fun at her elders.

Such was the frank openness with which Cristina welcomed her to Smith and Weisskopf that in early August, after an office lunch when they expressed their common interest in Victorian novels (Cristina preferred Dickens, Agnes preferred Austen), Cristina invited her to spend a Saturday afternoon together.

"Unless it rains, Angelo and my father are fishing on the Schuylkill. Why don't you and I have a day together? We can go for a walk, have lunch, and I can introduce you to my mother. It would be squoodles of fun."

Agnes hesitated. Yes, she'd saved enough money for a light sandwich. "As long as I'm home before five. We go to prayer vigils late Saturday afternoons."

"We never worry about schedules in our family, but sure."

After waking up Saturday morning, Agnes looked out her bedroom window at the blue sky and promise of a warm, sunny day. After putting on a white summer dress, doing her usual household chores, and having breakfast with Mama and Granny, she grabbed her wide-brimmed white hat. She didn't want any more freckles on her alabaster face. She'd arranged to meet Cristina at eleven on the southeast corner of Washington Square across the street from the building where Adams, Franklin, Jefferson, and the other patriots had signed the Declaration—a list that included George Taylor, the man who'd built Mama's house back in the 1770s. It took Agnes less than five minutes to walk to the park.

She arrived first. What a glorious morning! A cluster of teenage boys, shirtless and dirty, were playing a game of tag football on the far side of the park. A group of mothers with baby carriages were sitting on benches in front of the Athenaeum, their negro maids chattering nearby. Ebony and alabaster faces alike shone in the sun, too early for shade from the surrounding buildings.

Agnes could hear the din of another busy Saturday morning on Walnut Street. It reminded her of the Reading Terminal Market uptown and how much she enjoyed the endless rows of produce, fish, meats, bakeries, and Jewish delis. Everyone was doing something this morning, anxious to get chores out of the way, so as to enjoy the afternoon like she always did.

Her eye caught sight of a lone man running on the south side of the park. Wearing navy blue shorts and a white sleeveless shirt, he looked different from most of the men she knew, athletic with prominent shoulders, narrow waist, and muscular legs, the expression on his chiseled face focused like a pointer—on his exercise, she supposed. He turned the corner, and before she knew it, passed by her without a gentleman's glance. Her eyes followed his figure as he passed the group of young mothers. They also turned their heads. No one exercised in public like that, she thought as he passed Independence Hall. As strange as a pink elephant in a tutu.

"Agnes," Cristina cried out, approaching her a few minutes later. "I love your dress, so summery and light."

Thank heavens, their day could begin. "I got here a few minutes ago. I've been watching the people, those boys playing football, those mothers over there with their babies."

Cristina gave her a pouty look. "Babies don't interest me that much. What do you think? Let's go for a walk. The weather's breathtaking and so are those boys. Let's have a closer look."

"Why not?" Agnes said after a blushing pause, a little uncomfortable. She followed Cristina toward the shirtless boys but looked back at the mothers and their carriages. The women seemed so content.

She could see Cristina was prepared for a warm afternoon. Like Agnes, she wore a light dress, light green and more revealing in the chest than Agnes's demure frock. Agnes's skirt hung low, but Cristina's went no farther than her knees. She supposed Cristina's mother, like Mama, had sewn it for her years ago. She wore a tiny white ornament of a hat that seemed to disappear in her bird's nest of long, wavy hair.

That surprised her. Cristina rolled up her hair into a bun at work, and Agnes knew no women who let their hair fall onto their shoulders in public. But like Agnes, Cristina wore no rouge, though she didn't need it. Her olive skin glowed in the sun. Agnes felt positively ghostly.

After watching the boys playing football, conversation shifted to Cristina's husband and father. Agnes asked if they'd gone fishing.

"Oh, yes, much ado about nothing."

"You quote Shakespeare."

Cristina laughed. "Agnes, you noticed. Men make such a big production out of things. We women make no fuss, but when Angelo and Pop do anything, whether it's fixing the roof, cleaning the gutter, or fishing, they telegraph the news to the entire neighborhood."

They turned away from the football game. Casting out the thought of men, women, and their fussing, Agnes led them toward Market.

"Just like my Uncle Collin," Agnes said. "He's the priest at St. Patrick's on 21st Street. He spends half the time during homilies talking about all the repairs he's done to the parish buildings, as if he'd done them himself."

Up ahead, she saw a little mouse dart out of a sewer gutter into the busy street. She rooted for the scrappy little fighter, scampering between puttering Fords and Oldsmobiles, but a Duesenberg—probably owned by some snooty Hooverite—flattened the poor thing. Agnes covered her mouth and suppressed the urge to retch.

Cristina seemed not to notice. "No doubt with an eye on the collection plate. Guilt usually yields a few coins. So your uncle is Monsignor Doherty. When I was in high school at St. Monica's, he came every year to speak to our class about service to the poor."

Agnes did her best to forget the image of the squashed mousy-poo. "One and the same. But St. Monica's ... I worked in the parish office this year and *loathed* it. Except for my Aunt Lucy, the nuns watched me like hawks. She's taught there thirty-two years. Do you know the one with red hair just like mine?" Ah, Aunt Lucy, a cloistered, younger version of Granny.

"Sister Lucy," Cristina said. "I was her hands-down favorite in English and Latin, can't you tell? But I couldn't learn Latin like she wanted. So she's Monsignor Doherty's sister?"

"No," Agnes said, a little louder than she intended. "She's a Limerick, but he's a Doherty. I've got religion on both sides."

Cristina paused. "How interesting."

Agnes looked down Market Street, the long row of tall stone buildings on both sides crowding toward City Hall. As they walked, she tried to ignore the empty storefronts and out-of-business signs.

Agnes thought of the years of Latin swirling around her head at church, home, and school. She hadn't liked it either. It seemed there'd never be a chance to use it, even if she spent her entire life in Rome. And that she never would do. She planned to live in Philadelphia. Where else could she find the freedom to do whatever she wanted when she was out on these streets?

"That's my family, or at least the part of it I see every day." Agnes summarized the rest — her aunts, uncles, cousins, Patrick in Washington, Aunt Julia in Manhattan.

"You haven't mentioned your father," Christina said as Agnes trailed off.

They stopped in front of John Wanamaker's. Agnes eyed a beautiful green dress in the window, but why bother? She couldn't afford it. She considered Cristina. She didn't know her well enough to talk about Daddy. Mama and Granny might talk about him every day, but she couldn't. Why feel that sharp stab of pain, even thirteen years after he'd gone?

But she looked at Cristina's brown eyes and felt safe. "Daddy died when I was a little girl."

"I thought that might be the case. I'm so sorry, honey. Listen, are you hungry? Let's stop some place quiet for lunch and have a cozy talk."

Their walk had taken them to City Hall, the stone monument to Gothic architecture. They meandered around the cobblestoned courtyard and gazed up at the William Penn statue, the tallest point in Philadelphia. The epicenter of government in America's third-largest city, it was busy even Saturday at noon. Cristina led Agnes to her first lunch choice, the Reading Terminal Market, of course, opposite the east side of City Hall.

It hardly would be quiet in the chaotic market overflowing with shoppers bickering over produce, meats, and fish. Plenty of people shopping, but few actually buying. Agnes ordered tuna salad, and Cristina chose salami on rye at Lefkowitz's, Agnes's old favorite.

They sat at a table with their sandwiches in the middle of the hullaballoo and took off their hats. Agnes noticed Cristina's thick eyelashes, so unlike Agnes's wispy red ones.

Cristina spoke first. "So here we are. Tell me about your father."

How to start talking about Daddy? Dr. Martin Limerick, ambitious, driven, and passionate, carrying her on his shoulders to a lecture he gave at City Hall—the benefits of hygiene and fitness in avoiding influenza and consumption. Daddy, playful and engaging, making goofy faces at her during Uncle Collin's homilies, giggling when Uncle Collin cast sharp glances their way. Her father and greatest advocate, bidding her to be his good little girl as they walked the dog evenings. Martin Limerick, the man whose funeral after Thanksgiving '18 overfilled St. Patrick's with seven hundred mourners.

By the time she finished, they'd eaten their sandwiches and Cristina had smoked her third Pall Mall. Three cigarettes at lunch, how audacious. Then, she saw her old piano teacher at a fish counter over Cristina's shoulder.

"Why, there's Mr. Larney," Agnes said, grateful for a diversion. She'd been talking about Daddy for an eternity, at least thirty minutes, and she'd forgotten about the swarms of people.

She hadn't seen him in a year. He hadn't changed except for some extra pounds on his waist and a little less blond hair around his balding head. He still wore bright colors and a jaunty smile below the clipped moustache—and today, navy blue slacks, white jacket, beige hat, and bright-green bow tie. Still cheerful in these gray times.

Mr. Larney didn't notice her. He was animated in conversation with another man of the same age, each pointing at the fish, smiling, addressing the fish man, nodding their heads and laughing. Agnes thought about greeting him, but she hated to interrupt.

Mr. Larney and his friend dashed away as soon as they completed their purchases. She felt a twinge when he left. Odd seeing him at the Reading Terminal Market. In twelve years of piano lessons, she'd rarely seen him anywhere but at Mrs. O'Toole's house or the concert hall of St. Monica's. Even odder seeing him when she was talking about her father. It'd been Daddy who'd insisted she take lessons from Mr. Larney when she turned six.

"Cristina, it's nearly two o'clock. I've been monopolizing the conversation and wasting an hour. Let's change the subject ... Tell me about your family and your husband."

"Angelo!" Cristina rolled her eyes behind her glasses. "My husband, well, if you'd like to know something about marriage, but perhaps I shouldn't say ..." Cristina giggled, and her olive cheeks blushed a deep red.

Cristina didn't seem like the blushing type. "Oh, come now, I told you about my father. I'm entitled now."

"That's true, you shared your secrets, so I guess I can share mine. But I warn you, it's not suitable for virginal ears. If Angelo ever found out I told you—"

"Why do people always say I'm too young to hear things?"

"It's about our married life. Are you comfortable if I talk about that?"

Cristina was referring to marital relations—how fascinating, but oh, so scandalous. She wanted Cristina to continue, but she cringed at the thought of knowing what her bespectacled friend did behind closed doors. Surely a woman with heavy eyebrows and thick glasses who read Victorian novels wouldn't talk about marital relations. It would be indecent.

But Agnes closed her eyes, held her breath, and took the plunge. Perhaps she finally might hear the truth about *it*, and from the most interesting friend she'd ever made, so different, so alive.

"Yes, Cristina, do tell."

Cristina paused as if trying to find the right words. "I had an eye-opening Saturday afternoon last week, to say the least. It was nothing like we've read about in our fine English novels.

"Angelo and I sat around the kitchen, enjoying the heat, drinking Chianti. Ma and Pop were still at the market. I was nearing the end of *Great Expectations*. Angelo had been working all morning at the store, so he was hot, sweaty, and a little stinky. So Angelo takes off his shirt, and I say, 'Angelo, not in the kitchen. Be a gentleman.' He hadn't shaved and looked like a wolf. There he was, hairy chested, stinky, barefoot, wearing nothing but dungarees.

"The wolf, Angelo I mean, looks over at me and says, 'Ain't no gentleman in me now.' So he comes over and kisses me like he's got one thing on his mind."

Agnes barely could breathe. "What was that?"

"Agnes, if you really need to ask ... he's my husband, you know, so you can imagine what happened next." Cristina began to chuckle. "Let's just say he had great expectations."

Agnes forced herself to laugh, but her insides were in the midst of an uncomfortable skirmish. When would it be her turn to have these kinds of experiences?

Cristina continued. "Except for one thing, I put the book down and tried to lead him up the back stairs, but he grunted and stopped in his tracks. Picked me up and sat me down on the kitchen table. He was acting like a juvenile delinquent. And that's how it happened, right there on my mother's kitchen table."

Agnes clutched her necklace, surprised she still had a heartbeat. She'd never known married people would do *that* anywhere but under the sheets, late at night, draperies drawn, and lights out. She recovered enough to ask, "Did your parents find you there?"

"It happened quick, so we got dressed and walked down to Washington Street." She gurgled a deep laugh. "Angelo, the fool, left his undershorts behind. You'd think he'd have noticed, but no. When we came back, Ma was preparing dinner and called out to me. When I walked into the kitchen and saw the shorts sitting on a chair, I wanted to crawl behind the walls. But I grabbed his shorts and slunk up the stairs. Ma was laughing into a pot of marinara."

Agnes's mouth popped open. Did every marriage erupt in passion like that on kitchen tables? She had no way of knowing. She'd only known one marriage, and it had ended when Daddy died. And every woman in her family was a widow, a nun, or a spinster like she.

She found it difficult to look Cristina in the eye. "Goodness, how the time has passed. Shall we leave?"

"I can see my adventure has embarrassed you. Perhaps I shouldn't have said anything."

Agnes gulped and looked at Cristina tapping her chin with an index finger. "Not at all, Cristina."

They emerged from the building minutes later. Cristina turned to walk back down Market Street, but Agnes demurred.

"Oh, dear, we're about to walk by that dead mouse."

"What are you talking about, a dead mouse?"

"You know, the one that got smashed by that Duesenberg back at 9th Street."

"Funny, I didn't see that happen."

Cristina filled in the blanks about her family as they walked. "Just like you, I've got a brother, Salvadore. That's also Pop's name. He lives across the street from us, married and five children already. Ma harps on me about that. I'm only twenty-four, and she says I'm waiting too long for children, reading books and working for architects. I tell her, not everyone's having children at seventeen."

"My father turned forty a few months before I was born. Mama was in her thirties," Agnes said, her heart warming up. "I guess they started late."

"All I ever hear is grandchildren this, grandchildren that, Cristina, why don't you have children? Lord almighty, it's not as if we haven't been trying."

"On the kitchen table, no less."

Cristina popped open her mouth. Agnes laughed, delighted to be the one to shock for once. "How did you and Angelo meet?"

"Last year, Pop hired Angelo at the store to clean fish. He did real well and now he's running the fish counter. He took one look at me and swept me off my feet. Told me he fell in love with me soon as he saw me. We didn't wait for anything. Pop caught us kissing in the back room of the store, told us if we wanted to get any closer we'd have to get married, else he'd have to fire Angelo. So we did. Just had our first anniversary two weeks ago."

None of this made sense. It was as if the school librarian turned out to be—well, she barely could think the word. It gave her butterflies to think about doing that with a man. And yet, the image of Angelo, hairy chest and nothing but dungarees, made her throat tingle and her heart quicken a beat. What was Cristina talking about now?

"So we moved in with Ma and Pop to save money until business gets better. I've been at Smith and Weisskopf almost two years. No plans to leave, except I want to be a librarian. Angelo doesn't want me working, but I tell him the more money we make, the sooner we'll live on our own and start having children."

"Angelo sounds bossy."

"Not really. He's a teddy bear, all cute and fuzzy. He makes me feel good.

He's warm and funny, but not too bright. He never did too well in school, though it hardly matters. He melts my heart because underneath he's just a little boy. He says, 'Come to Papa, little Mama,' and I tell him, 'Calling me Mama isn't going to seduce me.'"

Agnes only could imagine the shocked look on Mama's face if she knew her daughter was privy to such a conversation. She'd never hear the end of it from Uncle Collin, and they'd forbid her to see Cristina. Perhaps they'd insist she quit her new job? She and Cristina walked slowly, stopping at a bookstore just before Washington Square, the only one they'd encountered since lunch not out of business.

Cristina browsed through a row of American authors, commenting only on a collection of Hemingway short stories called *Men Without Women*. Sounded like monks, she said, the worst way to live. Agnes perused a Beethoven biography she couldn't afford to buy. She looked at her gold watch, Granny's graduation gift back in '28. No money for gold watches these days, but she could afford a little dessert for supper.

"It's quarter to three. I'd like to buy a dessert at your parents' market. It'd be nice to surprise Mama."

"Beautyful! Our market's right around the corner from the house. We'll give you a bag of cannollis, and you can meet my family. Pop and Angelo should be back from fishing. They'll adore you."

When they reached Cassatas, Agnes surveyed row upon row of baked goods on the left side, salamis, prosciuttos, and hams on the right, and cheeses in the center. Fresh New Jersey tomatoes in luscious reds, oranges, and yellows had her salivating. She ordered four cannollis and éclairs that cost forty cents, and pulled out a dollar bill. But Cristina covered the bill with her hand.

"Cosmo, this one's on us," she ordered the man behind the counter, gathering a bag of savories for herself.

This embarrassed Agnes, so she'd invite Cristina and Angelo for dinner. But she wouldn't leave them alone in Mama's kitchen.

They reached the Cassatas' house in no time. It surprised Agnes how small the narrow row house was compared to her mother's fortress. Cristina pointed out several houses on the block. Her late grandparents had owned the house across the street. Her uncle and aunt lived with their spinster daughter three doors down. Her brother and his wife were raising their brood across the street and a block down. Angelo's parents lived two blocks away.

Agnes felt dizzy imagining all the relatives and their houses, but it warmed her heart. Cristina seemed out of breath. "Come this way. Family comes in the back door. Only strangers use the front." Cristina led her down a passageway between the houses so narrow, they had to navigate it like crabs.

Agnes let out a little squeak when they walked into the room. There it was: *the kitchen table.*

The large oak table filled the kitchen. It was certainly a large kitchen for such a small house. Three people greeted her. Mr. Cassata kissed the back of her hand and made a polite bow. He had a gentle smile and Cristina's abundant nose, his heartiness accentuated by a fat stomach and wild gray hair on both sides of his bald head. Angelo, the younger man, struck Agnes with his sinewy looks, a hairy wolf just as Cristina had described. She could see the veins in his biceps and forearms. Both men had blood on their T-shirts and were cleaning fish in a large, deep sink. Mrs. Cassata, a tiny woman with black-and-gray hair bundled into a net, hummed over a pan sizzling with tomato sauce. She turned around and wiped her hands on her apron.

Cristina plopped her purse and grocery bag on the kitchen table. Agnes couldn't bring herself to touch that table. Not just yet.

"Ma, this is Agnes."

"Don't you look pretty. Let me wash my hands, and I'll come say hello. You sit down at the table." Her dimpled smile made Agnes feel welcome. Mrs. Cassata elbowed her way past her husband to the sink. Agnes sat down and placed her hands on the table. It felt like an ordinary table, didn't it?

Angelo picked up the fish and gave his wife a wide-eyed look and a laugh. "Cristina, look at the *pesci*. We'll be having shad for dinner." He gave his wife a juicy kiss. She laughed and skirted away.

"Scoot away, Angelo, you're all blood. Pop, I thought you were fishing on the Schuylkill. Aren't the shad usually in the Delaware?"

"We changed our minds, *principessa*. Launched the little boat from the Jersey side where all the best fish are. They like Camden better than Philadelphia."

"Hah, how can anyone, even a fish, prefer Camden?"

Mrs. Cassata dried her hands and walked over to Agnes. She looked her in the eye, gave her a rock-hard handshake, and offered a warm Granny-like smile. "Cristina's told us all about you, all that beautiful red hair. You're the girl who reads just like our little bambina. Would you like to have some wine? We were going to wait for the boys to clean the fish, but why ever wait for a man?"

The little bambina, who towered a head over her mother, started a Puccini record on the victrola in the dining room. The elder Cassatas hummed along. Mrs. Cassata leaned into her husband and kissed him on the shoulder. Mr. Cassata slapped her behind.

So this is what a marriage can be like. Agnes laughed, marveling at the two couples having fun. Bloody T-shirts, slapping behinds, juicy kisses.

"Salvadore, not in front of Agnes. She's an unmarried girl," Mrs. Cassata scolded, darting behind her husband and slipping into a chair with her red wine. She placed a plate of olives in front of Agnes.

Cristina winked at Agnes. "Ma, she's twenty-one. She can handle it."

Agnes savored the bright-green olives. Everyone seemed to buzz about the kitchen, happy bees drinking and eating. Sizzling olive oil and marinara floated under Agnes's nostrils. Cristina announced she'd cook the pasta.

"Ma, look at these salamis, cheeses, and tomatoes I picked out today." Mrs. Cassata rose and inspected the food with a frown, then sighed and went back to chopping onions and garlic. She prepared the antipasto and began to sauté the fish while keeping up with the girls' conversation and her humming.

"Agnes, would you join us for supper?" Mrs. Cassata refilled her glass and refreshed her own.

The wine went straight to Agnes's head. What a topsy-turvy afternoon, she giggled. But then her stomach dropped as she remembered church at five, prayers for the dead Limericks and Dohertys. She peeked at her watch and felt her blood pressure rise. Not a minute to spare. Mama would be furious if she ran late.

"Thank you, Mrs. Cassata, but my mother's expecting me. We're ... meeting my uncle at church. I need to head home."

Cristina puckered her lips. "Agnes, how will you ever get to St. Patrick's by five? That's little more than an hour from now, and it's twenty blocks away."

"Mama drives us over at 4:30."

The four looked at each other. Agnes knew they were thinking that she was rich, but they should really see their ancient jalopy before jumping to that conclusion. She peeked into her bag of desserts. "Cristina gave me some desserts to surprise my mother. Look at these."

Mrs. Cassata inspected the cannollis. "Yesterday's. I'll have to chide Cosmo on Monday about this. Cristina, shame on you. Agnes, you'll take mine instead."

"Ma, you're embarrassing Agnes," Cristina said.

Mrs. Cassata eyeballed Agnes. "Am I embarrassing you? The way my bambina talks about me. She knows perfectly well I never let anyone out of this house without a bushel of food."

Mr. Cassata patted his wife's behind and kissed her. "You feed everyone in the neighborhood, my luscious tomato of a wife. Agnes, you wait here a moment until we come back."

"Nonsense, Salvadore," Mrs. Cassata said and insisted Agnes visit again. "And use the back door, because we don't always answer the front."

❧

On Monday morning, Agnes was preparing coffee in the office kitchen when Cristina walked in. "Ma thought you were real sweet, Agnes. She wants to invite you all for dinner next Sunday. It's a tradition with her. She always invites friends for family dinner."

She couldn't imagine Mama in the Cassatas' kitchen, let alone Uncle Collin. But Granny would have a lot of fun. Nonetheless, she smiled and told Cristina she'd check with Mama. Cristina headed back to her desk, and Agnes went to the bathroom across the hall while the coffee brewed.

She dawdled Monday mornings a little, reluctant to shake off the weekend's carefree idleness. She'd enjoyed Saturday with Cristina and her family more than she'd thought possible. They were so alive, so real, so much fun. She thought about their long walk, Angelo and Mr. Cassata cleaning fish, tiny Mrs. Cassata's strong handshake, and that kitchen table.

Nevertheless, she did want to keep her new job, so she made a mental list of revenues and expenditures she needed to tabulate while she washed her hands. She looked in the mirror. If only her complexion weren't quite so white. She wished she had Cristina's dark features, or at least something closer to it. She looked like an Amish farm girl with her freckles. But at least she had pretty green eyes and long red hair. She was combing her hair when the bathroom door opened. *What in heaven's name—*

In barged a man she didn't recognize wearing a dark-blue suit, Agnes saw in the mirror. She screamed a little shock of protest and turned around to face him.

"Don't you knock, sir? Please leave at once."

"My lord! I'm terribly sorry, miss. I thought it was vacant." He averted his eyes and shut the door as quickly as he'd opened it.

How rude, so ungentlemanly. She stalled, staring in the mirror, hoping he'd go away, but a crisp knock ended that.

"Miss, please excuse me, but I need to use the restroom," he said from the other side of the door. He sounded like a bassoon.

She sighed. His piano wire-tight baritone irritated her. "A moment, please. I'm finishing up."

When she opened the door, he stood with his arms folded, tapping his right foot. He rushed inside before Agnes had a chance to look at him. *Of all the nerve!*

The coffee wasn't ready. Hurry—she didn't want another exchange with this stranger. But he marched out of the restroom all too soon. She could feel his gaze lingering on her back and froze, wishing he'd disappear.

"Sir, may I help you?" She felt obligated by good manners to turn around.

Something about him looked familiar, but she couldn't place it. He was quite handsome and clean-cut with a square chin, a sharp and wide jaw, deep-set blue eyes, and dark-brown hair trimmed crisply on the sides but long on top. Only a little taller than she and perhaps twenty-five, he had an imposing physique, shapely and muscular, a narrow waist, broad shoulders, and a thickly muscular neck. He looked taut and tight all the way around.

"Miss, I hope you don't feel too embarrassed about leaving the door unlocked. Please don't give it a second's thought."

A sharp note in his voice provoked her. What if she wanted to give it more than a second's thought, and what if she minded? She detected an articulate whisper around the edges of his words that made her scalp tingle. She didn't know what to say.

"Miss, I would like you to answer me when I'm speaking to you."

Was he one of the lead architects? Mrs. Findlay had warned her to keep a formal, professional distance from them, but this one stared her in the face. And what a face! Long sideburns framed the closely shaved stubble of his cheeks. Dark eyebrows accentuated his forehead, his blue eyes penetrating, the bridge of his nose high. Most of all, his mouth commanded her attention. He had thin lips and a narrow mouth. He looked clever, perhaps too clever.

"Yes?" she stammered.

"What's your name? Mine's Balmoral."

"It's Miss Limerick. I've been working here since July."

"A pleasure, Miss Limerick. Might I ask you to lock the bathroom door next time?" She detected sarcasm, but also something playful.

"Yes, indeed, that was clumsy of me, and I'm sorry. But I wasn't exactly expecting a blue suit to walk in on me. I practically jumped out of my skin."

"It is the blue suit, as you put it, who must apologize." He laughed. Even teeth and sharp canines.

She turned back to the coffee. "I accept your apology. Would you like to have a cup of coffee, Mr. Balmoral?"

"No, thank you. I always wake up bright and early in the morning, ready to go. No need for caffeine. Have a good day, Miss Limerick." He bowed his head. "It is a pleasure to meet you."

He walked out of the kitchen with a jaunty gait and long strides, despite his compact height. Agnes watched him turn into the design studio and close the door with a crisp snap.

Agnes served Mr. Smith his coffee, jotted down his endless list of detailed instructions, and then returned to her desk. She was bursting with curiosity. "Cristina," she beckoned, "you haven't mentioned the Balmoral man to me."

Cristina's mouth dropped open, exposing an elongated oval but no teeth. "Him," she groaned, "of all people. He's been still as a mouse since his project was cancelled. He designed a new wing for the Pennsylvania Hospital. Everyone was talking about it. 'Good use of modern design techniques,' Mr. Smith said. Gave him a lot of prestige. Been here a little longer than me.

Spent a year in Florence after he graduated from the Philadelphia School of Design. First man in his family to go to college. They run a general store up in West Philadelphia."

Agnes computed his age — about twenty-five, just as she'd thought. "I could swear I've seen him before."

"Could be, but he doesn't come out of that design studio much during the day. They say he's always got his nose to the draughting board, even now that the hospital cancelled his project. Few people around here like him. Has a chip on his shoulder and keeps to himself. Never goes to lunch with the architects or talks about his life outside of work. Mr. Smith would get rid of him if he weren't so talented."

This made sense. "It sounds like you don't like him either, Cristina."

"I like most people, Agnes, but something about him rubs me the wrong way. He's brash and arrogant. Even Mrs. Weisskopf steers clear of him. He had a dalliance with a friend of mine here and broke her heart. After going out for two months, they went to Bookbinder's one night, you know — at 2nd and Walnut. The next week, he told her he'd lost interest and she was responsible for herself. She quit her job a week later. Said she didn't need the money badly enough to be insulted."

Agnes thought about the food lines, the hungry faces on the city's streets. "For a regular paycheck, I'd deal with being jilted."

Cristina paused. "Mary Alden — that was her name — ended up marrying her high-school sweetheart back in Doylestown. Last I heard, she was having a baby."

"It sounds like things have turned out for the best. Are there any other ladies in Mr. Balmoral's life?"

Cristina lowered her voice. "None that I know, probably because he never looks up from his blueprints. Yet, it's obvious he's experienced with women. Of course, he lived in Italy, and we Italian women will do that to a man. His name's Norman, but no one calls him that. They refer to him as Balmoral."

"When we met in the kitchen, I called him the blue suit, and he laughed. He's striking, like a vampire but without the bite."

"Vampire or architect, I'd keep my distance. There are plenty of men in this city without risking Norman Balmoral sinking his fangs into your neck."

Mr. Smith apparently heard them laughing and bellowed from his office. "Back to work, young ladies." They stifled their laughs. Cristina arched an eyebrow at Agnes as they settled at their desks. Cristina's gossip lightened her mood. Yes, there would be plenty of interesting men in this city. She entered figures into the adding machine as if playing Mozart on Granny's piano.

While half her brain flew through the numbers the other half wandered. She thought about the blue suit walking away from her so sure of himself, his compact, muscular physique, his narrow lips and blue eyes. And then she remembered where she'd seen him before. Mr. Balmoral was the man who ran by her Saturday morning in Washington Square. She pictured his muscular shoulders, arms, and legs—and blushed.

3

AGNES BROUGHT GRANNY'S TATTERED RED BLANKET to Washington Square to enjoy October's Indian summer warmth. She'd spent much of the last month outdoors trying to squeeze some color out of summer's end, but all she got was a fresh batch of freckles. Unlike Granny, who thought freckles becoming on her, she hated them. She spread the blanket on the grass of the park's sunny south side near a cluster of wild rose bushes.

She'd brought Racer. Today was sunny, warm but not hot, and she savored the oaky scents of the changing leaves. She walked her dog around the square and lay with him on the blanket for the afternoon. Racer didn't seem to mind when she used his side as a pillow. She looked up into the branches of a chestnut above her. A pair of white-throated sparrows tweeted at each other.

Granny had bought Racer for them two years after Daddy died. When her brother left for Washington a year later, Racer became hers alone. And Agnes loved golden retrievers, even those with doggy breath like Racer's.

She'd done a good job training him. He still had a healthy spark of energy at eleven. All those years of playing fetch had paid off. Why, she couldn't imagine life without him.

Sometimes she felt closer to Racer than she did to Patrick. She'd always wanted a younger brother to play with, and Racer fit the bill perfectly, even if he had four paws and a wet nose. And she had more to talk about with Racer than she ever had with her brother. After all, Racer lived with her here on the third floor of Mama's house, not a hundred miles away. And she was a few months closer in age to Racer—separated by little more than ten years—than she was to her brother. And, yes, she'd done the math.

After spending some time enjoying the sky, trees, bushes, and the Philadelphians in the park, she opened *Wuthering Heights* and continued from where she'd left off: Heathcliff, overhearing Cathy confess her misgivings about him to Nelly, running off before Cathy expressed her undying love. Agnes had read this book half a dozen times and knew the plot inside and out, but she wished she possessed magical powers to change the destinies of Emily Bronte's characters. If only she could transport herself into the novel and whisper in Heathcliff's ear: "This time, stay until the end. You won't regret it." Reality kept her on this side of the page, however, a helpless witness to their heartbreak.

"Their tragic flaws led Bronte's characters to a series of unfortunate events," Sister Kathryn James had instructed in English class. "The tragedy of *Wuthering Heights* is not due to one specific crime. Rather, it is due to a chain of calamitous events made inevitable by the characters' flaws, namely desire. They paid for their sins in death because they could not control their desires. One must always have one's desires under control, especially desires of the flesh."

She'd recalled these remarks a number of times since she'd learned about Cristina and Angelo. She'd always kept her desires under control—how could she not with her romantic experiences confined to Tommy Callahan with the overbite? Was she destined to be a spinster like Mr. Smith? Would she end up in the cloister like Aunt Lucy?

She'd thought about little else in the six weeks since spending the afternoon with Cristina, especially in those late summer evenings alone in her bed, the night's air blowing her drapes about, Mama's silky sheets tantalizing her skin. She wanted to know what it'd be like cuddling with something so warm and exciting as a man, resting her head on his chest. Not Angelo, but a man of her very own. She wanted to know what it'd be like to be swept off her feet. Would she end up on a kitchen table? So long as it wasn't Mama's kitchen table ...

But she'd wait until marriage. She knew more than one girl who'd gotten "in a delicate condition" (Mama's words) or "in a nasty fix" (Granny's words) and had rushed to St. Patrick's with a red-eared boy for a quiet wedding in the middle of the week with no one except Uncle Collin and four angry parents. No, she'd wait for a nice boy who'd propose with violins and roses. They'd have a beautiful wedding on her birthday and would be together until death did they part. But she wasn't getting younger. Cathy already had fallen out with Heathcliff, married Edgar, had her baby, and died before reaching twenty-one.

Life was passing her by, just like the Fords and Duesenbergs driving past Washington Square on their way uptown. All she had close to love were a few brief evenings with Tommy Callahan. He'd been very kind, but he talked too much about his father's shiny Chrysler in Chestnut Hill. Tommy had big glasses and clammy hands. When he tried to kiss her one Tuesday after school, a chaste peck that landed somewhere near her nose, Uncle Collin had snuffed out their friendship. She had no idea how he found out and didn't regret his edict, but it irked her that he always knew everything.

Robert Bernardo, his dimpled chin, his long black hair, and his black eyes were a different story. Oh, how she'd wanted to walk with him in the square with the April tulips, the May rhododendrons, and the June geraniums. That was a boy every girl had wanted, at least until he'd gotten Helen Clifford in a delicate condition (or a nasty fix), and Uncle Collin had married them one quiet Wednesday morning. That ended her dreams of Robert Bernardo.

She buried her head in *Wuthering Heights* until Racer forced her out of position, his tail wagging in her face. A man stood near her, his frame a black silhouette eclipsing the October sun and surrounded by azure sky, as shadowed as if he were Heathcliff.

"My dear Miss Limerick, you are making the most of our weather, I see."

It was the appalling Balmoral man. He offered her a hand, and she said her thanks as she stood. He leaned down to pet Racer, who frolicked at his attentions.

"I had no idea you had a dog, Miss Limerick. How delightful. I love dogs. What is his name?"

No dog lover could be all bad. "Racer, this is Mr. Balmoral. He is an architect where I work. Mr. Balmoral, this is my doggy, Racer."

Balmoral laughed, bent down to kiss the dog on the forehead, and muttered something to Racer. He stood and addressed her. "Do you always observe formal introductions between your dog and your friends?"

Since when were they friends? But his eyes danced, and his smile was so contagious, she couldn't help laughing. "I do like to include Racer in my innumerable social engagements. He gets upset if ever he feels left out."

"With a name like Racer, your dog and I will get along well. I ran track and field in school, and I still run as much as I can. It's the best way to stay fit, I say. More than anything, though, I like it because I have time to myself."

"That's exactly why I'm here today, Mr. Balmoral."

"Then I am disturbing you, Miss Limerick. I must apologize and be on my way."

He seemed so sincere, quite the opposite of her expectation. She decided to give him a chance. "Not at all. Please stay. Would you like to sit down?"

She waited until he'd sat down on the blanket to take her place on the opposite side, keeping the proper distance. A group of bluebirds and yellow-tailed blackbirds frolicked around the rose bushes. Mr. Balmoral wore a light-blue suit, an open-collared plaid shirt, but no hat, which she thought odd for a man about town on a Saturday afternoon. She noticed dark hair peeking out the top of his shirt collar.

"What brings you here today? The weather?" he asked.

Agnes held up her book. "I'm reading *Wuthering Heights*."

"The tales of Cathy and Heathcliff." He smiled and exposed a dimple in his right cheek. "So you've never read it before?"

"On the contrary, I've read it many times. It's my favorite novel."

"Why so many times? It's not as if the ending will change, is it?"

"That's just it, Mr. Balmoral, it always feels like it might change. I find myself hoping, somehow, Cathy and Heathcliff will end up together."

"You must be a hopeless romantic, Miss Limerick." His baritone oozed a velvety smoothness.

"Not hopeless, Mr. Balmoral, hopeful. And literary, I suppose."

In the six weeks since their encounter, she'd avoided him except when he passed by her desk in his dark-blue suit, smiling those vampire teeth, cocking his eyebrows, and winking. Cristina poked fun at her, "Looks like the Balmoral man has a nervous tic around you."

He had no nervous tics today, and his happy smile evoked not a whit of the vampire. He chattered on about the weather, made small talk, all friendly rather than sarcastic. Perhaps she'd been too quick to judge — one exchange really, too little to go on, except what Cristina had said about Mary Alden. That thought gave Agnes pause, but only for a minute. He seemed so friendly, so genuine, there had to be more than met the eye.

When the conversation meandered and they resorted to playing with Racer, she asked what had brought him here. He looked over her shoulder and pointed at the east side. "Do you see that building? It's the Athenaeum. I spent the morning in the library doing research."

She couldn't quite see through the line of elm trees, but she knew it anyway. "I know the Athenaeum quite well, though I've never been inside."

"I've spent many mornings there since coming back from Europe. It's an architectural library, a treasure trove of inspiration. Someday I'll show it to you, particularly if you're going to work at Smith and Weisskopf for very long. You strike me as smarter than the average girl. Perhaps it would interest you."

"What can you learn there that you can't find at the firm?"

"Miss Limerick, Smith and Weisskopf is a business. We'll build anything our clients are willing to pay for. Our architectural history, the masterpieces of the world's greatest architects, you won't find them at our firm. It's pretty rare to get a client who's willing to let the architect take risks and do exciting work. As a matter of fact, there's one great building going up right now —"

"Have you had any projects like that, Mr. Balmoral?"

"I designed a new wing for the Pennsylvania Hospital." His face lit up, his eyes wide, his nose twitching, his mouth moving rapidly — and that dimple on his right cheek jumping around as he spoke. "I tried to introduce new materials and streamline the structure with simple lines. I wanted to use poured concrete rather than a wooden frame with bricks. I've always felt hospitals should be oriented horizontally—lots of windows from one end of the building to the other end, lower floors, horizontal lines everywhere. But no, they wanted a carbon copy of the rest of the hospital with Victorian arches, elaborate curves, and ornate moldings."

"What happened?" She wondered if he'd tell the same story as Cristina.

He breathed in through his teeth with a whistling sound, and then he continued at a fast pace. "Turns out we'd been competing with two other firms for the contract. I had to bite my tongue when Smith gave me *that* news. A grave disappointment they wanted a conservative design instead of mine. Everyone, Smith included, had wonderful things to say about how I'd envisioned a hospital as no one had before."

Almost exactly as Cristina had related. "How dreadful to lose a project like that. You sound like you were so committed to it."

"Thank you. I was, but now I've got another project, and it's why I spent the morning at the Athenaeum. What's grabbing my attention these days is the library."

"I haven't seen any library projects in Mr. Smith's monthly ledger."

"Not the firm's project, Miss Limerick, my own. One day I hope to build it for my city, or if not Philadelphia, somewhere else, perhaps New York or Boston. But it's a secret, so don't tell anyone at the office, especially not Mrs. Rosamilia or Mrs. Weisskopf. They've got the biggest mouths."

He slowed down. Agnes sighed in relief. The conversation felt like a fast ride down Market Street in an open rumble seat.

"What makes the library project so special?"

"A lobby with a huge vaulted ceiling. Eight floors of bookcases, each with a long balcony overlooking the lobby, all glass on the façade bringing natural light to every floor. I'm using minimal structural supports for the glass façade—steel beams mixed with some dark woods. I've designed a restaurant in the atrium where people can spend the day, have lunch, and read books."

Mr. Balmoral's face settled into a soft smoothness, and his dimple relaxed.

"The idea, Miss Limerick," he said slower, "is to bring the outdoors in, not keep it out, like most Victorian architecture does."

Agnes thought of her mother's dark-red draperies, her heavy mahogany. Imagine opening those drapes and bringing in the light. Why, she could just picture Mr. Balmoral's library. It'd be the kind of place she could spend a sunny afternoon, even in January, losing herself in *Wuthering Heights.*

"Have you approached anyone with your idea?"

He talked some more about his library design, but their conversation quickly turned to their biographies. She'd learned much of this from Cristina, except a year ago he'd moved back to his parents' house in West Philadelphia to save money. When she told him that Uncle Collin was pastor of St. Patrick's, he became animated again.

"How lucky you are. I know that church. It's beautiful, outside and in. I've seen the stained-glass windows, little miniatures of the rosetta at Notre Dame in Paris. And the flying buttresses supporting the main structure — beautiful, also just like the Notre Dame."

This confused her, so she made a joke. "Are flying buttresses anything like *The Flying Dutchman?*"

He laughed as she'd hoped. "Flying buttresses are columns that support the structure of the building." He drew lines in the air with his fingers. "And *The Flying Dutchman* is a tedious Wagner opera about a ghost ship."

"I don't understand what *this* meant." She imitated his imaginary lines in the air. "And I think you're unjust. Wagner was a great composer, and his operas were nothing short of magnificent."

"Pardon me, Miss Limerick. I'm tone deaf and not qualified to talk about music. But I have to be honest. The politics in his operas have always rubbed me the wrong way, and they never bothered me more than when I attended the *Ring* cycle in Nuremberg. Fifteen hours of bombastic German nationalism."

His speech became rushed again. It made Agnes's heart beat fast.

"Please forgive my opinions," he continued, "but that nonsense caused the last war and could very well cause another. It bothered me, the things I heard in the Munich beer gardens in the summer of '29. Beer, pretzels, and an obsession over the Jews. I can't understand why the Germans can't leave them alone. They work hard and mind their own business. Look at Mr. Weisskopf."

"You're as committed to fairness as you are to architecture, Mr. Balmoral."

"I'm sorry to make a speech, but I really feel strongly about this. The Jews are quite a remarkable people, and the Germans should be emulating them, not blaming them. These days they seem to be blaming everyone else for their problems, rather than working hard and taking responsibility."

She had to admire him for thinking the subject through, even if he was making her head ache and her heart beat fast. He sounded like one of Uncle Collin's homilies about the underprivileged. She'd rarely given a thought to Germany's troubles. There'd been the Great War, but that was so long ago. Was he suggesting ... heaven forbid ... there could be another ghastly war?

"Are you saying the Jews will cause another war in Europe?"

"With all due respect, Miss Limerick, you are highly misinformed. The Jews didn't cause the last one, and they won't cause the next one. I hope your uncle hasn't been saying this in his sermons."

"Uncle Collin says we should love the Jews because they gave us the Old Testament, and they gave us Christ."

"He's right. Based on the madness I saw, if there's another war, responsibility will lie at the Germans' feet. *Il Duce* is causing trouble in Rome, but it's nothing compared to Munich. I feel sad for Europe when I think of the petty street violence. The greatest architecture in the world stands there."

"All this talk, you'd think the Jews were like the colored here in America. It's not as bad as all that in Germany, is it? The Jews haven't been enslaved."

His voice took on new urgency and speed, and Agnes felt her pulse quicken. "Miss Limerick, they were enslaved in Egypt. If *Mein Kampf* is to be believed, they'll be enslaved again in Germany. But what they really share is working hard and not being paid for it—which is morally wrong."

Agnes remembered the mothers in Independence Park, their maids behind them with their baby carriages. She saw the ladies' white gloves and hats ... and the maids' sweating black faces.

"Take the women, for example. Our mothers tend house because our fathers go out into the world and support them as much as their children. Wives are compensated by the security of their husbands providing them homes. It's as it should be. But the colored here, they've been given no homes and no security."

The notion of Mama and Granny being their husbands' servants struck Agnes as ridiculous, whether or not Daddy and Grandpa Andrew had paid the bills. And she wouldn't want to be any man's servant. She didn't know how to respond, so she asked him once again to explain flying buttresses.

"My political views have gotten to you. You're biting your nails," he said. "So I'll answer your question. No, Miss Limerick, flying buttresses are on the outside. Why don't we walk over to St. Patrick's, and I'll show you?"

That was fifteen blocks away. She had to be home by four o'clock to go to church. It seemed silly to walk all the way up to St. Patrick's, only to head home and right back again in Mama's rickety Ford. But Norman Balmoral and his opinions intrigued her, so she agreed. They gathered up Granny's blanket and *Wuthering Heights*. He took Racer by the leash on one side and offered his arm to her on the other. She rather liked his formal manners, and what a handsome man to have by her side.

They remained silent for some time while he led them up 6th Street. Now that they were walking, she could think of nothing to say. Perhaps the weather? No, they'd already covered that.

"That these united colonies are and of right ought to be free and independent states," Norman quoted as they passed Independence Hall, "and that they are absolved from all allegiance to the British crown."

"Did you memorize the Declaration of Independence?" Agnes said, grateful for a new topic.

"Only the important parts." He laughed. "The rest I ignored. Same with the Bible. Love thy neighbor, yes. Fire and brimstone—no."

"Where does your family worship, Mr. Balmoral?"

"We've belonged to St. Mark's Episcopal for years. We'll pass it, perhaps on the way to St. Patrick's. The two are very similar in terms of architecture."

If that was his intention, why was he leading them in a different direction? They turned onto Market Street.

"I have a reason for bringing you so far out of the way. An hour ago you asked me about great architectural masterpieces. There's an extraordinary structure being built here on Market Street, and I wanted to show it to you."

Agnes knew exactly which building he meant. She could see it five blocks in front of them — the new skyscraper for the Philadelphia Savings Fund Society, rising hundreds of feet into the sky, dwarfing the other buildings and shops up and down Market Street. Even from a distance, she could hear the cacophony of cranes, the clanking of steel, the groans of machine gears. They'd been working on this project two years. It seemed like they'd never finish. She hadn't looked at the site in a long time, even when she and Cristina had passed it on their way to the Reading Terminal, and she usually avoided it, for the smell of sewers, burning metal, and dust made her feel ill. However, she looked more closely when they reached it, prodded by Mr. Balmoral.

He turned to face her. His eyes danced, and he made wild gestures toward the building, detailing its revolutionary design. She listened with wide eyes, hypnotized by the scientific facts, his enthusiasm, the way his eyes penetrated hers.

"It will be the tallest office building in Pennsylvania. Look at those slab masses, the vertical steel beams, the simplicity of its lines. That's exactly what I'm talking about, Agnes — I mean, Miss Limerick — when I mention European modernism. We're trying to bring that to America. I saw so much of it when I was in Milan and Paris two years ago. And in the States, just west of the Grand Canyon, there's a dam being built at the mouth of the Colorado River separating Arizona from Nevada. It's the ultimate symbol of this new style — the French call it *l'Art Decorative*. Have you heard about the new suspension bridge Strauss is building across San Francisco's Golden Gate?"

She had no idea who Strauss was but decided to pretend she did. "I've seen the drawings in the *Public Ledger*. How can they build a single span across a mile of ocean water?"

"It's a rather shallow channel, Miss Limerick, but I mention it only because that bridge will be a masterpiece of *l'Art Decorative*. The Strauss bridge will be the greatest ever built and will remain that way for hundreds of years. What I'd do to work on a project like the canyon's dam, the Golden Gate's bridge, this skyscraper. When I got back from Europe, I'd have given anything to work for Howe and Lescaze, but they weren't hiring in '30."

Howe and Lescaze, he explained as they resumed their walk, was the architectural firm behind the new P.S.F.S. building. He liked his work at Smith and Weisskopf, he told her, but would've been happier at Howe and Lescaze.

"My mother and her friends don't like the building," Agnes remarked. "They don't understand why there aren't more sculptures on the façade, why they're using so much steel, why the windows are so long and narrow. But I like it very much."

"Typical of the older generation." He continued to look at this building and others, but not at her. "In fact, that's typical of older people, period. They forget that life's always evolving, always has, always will. You have to stay with the future, Miss Limerick. A good architect builds for the future. A poor architect just copies what's been done a thousand times. Look at this building here ..."

It was the train depot, the Broad Street Station built in the 1880s for the Pennsylvania Railroad. Dogwood trees dropping leaves dotted the west and south boundaries of the building. She'd gone there frequently to meet Aunt Julia arriving from New York City.

"Do you know about the glass roof in the main lobby? That's where I got the idea for my library's multi-story glass wall. Frank Furness, Philadelphia's most famous architect, designed the 1892 extension, one of his most ambitious projects ever. He turned an ordinary station into an expression of Victorian magnificence representing progressive technology. Do you see those pinnacled gables, the terra-cotta sculptures, the tympanum above the Market Street entrance?"

She'd always loved Philadelphia's most famous sites, and his words excited her. He continued. "And yet, if he were to propose that structure today, not even forty years later, I'd yawn with boredom. That's progress, Miss Limerick. Architecture has to keep up with it all the way."

He pointed at City Hall and talked about the structure, a tribute to the Second Empire style of France's Napoleon III. He told her about John McArthur, the architect who took thirty years to complete the massive structure of limestone, granite, and marble in 1901. Few people would've thought to build a city's executive offices in such a style, she learned, yet McArthur had the foresight to take those risks—risks that paid off, for

Agnes knew City Hall, surrounded by majestic oaks, to be the crowning jewel of Philadelphia. And by the gentlemen's agreement among the city's leaders, the thirty-foot statue of William Penn on top always would be the tallest point in the city.

And was that a bald eagle atop William Penn's head? No, she thought, eyeing the hawk's red tail. Mr. Balmoral continued, practically shouting above the passing cars and throngs of people.

"Do you realize we can see masterpieces of French Empire, Victorian, and European modernism just by turning our heads? That's the progress of architecture in the great city of Philadelphia, Agnes."

He bowed his head. "I'm sorry, I erred again, Miss Limerick."

"You may call me Agnes. It sounds almost musical when you say my name. And I play the piano, so —"

"Thank you. My name is Norman. Shall we continue?"

He took her arm again and led her through the passageways on the ground floor of City Hall. Yes, she liked walking by his side. He was taking the lead. It felt as though they'd been taking walks together for years — and would continue doing so for some time to come.

They said very little until they reached St. Mark's, where Norman pointed at columns, stained-glass windows, and the church's red door. Most Episcopal churches had red doors, a symbol of the blood of Christ, he explained. She knew that, but hardly cared. He could've been talking about sewers, painful diseases, and wringing chicken necks, and she'd still be enjoying it.

All she noticed were the blue and purple birds circling. She wondered if he felt the same warm glow, if he was smiling all over and tingling just like she. How could she have likened him to a vampire?

They walked the four blocks across Rittenhouse Square to St. Patrick's, passing under the sycamore trees on Chestnut Street. "Do you see those support columns on the side of the church? There are your flying buttresses, Agnes."

"Oh, of course." She laughed, noticing the columns she'd always thought were supported by junipers. "Nothing like *The Flying Dutchman* after all. To think I've been coming here all my life and never knew what they were called."

"Then you must have no architects in your family. You were raised here in Philadelphia?"

They sat on a bench near the front entrance with Racer at their feet. "Yes, Uncle Collin baptized me here in October 1910. I was confirmed here too and attended the school until I graduated in '28."

"Do you live nearby?"

"Not exactly. Near Washington Square on the corner of 6th and Pine Streets. My grandparents bought the house fifty years ago. I was born there."

"Old City is a beautiful neighborhood. Your parents and grandparents must be very proud of you, working so hard at our architectural firm."

"It's just my mother and Granny Limerick." Now she'd have to tell him about Daddy, but hopefully he wouldn't pursue it like Cristina had. "My father died when I was a little girl."

"I'm sorry to hear that," he said with an even voice and squinted. "Your mother must have her hands full, keeping a house like that when times are as tough as now. My parents are having a very hard time at the store. And the bank has been breathing down their necks about the mortgage."

"My father was a very careful planner," she said, thinking about chasing Daddy around the square. Only a short distance from here, but so far away in time.

"He couldn't possibly have planned for this mess." Mr. Balmoral shook his head slowly.

She paused. "Money is scarce, but we're surviving."

"I'd like to hear more about your father."

Why did everyone want to hear about Daddy? He was the one special thing she'd always kept to herself. Agnes stalled, looking at a woodpecker perched on the bench next to her and cocking its head at them. Did the bird also want to inquire about Daddy? She felt a nervous rumble inside and avoided Mr. Balmoral's eyes by patting Racer on the head.

Sharing Martin Limerick with Cristina had been one thing. Doing so with Norman Balmoral would be quite another matter. But she ended up repeating many of the stories she'd told Cristina and even more: how he'd take her on home visits to sick patients, encouraged her with Mr. Larney, written

"My little Agnes" notes to her when she was first reading, insisted she be allowed to write with her left hand. Yes, Mama had been the disciplinarian, but Daddy had been her friend.

He spoke in a measured tone. "May I ask, how and when did he die?"

"Flu epidemic of 1918, on Thanksgiving Day. He'd been tending so many people who were ill and caught it himself. I'll never forget that day."

He was silent for some time. "It's remarkable, Agnes. You must've been quite young in 1918, perhaps eight?" She nodded. "Yet, you speak about your father as if you'd known him for decades."

"He had that effect on people. Friends would say it always felt like they'd known him forever. My piano teacher, for example—"

"One could say the same about you, Agnes Limerick."

Her eyes lingered in his, crystal clear and deep blue. Her head tingled with delight. She thought of nothing but the clarity of those eyes, the triangular jawline, the square chin, the echo of his bassoon-like baritone. How long had they been sitting on this bench?

"You're very kind, Norman." It astonished her how beautiful his name sounded coming from her voice.

"Not kind, merely accurate. When I first met you at Smith and Weisskopf, I couldn't understand why our first encounter embarrassed you so much. But as I observed you in the weeks that followed, I noticed how hard you worked. Every time I passed your desk, your head was down, and you were writing feverishly. And I thought Miss Limerick must be a very determined young woman."

His kindness warmed her heart. She looked him in the eye. "I like to finish whatever I start."

He met her stare. "I never leave a job undone either, the only way to live."

A familiar voice boomed from above. "What have we here, Agnes?"

Uncle Collin stood above her, his cleric's black and white stark against the red maple behind him. An uncomfortable grimace crossed his face, and he looked from Agnes to Norman and back to Agnes. Racer jumped up, wagged his tail, and sat at Uncle Collin's feet, expecting a pet.

"Uncle Collin, what are you doing here?" Agnes stammered.

"Saturday prayers, my dear, and aren't you supposed to be coming here with your mother?" Uncomfortable lines formed across his forehead. "I wish it's knowing you're here she was, for the poor woman went to find you in the park and called me in a panic."

"Blessed Mother Mary, the time completely flew out of my head. Uncle Collin, can it possibly be time for prayers already?"

"It's now close to four-thirty, and prayers are little more than thirty minutes from now, missy. Agnes, where are your manners? You might have offended your mother and grandmother, but you don't need to forget the proprieties. Please introduce me to this young man."

Could it get any worse? She looked at Norman, one side of his mouth down, one side up. "Norman, this is my fa—uncle, Monsignor Doherty. Uncle Collin, this is Mr. Balmoral. He is an architect at Smith and Weisskopf."

Norman rose and offered Uncle Collin a slight bow of the head. It surprised Agnes that Norman was nearly a head shorter. "A pleasure, Monsignor. I fear I've monopolized your niece this afternoon. She and I had a chance meeting in Washington Square a few hours ago. We went for a walk and got caught up in conversation. I hope I didn't inconvenience you."

He hadn't spoken this way with her, so formal, so proper, so British. You would've thought he'd been the elder Mr. Earnshaw from *Wuthering Heights* speaking to Mr. Linton at Thrushcross Grange, rather than Norman Balmoral of Philadelphia, a man who gave speeches about politics and architecture during city walks.

Uncle Collin apparently took the bait. "You are kind, young man, and it's a pleasure to me that Agnes is with a gentleman of such impeccable manners. Would you go to the rectory over there and ask the woman inside—she's Mrs. Mallory—to call Mrs. Limerick and tell her Agnes is here?"

Norman nodded and dashed off without a word.

"Agnes, how could you be so careless?" Uncle Collin said, his mouth becoming firm. "Haven't your mother and I raised you better?"

Her old sense of guilt bubbled up. "I'm sorry, Uncle Collin, I didn't pay attention to the time."

"Your poor mother. But alas, here she is now."

The old Ford sputtered down Locust Street toward them, her mother at the wheel of the open sedan, and stopped in front of them. Mama pushed her globby figure out of the car quicker than Agnes thought possible.

Her mother's eyes jumped, and her cheeks trembled. "Agnes Mary Limerick, where in the name of Charles Dickens have you been? It's torturing your mother what you've been doing, wondering the last hour where you'd gone. We imagined you'd be at County Meath by now. And your poor grandmother practically in the grave from fright."

Agnes wondered how Mama had concocted County Meath out of a Saturday walk. She caught her mother's sharp eyes and curled lips as she offered to help Granny out of the car, and knew that rosaries and novenas were in the offing. She saw Norman walking back to the group. Yes, it could get worse.

Granny slapped Mama's hand. "Leave me be, Siobhan. When it's to the grave I'm going, it won't be from fright that my granddaughter's gone afoot. Just look at the lass. She's glowing. What's in your head, my dear? You have the look of Sister Bernadette at the Lourdes grotto."

She might've enjoyed the afternoon, but not because the Virgin Mary had paid her a visit on Locust Street. Agnes felt all eyes upon her. She had no idea how to proceed — Mama, a wreck of anxiety and hairpins, Granny, squinting and pursing her lips, and Uncle Collin, looking at her anew. And Norman, six feet behind Mama, as yet unnoticed.

Uncle Collin saved her. "The child met a colleague from her new place of employment in Washington Square. They lost track of the time, and he escorted her here. Siobhan and Annie Kate, may I present Mr. Balmoral, an architect in Agnes's firm."

Two pairs of eyes shifted from Agnes to Norman as if it were a tennis match. "May I be so bold," Norman said, "as to guess that in addition to Monsignor Doherty, we have Mrs. Limerick the younger and Mrs. Limerick the elder?"

Mama relaxed a bit. "It's concerned about Agnes's safety we were that had us in a tizzy. Thank you for taking care of my child this afternoon."

"Mama, I'm not a child." Agnes said, groaning.

Granny sniffed Norman up and down. "Not bad, Agnes. He's an architect, and that's an upright profession. And the young man's got manners, more than the boys who asked for my hand before your grandfather snatched me up."

Norman met her match for match. "A pretty lady like you, Mrs. Limerick, would've had suitors from every town within a day's motor tour."

Granny let out a throaty laugh. "No one had automobiles in Ireland back in the 1860s. We counted ourselves lucky to have a horse."

"Even the horse would recognize your beauty, Mrs. Limerick, enough to make up for the lack of automobiles."

This was too much, even for Agnes. Would Norman propose to Granny right here in front of St. Patrick's?

Apparently Mama agreed. "All right, then, enough of these introductions. Mr. Balmoral, we're attending prayers, and my brother is leading the service. Would you care to join us and stay for tea afterward in the rectory?"

"Thank you, Mrs. Limerick, but I'm expected for tea at my parents' house in West Philadelphia. And my family worships at St. Mark's Episcopal on the other side of the square."

Mama looked at Uncle Collin; Uncle Collin looked at Granny; and Granny broadcast an "Ah, well" to her. The silence stretched the next five seconds into an epoch. Agnes shivered, despite the day's bright sun.

Uncle Collin cut through the silence. "Shall we go inside, then? Agnes, Racer can stay in the rectory during prayers. Give him some water. Just look at how he's panting. That walk was too long for the old dog. Mr. Balmoral, it has been a distinct pleasure."

He extended one hand to Norman for Racer's lead and took Agnes by the arm with his other. Mama and Granny followed them inside, mumbling something, but all Agnes heard was "English, possibly Scottish."

Agnes noticed leaves falling and smelled fall's air. She felt a chill as she looked behind her. Norman stood alone on the sidewalk. He waved to her, then turned and left.

4

WHEN SHE AWOKE TO REPEATED CLAPS OF THUNDER on Monday morning, Agnes found Racer dead on the floor by her bed. Heavy rain pounded the roof.

She tried jiggling the dog awake but knew instantly he had died. She screamed for Granny and hugged him, rocking him back and forth on the Oriental rug. No evidence of vomiting, no evidence he'd struggled, just Racer lying on the floor. His head bobbed down, lifeless, numbingly cold. His body was still limp; rigor mortis had not set in. He must've died within the past couple of hours.

Agnes heard Mama and Granny's footsteps rushing up the stairs. She saw them standing above her through blurry eyes, looming large against the green background of her room—Granny in her black robe pulled close to her throat, her hair falling down her back like a red shawl, and Mama, her hair squeezed up into a brown-gray ball at the back of her head, dressed in a gray frock, ready for volunteering at the Pennsylvania Hospital maternity ward.

Granny made a sign of the cross, and so did Mama. "Saints preserve us," Mama said. "What happened, sweetheart?"

Agnes clasped her dog tighter. "I don't know, Mama. A heart attack? My little doggy boy, I can't believe it. So spry and healthy, how could this happen?"

She sobbed until she choked on her tears. The room closed in, and everything pressed against her. She wanted to crawl into bed with Racer, pull the covers over them, go back to sleep, and pretend this hadn't happened.

Granny leaned down and stroked her head. "It's all right, sweet lamb. Racer was a wonderful dog for all of us. We'll get you another dog."

Agnes looked up into her grandmother's eyes, and saw compassion in her tears. "I don't want another dog. I want Racer. Why'd he have to die now? I didn't get a chance to say good-bye." She'd been cradling his head in her lap, but placed it on the floor and stood to hug Granny.

"Agnes, you go downstairs to the kitchen." Mama said. "We'll take care of Racer. He needs to be buried."

"No," she blurted. Racer had been her dog. How dare they suggest anyone but she should take care of her darling baby! "I'm going to take him to Uncle Collin and have him buried next to Daddy."

Mama's eyebrows arched. "We'll talk about that later when you're less upset. I'll ask Mr. Shaughnessy to come over and put him in the garage."

Granny tugged ever so gently at Agnes. "Come with me, pumpkin. It's breakfast you'll be having before you head off to work."

Work? How could she possibly go to the office this morning? "No, Granny, I couldn't. I must stay at home with Racer."

Mama's lips tightened, and she raised her index finger. "Daughter, you must go. We can't have you missing work and getting yourself fired. And you, working there only three months. Imagine carrying on so much. What would Mr. Smith think, you fussing so about a dog?"

"Phooey on Mr. Smith. I can't go to the office. Granny, talk to Mama."

"Siobhan, I think she can stay home one day. After all, she did find the dog herself. A shock for any girl, let alone our Agnes who doted on the boy."

Mama relented, and Agnes went down to the kitchen. She drank coffee but couldn't touch the rolls Granny had baked that morning. Mama came downstairs, patted her on the shoulder, and puttered about the kitchen sink. She heard Mr. Shaughnessy's scratchy voice a half hour later at the door, then his heavy steps coming down the stairs. He came through the kitchen with Racer wrapped in a blanket and took him outside. Agnes cried anew at the coldness of the process.

Agnes stared into her empty coffee cup, her face feeling all puffy and moist. Granny came over. "Cheer up, sweetheart, there will be other dogs. We'll talk to your uncle and figure out what to do with Racer."

She called Smith and Weisskopf. She tried to tell Mrs. Findlay what had happened, but her voice broke halfway through, and she handed the phone to her mother. Mama explained the situation and said Agnes would come Tuesday morning, prompt and ready to work. She hung up the phone and faced Agnes.

"No worries. Mrs. Findlay says you should rest today, but she expects you at work tomorrow morning before nine o'clock."

Agnes crept about the house all day, haunted by the image of Racer. She eyed his bowls in the kitchen, food in one, water in the other.

Why hadn't she noticed anything? Surely there'd been some clue? Why, she'd been walking him all over town with the Balmoral man on Saturday, and he'd been playful the whole time. True, he'd been sleepy all day Sunday and hadn't eaten much of his dinner, but there'd been no inkling something like this would happen. Her very own dog taken away, just like Daddy. Everyone she loved, she lost. She lay on the parlor sofa, buried her face in Mama's pillows, and cried salty tears until she could no longer taste them.

With Mama volunteering at the hospital and Granny upstairs knitting in her bedroom, she hated the dead silence in the house. She wandered from the kitchen to the parlor to the dining room to the back office and back to the parlor. To break the silence, she sat at the piano to practice. But all she could play was the funeral march from Chopin's first piano sonata, which brought Granny out from her room, asking her to play something less morbid.

She dared not go outside on this terrible day. She thought of Racer covered with blankets in the garage on the workbench in front of their old Ford, the car no one liked. She thought about going to pet him, but couldn't bear the thought of seeing his body hardening.

Back to the piano she went. This time, she played Beethoven's final E major piano sonata, Opus 109, the *Brentano* sonata. The last movement made her cry—the introspective main theme, six variations, and a melancholy return to the theme. She'd always thought of Daddy when she played it, but now she could think only of Racer. The final conclusion made her weep, but it was even worse when the music stopped and all she heard was silence. Dead silence.

The bleak weather of the day cast a chill on the house, and she felt cold right to the bone. She lit a fire in the fireplace and sat on the parlor sofa, staring at her piano. Perhaps she could read a book? No, she had to finish *Wuthering Heights*. But that would make her think of Saturday in the park, Racer, and she'd cry her heart out. Had Mrs. Findlay broadcast the sad news to everyone at the office? Cristina must've found out. But what of Norman?

The soggy day crept along, but she began to feel a little less morose after Mama's dinner of roasted pork tenderloin and cabbage warmed her. Mama told her quietly after dessert that Uncle Collin had agreed to read prayers for Racer and bury him in the backyard. He'd come by tomorrow afternoon.

She cried out, imagining Racer all alone in the empty backyard. "No, Mama. Racer should be buried next to Daddy at the cemetery."

"Your uncle cannot do that, daughter," Mama said, her mouth, cheeks, and eyes hardening like clay. "You know perfectly well that St. Mary's is consecrated ground. Racer was a dog. No, he'll be buried here. It's enough that your uncle has agreed to come and read prayers."

"Then can't he at least wait until I come home from work tomorrow? I want to be here for Racer's funeral."

"Perhaps, Agnes, it would be best that you don't see your uncle bury him. It's enough that you've endured. Besides, it will be dark when you get home, and we can't wait until Saturday to bury him."

She continued to protest, but no amount of pleading could sway Mama.

"You must trust me on this, Agnes. He was like a child to you. Much better if you don't see it happen." Mama's voice rose as if about to cry, but she looked away. When she looked back at Agnes, her eyes were moist, but her lips steady. "Yes, Agnes, much better for you not to see your dog buried."

Agnes finally agreed. She went to bed early, anticipating a rough day at work, unsure how she'd concentrate on Mr. Smith's numbers or Mrs. Findlay's orders. She began to cry again and couldn't stop. Racer's absence made for an intolerable emptiness, a circle of pain in the middle of her chest she couldn't shake. She got up, circled the room, got back into bed, and cried into the pillow. Sleep came and went that night, with dreams of Racer running home, and Mama and Granny saying it'd all been a colossal mistake. Then Agnes woke up, and reality hit her. Racer never again would plop his head in front of her when she woke up.

She dragged herself to the office Tuesday morning. Monday's hard rain had brought Indian summer to an abrupt end, but she barely noticed the drop in temperature as she plodded her way to 20th and Locust. She found a vase on her desk stuffed with bright yellow roses, tall and thin like the new P.S.F.S. building.

Agnes took off her coat, sat at her desk, and looked closely at the beautiful arrangement. Why thirteen roses rather than twelve? She opened the envelope to read the card, *I'm very sorry to hear about Racer. My heart goes out to you and your family. Very truly yours, Norman.*

She had to swallow a stubborn sob clutching her throat. Too early in the day for crying. But how kind of Norman Balmoral to understand.

His penmanship intrigued her. The consonants were thick, the vowels thin, and the form was almost medieval. He exaggerated the capitalization, the *N* of his name dwarfing the other letters. It seemed deliberate, even premeditated, like the text he'd write on a blueprint. But surely, though, his yellow roses reflected a sincere gesture?

"Good morning, Agnes."

Cristina's voice startled Agnes out of her reverie, and she looked up. "Goodness, Cristina. You surprised me."

"Sweetheart, how are you feeling?" Cristina asked, her tone muted as if in a funeral parlor. She came around to Agnes's side of the desk. "And what are these, a condolence gesture from Mr. Smith?" She grabbed the notecard.

"Norman, who's Norman?" Then her eyes expanded behind her thick lenses. "Not Balmoral. He wouldn't know what roses are."

Agnes could sense that Cristina's pointy jabs were bringing her back to herself.

"Actually, it's Norman the Conqueror."

"Nice try. That would be William the Conqueror of Normandy."

Agnes relented. "Whether Norman the Conqueror, William the Conqueror, or Attila the Hun, these roses did come from Norman Balmoral. He encountered me in Washington Square on Saturday afternoon. We had a pleasant conversation, and he invited me for a walk. It was most enjoyable. Racer was there." A rising tide of a sob approached in her throat.

Cristina's eyes were still wide, but now she was shaking her head. "I can't imagine the two of you having a real conversation. You've got too much common sense, and he, well, he—he's just not the type to send flowers after a Saturday afternoon walk. You must trust me on this."

Odd, Mama had said the same thing about burying Racer—trust me, she'd said. "Well, he loves dogs," Agnes said. "He's a great architect, and he loves his craft. And he has an older brother, just like I do. And you too, Cristina."

"And on that intimate connection, may people's lives be forever changed."

Her life changed by a walk across town? That seemed a bit over-dramatic, like something in an Italian opera. "I just went for a walk with him. I don't want to marry him."

"Marry whom?" Norman's voice came from behind her. Agnes turned to see him approaching, and she lowered her gaze, excited but embarrassed. Odd to feel this jittery excitement when she'd been feeling sad only moments ago.

"Oh my, does anyone still say 'Marry whom' anymore?" Cristina said, turning one corner of her mouth down. "Agnes, I'm going to the kitchen to get coffee. Would you like some? What about you, Mr. Balmoral?"

"No, thank you, Mrs. Rosamilia. I don't drink anything with caffeine. It's bad for the heart, and I prize my heart, unlike some people."

Agnes detected a barbed sarcasm that squelched her excitement. Cristina walked toward the kitchen, ignoring him.

"Mr. Balmoral, I appreciate your flowers and the notecard. How did you know yellow roses are my favorite? Granny tended her own rose garden, and we always liked the yellows the best."

His eyes danced, but his fluttering eyelids, so long and thin, calmed Agnes's heart. "Please call me Norman. I was so sad for you, Agnes. It was so clear how much you loved Racer. I couldn't believe it when I heard."

Agnes felt a dull pressure behind her eyes. "I don't want to talk about it—not here, at least."

Norman gave her a gentle smile from the right side of his mouth, and she saw that dimple again. "I understand. I have only a minute to get back to my desk. I wanted to invite you to dinner this Friday after work. Perhaps an evening at a fine club would help get your mind off your troubles. The Richmond Club on Chestnut Street is my favorite, just beyond the University of Pennsylvania."

He was asking her to go out, alone with him, on a Friday night. The excited discombobulation that coursed through her made her briefly forget about Racer. But disappointment quickly extinguished the feeling.

"I'm afraid I can't. My uncle has a bingo game planned for us this Friday evening at the church." She hesitated to weigh the two options — bingo with Uncle Collin and the parish widows, or dinner with Norman. She changed her mind. "Perhaps I can, after all."

"Terrific. We can go directly from work." With a shallow bow, he turned back to his office, his gait jaunty as before.

She thought about Uncle Collin and her weeks-old promise to help him on Friday night. How would she wriggle her way out of the obligation? Well, she'd just have to figure it out.

The week went slowly, too slowly. Torn between anguish over Racer's sudden death, creeping about the office Tuesday afternoon when she knew he was being buried, and anticipation over dinner plans with Norman Balmoral, she procrastinated in telling Uncle Collin. She couldn't think of a good reason to miss bingo. What would she ever say?

"Uncle Collin," she imagined, "Mr. Balmoral is just so handsome, and I like him a lot. He invited me to dinner at a nice restaurant in West Philadelphia. May I go even if he is an Episcopalian?"

She didn't think Norman's religion disqualified him as a dinner companion. And this was her first real date as an adult, even if it was with a Protestant. A date, and all she'd had in her meager twenty-one years had been a kiss from Tommy Callahan and dreams of the wayward Robert Bernardo.

She saw Norman only a couple of times during the week. Once, he was deep in discussion with Mr. Weisskopf as they passed by her in the kitchen. The other, he walked by her desk carrying blueprints, winked, and flashed a broad smile.

Cristina noticed and whispered to Agnes, "There he goes again, those nervous facial tics."

She didn't want to risk more operatic drama at the office, so she kept her dinner plans from Cristina. "Cristina, please, he's simply being friendly."

On Friday, Agnes paid a lot of attention to how she dressed for work. After trying on three dresses, she settled on a dark-blue wool dress with a laced white collar and cuffs, narrow waist, and long skirt. The crisp look pleased her, and she hoped Norman would like it too.

Midway through the day, she called the rectory at St. Patrick's. Mrs. Mallory put her through to Uncle Collin.

"Hello, my dear. And who should we be praying to win tonight, I'd like to ask? For all the old ladies of the parish will be fighting each other for bingo cards. There we'll be, calling numbers and making for certain that ladies remain ladies."

The moment had come. "Uncle Collin, that's why I wanted to call. I can't come tonight. Mr. Weisskopf needs me to sort through a large stack of statements. I was supposed to do them earlier this week, but I missed work Monday. I've been behind ever since. I won't be done in time to get to St. Patrick's."

She cringed at her lie but also wondered how it could come so easily.

"What will I ever do without you? Well, no matter. This job is very important, and I understand. Just don't let it become a habit, and don't work too late. I'll call your mother. Otherwise, she'll worry herself silly."

Agnes hung up the phone, looking at it with disbelief. She'd never once lied to her uncle. This was a lie about a man she barely knew, whom until this past week she hadn't even liked, and now she was making up stories to Uncle Collin, who'd practically walked on hot coals for her these past thirteen years, making sure she had everything from shoes to books to dresses. All so she could dine with Norman, whom she hadn't known even three months. She said a quick prayer asking for forgiveness. What would Daddy have thought?

But dine with Norman she would. Norman had dressed for a festive evening. When she met him in the downstairs lobby at five-thirty, he'd exchanged his conservative blue-and-black tie with a fancier red and white. As they left, he took her by the arm, talked to her about the week's work, asked her how she was feeling about Racer. His consideration gratified her. He entranced her as he leaned down to her in conversation, smiled into her eyes, opened doors for her, acquired a taxicab with a careless raise of the arm, greeted the maitre d' ("Mr. Balmoral, come this way, your table is waiting"), held a chair for her, and ordered wine and entreés for them. He made it all so easy. She didn't have to do a thing.

Their dinner conversation gravitated toward Europe, Norman talking about his year in Florence. She asked about his journeys to Germany, France, Spain, and England. "Not England, Agnes, I never made it that far. But one day ..." The discussion veered toward politics, Norman expressing his belief that the Democrats would capture the White House for the first time since Woodrow Wilson ("but not with Al Smith, who lost the last time around ...").

That flew in the face of Uncle Collin's prediction that Smith would indeed win the presidency in '32, but she put it out of her mind. No need to have thoughts of her uncle making her feel guilty—especially not in this lovely setting with its white-draped walls, linen tablecloths, fine crystal, and sterling silver. And the food! She'd never enjoyed beef Wellington and Yorkshire pudding at home like this.

She enjoyed the conversation with Norman so much, it wouldn't have mattered if he'd been saying Herbert Hoover had joined the Ringling Brothers as an acrobat. Norman's blue eyes danced and melted into hers. She wondered what she looked like to him. Perhaps a little mousy, but pretty enough. She hoped he found her more interesting than the other girls he must have courted—even those in Italy, she imagined.

He squired her home and left her at the front door with a bow. The evening had excited her and made her forget her troubles—until she heard nothing but silence and missed Racer's breathy panting upstairs in her third floor bedroom. She wanted to see Norman and feel the excitement again—but not until Monday morning, and then they'd be busy working. She replayed their dinner scene but couldn't help but go to sleep sad once again.

She came down the back stairs Saturday morning and stopped just before reaching the landing. She overheard Mama's voice, high and tremulous, in discussion with Uncle Collin.

"Why would she worry me so? After all the babies I buried, why would she ever behave this way? Her behavior's a disgrace to our family. I'm never able to handle this kind of scandal, you know that, Collin."

"Siobhan, settle yourself. It's no reflection on you or us. The fault lies squarely at her feet alone."

"All the work I've done, all the effort I've put into this family, and she disgraces me in just one evening. All of my friends were at bingo. I shall hear about this for weeks. It will be an ordeal going to Mass tomorrow morning."

"It's hardly necessary to blame yourself for someone else's sin."

Agnes felt an electric jolt of guilt coarse through her veins. She'd be punished as she'd never been punished before.

"Not to mention my suffering all those years ago, burying four babies in the cold rain. It was bad enough burying Racer in the backyard this week and being reminded of those horrible years. But now this?"

What four babies? Agnes forgot about guilt, and her mind percolated with a thousand questions. There'd only been Patrick and her as far as she'd known. She heard her mother sobbing and Uncle Collin comforting her.

She dreaded going any farther, but she had questions for Mama, so she went into the kitchen. Uncle Collin looked at her while her mother remained rooted at the stove, her back to them. Agnes cast a sideways glance at her uncle as she took her seat.

The avenging angel of death could not have seemed more threatening than the hard lines of Uncle Collin's ridge-like eyebrows. And those thick black eyeglasses—they seemed enormous. She forgot about Mama's revelation. Nervous and dry-mouthed, she asked him who'd won bingo.

"We have something very serious we need to talk with you about. I expect it will come as no surprise to you, Agnes Mary. Of course, it's all about last night."

The electric jolt of guilt returned. "Uncle Collin, I'm so sorry. I shouldn't have done it. Will you ever forgive me?"

"Whatever do you mean, child?" She heard irritation in his voice.

"Last night, Uncle Collin, I shouldn't have skipped bingo."

"For heaven's sake, Agnes. I told you I understood. No, I'm talking about Sister Lucy. She drank too much wine before the game began last night. It was most embarrassing and so inappropriate for a woman at her station in life. You know how people talk.

"Of course, they will know that no one on the Doherty side has ever had such a problem. When old Andrew Limerick lived, everyone said he drank too much. Your Aunt Lucy inherited that particular curse from her father."

Agnes sensed her blood calm down but still felt jittery all the way to her fingertips. "Aunt Lucy might drink a little too much wine on occasion, Uncle Collin, but I'm certain it's not a problem."

"Lucy may partake of fellowship on occasion, but she cannot do it too much. She has the family name to consider, you know. As head of the family, it's my responsibility to consider our standing in the community first and foremost. We have a reputation to uphold."

Why did it annoy her so when Uncle Collin reminded them he was head of the family? She thought that honor lay with Granny, not Uncle Collin. Mama said nothing, but she usually avoided any dissension in the family.

And speaking of dissension, Granny would pop a blood vessel if she heard Uncle Collin talking about her favorite daughter this way—or her husband. Granny doted on Aunt Lucy, her thirty years' service to St. Monica, and held Grandpa Andrew's memory dear.

The doorbell rang. Mama turned around, her face still a splotchy pattern that reminded Agnes of a geography lesson—perhaps those islands near Siam?

"That will be the shoemaker. I had my good shoes resoled last week." Mama made her way to the front door, her bad shoes clickety-clacking across the floors.

Agnes heard a man's voice at the door, and her heart throbbed. It was Norman. She ran a hand over her hair, wishing she could make herself pretty in the mirror, but then looked at Uncle Collin, who was eavesdropping as best he could. Her stomach dropped when she realized Mama was bringing Norman into the kitchen.

Mama's voice was a tinny vibrato. "Agnes, a visitor. Mr. Balmoral says you left your scarf with him yesterday evening."

"Oh-h-h-h, that's right, Mama," she stammered. Panic returned. With all this back and forth, would her blood turn to acid? "I must've forgotten it when I left work yesterday."

"You need to be more forthcoming," Mama said. "Mr. Balmoral said you left it in the restaurant where you and he dined. Last night."

She panicked and dared not look at Uncle Collin. "Oh, is that so?"

"Yes, Agnes," said Norman, who gave her uncle a brittle smile that reminded Agnes of the undertaker at Uncle Daniel's funeral. "I walked home after bringing you here. I passed the Richmond Club, and the owner, whom I know, fortunately, gave me the scarf. 'Your companion,' he said, 'must've dropped it on the floor under the table.' They know me quite well there."

"How fortunate," Uncle Collin said, his tone dropping an octave. His forehead became stone again.

Norman's smile died in the face of dead silence. Mama finally spoke. "Please sit, Mr. Balmoral, for coffee and marmalade."

"Thank you, but no. As Agnes well knows, I don't drink coffee. I only wanted to return the scarf. I'm meeting a group of men with whom I exercise regularly."

"I must compliment you," Uncle Collin said, finding his voice. "A healthy body is the guardian of the spirit."

"Yes, well, then I must be off." Norman glanced at her. She knew he expected her to escort him to the door, but it frightened her to think of what Mama and Uncle Collin would say once he'd left the house. She couldn't budge.

"Agnes, where are your manners?" Mama scolded. "See Mr. Balmoral to the front door."

Agnes led Norman through the hallway just as Granny came down the stairs, her left hand on the marble-and-wood handrail. "Good morning, Agnes. What is the dapper Mr. Balmoral doing here at this hour of the morning?"

Thank goodness for Granny. She always could dull the knife of impending doom when it was pointed at Agnes.

"Granny, he came to return my scarf."

"Any good reason will do. Young man, come visit us soon again." Her eyes danced a merry widow's waltz. "Give this old woman some white hairs she can brag about to her jealous friends."

"My pleasure, Mrs. Limerick. Next time, I'll bring you a variety of roses. Agnes tells me you once grew red, white, and yellow roses."

Granny turned to Agnes. "That's a dear, telling the young man about me. Now you two be on your way and make the most of the morning."

"Come outside with me a moment, Agnes," Norman said. Once outside he said, "Your grandmother is a treat. I like her. She's got *chutzpah*. What was that all about in the kitchen?"

She sidestepped both *chutzpah*, a word she didn't understand, and his question. "Granny flirts with any unattached man under the age of sixty, even my piano teacher, and he's hardly someone she'd marry."

"But Agnes, why did your mother and uncle seem so perturbed?"

There was no avoiding it, right there on the Pine Street sidewalk in front of the house. A cold breeze chilled Agnes.

"I told a little white lie to Uncle Collin about yesterday. I made up an excuse for not being at bingo. I didn't tell him about our dinner. When I go back inside, it's the Spanish Inquisition for me."

Norman scrunched up his mouth. "What a tangled web we weave, when first we practice to deceive."

"You quote Shakespeare."

He laughed. "Do your research, my dear. It's Walter Scott's *Marmion*. I don't want you lying on my account. It doesn't fit my image of you."

"Sometimes my uncle scares me. I feel like I'm four years old again when he wears those black glasses and stares at me like that."

"My image of you isn't that of a four-year-old child. When I'm walking home from work, I see your red hair and freckles, your green eyes, the way your fingers move about, so long and graceful."

Like Granny, his words assuaged Agnes's dread of facing Mama and Uncle Collin. How romantic too that he had a noble image of her.

Norman continued with a soft resonance. "You remind me of my first-grade teacher, Miss Manning. My eyes followed her for a year. I adored her, but alas, she got married and moved away."

He had a dreamy way of looking at her that took her imagination to another place, somewhere unknown with quiet fields of spring flowers and singing birds, and she'd forget the where and when of the moment. She had to think—yes, Mama's house, October 1931.

Just as she came back from her spring fields, Norman lifted her chin and kissed her on the lips ever so quickly. Agnes felt the imprint of his lips, a little jolt, part hope, part anticipation, and she wanted to feel his lips again. His mouth lingered in front of hers, his blue eyes mesmerizing. Then he kissed her a second time, much longer. The magic returned, and she felt waves of warmth pass from her lips, into her throat, up onto her scalp, and down into her heart.

They looked at each other after he released his lips. Agnes came back to her world—Mama's house, Pine Street, October 1931, awaiting Uncle Collin's punishment. What if the neighbors had seen their kisses?

"Good-bye for now," he said, straightening his coat. "I'm off for my morning run. Monday at work, Agnes."

She stood there a long time, reliving his hypnotic kisses, wanting more, wishing he were standing there, his face eclipsing hers. But then she went back inside and tried tiptoeing up the stairs to her bedroom.

"Agnes, come into the kitchen at once," Uncle Collin said.

She crept back into the kitchen, sat down at the table with the other three, their faces three points on a triangle—Mama pouty, Uncle Collin sphinx-like, Granny in the middle with her eyebrows raised but her purple eyelids closed. Agnes decided to play Miss Demure and cast her eyes downward.

"You lied to me," Uncle Collin began, his black glasses growing to huge proportions. "Tell the truth now, young lady."

Her stomach lurched as if caught in a whirlpool. "I didn't lie, it's just—oh, all right. Mr. Balmoral invited me to dinner, and I didn't want to tell you. I'm sorry."

Mama groaned. "Why would you be lying to your Uncle Collin who's done so much for you ever since your poor sainted father died?"

"I don't know really. I didn't want Uncle Collin to feel bad that I chose dinner with Mr. Balmoral over bingo."

Uncle Collin scowled. "I don't feel bad. I'm angry. My favorite niece has disappointed me, Agnes Mary. Until sundown it's rosaries, novenas, and—"

"Oh, poo." Granny stood and came behind Agnes, placing her hands on her shoulders. "You leave her be, Collin Doherty. Can't you see the lass is smitten? And she's far too grown up now to be her uncle's little helper."

"Woman, mind your manners. May I remind you, he is an English heathen."

"I am minding my manners," Granny bellowed. "Don't be impertinent with your elders. I've seen more in this life than you'll ever pontificate over."

Agnes made a silent prayer of thanks for Granny. "It was my fault, Granny. Mr. Balmoral invited me to dinner last night at the Richmond Club."

Granny continued. "He's a bully young man and very handsome. A nice twinkle in those blues. There's something about him that has me liking it."

"I smell a rat," Uncle Collin said. "He conspired with you to deceive me. He's obsessed with how he looks. And the heirs of St. Patrick do not break bread with the heirs of William of Orange."

Uncle Collin stood, towering over the others. "My dear niece, we cannot have you socializing with Episcopalians. It's one thing to work with Protestants and Jews, even do business with them at the market and the bank. But it's quite another matter to break bread with them in the evening. Do you remember what they did to us in Ireland?"

Granny rolled her eyes. "How could she ever forget? You drill it into their heads night and day."

"That's enough, Annie Kate. Agnes, I command you, you're not to see that young man again outside of work. Do you understand?"

When she didn't reply, he turned to Mama and said, "Siobhan, I'll see you tomorrow morning. Make sure you all come to Mass." He gave Agnes his final glance and banged the back door shut.

Granny patted Agnes on the shoulder. "Don't worry, princess. You have dinner with your young man and bring him around here whenever you like. So there's nothing more to be done about the matter."

"There's plenty more to be done," Mama said, her words quick and sharp. "You and I will have a long talk in the parlor after supper. You need to hear a few things about what the English did to the Dohertys in Ireland. Only heartbreak and unhappiness can come from associating with Mr. Balmoral. And I will not have that for my only daughter."

5

ON THE FIRST SATURDAY OF THE NEW YEAR, Agnes found herself on a walk with Norman through Old City neighborhoods. The gray ugliness of winter depressed her. Yes, the temperature had warmed to a toasty forty-five and the Christmas snow had melted, but 1932 promised to be no happier than 1931. Everyone she saw on the street moped about as if they'd lost their nearest and dearest grandmother. No one had money, especially not Agnes, whose earnings Mama used for paying household expenses, and the new year generated no special reason to celebrate. Still, she enjoyed walking along the cobblestoned streets with Norman, discussing music with him.

"Whom do you prefer, Agnes, Mozart or Beethoven?"

She tightened the belt of her tattered old Loden coat before answering. If only she could buy a new one, but at least her hat with its red-and-yellow plume was new, a handmade Christmas gift from Granny. "I have to choose?"

"You talk so much about playing Beethoven and Mozart, I wondered, why these two so much more than the others? Why not Bach, Schubert, or Brahms?"

They continued their walk by the open market at 2nd Street. Fall's leaves had yielded to dried twigs and loose branches. She shivered in the day's dampness, so she stayed close by Norman's side, drawn into the warmth of his body.

"I see. Mr. Larney encouraged me in the classics, and somehow I always gravitated toward those two. Mozart was always the greater challenge, especially the piano concertos. In Mozart, every mistake is glaring and ugly. The notes, arpeggios, and scales have to be as crystal clear as an ice sculpture."

Norman brightened. "An ice sculpture. Now we're talking my language."

"Like the sharp edges and smooth planes. One flaw and it falls apart. That's Mozart, but Beethoven—"

"Don't they come from the same era?"

"Yes, but Mozart worked within the classical structure. Beethoven revolutionized it."

"You're thinking about the *Eroica*, aren't you?"

"Not just his third symphony. His final piano sonatas challenged the entire sonata form, which was the foundation for all classical music. Nothing's been the same since. Listen to his final sonata and you'll hear the origins of American jazz. It's inconceivable to imagine the world without Beethoven—or Mozart."

"The world survived a long time before Mozart and Beethoven."

True, Agnes had to admit, but they'd changed the world nonetheless. Norman shifted their conversation to architecture that had changed the world, using Old City's eighteenth-century buildings to make his point. His enthusiasm intoxicated her. Those bricks, windows, and rooflines had been etched onto her mind from walks with Daddy long ago. Walks like this one.

Beneath her happiness, apprehension grew with each block they passed. What if someone saw them? She hadn't promised Mama and Uncle Collin she'd never see Norman outside work, but she hadn't said she would, either. Their first dinner had been October, followed by three months of awkward silence at home for Agnes, who kept outings with Norman to herself. But today, walking about her own neighborhood?

Oh, why did Mama and Uncle Collin care so much? Though Norman's views intrigued her and she liked the hard muscles on his upper arms, surely it wouldn't go further than a good-bye kiss? At least Granny had said, "Make the most of it."

Mama indeed had lectured her on what the English had done to the

Dohertys. It had made Agnes's skin crawl. She'd never known about the English landlord who assaulted their Doherty great-aunt. When she poisoned his brandy late one night, he had her hanged for attempted murder, the whole family watching. Shortly after that, he evicted the Dohertys from their damp hovel, leaving the family to wander the streets of Dublin until they could scrape together enough money to escape to America.

But did that mean Norman had to accept blame for things his Protestant ancestors had done to hers? He had about as much responsibility for the Battle of the Boyne as she did for the Inquisition. But she kept these radical thoughts to herself at home.

That question drew her to one of the back pews at St. Mark's Episcopal just three Sundays after Mama's lecture. She had to see the evil rites of Protestantism, knowing she risked Uncle Collin's thunderbolt. But the Anglican Church differed very little from her own. Yes, they had no pope, their priests could marry, and they spoke English in services. But they recognized the saints and celebrated the sacraments the same way. More importantly, they sang the same music.

So she enjoyed her new friend regardless of her family. Being around him excited her. He had vital opinions. To Norman, neither Herbert Hoover nor any of his Democratic opponents could get them out of their mess. Only individual responsibility and dedication to work would do it. And physical fitness ... Norman seemed obsessed with exercise.

She admired his perfectionism and tried dedicating herself anew to perfecting her music. Invariably, though, her mind would wander and she'd want to read a book. But when she read, her mind would wander again and she'd want to play the piano.

Norman might expect much of others, but he expected even more of himself. He criticized his architectural draughts and revised them over and over. When he had his own architecture firm, he told her, he planned to choose only projects that advanced architectural modernism, even if that meant less income. Even Norman's favorite way of relaxing, by running along the Schuylkill River, revolved around discipline.

Somehow, this added to his appeal. She had to admit he was growing on her. Maybe she did want more than friendship? She couldn't sort it out, so she let the days and weeks pass, juggling her friendship with Norman with her obligations to family, at least until she had an answer.

They would lunch at the office a few times every week and take private walks around the office building. On the rare occasions they could afford it, they would share a dinner after work. The first time Norman walked by her desk in the afternoon suggesting they meet for dinner, she said to herself, "A minute here, a minute there, Mama won't notice I'm home late." She never told Mama why she came home late and not terribly hungry for their light suppers of corned beef, cabbage, and stewed carrots. The occasions multiplied with the weeks.

She'd return early evening to a quiet house. Granny would have retired to her bedroom, no doubt knitting. Agnes would knock on Mama's door before heading up to her bedroom. Their courtesies had become alarmingly pleasant, almost too pleasant. She'd tell herself that disclosing her time with Norman would upset her mother. After all, she didn't want to marry Norman Balmoral.

Only on Saturday mornings when Agnes came down the stairs for breakfast did their family resume its routine. Mama would grill bacon and eggs while bickering with Granny, who'd rattle off questions to Agnes about her job.

"Agnes," Norman said, "you're a million miles away. You haven't been listening to me."

Agnes turned her head at him and laughed. "I'm sorry. I was thinking about breakfast this morning. My grandmother asked me about my job, and the way she did it reminded me of Mrs. Weisskopf."

"If she reminds you of Mrs. Weisskopf, then you have no privacy at home. That lady makes it her business to know everything about everybody."

"Little does she know, we've already had lunch fourteen times, met for dinner five, and walked away eleven Saturdays. If Mrs. Weisskopf could spy on us right now, she'd have the wedding silver engraved."

"You've counted our lunches and dinners? Don't joke about Mrs. Weisskopf. Marriage is too far off for either of us. You're just a child and I have no money."

A child? A shiver ran up her spine, but she hardly cared. Sometimes he behaved like an obtuse know-it-all, pointing up to gables, balustrades, and those silly flying buttresses. Agnes frowned, and even this walk down Locust Street with the pleasant fragrance of brownstones' chimneys failed to squash her irritation.

"I've got a mother already, and she has her own opinions about marriage for me, and I'm not a child. I'm almost twenty-two. And my mother—"

She was about to tell him Mama didn't approve of arrogant architects when she saw a heavily clad man accost a bony pear-shaped woman at Locust Street. The older woman kicked the man in the shin, but he knocked her to the ground, tore her purse from her arm, and ran off.

Agnes stepped back, feeling as though the man also had struck her. "My God, Norman, look at that."

His head darted from Agnes to the victim and back. "Blasted vagrant. Agnes, you tend to the lady. I'm going to catch that thief if it's the last thing I do—"

He was off like lightning. She'd never seen a man run so quickly. Passing the fallen woman without a glance, Norman turned the corner where the man had disappeared. Agnes rushed up to the woman.

"My Lord," the lady said, sobbing, blue-gray hair strewn across her face. "He stole my purse and the money for Sunday's dinner. And pictures of my Jimmy."

It was Mrs. O'Toole, the lady who owned Mr. Larney's house. The sight terrified Agnes. What if it had been Mama or Granny? She leaned down to help the older woman stand.

"Mrs. O'Toole, it's Agnes Limerick. Let me help you up."

Her right hand was bleeding, and her glasses lay shattered on the ground. Mrs. O'Toole seemed a sliver of the stolid matron Agnes had known, now reduced to scrawny and frail. Agnes gave her a clean handkerchief for the blood. They sat on the nearby stoop, and Mrs. O'Toole continued to cry while Agnes, remembering how her father had examined injuries, took a look at her cuts and bruises. She asked Mrs. O'Toole to move her arms and legs. No broken bones.

"Everything will be all right, Mrs. O'Toole. We'll take you home when my friend returns. Tell me what hurts."

Despite numerous groans, it became clear the scrapes were only superficial.

The lady settled down after several minutes. "Agnes Limerick, I've never been so happy to see anyone. What are you doing here?"

She explained that they'd witnessed the attack and Norman had run after the thief. Norman returned fifteen minutes later with a policeman who carried what must've been Mrs. O'Toole's purse, ragged but in one piece.

Norman spoke first. "Ma'am, I believe this is yours. This officer noticed me just as I caught up with the man and wrestled him to the ground."

"Norman, this is Mrs. O'Toole. Would you believe it? She owns the house where my old piano teacher lives."

"Mrs. O'Toole, is it?" The policeman spoke, his voice weary and slow. "I'll have to make a report."

"Kathleen O'Toole, sir, 1005 Clinton Street."

He raised his eyebrows as he jotted down her name. "Why do ladies walk about alone in this neighborhood? Too dangerous these days for a nice Irish lady like you. We'll need you to make a statement so we can prosecute the man."

"Thank heavens," Mrs. O'Toole said, ignoring the policeman while she took inventory of her purse. "It's all here, my wallet. Agnes, here's my photo of Jimmy at twelve, God rest his soul. Young man, who are you?"

"Balmoral, ma'am. We saw that man attack you. Are you all right?"

"I am now, thanks to you. God bless you, son—"

The policeman took over and insisted Mrs. O'Toole accompany him to the station to identify the criminal, to prevent him from doing it again. Mrs. O'Toole grumbled, but Norman convinced her to make the effort. An hour later, Norman and Agnes deposited Mrs. O'Toole at her house—the very one where Granny and Grandpa Limerick first had lived in Philadelphia, she pointed out to Norman.

"It's been quite an afternoon," Norman said at the corner of 10th and Clinton. "I certainly hope they put that man in jail."

"Yes, it is unfortunate, a vagrant driven to attacking an innocent lady. If only people weren't so poor these days."

"Hogwash, Agnes. Any man can get a job if he wants to. I know times are tough, but there's work out there for men who want it. Men who end up stealing from ladies like Mrs. O'Toole belong in prison, sweetheart."

Agnes was too tired to disagree. "I suppose you know best."

True, he deserved to be punished, but surely their society could find a better way to help indigents? So many mulled about town these days, she found it impossible to believe there really was work for all the people who wanted it.

And, Norman had called her sweetheart for the first time. No man had ever called her that except Daddy, and then she'd been eight. She felt transported above herself, looking down at them on the sidewalk talking love and work. And did she just think *love*?

The winter's sun shone through Norman's hair, and smoke rose from the neighborhood's chimneys. Agnes's eyes lingered on Norman's. She couldn't think of anything to say. His gaze lowered to her mouth, and her body warmed up. He leaned in and kissed her.

Her heart jumped at the touch of his lips, and her mind wandered. She squirmed, excited as he pulled her close to him and wrapped his arms about her. She'd never felt this way when anyone else had kissed her—not kisses of affection from her family, not Tommy Callahan's. His lips stayed glued to hers for how long, ten seconds? She liked the feel of him, his smooth lips and his chin's stubble on her face. Kissing seemed very natural, as if they'd been doing it for years.

At long last, he released his lips. "So sweet," he said. What was it about his eyes, as blue as the spring sky? The oblique jawline, square chin, long nose—Agnes felt a rush through her abdomen. Her scalp tingled as if he'd cast a spell, all with those blue eyes and a kiss.

"I must be going. Until Monday, Agnes. We'll have lunch. I have a morning meeting with Weisskopf, but you and I can have some time together after that."

She walked the six short blocks home in a happy daze, reliving his lips on hers, his dizzying blue eyes, his crisp haircut. Norman Balmoral had kissed her on the front steps of the same house where Granny had loved Grandpa Limerick. Walking into Washington Square, she remembered her first encounter with Norman just a short three months ago. How had that day led to this one? How could his lips have put her in such a tizzy, his eyes boring into hers, his mouth surrendering an involuntary smile?

Tossing and turning that night, she couldn't get him out of her mind. At times his image faded and she forgot the outlines of his face, but then he'd reappear and she'd feel the graze of his stubble. On her soft mattress in the privacy of her bedroom, she purred in anticipating the next time her face touched his. And she began to wonder if she wanted more than just a kiss.

She slept only a few hours and yawned her way through church, the words from Uncle Collin's Mass flying right through her head. Only the music stayed—and what beautiful music, so magical. She'd always found God in the music, but this time it made her think about Norman.

Throughout the long Sunday, she counted down the hours until Monday morning. Eighteen, seventeen, sixteen. She tingled at the thought of seeing him again, and her heart throbbed. Fifteen, fourteen, thirteen.

The bomb dropped Sunday evening after supper. Mama called her into the kitchen, her voice vise-tight. She was cleaning dishes, her back to Agnes. Mama's shoulders were hunched up to her neck.

"Kathleen O'Toole tells me Mr. Balmoral rescued her purse from an indigent. You were out walking with him yesterday. How long has this been going on?"

Agnes stood in the doorway, prepared to turn away. "Mama, he's simply a friend from the office. He is a good man. He caught the man who attacked Mrs. O'Toole and got her purse back."

"This is not about Mrs. O'Toole. You've been sneaking around here ever since you went to work at that office. You've obviously been seeing quite a lot of the heroic Mr. Balmoral, and that means you've been lying—to all of us, chances are, quite often. I don't care if he's a good man, Agnes. He's simply not suitable for you."

But Agnes regained her courage, hearing Mama admit Norman was a hero. "I'm twenty-one years old, Mama. I can spend time with whomever I like."

Her mother's eyebrows rushed together above stormy eyes. "Not while you live under my roof, young lady. You cannot oppose what your uncle and I say. I wish you would take your family's feelings into consideration. Blood is thicker than water, you know."

Agnes's head cleared. "Then perhaps I should move, because I'm not planning to give up Norman's friendship."

"Just exactly how? You don't have the money to support yourself."

"I'm a grown woman, Mother. I can make my own decisions. Why, I'll rent a room in a house, just like Mr. Larney."

Why—she *would* be able to do this. She made sixteen dollars per week, and Mrs. O'Toole charged Mr. Larney only twenty-five dollars per month. If she found a landlady as nice as Mrs. O'Toole, she'd have almost forty dollars left every month for food, clothes, and shopping. But what would that mean in the evenings when she sat in her room alone? No, she'd be walking about town with her new friends from the office. Norman, he'd be there too.

Mama threw the silverware into the sink and jolted Agnes back to reality. She leaned on the counter and turned to face Agnes. Her face had become puffy; her chin and neck sagged.

"Have you any idea what this will do to our household if you leave? Daughter, how will I ever pay the taxes this fall?"

God in heaven, she hadn't contemplated this. The severity of Mama's situation weighed Agnes down like a stone-laced quilt. Mama had breathed a sigh of relief about the taxes when she'd started at Smith and Weisskopf. Would Mama and Granny be put on the street if she insisted on her independence? Agnes felt her veins stretch like piano wire. No, she couldn't desert her family, nor could she betray Uncle Collin.

There had to be a way to figure this out. She'd always been able to solve algebraic equations, but finding a value of X to balance this one would be a real challenge. Norman stood on one side of the equation with his magnetic smile, resonating baritone, and architecture lessons. Mama and Uncle Collin stood on the other with their rules and pronouncements, backed by the cozy red-bricked house with her books, her music, and Granny.

She looked around the kitchen at Mama's gas stove, the Frigidaire refrigerator she'd been so proud of buying, her heavy oak table, the marble floors. Daddy moved back here with Mama and Patrick after Grandpa Limerick died, just before Agnes came along. After Daddy died here, Granny had come back to live with them. The red drapes, the dark furniture, the smells of roast beef and stewed cabbage, how could she ever contemplate leaving? How could she survive without Uncle Collin's warm embrace to protect her from the world?

"Mama," she said, seeing Mama's chin begin to shake. "Please don't cry. I didn't mean it. I promise I won't leave. And I won't see Mr. Balmoral again."

Mama turned back to the sink. Agnes trudged up the back kitchen stairway to her room, nervous and miserable. No, she never could leave this house. She waited until Mama retired to her bedroom to come down to the kitchen to look up the Balmorals' telephone number. She wanted to telephone him before her resolve melted away.

"Cheltenham 591," she said. It rang once, twice, indefinitely, no answer. She sighed, put the phone back in its cradle, and sat in the nearby chair. She slouched, knees touching, feet wide apart.

"I'll talk to him tomorrow at lunch," she said. "I'll tell him the truth. He'll understand. He'll know I can't give up my family."

But a chaotic uproar greeted her at work the next morning. Mr. Weisskopf had called the architects into the conference room and announced that half would be furloughed indefinitely. The administrative staff, already greatly reduced, would be unaffected.

Agnes asked Cristina for details.

"We don't know yet, but they're all in there." Cristina raised and lowered her eyebrows as she spoke in a hushed, hurried alto, as excited as a down-on-his-luck lawyer reading a headline such as *Wealthy Industrialists Lost at Sea; Sinking Blamed on Captain's Error.*

Agnes sat at her desk, ignoring Cristina's blazing eyes. "How bad can it be? They can't possibly keep the firm in business without the architects."

"It's a miracle they've been able to do it this long. No one is building in Philadelphia. No one is building anywhere."

Dear God, Agnes thought as she sank into her chair, what if Norman lost his job? His family depended on him. Her heart melted at the thought of him unemployed. He loved his work like no one she'd ever known. She could see the passion in his eyes when he talked about the P.S.F.S. building or his library design. No one had the right to take that away from him.

After ten excruciating minutes, the door to the conference room burst open. Norman was the first one out, and she saw fury in his eyes. Agnes rose, but before she could say anything —

"I've been fired, Agnes," he yelled, heading to the elevator, his face purple. "And I'm not staying here one minute longer."

His anger made her mind go blank, her knees weak, and she could only stutter. "But I want to talk with y-y-y-you —"

The elevator arrived, and Norman opened the doors and marched in. "I'm not in the mood to talk, Agnes." He closed the doors, leaving without even his overcoat.

What had she wanted to talk with him about? She couldn't remember. But Norman, out of a job, no income, no work, a devastating loss. She had this image of a talented and handsome man, his face ashen white, swinging from the William Penn statue on top of City Hall—then jumping off.

Her heart contracted at the thought of Norman fired, so wrong and unfair. And now he was gone from her too, perhaps forever. Since their first walk about town, she'd counted on seeing him in the kitchen, waiting for him to pass her desk and make some witty remark. A thousand thoughts swam through her mind, all circling Norman. But what had she wanted to discuss with him?

Agnes couldn't work the rest of the day, glancing at the elevator every time the doors opened. That night, she barely could eat or sleep. The next morning, she discovered he had come back to the office before anyone had arrived to collect his personal items. He left a note on her desk.

My dear Agnes,

I hope you forgive my departure yesterday morning. I was quite angry and did not care to speak with anyone, not even you. Please forgive my rudeness.

I would like to see you very soon, but for now I need some time to myself. I also need to find a new job, which will take a considerable amount of time. It's a difficult environment for an architect these days. But find work, I will.

I'll be calling on you soon.

Sincerely,

Norman

Sincerely? Flabbergasting. After all the time they'd spent together, after the upsetting incident with Mrs. O'Toole, after their special kisses (two!), she rated far better than *Sincerely*. The assignation made her blood boil. Had he toyed with her, like he'd toyed with Mary Alden? She decided to confide in Cristina.

"I've had a most annoying letter from Norman."

Cristina read it through her thick glasses and groaned. "He's leaving you, Agnes, just like he left Mary Alden. He turned around and ran away as soon as she expressed an interest in him. I hope you haven't told him you love him."

Dear God, had she said that? She couldn't recall. Perhaps she really was a child, a naïve girl who thought an older, more worldly man actually might fall for her.

But she couldn't admit this to Cristina. "Of course not. It's not like we're engaged, after all. We spent all day together Saturday, and then this happened." She smacked at the letter.

"Even if you haven't said anything, I'll bet he thinks you've developed a mad crush. Men are such crazy creatures. Never let them know you love them until you're absolutely sure they're going to respond in kind. I waited until the day before Angelo and I got married, and we'd been engaged for three months. If you push men too fast, they'll run faster than Jim Thorpe. Looks to me Norman's using the furlough as an escape hatch."

"That's impossible. He has far too much integrity to do something like that."

Cristina grunted. "Did I hear integrity and Norman Balmoral in the same sentence? I'll be surprised if you ever hear from him again."

"You read the letter, Cristina. He said he'll be calling on me soon."

"No man ever says that and actually calls."

"We'll see about that." Mama, Uncle Collin, and now Cristina. Did no one believe in Norman?

She crept around the office like a wounded animal that week peeking around every corner, hoping to find Norman. She jumped when the phone rang or the door opened. She knew he'd never come back to this office, but that didn't stop her from looking.

Then she realized he'd have to return Friday for his final paycheck. Since she did the payroll now, he'd have to get the check from her.

Friday came, but no Norman. While reviewing the week's transactions with Mr. Weisskopf that afternoon, she mentioned the unclaimed check. He told her he'd be mailing Balmoral's check to him.

Mr. Weisskopf added, "He used a few ugly words with me in Monday's conference. I told him not to come back. He's a loose cannon, that one."

On Saturday, Agnes went to Rittenhouse Square, hoping Norman would meet her as he'd done so many weekends before. But the tolerable weather of the past weekend had yielded to bitter cold. She sat on the dreary, bone-chilling bench for an hour. She gave up at last and walked home, her hands and feet frozen, her shoulders sagging.

She'd been still as a mouse at home since Mama's explosion Sunday afternoon, staying close to Granny. But perhaps her mother and Uncle Collin had been right—she had taken leave of her senses with Norman. Perhaps he wasn't right for her.

The icy silence gradually had thawed through the next week, and by that afternoon, Mama was issuing her usual domestic directives. "Lass, it's getting to be time for dinner, and I need your help."

Agnes dutifully dragged herself into the kitchen, but the promise of a hearty meal failed to energize her. She couldn't muster any enthusiasm for the piano that evening but played anyway. Everything came out hollow. Even the Chopin nocturnes had no feeling, just dead.

Anger gave way to depression, depression to resentment, and resentment back to anger. She'd been angry with Mama and Uncle Collin, and now Norman had jilted her. She alternated between happy highs when sure he'd return, desperate lows when certain he'd abandoned her.

She awoke Sunday morning with a brainstorm. She'd attend Sunday morning services at St. Mark's Episcopal to see Norman. She told Mama and Granny she was going for a morning walk ("In this foul weather?" Mama asked). She scanned the pews once inside, but saw no sign of Norman, just well-dressed people wearing affluence on their pouty faces.

Norman had drawn a detailed picture of his parents. But only a few men were short, overweight, pink-faced, round-spectacled, and bald, although most of the women were tall, full-figured with high cheekbones, jutting chins, and grayish swept-back hair. But none of the Johnny Bulls were paired with the

Queen Marys. She strained to hear their names in the crowd—Victoria and Cornelius, Norman had mentioned—but left disappointed.

She was eating very little these days. Granny remarked on it one afternoon as they sat at the kitchen table sipping tea that had turned cold.

"Lamb, it's like a bird you are, picking at your meal," Granny said, the lines above her nose pinched together. "You'll grow thin and irritable like your Aunt Lucy. What ever is the problem?"

Agnes searched her mind for an easy culprit. "I'm sorry, Granny, I'm all upset about the office. They've let half the architects go, and it's a bucket of nerves we are these days. I never realized working could be so upsetting."

"You need to have your nourishment, Agnes Mary. You can't let this turn you into a skeleton. Remember those of us who dote on you."

"I know, Granny, I must have an upset stomach. Nothing to worry about."

"There's something you're not telling me. It's that fetching Balmoral man, I'm sure of it. Was he one of those who lost his job? Remember, I'm your granny. I know you better than anyone."

She sidestepped the question. "I could never keep anything from you, Granny. I'm worried about keeping my own job. What'll we do if I lose it? How will Mama keep the house?"

"You just set your mind at ease. We've been through much harder times, and we'll get through this rough patch, no matter what."

She kissed Granny's wrinkled cheek, uneasy and unsure despite her assurances, and headed to the piano. She kept her feelings from everyone—Norman's firing, his disappearance, her family's opposition, her own turbulence, the lonely hour she'd spent on the frozen bench in Rittenhouse Square. All of these things remained locked away.

She accomplished nothing at work that second week and could not lose herself in numbers for the first time. She couldn't get Norman out of her mind. Nothing was the same at work without him. Even though she'd said nothing to Cristina in recent days, Agnes felt as though she knew. She could feel Cristina trying to lighten the mood with jokes about Mr. Smith's pencil-thin moustache, the chicken soup and matzah balls Mrs. Weisskopf brought to the office, even Herbert Hoover's starched shirts, but nothing could raise Agnes's mood.

To make matters worse, chatty Limerick and Doherty relatives, including Patrick from Washington and Aunt Julia from New York, filled Mama's house that Friday for Uncle Collin's birthday. Listening to the happy chatter felt as excruciating as scratching a chalkboard. Normally, she'd enjoy visits from Aunt Julia, Aunt Lucy, and her relatives. She'd always delighted in Uncle Collin's birthdays, but not this year. She wanted to hide in her bedroom and lick her wounds, like Racer would've done. But he was gone too.

She wanted to see Norman; she couldn't deny it. She missed him, and yes, she liked him more than just as a friend. She despaired of this truth, but she had to admit it. How had it happened? It seemed like she'd been in love with him right from the start. Love had been there, in their awkward meeting in the bathroom, in the sun shining behind his head in Washington Square, in their kiss in front of Mrs. O'Toole's, and even as the elevator door shut in her face.

Her patience reached its limit the next morning, and she telephoned his house again. No answer. She went for a walk after lunch and her feet led her west. She barely noticed the snow. Norman's parents' house at 36th and Hamilton became a magnet. With each block, Agnes felt the urge to turn back but somehow her feet persisted. She trembled when she reached his block, certain she'd be discovered. But she had to see him.

Though she'd never seen his family home, she recognized the white-bricked, black-trimmed house based on his description. She could see into the windows, an empty void that horrified her. She walked up to the porch. No furniture, no rugs, no wall hangings. The emptiness terrified her.

What had happened? Norman had said nothing about trouble at home. She walked around to the other side and peeked in the kitchen window. She saw rusty dirt on the steel countertops, an old telephone on a desk, its cord pulled out of the wall, two mice nibbling at scraps of food. She turned away, her mouth dry and her head dizzy.

Then she saw the large sign on the opposite corner of the block. Balmoral's General Store. The lights were on.

She'd inquire at the store. Perhaps she would meet Norman's parents. He'd told her they ran the store. His father ran the counter while his mother did the books. And if they weren't there, someone else could tell her where they'd gone.

She crossed the street to the corner entrance, unsure whether she'd be welcome. Her hands shook. Would they think her too forward? Her feet seemed to know better, and they led the way.

Her heart pounded in her ears as she opened the front door. She took off her gloves. Her palms had become clammy, her empty stomach a bundle of nerves. The store was deserted except for a wrinkled sack of a man at the register. Norman's father? She hadn't expected him to be so old.

"I've come to see Mr. Balmoral," she said as she approached the register. She looked around at the tall shelves stacked with food, organized just the way she had imagined Norman's family to be.

"Mr. Balmoral the older, or Mr. Balmoral the younger?" The man's stuttering echoed Agnes's nervousness.

"Mr. Norman Balmoral. Are you his father, sir?"

"Certainly not, I am Mr. Soltham. Mr. Balmoral's in the back office. Who may I say is calling?"

"Miss Limerick."

The old man arched his eyebrows and walked to the back. Agnes wandered about, noticing counters of cold medications, magazines, restoratives for the elderly, grooming supplies for men, toothpastes, shampoos, even a wall shelved with row-upon-row of books. She pretended to be unconcerned, even careless, but her nerves assaulted her stomach.

"Agnes, what ever are you doing here?"

Her heart jumped into her throat. Norman was two feet behind her. He wore light slacks and a red flannel shirt, dark chest hair peeking out over the open collar. She gasped. He'd almost always worn a tie except when running. This new image in working man's clothes ignited a range of feelings — feelings she didn't understand and hadn't expected.

"What a surprise," Norman said. He wore a thin smile betrayed by eyes as sad as a lost puppy dog's. "I barely know what to say."

"Norman," she said, her voice far away.

He smiled but looked down. "How wonderful to see you. Give me just a moment."

He turned to the older man. "Mr. Soltham, thank you for coming today. I know it was difficult to spare the time. Monday, then? I can manage now."

"Yes, of course," Mr. Soltham said, focused on the cash register and receipts.

Norman looked back at her. "Mr. Soltham, you may go." It pleased Agnes that Norman wanted them to be alone. Why did such a cozy warmth spread into her chest and abdomen?

"All right, sir, but I haven't finished with these receipts. You won't be needing anything beyond that?"

"I repeat, Mr. Soltham, that's quite fine. The receipts I can finish. Goodness knows, there aren't many."

The older man fussed about with drawers, receipts, and bottles, going through some sort of nonsense while Norman and Agnes exchanged glances. Norman's cheeks turned red, though the store had plenty of heat. He fidgeted while Agnes's eyes caressed his figure. Had he really become so alluring in the twelve days since she'd seen him? He wore casual clothing well. She wanted to wrap her arms about herself. It felt so good to watch him move, his eyes smiling at her. She barely could contain her joy, but it felt different, something basic and simple.

Why didn't the pesky Mr. Soltham just leave?

At last Mr. Soltham finished fussing, and Norman escorted him to the door. Agnes wondered why he'd delayed so long. Perhaps he'd thought to act as chaperone? She heard their endless exchange — Mr. Soltham's refrain, "Mind you . . ." and Norman's reply, "Yes, that will do . . ." — it seemed Norman was ready to push the old man out the door any moment.

"Mr. Balmoral, mind you . . ."

"Mr. Soltham, that will do . . ."

It occurred to Agnes that Norman felt agitated about her, that she presented a quandary for him, just as much as he presented one for her. Her heart throbbed, and she noted his gestures, clearly eager to get rid of the oblivious clerk. She knew, of a sudden, why he wanted to be alone with her, why he acted so nervous, why his complexion turned red. Mrs. Weisskopf and Mr. Smith notwithstanding, despite her mother and Uncle Collin beating the Irish drum of the Boyne, they'd broken the rules, they'd been drawn together at work, they'd kissed in front of Mrs. O'Toole's. Norman wanted to be alone with her because he desired her.

But a man shouldn't desire her unless he'd declared his love, proposed, gained permission from Mama, and had Uncle Collin bless their betrothal at St. Patrick's. She could hear voices in her head—Mama, Uncle Collin, Granny, Daddy—a crowd of people, her people, warning her, "Get out of this office before you commit a venal sin. Now, Agnes Mary!"

She stood rooted, her heart pulsing, her hands clammy, her mouth dry, her throat parched, and her stomach sizzling, unable to move. She saw a small, narrow path to the open door. Mr. Soltham and Norman stood in the way talking about tonic supplies. Her head told her to leave, but her heart fixated on Norman's oblique shape, his silky baritone, the zippy way he shook his head. Faith and obedience ordering her to leave, and love and joy pleading with her to remain. Her heart commanded her body to stay and snuffed out the voices in her head.

Norman remained at the door after Mr. Soltham left, looking out the window. They remained silent. Somehow, she knew he felt her eyes on his back. He turned around. His eyebrows made steep angles above his eyes, and his gaze penetrated her. The enigmatic vampire who'd hypnotized her on their first meeting returned in that stare.

He walked slowly, reached for her left hand, and clasped it to his chest—a warm, contoured chest. Would he know how clammy her hands were? Would he feel the rapid beat of her heart?

"I couldn't bear seeing you. Now you know we lost our home," he said.

Her throat turned dry, so she did her best to convey her thoughts through her eyes. *I missed you, Norman. It's been two weeks. Why didn't you call me?*

"I've avoided you these past two weeks because I was ashamed," he said. *What have you to be ashamed about?*

He brought her hand up to his chest and started stroking it. "... Ashamed of not working, losing my job, losing my temper. Can you understand that?"

She nodded, *Of course, I understand.* She'd thought of little else in those twelve days. Why couldn't she speak? All she could do was look at him. She felt her face flush and felt exposed. *But what about the house, Norman? What about your parents losing the home where you were born and raised?*

"It's painful enough living upstairs, looking out the window across the street to the empty house, waiting for the bank to sell it at auction," he added, circumventing the question she hadn't even formulated in her mind.

What that must be like—Norman and his parents living above their store's dwindling business, its windows looking across the street to their house, waiting for the highest bidder to yawn his way to the front of the line. Indifferent strangers would move into the Balmoral home at a bargain price.

A wave of love came over her, and she reached for his face and caressed his cheek. *Don't be ashamed. You make me feel happy, like I belong here with you. You make me feel connected to my heart. Connected to your heart too.*

Without letting go of her left hand, he turned his lips to kiss her right fingers, wet and needy. She felt the rough, spongy texture of his tongue sweep across her hand, electrifying Agnes and sending tingling jolts down to her feet.

Her heart pulsed a strong fortissimo, but her hands stopped shaking and her stomach settled. The sensation overwhelmed Agnes, and she knew she wanted Norman the same way he wanted her. They reached to kiss each other at the same time. This one was different. It was urgent, vital, and alive. Agnes felt unsatisfied need in his kiss. And so she kissed him back.

Faith and obedience, or love and joy? Her family's tribunal receded as she struggled to control her body. But wrapped by Norman's arms and feeling his lips, their judgment faded away. *I want you, Norman.*

His body melted into hers. She felt the contours of his chest, his flat stomach, his straight hips, his left leg against her right, and his right against her left. She felt something hard pulsing on the inside of his leg, pressing against her middle. An altogether new feeling drew her into that sensation, an alluring temptation between her own legs to surrender to his will.

Words failed her and she moaned. She pulled her head back and told him with her eyes what she wanted—no, demanded. She forgot her past, her breeding, her family, and surrendered to the joy in her heart. *This is what I want from you, now. It's your purpose for me, the one thing you can give me that matters.*

But his spine stiffened and he pulled away. The blues of his eyes blazed into her. "We cannot do this, my love," he gasped between heavy breaths.

"Yes, we can. Kiss me again."

Without taking his eyes off her, he buried his lips into hers, his tongue deep inside, kissing her in a way she never knew possible. It felt exactly right, and she did the same. He broke free and breathed hard. He took hold of her again and pressed the bulge in his trousers against her. *Take me with you now, Norman. I need to be connected to you. Now.*

Norman locked the front door, his eyes never leaving hers. He grabbed her waist and led her to the back office, smothered by stacks of paper and musty books. Agnes leaned against the desk, facing him, as he closed the door.

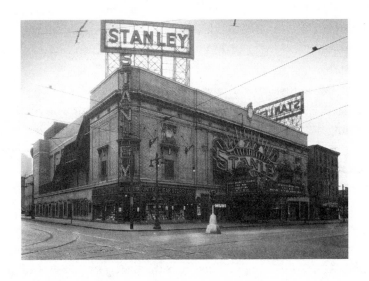

6

CRISTINA TALKED RIGHT THROUGH HER TURKEY PASTRAMI SANDWICH, attacking it as if her face were kneading bread. Mustard dripped down her mouth. "Can you believe we spent ten cents for that picture? Should be no more than five cents."

"I loved it, Cristina. It's a lot of money for John Barrymore and Billie Burke, but worth every penny."

They'd discovered they liked going to picture shows together. This Saturday in late February, Agnes had spent the sunny morning walking with Norman in Rittenhouse Square and then seen *A Bill of Divorcement* with Cristina at the Stanley on 19th. After the movie, they went to Nussbaum's Diner across from the theater. Sitting with her back to the deli counter, Agnes savored the sausage, sauerkraut, and latke scents while eating corned beef pastrami on rye.

"Agnes, who was the actress playing the daughter? She was the best thing in the picture. Something like Hesbourne."

"Katharine Hepburn. She's our age, *veddy* upper crust, *veddy* Main Line Philadelphia. She graduated from Bryn Mawr or Swarthmore, one of the two. I've been reading movie magazines since we started going to pictures. She made a big splash on Broadway and is having a go at the movies."

Going to the movies helped Agnes get her mind off Norman, their topsy-turvy relations, and the deadly sins they'd committed in his office. The more time she could place between herself and the event, the easier she'd breathe.

"That movie upset me, Agnes. I don't believe in divorce, even if they stayed together in the end. Those movie types always get divorced," Cristina said, rolling her eyes. Her voice sharpened into cutting tones. "Look at the Barrymores. Look at Billie Burke, Ziegfeld's second wife after *he* got a divorce. Terrible people, they should be ashamed."

Divorce just seemed unnatural to Agnes, something against God's plan, something no respectable person would consider. Like the movie, Agnes supposed—pure fiction, so she wasn't going to get in a tizzy. Didn't those Hollywood movie stars spend their lives obsessed with make-believe?

"They're creative types, Cristina, and these are just stories. No need to get upset about the people who make them. Billie Burke did go back to John Barrymore, so we got our happy ending."

"Our last movie didn't have a happy ending, but we loved it anyway."

Agnes didn't want to think about *A Farewell to Arms*. The image of Helen Hayes unmarried and pregnant with Gary Cooper's baby hit too close to home. Her monthly time hadn't come in the six weeks since that back office. Even Agnes, inexperienced as she knew herself to be, recognized what that could mean.

Cristina plowed ahead. "Now that's my kind of romance, Italy in the Great War, staying in that beautyful hotel. La bella Stresa and the Grand Hotel des Iles Borromeo, northern Italy and Lago Maggiore, Switzerland on the other side. I'd have given anything to spend my honeymoon there, but no, we chose Coney Island. Just like everyone else in America, no money to do what we wanted."

Agnes struggled to listen, her mouth dry at the thought of how her body was changing. Headaches, frequent bathroom trips, every day more exhausting than the last—and no blood in six weeks.

"Look at Frederic and Catherine—I mean, Gary Cooper and Helen

Hayes. Against all the odds, they stayed together right up until she died. Agnes, are you paying attention? You've barely heard a word I said."

"What? I've been listening. I just don't want to think about it, Cristina."

"Well it *was* a war. You've read the book, so why are you so upset now?"

Agnes remained silent, scared to death Cristina might figure out her worst fears. Though, how could she know? She'd told Cristina nothing about that day.

"I know why," Cristina blurted. "It's because Norman's a dead ringer for Gary Cooper. Am I right, or am I right?"

Norman had a square chin, milky skin, dark hair, and blue eyes. Gary Cooper had a long face, a narrow mouth, and a pointy chin. The only thing they had in common were voices ranging somewhere between a bassoon and a trombone. How could Cristina possibly see Gary Cooper in Norman?

Her eyes wandered to an old couple bickering behind Cristina. Married for years, she supposed, as used to each other as an old pair of shoes. No, she didn't want to think about Norman in the same context as *A Farewell to Arms*. It forced her to confront their sin. Every new day made her more certain she'd pay for her sin ... just like Helen Hayes did in the movie.

She thought about her years of religious training, catechism, thousands of Hail Marys, the Nicene Creed, the Mother of God, her uncle, her grandmother, her parents. All the beauty she'd ever known in the world except for piano music, she had tarnished it with her sin. She couldn't even talk about it at confession, knowing there'd be hell to pay if Uncle Collin found out.

She blushed at the exalted joy she had felt once she'd gotten beyond the terrible pain of his first penetration. Only the climactic ending in *Isle of Joy* had approached it. Why, she went crimson with shame every time that warm feeling of desire came back, and it came back all too often. She'd started throwing up mornings, so upset had she become over their tryst. Despite this, she found herself unwilling to refuse Norman's weekly invitations for walks.

Whom could she tell? She looked at her friend, but Cristina would go beet red. Norman, penniless and working for his parents, would resent the imposition. Her family would cast her out. Her friends at work would shun her. Her father, thank heavens, couldn't see what a sinner she'd become. Her friends, her family, even her memories of Daddy, all would be lost to her because she'd surrendered to a single moment of passion. Perhaps she could run away to New York, California, or Florida, though she hoped a vengeful God wouldn't inflict so hot, humid, and buggy a place as Florida on her.

Cristina tapped her fingers on top of Agnes's hand and lowered her head closer to her. "Agnes, you're not listening. What is with you today?"

Flustered, she put her head in her hands and wept into her food. Her sobs echoed around the diner's glossy walls. Mortified, yet unable to stop, she felt the weight of a million eyes on her. When Cristina came around to her, she buried her head in Cristina's soft stomach.

She quieted down after a while. Back in her seat, Cristina whispered to her. "There, dear. Why don't you tell me what's wrong?"

Squinting through the sun's glare and her tears, she whispered back, "I'm going to have a baby. I've suspected for a week. I know it in my heart."

Cristina swallowed before whispering, "Are you insane?" She became silent, her hands shaking and her face freezing.

Agnes would've preferred burning at the stake to the revulsion she saw in Cristina's face. Cristina continued after a minute. "We should pay and leave. I'm as jumpy as a November turkey."

Agnes paid her twenty cents. Why was Cristina so agitated? Did she dislike Norman that much? Did she disapprove so greatly of their conduct? Cristina hadn't seemed the least bit prudish before.

"You need to see a doctor right away. I suppose you're telling me Norman is the father, but it's really not my business. Have you told anyone else?"

Agnes had to shield her eyes from the sun to see Cristina's face, which had settled back into its practical lines. They hurried in the brisk cold down 19th Street toward the square. "No."

"Not even Norman?"

Agnes didn't want to hear his name. "No, not even—him."

"Well, you're going to have to. I could've told you something like this would happen. Norman Balmoral is just the type. Damn him anyway."

"Your language, Cristina." Her voice wavered again, and she had to swallow hard to avoid crying again.

"You can come to my neighborhood doctor, Agnes. Monday. He'll respect your privacy. And don't cry. You need to be very strong now."

It felt like ten years passed until Monday, and then the doctor couldn't see her until Tuesday morning. She surrendered to his examination, his request for a urine sample, and waited forty minutes while he analyzed it under the microscope. He gave her the sentence: pregnant and in excellent health. He'd have to confirm the result in the laboratory, but yes, he was certain.

She shivered in the antiseptic room. Consumption or cancer would've been easier to bear.

"I see you're unmarried," he added. "I'd advise you, young lady, to tell the young man at once and for the two of you to see your priest without delay."

Her body went numb as she pictured the scene, Norman sitting with her, Uncle Collin on the opposite side of the table, discussing marriage vows. Or, would they visit Norman's priest at St. Mark's? Not possible. Mama never would allow marriage in a Protestant church. And she remembered Norman's words on the topic of marriage, "Too far off for either of us, Agnes."

Prying open the heavy steel door of the room took all the strength Agnes possessed. Cristina gulped at the news. "Come with me. Ma will have lunch for us, then we'll go back to work."

Agnes made her way through lunch barely smiling or talking, hardly noticing the linguini and antipasto Mrs. Cassata served. Cristina also remained quiet, while Mrs. Cassata, a question mark in her voice and on her face, tried to entertain Agnes with neighborhood gossip.

She thought about the awkward boxing match this situation created, being squeezed in the middle, her family in one corner and Norman in the other. They'd all condemn her.

Norman had no money, no job, and his family barely could make ends meet. She remembered a rueful cartoon she'd seen last month in the paper. Herbert Hoover had run for president back in '28 on the slogan, "A chicken in every pot and a car in every garage." Well, it was now '32, and its latest incarnation showed an emaciated half-plucked old chicken, in an empty garage. The caption: "A chicken in every garage." How times had changed.

They had no chicken, only a small garage, and their car coughed out a few fumes when it chose. But her family did have some money, though they'd toss her out penniless once they knew the truth. She had nowhere to turn, not even to Cristina, whose silence after the doctor's visit spoke volumes. All alone except for her baby. How would she ever be a good mother like her mother had been, like Granny had been? But they'd been smart and waited until they'd married Daddy and Grandpa Andrew.

She tried to work that afternoon, but nothing turned out correctly. Two tries, three tries, each in error. She started to pick at her dry and flaky lips. She walked home at the end of the day, not caring about the windy weather or the swirl of public events. That first day in March in Hopewell, New Jersey, fifty miles away, someone had kidnapped Charles Lindbergh's baby in the middle of the night.

She walked down Locust Street and barked a bitter laugh. "Me and the Lindbergh baby. What a horrible way to start March."

She ignored the wind swooping through the city streets as she passed Rittenhouse Square and continued the long walk home. And then she saw Norman emerge from the side door of St. Mark's Episcopal twenty feet in front of her, wearing his black coat and derby.

His face lit up at the sight of her. Her heart jumped, but it landed with a thud. Norman was the last person she wanted to see.

"Agnes, look at you, my rosy-cheeked love. Never more beautiful!"

He rambled endlessly about his day, a morning run at Penn, a few hours writing letters to prospective employers, working at his parents' store, serving food to the poor in St. Mark's basement. Never an idle moment.

"I came outside to look at the afternoon's headlines. I'm going back inside in a minute. Did you hear the terrible news about the Lindbergh baby?"

She nodded. "Yes, Norman."

"Quite a number of parishioners at St. Mark's are friendly with Lindbergh. We're having a prayer vigil. Would you like to come inside?"

Go inside his church with its forbidding marbled floors and columns? She had no business entering any church, not now or ever, a cursed woman with the mark of the devil who was about to destroy this man's life. She turned her head toward the gray stones as the tears fell.

"What ever is the matter?" Norman said, his voice smooth as he took her hands in his and pulled her into an embrace. "Can the Lindbergh kidnapping have affected you so much?"

She looked at Norman, his eyes soft but his lips thinner than ever. "I've made such a mess of our lives."

"We'd better sit." He led her to a wooden bench near where they'd admired the building's stained-glass windows.

"Tell me what you mean, making a mess of our lives?"

She looked him in the eye. She found her voice, reassured by the warmth of his hands. He had a right to know — no holding it off.

"I'm going to have a baby."

She heard the jumpy gallop of cars on the cobblestones. She heard the whistle of leafless trees in the wind. She heard winter birds tweeting in the raw cold. But nothing from Norman. A vapid blankness masked his face, his skin turned gray, and his hands fell lifeless.

He turned his head away. He spoke in a hollow monotone. "My God, it was only that one time. Just once, one time together, how is it possible? Is it true then, Agnes, for real?"

She nodded. "Yes, Norman, it's true."

What coursed through his veins? Anger, shock, revulsion, disappointment, fear, love, or some combination? His stare revealed nothing.

"I found out late this morning from Cristina's doctor. I have no idea what to do."

His head darted back to her. "What does Cristina have to do with this? Does she know?"

"Yes, Norman, I told her my suspicions Saturday afternoon. She arranged for me to see her doctor, privately, this morning."

"Please don't tell anyone else, not just yet," Norman said. His voice's soft smoothness that had comforted Agnes dissipated. He crossed his arms and moved an inch or two away.

"Just one moment. You told Cristina on Saturday afternoon? We saw each other that same morning. Why didn't you tell me then? You concealed this from me but told Cristina?"

His face turned blood red. Agnes could feel fear heating up her body and longed to free herself of her stifling coat, despite the cold weather.

"Cristina sensed something was wrong and asked. I didn't want to worry you until I knew for certain. It's been agony, sweetheart, wondering how I'd break it to you."

"Couldn't happen at a worse time. No job and no money to bring a child into this world. How are we supposed to do it, Agnes? My parents can't help us."

The silence grew. Would he take charge and tell her what they'd do? The seconds grew into minutes, Agnes's tears freezing on her face, Norman's anger percolating.

Would he ask the question? She waited. Her mouth went dry and her stomach felt empty. Yes, he'd jilt her, just as Cristina had been warning her for months.

He stood, looking down at her, his face and hands shivering. The wind wasn't helping. Would he propose? He stuffed his hands in his pockets.

"I can't think right now, Agnes. I need to go back inside. I can't think."

He walked away, his shoulders hunched, his body tense. Before he got to the door, however, he turned around. He shrugged and shook his head. His face wrinkled up, and she thought he'd cry, but he mouthed the words, "I'm sorry," and disappeared inside.

She managed her way through dinner that evening. They were beginning the second week of Lent, and Mama had invited Uncle Collin, putting aside money worries. She'd splurged on trout from the Italian market—the Cassatas, no less. Agnes worried Mrs. Cassata might've said something, but Mama breezed right through the topic of conversation without even a suspicious glance.

They sat in their usual places—Mama and Uncle Collin at either end of the table, Agnes and Granny on the sides—for their most generous meal since Christmas. Mama served the trout on Granny's silver platter with a colorful medley of winter squashes and wild rice, but no wine. Uncle Collin always provided the wine—he could rely on Prohibition's religious exemption as pastor of St. Patrick's—but not during Lent.

Ordinarily, Agnes would have savored such a feast during these lean times, but that evening she struggled to finish her plate. The savory flavors brought on a queasiness she fought to control. She threw furtive glances at her family, wondering if they noticed. The conversation revolved around her brother's job as a bank clerk in Washington. She found it difficult to follow Mama's tales about Patrick. Two questions kept repeating in her head. *What would Norman want to do? What did she want to do?*

"Patrick has been so anxious about his job," Mama said, "that he has begun talking to other people about a new position. Something in government, not in banking."

Agnes interpreted "talking to other people" as meaning that her brother had wandered into a pub and struck up a conversation with a curvy secretary. He'd had the same situation for so long, she doubted he'd done much more than that — unlike Norman, who in six weeks had applied at sixty-seven firms in the Philadelphia area.

She stared out the dining room window, wondering what would happen if Norman left Philadelphia. Would that eliminate marriage as an option? What would she do if he left and her family tossed her out?

"Thank the Lord," Mama said. "We can always count on our Agnes. She's done so well at Smith and Weisskopf."

Agnes's heart sank. It wouldn't be long before she'd have to resign and disappoint her mother. She looked about the table, knowing it might all soon come to an end, her friendship with Norman, her job at Smith and Weisskopf, her life at this beautiful house.

"That's because she's doing something she loves," Granny said. "It's hard enough to succeed in this world, and if you're going to do it at all, you have to love your work better than anything."

Agnes wondered if the men selling pencils on the street loved what they were doing. Would Norman be reduced to peddling anything he could get his hands on? Her eyelids burned, and she tried to put it all out of her mind, focusing on her food. But she only picked at the fish and shuffled bites around her plate.

God forbid she should escape her uncle's eagle eyes. "Agnes, quit playing games with the trout. You don't usually pick at your food, child. And what's with you this evening? You've been silent as a duck during hunting season."

She looked at Uncle Collin, the familiarity of his thick jawline and nose calming her mind. Perhaps he'd find a way to help, just like he always had ...

"I'm sorry, Uncle Collin. Cristina and I went to Mrs. Cassata's for lunch today and I overate. She served a delicious antipasto and linguini."

"Agnes, you're acting very strange these days. What were you doing all the way down Christian Street for lunch? Your office is on the west side of Rittenhouse Square. That's a forty-five minute walk."

Agnes, Agnes, Agnes ... Why must they harp on her, now of all times? She had to think fast. Uncle Collin on the scent was like a Kentucky bloodhound. She could sense his curious nose twitching. He rarely allowed one of her misdeeds to get by him.

"Oh, Cristina had a doctor's appointment late this morning. Her cousin picked her up at work in their Olds, and I went along. We had lunch with Mrs. Cassata since it was in their neighborhood."

"Saints preserve us," Mama exclaimed, clasping her hands and smiling cheek to cheek. "The young woman is having a baby. Well, congratulations to the young lady. How fortunate for her family."

"I can only imagine her parents' relief," Uncle Collin said, "for she and her husband have been married almost two years without child. It's a sinful state to have marital relations but no children."

Granny groaned. "Collin Doherty, if you think every young married couple wants a baby every year for fifteen years like I had, you've got another thing coming. That couple had eyes only for each other, and I don't think babies were on their minds. Don't tell me it's sinful for them to be happy."

Uncle Collin's face turned red. Agnes would've enjoyed the fireworks but for her mood. She wanted to slip between the cracks and hide with the mice. Life would be a lot simpler if all she had to worry about were cheese and cats.

"Enough of that nonsense, Mother Limerick," Mama said and volleyed the discussion back to Agnes. "Back to my question, is Cristina having a baby?"

"No, Mama, and it's nothing serious. I enjoyed the food. They've been very kind, Mama, and so much fun to be around. I've never laughed as much as when I've sat at their kitchen table."

They continued with their usual threads of conversation. She hoped no one noticed her breathe a sigh of relief as the topic of babies subsided. Uncle Collin worried about the young men in the diocese who couldn't find work. Hard times were here to stay, he reminded them. Money had evaporated, and there were few choices for hard-working men.

Granny disagreed. "Oh, pooh. It's cowardly attitudes like these that make the times so much worse. If Grandpa Andrew and I had behaved that way during the Panic of '73, we'd have ended up back in the fields of Ireland eating potatoes. You all remember this. It's when the times are tough that the tough get to work."

"Granny, I love you, but that's such a cliché, and besides, times are much worse than back in '73," Agnes said.

"How would you know? When you get to be my age, you realize it's always going to be a challenge. Life's hard for everybody, and you have to stand up and fight, no matter what." She broadcast a stone-hard mouth to the table. "My husband never gave up, and I expect my granddaughter to be just as strong."

Uncle Collin proffered his opinion as usual. "Annie Kate, everyone has to fight for something. We fight for our belief in the Resurrection and the Church. We've had to fight the English and the Protestants for centuries, but look around the table. Here we are now, a family united in faith."

Mama redirected the conversation toward Lent and Easter events at St. Patrick's. The mood lightened, but Uncle Collin's words reminded Agnes that he'd ministered to young girls having children out of wedlock many years ago. He even arranged homes for their confinements after their families turned them away and placed their newborns in homes for adoption.

"Poor young women with no one to blame but themselves for yielding to the temptations of the flesh," Uncle Collin had said, words that now haunted Agnes. "They will pay their penance now by suffering the separation of mother and child, and they will stand in peril of damnation in the next life."

Agnes froze at that thought. She looked around the happy table at the dark mahogany, the heavy draperies, the crystal chandelier, the artifacts of her most deeply cherished memories all the way back to being a little girl, running around the house and chasing her father. She looked at the chair where Uncle Collin sat, once occupied by Daddy, and she asked to be excused. She felt ill.

She stayed home from work the next day, throwing up that morning and staring at the bedroom ceiling, wondering what she'd do, what Norman would do. Cristina stopped at the house late in the day to check on her and told her that Norman had called for her at the office.

Agnes had dreaded coming home after the diagnosis (which made her baby seem like a disease) but now that she was home, she dreaded seeing

Norman. What if he wanted nothing more to do with her? Her stomach turned cartwheels.

A cold rain started as Agnes walked to work the next morning. She barely accomplished anything that day. He didn't try to contact her, thankfully. But it alarmed her when he didn't try Friday, either. What if he jilted her? She sent him a note by courier early that afternoon after agonizing through seven drafts.

She vowed she'd reach clarity by Saturday. If Norman proposed, would she answer yes? Could she tell Mama and Uncle Collin? She couldn't let the situation drag out much further, yet when she lost herself in the comforts of her mother's house, the warm food, Granny's prodding, memories of Daddy, she became desperate at the thought of losing her home and family.

She stayed inside the warm confines of the house all weekend, avoiding the damp chill of rain and sleet. Unable even to practice the piano or read a book, all she had were the fingernails she chewed and the chapped lips she picked at. Still, she had to be thankful for home. Surely the house where she'd been born would protect her from the harsh world? Perhaps she could remain in its cocoon forever, and her problems would go away ...

She walked to work Monday morning, looking down at nothing but slushy snow and her clumsy feet. Norman was waiting outside, shivering in the cold, his cheeks red. They crossed the street and went into Marshall's Diner to warm up. They sat as far from other customers as possible, though the tables filled up within five minutes. Agnes wished these people would take their happy lives elsewhere.

Norman spoke in low tones as soon as their waitress brought coffee and pastries. Everything on his face — his triangular jawline, narrow mouth, high-bridged nose, and even those blue eyes — seemed to take on a cold sharpness. "I've decided we need to get married as soon as possible."

His proposal was as cold and dirty as the slushy streets. Norman hadn't proposed, he'd barked an order. He continued speaking, talking about respon-sibility, their duty to the child — nothing she wanted to hear, and certainly nothing of love, nothing of his happiness that they'd be together. Agnes felt a cold pain pounding against her temples, and she heard only his voice and the quickening drumbeat of her heart.

He looked her in the eye, his face a mysterious blank. "We have a responsibility, Agnes, and I intend to honor my responsibility."

He didn't really want to marry her. She could tell by looking at him. No, he was only offering to do his duty. As relieved as she felt, the cold pain in her head became stronger. For years she'd dreamed of a marriage proposal with roses and violins — not cold wind, greasy eggs, and the dictates of a potentate.

"This isn't how I thought I'd start a marriage," she said. "You have to admit it isn't how we thought it would happen. I thought you might propose one day, perhaps three or four years down the road."

"Three or four years. I hadn't planned for this either, darling, but we've really got no choice."

"I need some time to make a decision. Can you understand that? We have a problem. The Church won't allow me to marry a Protestant."

Norman raised his eyebrows and spoke in a flat voice. "Then quite simply, you'll have to leave it."

In all the thoughts that besieged her, she hadn't contemplated this one. Leave the Church? Why, it was central to her existence. She wouldn't consider it. It'd be like amputating one of her arms and never playing the piano again.

"I can't possibly, Norman. There must be another way."

"Well, I can't very well become a Catholic. I'd be doing something I don't believe in."

Back and forth they went at an impasse. They had coffee, they had pastries, Norman ordered eggs and bacon. Agnes checked her watch; she'd have to be at her desk soon, or Mrs. Findlay would fire her. She reminded Norman she had a job, but he ignored her. She reminded him a again, but he still didn't acknowledge her. Her voice rose, high-pitched and uneven.

"Let me get this right, Norman Balmoral. You're expecting me to give up my home, my family, and my faith, and from what I can see, my job too? You're also expecting an answer now. And you dare talk about taking responsibility."

The diner's regulars looked their way. Norman motioned for her to *shhh* her wavering falsetto, the whites of his eyes boring into Agnes. She quieted down.

"All right, but it was you who put me in this fix, Norman. I know it's my fault, too, but you put me in this fix. You're going to have to be patient while I figure out what to do."

The minutes, hours, and days passed very slowly that week. The smell of coffee in the mornings triggered nausea. She imagined she might be gaining weight, even though she was barely eating—and only six weeks along. How long would it be before her waistline expanded and people noticed? A few weeks? A few months? And she dreaded the weekend. Norman wanted an answer, and she would have none to give.

How'd she get herself in such a fix? Would there be a way to end it? Women sometimes had miscarriages. Perhaps she could arrange some minor accident. She'd also heard about women who could visit the doctor to end it but she never could look in the mirror if she did such a thing. Even in her misery, Agnes loved this child deep down like nothing she'd experienced. She and Norman had created a miracle, not a disease.

Damn whatever insanity had led her to Balmoral's General Store that Saturday afternoon, and damn Norman for taking advantage of the situation. Yet, when she thought about him that day, so handsome, so caressing, so agile . . .

Agnes lay in her bed for a very long time when the weekend came around. Mama called up to her for breakfast, but she didn't have an appetite. She came downstairs at noon, and forced herself to drink coffee and eat a hard roll with butter and jam—for the baby's sake. That afternoon, she lay in the parlor trying to read her book. Norman intruded in on her thoughts. She forced him out, but he barged right back in. Her blood pressure spiked. How she hated him for putting her in this quandary!

She decided against attending Mass on Sunday despite Mama's protests. A note from Norman arrived by courier early that afternoon, before Mama and Granny returned. Agnes panicked anew; what if someone had been at home? He requested a meeting for early Sunday afternoon in Rittenhouse Square. The courier awaited her reply. No, she wrote in her own hand, she wasn't ready, but she'd contact him early in the week.

She bargained with herself for more time. Every time she promised herself the next morning would yield a decision, she awoke confused, one moment deciding to beg Uncle Collin for mercy, another moment gulping hard and deciding to marry Norman. She cowered at the image of Uncle

Collin's reaction. Her body shook at the thought of leaving the Church, her home, her family. And Daddy would've been aggrieved, having raised her to be a good girl.

Before she knew it, more than two weeks had passed since she'd seen the doctor. She had to make a decision, but her mind kept plaguing her with *what if?* And she kept reversing direction.

If only Daddy were around, he could decide for her, she echoed to herself that gray Thursday morning while adding up a column of receivables at work. She couldn't get it right, and she couldn't pay attention.

She'd been daydreaming apparently, because Mrs. Findlay rebuked her with an acid-tongued "Pay attention to your work." She loathed her supervisor with those cat-eyed glasses. Didn't Mrs. Findlay realize she had more important things on her mind? Couldn't she tell her nerves were ready to snap? Agnes looked at Cristina and rolled her eyes.

To Agnes's astonishment, Mrs. Findlay scanned page by page through her ledger. "That's the third time you've added those columns wrong. What is with you, Miss Limerick? If you can't do it right, we'll hire someone who will. It's not as if a hundred girls don't want your job, young lady."

"As far as I'm concerned, they can have it," she said, so angry she couldn't think, even though Cristina shook her head. "Because working under your snippy gaze is a big fat pain in the neck."

"All right, then, you're fired. Gather your belongings and leave at once."

"Fine with me, Mrs. Findlay. Good day—" Agnes began stuffing her purse with a stack of handkerchiefs, a desk calendar from St. Patrick's, and a childhood picture of her family.

Cristina groaned. "No, Agnes, you need this job. Mrs. Findlay, she didn't mean what she said. Please, let's calm down and sort this out."

The bickering drew Mr. Smith's attention, and he came out of his office, his bird's-nest eyebrows twitching. "What seems to be the trouble?"

Mrs. Findlay's face took on the same gray tones as her hair. "Under no circumstance, Mrs. Rosamilia, will I reconsider. Mr. Smith, Miss Limerick just committed insubordination. She's refused to do her work correctly, and she insulted me. What was it, my 'snippy gaze?' Is that how you put it?"

Mr. Smith shook his head. "Agnes, Mrs. Findlay is your supervisor. I'm terribly sorry, but I'm afraid you'll have to leave. We can't afford to have any problems in the office these days."

Agnes breathed heavily, regretting what she'd just done. Mama would grieve over the lost income. Agnes was sorry for that, but then another thought crowded out Mama. She no longer had a job, no way to support herself and her baby. What if Norman withdrew his proposal? What if Mama threw her out of the house? The abyss was drawing near, and she felt it in her empty stomach.

The house appeared to be empty when she got home and banged the front door shut, but Granny called from upstairs. "Agnes, my dear, come upstairs. I want to have a word with you."

She was practically in tears when she reached the landing and turned into Granny's bedroom. Her grandmother sat in an overstuffed chair by the front window, enmeshed in a sweater she'd been knitting for Agnes. She looked so cozy in that chair with the dark-green floral wallpaper behind her. Agnes wished she were old and smart like Granny, rather than a stupid girl who had ruined her entire life.

"Why are you home so early?" Granny said, her face an unsolved puzzle. "Something's been amiss these last few weeks, and I'd like to know what's troubling you. Spit it out and tell your old grandmother what's causing all those lines in your forehead."

Agnes plopped down on Granny's four-poster bed and stammered out that she'd been fired. Granny shook her head.

"Don't be fooling your grandmother. It's today they let you go. You've been moping about two weeks. It's another matter that's on your mind. Does it have something to do with the young Balmoral man?"

Agnes knew her grandmother was only one step away from the truth.

Granny placed her knitting on the end table next to a photograph of Grandpa Andrew. "Would it help, Agnes, if I told you I know? It's obvious just to look at you. You're expecting a child."

Of course, Granny would know. She nodded her head and burst into tears. "I don't know what to do, Granny."

"I figured as much. Every morning this week, the young Balmoral has been at that corner opposite my window pacing about, staring at the house.

Yesterday, I opened my window and asked him what the devil he was doing. Must've scared the bejesus out of him, because he ran away like a scared cat. He knows?"

"Yes, he wants to marry me."

"Good. We can plan the wedding right away."

Agnes gulped down her tears. Why hadn't she told Granny right away? Of all the people in her world, her grandmother had been the one she could always count on, the one person who backed her up, right or wrong, good or bad, left or right. Granny never judged her and never tried to change her. She only wanted happiness for her. Granny never complained about problems as long as Agnes could remember. She came up with answers.

"It's not that simple. He doesn't want to have a Catholic wedding, and he doesn't want to raise the child as a Catholic."

Granny fell silent. The clock chimed the half-hour above her fireplace. It was only ten-thirty. It felt like late afternoon.

"Child, I'm going to tell you a story you've never heard, but you're old enough now. Maybe it'll help you decide what to do."

Granny's memory must've been failing her, because Agnes had heard this story so many times, she could recite it with distant, impersonal objectivity: how Annie Kate O'Grady, born 1852, the year the Great Famine ended, had married Andrew Limerick back in their beloved Trim on the River Boyne at the foot of Tara Hill, County Meath, Ireland, escaping poverty in 1870 with their infant Martin, sailing to the United States from Queensland, Annie Kate four months into her second pregnancy, shielding her baby from the crashing waves of the angry Atlantic seas as they braved the six-week journey to New York, Andrew determined to make a profitable life for them in the New World.

Agnes sometimes found it difficult to imagine Granny had been the eighteen-year-old Annie Kate battling Ireland's poverty and enduring an Atlantic gale, and wondered how she and Grandpa had ended up in this comfortable Philadelphia home.

"When we arrived—October it was—we wandered the streets of New York for eight hours in a cold rain. I'd lost five pounds on the boat, even though I was expecting Uncle Daniel. Your grandfather thought I would collapse from fatigue, hunger, thirst, you name it, and then he met Mr. Adams coming out of the Union League. He saw us on the corner and asked if we needed help."

In previous tellings, Agnes hadn't heard of Mr. Adams or anyone else from before they came to Philadelphia.

Granny resumed her knitting. "I don't remember how we came about to stay with them. I was quite ill, and the young Mrs. Adams nursed me back to health. A good Christian woman she was ..."

Granny continued her long story with details of New York, her eyes cast down onto her knitting needles, her chin sagging, but her cheekbones still high—how Mr. Adams's brother operated a booming masonry on the Schuylkill River and was looking for men willing to work hard for wages. Hearing Granny's familiar scratchy voice brought a measure of calm to Agnes.

"Adams was a Protestant, and he was English. He didn't care that we were Catholics from Ireland. He only cared that we were a loving family and that your grandfather was willing to work. If it hadn't been for the Adamses, I'd have died on the streets, and your grandfather wouldn't have had his first opportunity."

Granny looked up, and her green eyes were liquid and soft. "When your Mama and Uncle Collin talk about Protestants, I think about Mr. and Mrs. Adams. And what I most remember about those six months in New York was how much I wanted a home for your father and my babies. That's all I cared about. I'd have given up anything to be with them. It's family that counts, not any church, not any job. Everything comes second to family, sweetheart."

Agnes had seen Granny cry twice—when Daddy died and when Uncle Daniel followed. But tears started down her grandmother's face as she spoke.

"You're my favorite grandchild, pumpkin, and you're just like your father, always so hopeful. You've got the same spark in your eyes. Dear, I hope you know you can always count on your Granny to love and protect you."

Agnes's voice quivered. "Yes, Granny, I know. I love you too, better than anyone except Daddy."

Granny sniffled but spoke evenly. "Good. I have a lot of money, even now. Never mind what your mother says about being broke. There's still enough, and I'll use it to defend you if I have to. So don't you worry. But I do have some hard questions for you. Do you want to keep this child?"

"Why, yes, Granny, very much."

"Do you love Norman Balmoral?"

Agnes paused. She thought about Norman, his enthusiasm for architecture, his desire for her, his laugh, his enigmatic smile, the magic in his eyes. Her heart thumped, her throat tingled, and she felt excitement up and down. She had to admit the truth. She nodded.

"And does he love you?"

"I believe he does. I hope he does."

"I certainly hope so. I've met him, and he's not the sort of man who'd be kind to a wife he does not love. Some advice, my dear. Make your decision now and stick with it. You've been very hard on yourself these past two weeks. It's been painful waiting for you to come to me, knowing how you were suffering. Now's the time to trust yourself, sweetheart. You're going to make the right choice, have no fear."

"What if I don't marry Norman? What if Uncle Collin makes me give up my baby?"

Granny's mouth tightened into a firm bundle, and her eyes went hard. "He'll do it over my dead body. I'll fight anyone who tries to take your child away from you."

"What about my faith? It's as much a part of me as anything else."

"You've got to decide which is more important, your baby's father or the Church. I know you well enough to know the answer to that. Same answer for me. Your grandfather's been dead more than twenty years, your father's been gone more than ten, Uncle Daniel two. I'd give up all the churches in the world if I could have just one more day with my husband and my sons."

Agnes gave Granny a big squeeze before she left the room. She wandered around the house to her bedroom, to the kitchen, to the parlor, dabbling on the piano. Mama would come home at noon for lunch, but Agnes had no appetite. She ended up on the parlor's red sofa staring outside and drifting off to sleep. The ringing doorbell startled her awake just before twelve. It was Norman.

He was breathless in his heavy black coat and fedora, hands in his pockets, cheeks again red from the March wind, his blue eyes luminous against the hallway's dark-blue wallpaper. He must've rushed over here.

She invited him in and took his hat and coat. He'd dressed in his best blue suit and groomed himself, fresh haircut and shave. Agnes's heart jumped into her throat. Why had she waited so long?

He took her hands in his and placed them on his chest. "I can't wait any longer, Agnes. Say you'll marry me today. Everything's all arranged."

Her mind swam in a million directions. "What do you mean, Norman, everything's all arranged?"

"I've spoken with my parents, with my priest, and I've even spoken with — well, never mind. I've gone to City Hall, gotten the application for a marriage license. We can have it all done today."

She looked away, surprised to the point of embarrassment at the happiness that she felt creeping into her cheeks. He turned her chin and kissed her.

"Norman, I —"

"I want us to be together, darling. I've thought about nothing else these past two weeks, and I want us to do the right thing. This is our child, and he deserves a home with both his parents."

She had to laugh. "*He*, Norman, are you certain the baby's a boy?" She looked at her hands, so large and gauche in his own, thin-fingered and delicate.

He leaned down on one knee, looking up at her. "Would you prefer a proper proposal?"

His voice drummed an even, melodic beat. "I love the way you laugh, the way you juggle numbers in your head and spit out funny formulas, the way you cock your head to the left when you don't understand something, how I can read your face so easily, how I know everything you're thinking without you even saying it. I love your red hair, your green eyes, your modest manners in public, but most of all, I love the fire behind your eyes, the determination to get what you want, and your passion for what you do. Yes, Agnes … I love you. I'd want to marry you even if you weren't having a baby."

Agnes stepped back, closed her eyes, and placed both hands on her heart. All those miserable clouds in her life seemed to vanish and leave only a beautiful blue sky of hope and beauty. This was what she'd needed to hear for the past two weeks, not all the talk of responsibility and duty. She breathed in the crisp, cool air of Mama's house through her nostrils. Mama, Uncle Collin, how ever would she explain this —

"What about my family?" she said.

"What about them? I don't know them, Agnes. Just your grandmother, and she's been very kind."

"Promise me one thing, Norman. If we do get married, I want to see them, and I want my baby to know both families."

"Of course, but they have to meet me halfway. I'm not blind. I know very well they dislike me."

So he had figured it out. "But, Norman, Granny doesn't hate you."

"Well, your mother and your uncle —"

"They don't even know you, except that you're a Protestant."

"I can't help who I am, Agnes. I can't become a Catholic, that much I know. But I've realized something that should make it easier. If you want to remain Catholic, I'll allow it. The choice must be yours."

"What about the wedding? What about the baby? Will he or she be a Catholic or a Protestant?"

"We can go to a justice of the peace. And decide later . . . about the baby."

With his last words she sensed the life within — her child, a human being who'd change her life — and she thought about Granny's last words. She'd be a *mother*. What did being a mother mean? Agnes knew right then and there what it meant. She'd lie down on hot coals for this child, if that meant her child could walk to safety. She'd play any game with her baby, if the child might laugh, frolic, and grow into a happy adult — boy or girl, it didn't matter. To be a mother, the job of a lifetime.

It began here and now, making the right choices. It's what a mother had to do. It's what Mama had done for her, and it's what Granny had done for Daddy.

"No," she said, not the last time she'd oppose him. Even in the gauzy glow of his proposal, she knew they'd disagree on occasion. "That's not what I want for us."

He looked crestfallen. His face turned white.

Agnes thought about the years ahead, what it'd be like to live with a husband in separate worlds, Protestant and Catholic, their family divided and the fierce arguments over how their child would be raised. No, that life was not for her. It was definitely not for her baby.

"If we're going to be a family, we have to belong to one church. I've looked at the Episcopal Church. I have no real objection to it. So that's my choice. Yes, Norman, I'll marry you, but I want a wedding at St. Mark's, not a justice of the peace. I want us to raise our child together as one family, not two."

She heard footsteps on the stairs and turned to face Granny. Her black dress and flaming red hair loomed large above them.

"Balmoral, you're quite the dandy," Granny said. "I see you got my message."

"Yes, Mrs. Limerick. Agnes has consented to marry me."

"Thank the Lord. Now you be good to her, young man, or you'll answer to me. I'm not so charitable as Collin Doherty when I've been crossed." She gave him a sharp look and smirked.

"We don't want that, do we?" he said, uncomfortable in his laugh.

"All I care about is that she be happy. Promise me you'll do your best."

"Never you fear, Mrs. Limerick. I always do my best."

"Yes, I imagine you do. Now the two of you had better be going. The house will be shaking when your mother comes home and brings your Uncle Collin into the picture. You'd best be gone before then."

Agnes shuddered at the image of Mama storming through the house with hunched shoulders and Uncle Collin's face turning to stone. But she couldn't have everything, could she?

"I need to pack my things," Agnes said and trotted up the stairs.

"Just pack a few things, princess," Granny called after her. "Don't forget your white lace dress. You should wear it for the wedding. I'll have Collin bring your trunk to you."

"He won't agree to that," Norman said.

"He'll do as I say," Granny said, her mouth firm again and her eyes penetrating. "I'll take care of him, and I'll also handle Siobhan."

Norman cocked his head to the right. "Who's Yvonne?"

"Not Yvonne, young man, Siobhan, Agnes's mother. Perhaps she hasn't shown you the family tree? About time she did. Next time I see you, I'll quiz you on distant cousins and shameful secrets."

Five minutes later, Agnes had changed into her gray tweed suit and returned with a stuffed satchel.

"Agnes, do you realize today is St. Patrick's Day, your father's birthday?" Granny said. "He'd be sixty-two. If you hurry, you can have your wedding today."

"Bye-bye, Granny. I love you best. You've given me so much. How can I ever repay you?" Agnes settled into a long embrace with her grandmother.

"You do one thing for me. Give my first great-granddaughter the best life you can. That'll be payment enough."

Agnes laughed. "Norman thinks it'll be a boy. You think it'll be a girl."

"We've got the bases covered between us," Granny said.

Agnes and Norman pulled on their coats and hats. She thought about her father. Maybe he wouldn't have been so ashamed, after all. "Just one moment, Norman," she said, tapping him on the chest with her fingers. She ran upstairs to her bedroom and retrieved the one item from her bureau she had to have at her wedding, her gold necklace and locket containing a picture of her father. She clutched it to her heart.

She wanted to remember everything about this moment. She took in the scene in Mama's hallway: Norman, his blue suit, black coat, and Fedora; Granny, her black dress, red hair, salty tears in her eyes; the dark mahogany surrounding them, the old blue wallpaper of the entryway, Mama's porcelain figurines. Alas, no need to delay her departure. Every detail would be etched on her memory.

As she and Norman stepped into the day's overcast gloom, she allowed herself one last look at Granny, that woman of ageless beauty—the high cheekbones, the emerald eyes that knew the world inside out, the resolute mouth that stormed to battle for anyone or anything she loved.

Agnes stretched the moment as long as she could. Finally, she turned and faced Norman, and they began their walk away from the Pine Street house. She didn't look back.

7

T HE BRIGHT SUN AWOKE AGNES THE NEXT MORNING. She had a hard time making out the room. Where was she? She turned her head away from the window, startled by unfamiliar surroundings. All she saw were white walls, two diplomas, a tall dresser of drawers, and a folded pile of clothes on the floor. It took her eyes a minute to adjust. Who'd opened the drapes?

Then Agnes gasped and buried herself under the heavy blanket. So soft, so smooth on her skin. Good Lord, she wasn't wearing a nightgown — nothing, not a stitch. She'd never gone to bed like this. What on Earth had happened? How common for a woman to sleep, well, she couldn't even think the word — without undergarments.

The previous day came back to her a snapshot at a time. Today was Friday, the day after St. Patrick's Day. She and Norman had gone to St. Mark's Episcopal late yesterday to be married by Father Thomas, the Balmorals' priest. They'd met Norman's parents there for the ceremony. No one else had come, not even Granny.

She must be in Norman's bed in his parents' house — no, the apartment above the store. But where was Norman? She remembered dinner with him and his parents. Norman's father had a laugh that made his roly-poly chins bounce, but deferred in most of the evening's topics to his wife. What was her name? Oh, yes — Mrs. Balmoral. Agnes remembered a good deal of Champagne, shrimp cocktail, and grilled salmon at some restaurant on Walnut Street. Norman spoke French to the waiters. She remembered blushing at the expense.

Agnes's forehead throbbed. Oh, what a headache. She wished Norman were here to rub her temples. Ah, Norman, how tender and caressing he'd been last night, rubbing her temples, the luxuriant feel of lying in his arms, their legs intertwined, before sleep. But her headache made it hard to relive the night. She must've drunk a lot of Champagne. Then her stomach lurched. She peeked out the covers and looked around the room. Her eyes adjusted to the light, but oh, this flash of pain in her head! A small room and closet, some photographs on the wall, light-blue drapes around a large picture window opposite the bed. A white nightgown, not hers, lay at the foot of the bed, too far to reach. Good, the door was shut. She had to expose her breasts to reach for the nightgown. Small as they were, what if someone could see through the window from the other side of the alley? So common and ordinary to be lying in bed with no nightgown. What if Mama ever found out?

She threw the strange nightgown over her head. Agnes took a closer look at the nightstand. Light cherry wood, a small Victorian lamp, a stack of books — *Classical Architecture, The Modern Form, The Great Gatsby, The Picture of Dorian Gray.* He read novels. She hadn't known.

The other wall had a desk with a small wooden chair. Next to the desk, he had a severe high-backed chair, its faded muslin print tattered. She saw her clothes neatly folded on top of the chair next to the satchel. Agnes remembered packing yesterday in her rush to leave home.

Where was he? If they'd gotten married yesterday, shouldn't he be here beside her? She started to recall the night, naked in bed with him, joyful, and then his thrusting inside her just like their earlier tryst. The memory thrilled Agnes, but her face felt hot. How could she ever feel modest now, carrying the man's child eight weeks?

She heard the sound of pots clanging from the other side of the bedroom door. Norman must be in the kitchen making breakfast for her. How romantic! Agnes rose from bed, wobbling from the pain. A wave of nausea sent a breath of unpleasant air into her throat, but she suppressed the urge to retch and sat down at the desk. What kind of things did Norman keep on it?

A block-ruled pad of paper stood in the center of the desk. An array of sharpened pencils, parallel to each other, waited for their master to use them on the notepad. On the other side of the notepad lay a stack of envelopes, half a dozen addressed to architectural firms here and in New York City. New York? Did he plan to move them to another city? A brush, comb set, and matching mirror lay on a silver tray at the far end of the desk, arranged to perfection around three engraved letters, a smaller *V* and *A* surrounding a larger *T*. Odd, she had no idea who or what those initials represented. No *B* for Balmoral?

Images of marriage had filled her childhood with hopes of idyllic hero-ism in which a handsome groom worshiped at her beslippered feet, vowing fidelity until death did they part. She had her handsome groom now, but this wasn't how Agnes had pictured the morning after her wedding. Here she was, twenty-one years old, pregnant, alone in a strange room, and her new husband nowhere to be seen — hardly her image of a romantic wedding.

The scent of sizzling bacon reached her nostrils. Her stomach churned and gripped her. To the bathroom! Every second mattered. She opened the door and, dizzy, saw it on the left. She pounced over to the toilet just in time, and vomited a choking stream of chunky acid.

When she was able to breathe again, she sat back feeling the bitter taste in her mouth, and noticed a ghastly wallpaper of red-and-gold pheasants. She looked down toward the doorway and saw a pair of women's shoes and dark stockings. An older woman stood there — tall, fair, with a tight face but wrinkled neck. Ashamed, Agnes turned back to the wall. The busy pheasants dizzied her, and she retched again, this time more liquid.

She felt something cool on her forehead. Mrs. Balmoral, Norman's mother, held a cold handcloth that soothed her throbbing head.

Agnes felt mortified. If only she'd shut the door, she could've turned on the water taps and pretended to shower. After that, she could've jumped out the window and run back to Granny and the safety of her red-bricked house. All a nightmare, Mama, time to wake up! But no, that avenue lay closed to her. Mama and Uncle Collin never would forgive her. She sat back and groaned in C minor.

"Ah, my dear," Mrs. Balmoral said in her silky alto with its cultured inflections from the New York of her childhood back in the 90s. "Everything will be all right. It was the same for both of my sons. Morning sickness every day until three months." The woman stroked the back of Agnes's head, long fingernails making wavy patterns on her skull. Agnes forgot her vomiting and headache. Her strength returned several minutes later and her head cleared. She looked up at Norman's mother.

Mrs. Balmoral was smiling. She had a dimple in her right cheek just like Norman. "Do you think you could come out to the kitchen and eat something?"

"Where is Norman? Where is my husband?" *Husband,* that had an odd ring.

"Norman's downstairs. He's managing the store with Cornelius. Mr. Soltham was overworked yesterday, all of us gone to St. Mark's for the afternoon. Yesterday was busy at the store, and Norman's catching up. He asked me to prepare breakfast for you."

She pictured Mr. Soltham, a pair of spectacles and twitching moustache greeting her that fateful Saturday afternoon, and how reluctant he'd been to leave. She might not be here now vomiting into Mrs. Balmoral's toilet if he'd refused.

"I'm feeling better, Mrs. Balmoral. Breakfast would be welcome. It takes me a while to wake up mornings, I'm afraid, especially now. I'd like to eat a little something before I see Norman."

"Agnes, you're now a member of our family. None of this Mr. and Mrs. Balmoral nonsense. My husband is Cornelius, and my name is Victoria."

Victoria? Agnes looked at the older woman, blonde-gray hair swept back from her face, a matronly blue dress with high-collared white lace, dark stockings, and firm shoes. She'd never addressed an elder by Christian name.

What were Mama and Uncle Collin doing? Granny certainly would have told them by now what had transpired. She imagined the arguments, the crying, the wrath of God, a hasty trip to St. Patrick's to pray for the damned souls — hers, Norman's, their baby's — Uncle Collin's remonstrations that all who repented would prevail in the end. Would they try to rescue Agnes? If they did, she had no idea what she'd say to them.

Her voice steady, she stood up. "Victoria, what a beautiful name. I apologize for making a mess of your bathroom. Thank you for helping me."

She recognized Norman's wide jaw, square chin, and high-bridged nose in his mother. Only the eyes really differed. Yes, they both had blue eyes, but his sparkled and danced while hers caressed and soothed. She must've had blonde hair. Streaks of blonde peeked through the gray, but her eyebrows and eyelashes remained silky yellow.

Victoria left the bathroom and motioned for Agnes to pass. She spoke again in clear, firm tones. "Perhaps you'd like to clean up and dress for the day. Norman tells me your uncle will be delivering your trunk, but you'll need additional clothes until then. My other daughter-in-law is petite like you, so I've asked her to loan you some clothes in the meantime."

Agnes looked in the mirror — her red hair in a wild bird's nest, her freckled face splotchy from tears, and reddish-orange stains on her nightgown — no, not her nightgown — someone else's.

"I'm afraid I've made a mess on this nightgown. Is this yours?"

"We'll be speaking nothing of it," Victoria said, nodding. Her jaw was even more sharply angled than Norman's. "It isn't as if a simple washing won't clean it up, my dear."

❧

Thirty minutes later, Agnes was dressed for the day. It felt tacky putting on the same gray tweed she'd worn to work yesterday, but the only other dress she'd packed was the white lace she wore at the wedding. She'd never done that before. Scents of sizzling bacon and eggs whetted her appetite when she emerged from the bedroom ... thank goodness, she must be feeling better. She'd noticed Norman's bedroom and the bathroom, but now she took a look at the scope of the apartment. Outside Norman's bedroom was a small living area with a worn beige sofa, two matching stuffed chairs, a stack of shelves adorned with numerous Royal Doulton figurines, and two end tables. Beyond it was a small wooden table with chairs for four, and beyond that, Victoria worked at a stand-alone sink, her back to Agnes, surrounded by white wooden cabinets, a small stove, and an icebox. To the left of the icebox was a closed door Agnes presumed led to Victoria and Cornelius's bedroom. A matching door and large picture window stood on the other side of the living room, their exit.

How could she possibly live here, or survive without a piano? Perhaps she could practice at their church. She'd had childhood friends who'd done that at St. Patrick's because, unlike the Limericks, their families couldn't afford pianos.

The entire apartment was smaller than Agnes's bedroom suite. Why, even her bathroom was larger than Norman's bedroom. How could four people ever live in this cramped space?

"Come sit at the table. I have some bacon and eggs for you," Victoria said with a hint of hesitation. "I know we're packed into tight quarters, but I've always found this to be a comfortable apartment. It certainly has been useful in the past when my Tasker relatives have visited."

Something behind Victoria's immobile eyes challenged Agnes to even try showing pity. Agnes offered none and sat down, looking out the picture window at the white house across the street. How could Victoria stand looking at it, knowing the house where she'd raised her children was now forbidden to her?

Victoria brought coffee, a plate of fried eggs, bacon, and potatoes, and a glass of orange juice. They sat at the table. "The chief benefit in having a general store is access to inexpensive food," Victoria quipped as they sat down, "We might live in three small rooms, but we'll always have food on the table."

Agnes nodded, unsure how to reply. She must be an unwelcome inconvenience. She'd vomited in the bathroom and soiled Mrs. Balmoral's nightgown, yet Norman's mother was going out of her way to make Agnes feel comfortable in a cramped space that had become even more cramped overnight. She was hospitality itself, but shouldn't that responsibility lie with Norman?

Victoria was watching her, her mouth open in a trapezoid shape that

Agnes interpreted as a smile. "Norman has told me a little about you, your love for piano, your parents living in Old City. Your father owns a bricklaying business?"

She corrected Victoria on these details and gave her biography, but she didn't mention how Limerick's Bricklayers had closed its doors or how Uncle Daniel had died. And she certainly didn't mention what Mama and Uncle Collin had said about Norman, but the smile on Victoria's face gave Agnes confidence.

"Your father sounds like my own. He'd bring people in from the cold, house them at night, give them a new start. Old City would've been in good hands with Dr. Limerick, just like my father in New York keeping an eye out for people's welfare. In the final analysis, Agnes, that's what we all must do, isn't it?"

Victoria squeezed Agnes's hand. Agnes looked up at her. The eyes had gotten serious. Agnes felt butterflies again.

"I appreciate how difficult this is for you," Victoria spoke in hurried but soft tones. "My husband and I will do everything we can to make you comfortable here. You and Norman are welcome to live with us as long as need be."

"Th-th-thank you," she stuttered, surprised this thought hadn't crossed her mind. "I haven't thought very far ahead."

"This is very sudden for all of us. When Norman told us of your situation, Cornelius and I told him we'd support whatever decision he made. We're delighted he chose to marry you. To be frank, we expected it of him."

Agnes blushed at the word *situation*. Would Victoria be quite so polite if she knew the child had been conceived in her back office?

Victoria patted her hand. "Enough of this awkwardness. You're blushing. You find Norman. Remind him that his older brother and the three Gs will be joining us for dinner this evening."

"The three Gs?"

"My grandsons, George, Gregory, and Glenn. Ages two through five, so be forewarned. Their mother will be here too. Chaos shall ensue."

Norman's brother, his wife, and their children ... why did they have to come? Surely she could spend the day after her wedding alone with her new husband getting to know his domestic life, rather than being smothered by new in-laws?

"Today is Friday and it's Lent. Fish for dinner. I hope you like trout."

Like Mama had served just two weeks ago. "Oh, yes, we always have fish for dinner on Fridays."

"We do it as well, so fish it is, for nine. I'd better get started. You will find Norman downstairs. Also, my dear, tomorrow we're attending a church bazaar in the afternoon. It will be a good opportunity for you to meet our friends at St. Mark's, then and at coffee hour after Sunday communion. We have a busy weekend planned for you."

Agnes gave a tentative smile and bumbled over her thanks, then excused herself. A busy weekend already planned? She'd speak to Norman about that. She wanted to spend time with him, not his family. She washed up, thinking about yesterday's wedding at St. Mark's — so like attending Mass at St. Patrick's, except that she'd been the only one to cross herself.

Giddy at the thought of seeing Norman, Agnes wanted to look attractive. For a month now, she'd sensed the new baby and hadn't felt like her usual perky self with a ponytail that bounced side to side when she was walking. Today, as she picked up Norman's silver brushes with the *VAT* initials — Norman's mother, of course — and brushed her hair, she wanted to be the Agnes he'd fallen in love with. But did he really love her, a little voice in the back of her head taunted her, or was he simply doing his duty?

It was just before noon when she walked down the creaking back stairs to the Balmorals' store. Yesterday's ominous clouds had evaporated, and the brisk, sunny day pleased her. How fun to spend a romantic afternoon with Norman! She'd always loved the anticipation of spring in the second half of March and looked forward to an afternoon outdoors with him on their first full day as husband and wife.

She reached the bottom of the stairs and turned into the corner entrance, the name Balmoral's General Store above her head. Norman had told her it was a neighborhood institution, and she saw a number of customers inside. A good sign, considering he'd told her business had fallen off sharply since 1930.

"Good morning, Mr. Soltham." Agnes blushed as she entered, wondering if the fidgety old man remembered her. She hoped not. "How are you today? I came to see Norman."

"H-h-h-how do you do," he stammered. Would he call her Miss Limerick, Agnes, or Mrs. Balmoral? Ah, she'd now be addressed as Mrs. Balmoral. Agnes Mary Balmoral — no, Agnes Limerick Balmoral. But Mr. Soltham babbled on.

"Norman is in the back office going through yesterday's receipts. You may go back there yourself, Miss Limerick."

She didn't like his nasal inflection. An old fuddy-duddy, just like Mr. Smith when Mrs. Findlay fired her. Mr. Soltham disapproved too, standing there with the same pursed lips and arched eyebrows Mr. Smith had used yesterday. Yesterday ... it seemed like a year ago.

But she didn't need Mr. Smith or Mr. Soltham, did she? She was married and had a home, even if it was a tiny apartment above a general store. Victoria and Norman, they mattered now. This strange man did not. So she lifted her chin and walked to the back.

She knocked the rhythm of Beethoven's Fifth Symphony twice on the door. "Norman, it's me."

"Just a moment," she heard from the other side. He kept her waiting. Ten seconds, twenty? He motioned her inside when he opened the door, and kissed her on the cheek. She thought he'd close the door, but he didn't. He sat back in his chair and buried his head in papers on the desk.

Agnes observed the cluttered office of drawers, shelves, and paper stacks, so impersonal for where she and Norman had been intimate that first time.

"Did you sleep well last night?" Norman asked in a flat monotone, his mouth a long, straight line as if speaking to Mr. Soltham. "I'm swamped with work, so I woke up early and ran at the University of Pennsylvania. I started here at seven thirty-five. We've got two days of receipts and bills to process. The bad news, too much paperwork. The good news, we have customers, God willing."

Four adults living in three small rooms with a baby on the way had Agnes uncertain of God's will, good news notwithstanding. But she buried her doubt in thoughts of Norman and a beautiful afternoon ahead for them.

She manufactured a bubbly brightness for him. "I thought we'd go for a walk into town this afternoon, perhaps Rittenhouse Square. It's a beautiful day, not a cloud in the sky."

Norman scratched his chin, looked at her with that straight-lined mouth and an unreadable puzzle in his eyes, and looked back at his papers.

"Darling, I'm afraid the books won't wait. If I don't do them now, there'll be twice as much tomorrow. Dad is sitting for my nephews this afternoon, and Mother is preparing dinner, so I have to do the work. Besides which, it's too cold for a leisurely walk."

All their Saturday walks together this winter, he hadn't once complained about the cold. Agnes groaned.

"That's enough. Why don't you go by yourself? I'll be finished here by five, and we can do something then."

"Your brother is coming for dinner and bringing his family. I doubt we'll have much time to ourselves."

"I know. I invited them. I want you to meet them. Perhaps you can keep Mother company while she prepares dinner. Even better, why don't you help her cook? Dinner for nine in that small kitchen will be quite a task."

"Can't we think about dinner later, sweetheart? I wanted this day to be for us. I didn't want to share it with anyone, not your parents, your brother, or his children. Just the two of us, please."

"This is your family now too. And speaking of family, have you thought how you're going to talk to your mother about our wedding? Shall we invite them to have dinner here?"

Her heart gave her a little zap. She didn't want to think about Mama or Uncle Collin. "Granny certainly will have told them. I'll write Mama a letter and go over there next week."

"Writing paper and envelopes are on my desk. Perhaps you saw them when you were snooping about in my room." He laughed and winked. "I'm not serious, you know. You'll have to get used to that about me. I'll make the most outrageous remarks, and you'll have to know when I'm speaking in jest. Tonight after dinner, we'll have our own quiet time in the bedroom."

He meant they'd have sex again—if he wasn't jesting, she fumed. Would their marriage be like this? He'd work, they'd have dinner with his family, and their only time together would be in bed? Perhaps yesterday had been a mistake.

She gave him a pungent glare. "We'll see. Maybe your family would like to join us for that too." She headed out the door.

Norman sighed. "Agnes, come back."

She stopped and looked back. He came over and took her in his arms, snuggling his nose against her ear.

"Please forgive me. I didn't mean for today to be like this."

She giggled, and a purring warmth invaded her body, as if Norman had turned the crank and started her up like a car. Where'd he learn how to make her feel so good?

"I'll finish my work, and you'll have your walk. And no more protest. I want you to get your exercise. It'll be good for you and the baby. Why not every day? I'll have my morning run, and you'll go for a walk. Best time of day to exercise in Philadelphia, bright and early, especially with spring just around the corner."

Bright and early, she groaned, alarmed by the prospect. Waking before nine with crusty eyes and a foggy head never had appealed to her, even during the past several months she'd been working.

"We'll wake up at six and be outside—rain or shine—before seven."

Not a chance in the world would she be popping out of bed at six. Maybe he'd forget about morning runs when he got used to waking up every morning with her beside him ...

"If we spend our mornings together, Norman, I can help you with the books. They may not want me at Smith and Weisskopf, but I can be useful here, at least until the baby is born."

Two customers, older ladies wearing coats and hats, walked by the entrance to the office. Norman smiled at them and bowed, then pulled Agnes back inside and shut the door.

"That's very sweet, darling," he said, no longer smiling. His jaw jutted at her. "But I'm going to be the breadwinner in our family. Don't you worry about money. Your job will be to manage the house and raise our children.

I won't have you working. Until I can afford to buy or rent a house, we'll live here. I want you to help Mother with household chores."

"Norman, don't *you* worry about money. Have I mentioned my inheritance? My father set up bond trusts for Patrick and me. I won't come into mine until I'm twenty-four. Sooner if, God forbid, Granny dies, but I'll be twenty-four in just two years. We could buy our own house with it."

"When is your birthday, Agnes? I can't recall."

She'd told him this twice already. "The ninth of May, exactly two months before yours."

"Of course. I'm not good with numbers like you. Maybe I should be having the baby and you should be doing the books."

If he knew how she'd been vomiting every morning, he wouldn't be quite so willing to trade places. She could still smell the bile in her nose. "That's exactly what I've been saying."

"Not serious, Agnes, pay attention. But I do mean this. We'll buy a house when I can afford it."

"I told you, you don't have to buy it. I will."

Norman shook his head, his eyes hard as rocks. "I'm just not comfortable taking money from you, Agnes. I'm going to support our family, that's just the way things are in the world. But listen, we can stay here and argue away the afternoon, or you can go for your walk and I can get some work done. Which will it be?"

She played out a quizzical expression. Who had kidnapped the fiery young idealist who squired her about Philadelphia's streets with all sorts of outspoken remarks about modernism, admiring the Jews and negroes for working hard, sympathizing with their struggles? When it came down to it, he ranked women's work below his own, just like everyone else.

"Stay here and argue," she blurted. "Now who's not being serious?"

They laughed. He patted her behind again. "Copycat. I really am sorry I can't spend the day with you, but I hope you understand why. Now go have your walk, and I'll see you upstairs after five. That's a good little girl."

Perhaps a quick departure would telegraph her annoyance with that remark. She turned to leave. "All right, then, bye-bye."

"Agnes," he said with a smirk, "a kiss, please."

"I'm a good little girl, and I don't kiss grown-ups," she broadcast, not caring whether Mr. Soltham or the customers overheard. Did marriage mean that she now had to obey Norman's rules instead of Mama's? She walked outside. Her feet felt like rocks.

8

AGNES PICKED UP NORMAN'S LAUNDRY BASKET late the following Wednesday morning. Yesterday she'd washed the clothes Norman's sister-in-law had loaned her, but today she wanted to surprise Norman by doing his laundry. That's what marriage meant to her, doing things for each other without being asked.

Sweaty undershorts, shirts, and socks, she saw — but folded and stacked in the basket, ready to be washed. Norman even organized his dirty laundry. When Agnes came out of the bedroom with the basket, she sneezed and stumbled into a set of shelves on the wall next to the hallway entrance. Three rows of Royal Doultons smashed onto the hardwood floor. The balloon lady fell last.

Victoria stood rooted at the kitchen sink. Agnes only could imagine what she'd heard. Icicles crashing against a cold slab of ice, organ pipes collapsing on a pile of glass shards, the demolition of the crystal palace after the 1851 Great Exhibition—none of those could compare to this cacophony.

But her mother-in-law stood solid as petrified wood, her gaze locked onto the salmon-colored wall. Agnes's melodic soprano rose to a tremulous falsetto. "I'm sorry. I'm so sorry, Mrs. Balmoral."

It'd all been going so well. What would Victoria think of her now? Victoria turned around from the sink in discrete, slow, clockwise motions. When her body reached six o'clock, the wide whites of her eyes eviscerated any hope Agnes held that she'd be forgiven.

Victoria clutched at the white lace of her brown dress's collar. Of course, she was devastated. Those figurines were the only valuables remaining from the foreclosure, and she'd made special mention of them to Agnes on her second day there. Now here they lay, smashed into a million pieces.

Agnes despaired at her mother-in-law's grief and anger. But then she sensed a horizontal line of composure come down over Victoria. Her face settled back into the serene calm Agnes had come to admire this past week.

She spoke in an even but scratchy tone. "Agnes, my dear, these are only transitory objects. You needn't concern yourself over them. And remember, dear, call me Victoria. You mustn't forget."

"Mama says I'm clumsy because I'm left-handed. Let me clean it up."

She dropped the basket on the floor. A broom and dust pan hung on the wall next to the kitchen, so Agnes broomed up the shardy mess into paper bags, while Victoria went back to preparing ham-and-cheese sandwiches for lunch in an aromatic cloud of onions and pickle juice. She cut her fingers on ceramic shards a few times but kept the stinging pain to herself and licked the blood off her fingers. She didn't want to exacerbate her problems by getting blood on another woman's frock. Oh, why hadn't Uncle Collin come yet with her trunk?

The boys, as her mother-in-law called Cornelius and Norman, were puttering about in the store downstairs. Agnes hurried so they wouldn't see what she'd done when they came upstairs for lunch. She looked at the clock. Eleven fifteen, enough time before lunch.

"What shall I do with these bags, Victoria?" she said as she swept up the last of the ceramic shards.

"Put them over by the door. Norman will dispose of them after lunch."

So much for keeping the incident from him. He might not notice the empty shelves right away, but he'd pay attention when Victoria spoke up. A tight cough gripped Agnes. To make matters worse, she'd started a cold. Odd, though, she hadn't developed the runny nose, fever, or aches and pains she usually experienced with her rare head colds—just sneezing and coughing.

She placed the paper bags by the door and was ready for the laundry. Mama had an electric washing machine, but all Victoria had was a noisy washboard to use in the bathroom. Too bad they kept it in the closet. Had it been in the bathroom, she wouldn't have sneezed the Royal Doultons off the shelves. Agnes's stockings and underwear had been drying on a clothesline that bisected the cramped bathroom, and she'd removed them earlier that morning to make way for Norman's undergarments—all of them white, she sighed. She'd have to use bleach, and that'd only make her coughing spells worse.

"I wouldn't do Norman's laundry if I were you," Victoria said. "He's quite particular."

How particular could he be? Someone knocked on the front door just as she was about to take the washboard over to the bathroom.

Victoria had put a kettle of water on the stove for hot tea at lunch and cast a sideways glance at the door. "Who could be calling at this hour?"

Agnes peered out the window and whimpered. Uncle Collin stood there in his black suit and clerical collar, his arms crossed in front like an Egyptian pharaoh. She'd last seen him wear that suit after Uncle Daniel's funeral. He wore a grim expression of tight lines and lowered eyebrows that hovered just above those black glasses. Had something happened to Granny? But then she saw her trunk behind him with two scraggly boys leaning against it. Students from St. Patrick's, Agnes guessed.

Her heart raced and her mouth went dry for the hundredth time in the past six months. Victoria opened the door. Agnes hid behind it. As much as she wanted her trunk, she dreaded seeing Uncle Collin.

"Madame, I'm Monsignor Doherty. I'm here on instructions from Agnes's grandmother to deliver her trunk."

"Agnes," Victoria said and turned to her. "I believe this must be your uncle."

She felt weak in the ankles when she appeared from behind the door, and her eyes stung when she locked eyes with Uncle Collin. They held no expression, just a flat stare, his features hard as granite. It reminded her of one of John Wanamaker's mannequins, not the cozy uncle to whom she'd run for embraces so many times. But she couldn't bring herself to approach him for a hug now. She shivered.

Uncle Collin only glanced at her and then addressed her mother-in-law. "Yes, her uncle. Where may we place the trunk?"

"Father Doherty, I'm Victoria Balmoral, Agnes's mother-in-law. A pleasure to meet you. Agnes speaks very highly of her family."

Was Uncle Collin trembling? Might he have been as nervous about this meeting as she was?

He sniffed and clamped his mouth. "That is frankly surprising under the circumstances."

Victoria ignored his remark and icy gestures. "We are looking forward to meeting your sister and old Mrs. Limerick. The wedding was six days ago, and it is time we meet them. Please do come inside. You may stand the trunk up against that wall. Just remove those empty shelves, why don't you?"

Uncle Collin ordered the boys to bring the trunk into the apartment. He seemed too large in the apartment, like a rhinoceros in a cave. Lucky for Agnes, the boys managed to position and open the trunk without breaking anything else. Agnes recognized her dresses, undergarments, jewelry, papers, books, and piano music. So many dear things, her favorite books and piano music, a happy picture of Granny with Daddy, a formal portrait of Mama and Aunt Julia standing behind Patrick. A whisper of a sob clutched her throat at the happy memories, but instead she coughed.

Her uncle dismissed the boys and told them to wait by the car.

"Father Doherty, would you care to stay for lunch?" Victoria asked, her posture as straight as an ironing board and her face emanating the formal lines of a grand duchess. "My husband and son are coming upstairs —"

Norman barged in the door, Cornelius behind. "We're ready for lunch, Mother. Father Doherty, this is a surprise. I'm pleased to see you."

Uncle Collin's face twitched, and he tapped his foot half a dozen times. He clicked his tongue like a parrot and turned from Norman to Victoria to Cornelius to Agnes. After a long pause, he turned back to Norman.

.

"Balmoral. Norman Balmoral," he said, flat as a lake in no wind. "Pleased to see me, indeed. Young man, what do you have to say for yourself? I'd like to have a word with you in private."

Norman's jaw clenched, and every muscle in his face tightened up. Victoria walked over and stood between them. She jutted her chin at Uncle Collin. "You may speak freely here, Father Doherty."

The tea kettle whistled like an oncoming train. Agnes practically jumped out of her skin. Norman groaned.

"I meant no disrespect, Mrs. Balmoral," Uncle Collin said. "I had a message for him from Agnes's mother, but I see now that it would be pointless."

Uncle Collin stomped over to the front door, and Norman stepped to the side as if dodging an assault. Agnes ran to the window and pressed her nose against the pane to watch her uncle descend the stairs and scoot out toward Hamilton Street. He turned and disappeared.

Norman relaxed his face and exhaled as if he'd been holding his breath two minutes. "Thank heavens that's over. Sweetheart, come to the table and let's have our lunch."

Lunch? Not for all Queen Mary's jewels. "In just a minute, Norman."

She grabbed one of Victoria's coats—a gray raincoat that nearly swept the floor on Agnes—and ran down the steps into a misty day. She saw her uncle in the distance. He'd parked Mama's car halfway down the block, where the boys waited. But her uncle had passed them and walked all the way to 36th. She yelled out his name, but he ignored her and kept walking. She broke into a light run and caught up with him three blocks later at Powelton.

"Uncle Collin!" she cried, out of breath and grateful for the traffic that kept him on the corner. "Why are you running away from me? Nothing can be so bad that we can't talk about it."

He clenched his fists while a storm gathered in his eyes, and his mouth protruded outward. "Is that really what you think, or is that what the Balmoral man has told you? It's very bad, Agnes Mary. It is very bad, indeed."

"But why? Granny said everything would be all right."

"She was wrong. Look, I need to clear my head before driving home, and we need to have a talk. So let's walk. It feels so awkward standing here on the street corner with cars sputtering by."

He didn't wait for her and marched across Powelton. Uncle Collin walked so fast, she became breathless trying to keep up. She waited for his cue to speak, but he remained silent as they passed Market, Chestnut, and Walnut. He continued into the cocoon of the University of Pennsylvania. Daddy had gone to medical school just two blocks away. He'd brought her here on several occasions to teach her about seasonal flowers—tulips in the spring, geraniums in the summer, chrysanthemums in the fall. If only she could transport herself back to that happy time when Daddy lived, away from all this heartache ...

Uncle Collin stopped in front of College Hall. Only a few students passed by them. Everyone must have been at lunch. The misty day illuminated the grass, green from the melted snow—emerald green like Granny's eyes and the hills of her County Meath—grass surrounded by tulip gardens, fragrant with hints of lemon and sage. Her uncle motioned for her to sit on a nearby bench. The seat was wet, but who cared?

"We promised Annie Kate we'd be civil to you and your husband, but I have to be honest. This turn of events has devastated your mother. She took to her bed last Thursday afternoon when Annie Kate gave her the news. I don't want to tell you about the crystal goblet she smashed, or the silver brooch she tore from her neck. She rose only to attend Mass on Sunday. For three days I've tried to convince her to come downstairs and cook dinner, but to no avail.

"It breaks my heart to see my sister so unhappy. What you've done is inconceivable to her. Hasn't she had enough to deal with in this life? She's lost your father, Patrick has gone to Washington, and she lost those babies before you came along ..."

When Uncle Collin had started talking about Mama, Agnes looked away, but at this remark, she brought her eyes back to him. "I've been wanting to ask you about that. A few months ago, I overheard Mama talking to you about four babies buried next to Daddy."

Uncle Collin told her the story. After Patrick was born, Mama had borne two girls and two boys, all of whom had died before reaching six months of age. Each time, the child lived longer—but eventually, they'd close their eyes and never waken again. Mama and Daddy waited five years before trying again, and along came Agnes.

"Poor Mama, that's why she always wore black and gray, even before Daddy died. I never knew. That's why Patrick is so much older. When I was born, Mama was already thirty and Daddy had just turned forty."

"You could've at least betrayed her to her face rather than running off without even saying good-bye."

Agnes sat on her hands and rocked back and forth. "I couldn't stay, Uncle Collin. I just couldn't face her. I was—I was so ashamed of what'd happened. I knew I'd have to face Mama eventually, but I couldn't bear it." She remembered the emptiness in her stomach, the dry mouth, how that decision had wrenched her, her old fear of making the wrong choice and never being able to take it back.

"No," he continued, "you left it to Annie Kate to deliver the bad news. I'd wait a while, Agnes. Perhaps a month, perhaps longer. Your mother needs time to recover from this loss. Tell me, though. I'm your uncle, and I've got a right to know. How did you get caught in Norman Balmoral's web? How did he persuade you to do all of this?"

She paused, as if hesitating at the edge of a cliff over water. Could she speak on such terms with her uncle? And then she dove off.

"I fell in love with him, Uncle Collin, it's as simple as that. He didn't do anything wrong—quite the opposite, he held me at arm's length. Can you understand that? He loves me too, I'm certain of that. All along, a little voice inside told me he was the right choice for me—to have the baby, to marry him."

They fell silent. She thought about Norman, so idealistic that he couldn't compromise on anything, not on his love for modern architecture, his belief in the value of hard work, even his routine at home. People didn't understand where his persnickety habits came from, but Agnes knew—discipline and the innate sense he could always do better. They didn't see his magic sparkle, how he lit up a room when he entered, especially when he looked into her eyes. Not all that different from Uncle Collin, all things considered.

He began talking. She'd thought he would condemn her, but that wasn't the case. Yes, she'd disappointed him, and he'd buried his head in his hands when hearing the news from Mama. He'd read a special Mass for Agnes and her baby, praying she'd repent.

"I told your mother, we'd better not see Agnes until she seeks forgiveness. And I say that to you now, niece. I pray that you repent …"

Uncle Collin's words trailed off as if he'd run out of steam. Agnes began to shiver, but she knew it wasn't from the March cold. She gripped herself and forced the shivers to stop. She changed the topic.

"How is Granny?"

He ignored her. "Your mother's shoulders are stooped over now that you've gone, wondering what will become of the family. Annie Kate doesn't mind any of this because she has no sense where you're concerned, but I mind for her. She's almost eighty and shouldn't have to spend her final years worrying about you or wondering where the money's going to come from. Your brother has settled in another city, and now you've married a strange man. So it falls to me to look after them."

Agnes stared at the tulips across the lawn and saw a pair of birds fly by. She thought they were whippoorwills, but it was too early in the spring. A leaden sadness weighed on her heart. Mama and Uncle Collin had raised Patrick and her for marriage, the Church, and grandchildren. Everything they'd done had been based on the premise that Agnes and Patrick would provide the family with a brood of grandchildren, and now Agnes had married outside the faith. And Patrick might never get married, for all she knew.

She covered her mouth and coughed several times. "Life hasn't turned out the way we planned, has it?"

He snorted out a staccato laugh. "You certainly can say that again."

Her uncle stood and looked down at her. "It would be best, Agnes, if you gave us time. You have a new husband. You're expecting a child. When is it due, October? Your mother needs to have peace. I don't know for how long. I'll do what I can to convince her to see you. For now, I'd wait for her to approach you."

Tears welled up in the lower parts of Agnes's eyes, but they didn't spill. She lowered her head. "But … Granny?"

"If Annie Kate wants to see you, I'll bring her here. But if I were you, I wouldn't try to visit the house until your mother calls you. Agnes, look at me." Through blurry eyes, she saw his chin protruding, his jaw sharp, but his eyes were soft. "You have to do things your own way. So stubborn, Agnes Mary, so determined."

Uncle Collin touched his fingers to her forehead and walked away. Agnes let the tears fall. She longed to see her mother, to hug her, and tell her everything would be all right. But she knew that wouldn't suffice. Mama felt so betrayed, she couldn't even speak about it. Agnes could see her mother, her mouth quivering, tears streaming down her face, her hair a wild mass of brown and gray—destroying family heirlooms, crying on her bed, unable to do anything except drag herself to Mass.

Perhaps Mama wanted to hear *suffer little children* in the readings, all those infants she'd lost, Patrick in another city, and now Agnes gone. How life might have been different if instead of two children running around the house, there'd been six? She'd have had three older brothers and two older sisters—five playmates instead of just Patrick, who'd always seemed more like a distant uncle than a brother. She might not have felt so alone in Mama's house if she'd had a sister who played the piano or a brother who liked numbers. An icy dagger stabbed at her chest. What if Daddy had survived the epidemic?

She saw what the future might be if Mama never accepted Norman. He'd have no patience for that, and the two families would never speak. The Limericks would go one way and the Balmorals the other. Agnes would be caught in the middle, forced to choose between her mother and her husband.

She wanted to run home to 6th Street but scolded herself that she must wait. So she headed back to Norman and his parents.

9

Agnes walked back to the apartment alone. When she arrived, she discovered they'd all left. Norman and Cornelius, no doubt, had gone back to work, and Victoria must've gone to her reading club. How long had Agnes been gone? She looked at the wall clock—two hours. Victoria had left her a plate on the table, slices of ham and cheese on a roll. The roll was so hard it almost broke her teeth, but she managed to eat it in only a few bites.

The encounter with Uncle Collin had exhausted her. She passed her trunk in the hallway on the way to the bedroom. She'd unpack later, perhaps tomorrow when her aching body could bear chores. She needed a nap.

She let out a gasp when she walked into the bedroom. On top of Norman's tall bureau, her books were lined up, alphabetized by type (history, fiction, or music), then author. Norman must've done this. Victoria and Cornelius wouldn't have gone through her trunk.

Norman had moved his things to one side on his desk, and placed hers on the opposite along with the photographs of Mama with Aunt Julia and Patrick, Granny with Daddy. He'd stacked her piano music on the lower shelf of the nightstand on her side of the bed. She opened the bureau drawers.

He'd unpacked her clothes, her undergarments stacked in two neat piles in the top drawer, blouses and scarves in the second drawer, skirts and stockings in the third. He'd moved his clothes into the bottom three, also neatly stacked. She opened the closet door. On the left were her dresses, four for winter and three for summer. Seven pairs of shoes were lined up in military formation underneath. On the shelf atop rested her four hats, one for each season.

He'd put everything in the perfect place, in perfect order, and made it all look so easy. A place for everything and everything in its place, just like Uncle Collin had drilled. How'd he found the space? She went into the bathroom and saw he'd washed his clothing and hung it to dry. Enough about finding the space, what about finding the time? She'd been gone barely two hours.

She couldn't rouse much energy over Norman's domestic gymnastics. Every muscle in her body ached, and every bone felt tired. This was the head cold she feared. She stripped to her slip and looked in the mirror, her face puffy and her skin white as a sheet. She had no idea, once she put on her winter robe, that it could feel so comforting to wear her own clothes. She lay on the bed with *The Great Gatsby* and fell asleep before turning the first page.

Agnes awoke to Norman sitting beside her, holding the copy of Fitzgerald. "You were dreaming, darling, mumbling unintelligible words and giggling."

How long had she been sleeping? She recalled the dream — yes, about Uncle Collin, Cristina, baked goods, and women serving as priests. She told Norman and he laughed.

"You're a born rebel, a revolutionary like Susan B. Anthony, Gertrude Stein, or Edna Ferber." He kissed her forehead.

She snuggled her head onto Norman's lap. "Sweetheart, I missed you."

He held her tight. "Well then, I guess I missed you too. It's five, darling. Mother's preparing dinner. Would you help?"

"Thank you for unpacking. You put everything away just perfect."

Norman straightened. "As I like to say, there's a place for everything."

"I thought you'd say something like that."

"We have such limited space, I figured it'd be best for one of us to organize."

"You even sorted my books like a librarian. Even the piano music is stacked in alphabetical order."

"Six days married and no arguments yet. I'm going back downstairs for an hour. I'll see you at dinner."

Norman leaned down to kiss her. He kissed her a second time, longer and deeper, and so it went. He closed the door and untied her robe. When he slid her slip up over her head, his stubbly chin and wet mouth tickled her into giggle fits. He stripped and stared at her from a distance. He reminded her of a Rodin statue she'd long admired at the Art Museum, although the statue hadn't made her tingle all over.

After they finished, she rested her head on his chest, and he ran his fingers through her hair, their legs intertwined and heartbeats synchronized. She loved these moments afterward when they lounged together. Tears emerged from one of his eyes. He smiled at her like he'd never done and said, "Sweet, oh so sweet."

Did this kind of joy really exist in the world, when so much misery walked about the streets? They had no money, but they did have this.

And they had music. Agnes heard one of her favorites from the other room. "That's the Mendelssohn Italian Symphony on the victrola. You know, the third movement, the lovely minuet. Would you care to dance, Norman Balmoral?"

"I'd better put on clothes first. But it is the man who asks for a dance, my dear girl. And I warn you, I don't know the minuet, only the waltz."

"Silly husband. They have the same beat."

They rose and Agnes took a deep breath. Clear sinuses. Her muscles didn't ache, and she didn't feel tired. Not a head cold, she decided.

Life settled into an ordinary routine for the four of them. They each took turns using the bathroom—Norman, who always woke up first, then Victoria, who prepared breakfast early, then Cornelius, who headed down to the store at eight, and finally Agnes, who lay in bed until tip-toeing out at nine with a vague spell of nausea.

"Rise and shine, Agnes!" Victoria crowed every morning.

She did very little in the morning these days, usually weak from morning sickness. Though she hadn't developed a cold, her coughing and sneez-

ing persisted, and she didn't usually reach her normal level of energy until
eating one of Victoria's sandwiches for lunch. Afternoons, she'd clean with
Victoria or do laundry and then go for a long walk. Living in this section
of town, she had lots of new areas to explore—West Philadelphia, the
University of Pennsylvania, Drexel University, the Pine Street mansions.
She enjoyed them all, especially after the tulips bloomed and the birds
came back to chirp.

On the second Saturday in April, a gray and ominous morning, she
walked over to the Cassatas at Cristina's invitation. She hadn't seen her since
the wedding. Cristina had coffee roasting and waiting. They decided to play
gin rummy.

"I had a dream about you a few weeks ago," Agnes said.

"Me? Why in the world would I be in your dreams? What crazy outfit
was I wearing?"

Nothing like the faded muslin print housedress Cristina was wearing this
morning, Agnes thought, not even one of her gold bracelets or necklaces to
spice it up. Ah, well, life at home . . .

"That's just it, Cristina, you were wearing a crazy outfit. Picture this—I
was sitting in the pews at St. Patrick's in the middle of one of Uncle Collin's
homilies. There were rows and rows of priests sitting across from me, at least
thirty or forty, all looking like Uncle Collin with pink faces, white hair, and
black glasses. I didn't know you were there until halfway through Mass."

"I wear black glasses, too, Agnes, but I don't have a pink face."

"Wait just a minute. Uncle Collin was having a bake sale during Mass. The
center aisle had a long table with a banquet of desserts on them—chocolate
cakes, carrot cakes, cherry pies, apple pies, pecan pies—"

"Gin!" Cristina said, throwing down aces and tens. "Did you say cakes
and pies at Mass?"

That was the third round in a row that Cristina won. Agnes gathered up
the cards, shuffled, and dealt another hand.

"Uncle Collin's delivering a homily about how women best serve God by
baking cookies and desserts. He kept saying that some women wanted to
become priests, but that would never, ever happen."

Cristina gave her a deep, throaty laugh. "You don't say."

"I stood up and danced the Charleston around the priests. I pointed to the pies and cakes and sang, 'You offer crumbs from your table, and we women worship you and serve you.' I must've been singing off-key because the priests covered their ears."

"You are a born instigator, Agnes Limerick. Where do I come in?"

"It's Agnes Balmoral. Remember, I'm married. Uncle Collin told me, 'Pipe down, Agnes, you cannot talk in the middle of Mass.' He went back to his homily about how 'morally wrong' it is for people to suggest women should become priests. All the men applauded. You marched right up the aisle, stood next to the desserts, and blurted, 'You're all a bunch of lunatics!'"

Agnes picked up a king. One more card, and she'd have—

"Gin!" Cristina said, laughing. "But what was I wearing?"

"I must dream in color because you had on a summer print dress with blue, green, red, and orange flowers. Everyone else was wearing black and gray. But there you were, zesting up my dream with your colors."

"Times are hard enough without dressing like you're dead."

"Mr. Larney would say that. As soon as you called them lunatics, the women applauded. As hard as I tried, though, I couldn't put my hands together to clap."

Cristina dealt their next hand while Agnes refilled their cups. She asked Agnes whether she knew who Sigmund Freud was, her eyes never leaving the cards. One of her teachers had talked about his book, *The Interpretation of Dreams*. Everything we dream means something in real life, the teacher mentioned, and every character in our dreams represents some aspect of our personalities.

"That's exactly what Norman said."

"You talked about it?"

"Yes, Norman woke me up from my dream. With all those priests who looked like Uncle Collin, he thought it represented my rebellion against the family." Ah, this hand—this time she'd win for sure.

"And?"

Agnes felt the telltale itch in her throat that presaged a dry cough. Pausing until the spell passed, she thought about a different dream from last night. She'd woken up screaming and soaked in perspiration. Norman had yelled at her, frightened by the noisy jolt in the middle of the night, but held her tight when comprehending her terror. She'd dreamed she saw her mother run over by a horseless carriage at 19th and Chestnut, in front of Longacre's Music. She shuddered at remembering the carriage's brakes screeching and wheels squashing her mother into a lumpy mass.

She didn't tell Cristina about this one. "Yes, I think it has to do with my leaving the Church."

"I was curious about that aspect. Oh — gin." Cristina spread out a seven-card straight.

"Cristina, that's the fifth hand you've won. I think you fixed the cards."

"They're from your own purse, Agnes. You decided to leave the Church?"

"It wouldn't be practical otherwise. Mama and Uncle Collin won't accept Norman under any circumstance. I've been going to the Balmorals' church since the wedding — St. Mark's Episcopal on Locust."

They'd been so kind at St. Mark's, she told Cristina. Victoria introduced her as "my clever new daughter-in-law." They complimented her red hair and green eyes and said she *simply must* play the piano. The organist eyed her for the choir, though she confessed she'd never been able to sing on key. Father Thomas, who performed the wedding, welcomed her most of all.

"But don't they drink grape juice for communion and wave their arms about singing 'Praise Jesus'?"

"That's only Baptists in the South. But it is rather odd. They don't have a pope, and their priests are allowed to get married. And they serve red wine for communion in addition to bread wafers. Cristina, you deal this hand."

"Let's stop playing, Agnes. I'm bored with the game. But the wine is reason enough to abandon Pope Pius the Whatever. I'll have to talk to Angelo. He'll like the part about red wine."

"The eleventh."

Cristina gave her a blank stare. "What does eleven have to do with red wine?"

"Pope Pius XI. Tsk, tsk, Cristina, you should know that."

The conversation steered toward Norman's family. Cristina had a lot of questions about Norman's parents. She clutched her gold St. Mary's necklace at Agnes's description of Norman's Johnny Bull father and his Queen Mary mother.

"What do they think about the baby?"

"They want me to name the baby Cornelius if he's a boy and Victoria if she's a girl."

"How royal. Have you bought a coronation robe for the child?"

"Norman wants a boy, but something tells me this will be a girl."

"Boy or girl, you've ruffled quite a few feathers. People have been asking at the office. Mrs. Weisskopf found out that you and Norman got married, and she's buttonholing people trying to find out why she knew nothing about your 'dalliance.' That's what Mrs. Findlay told me."

Agnes sneezed and started to play a fake piano at Cristina's table. She didn't like Mrs. Findlay or Mrs. Weisskopf talking about her, so she side-stepped the topic. "I have to get back to West Philadelphia soon."

"I want you and Norman to come for Sunday dinner next week, Agnes."

"I would love it. I'll ask Norman. Cornelius and Victoria are playing bridge with their club tonight, so we'll have a quiet evening just the two of us."

Cristina rolled her eyes. "Lovely, simply lovely."

Later that day, she bubbled over when she conveyed Cristina's invitation to Norman, but he hemmed and hawed. He felt they had nothing in common with the Rosamilias, but if it made her happy, he'd agree to it — just this once.

That next Sunday, tulip displays throughout the city put them in a good mood on their walk down to Christian Street. Mr. and Mrs. Cassata were having dinner that evening with Cristina's brother, so Norman and Agnes sat at the kitchen table with Angelo while Cristina prepared dinner at the stove.

Cristina served red wine, bright-green olives, and antipasto as hors d'oeuvres in the kitchen. Her pasta bolognese they'd eat in the dining room. Agnes savored the aroma of eggplant, mushrooms, and onions while they listened to Al Jolson, Fanny Brice, and Fred Astaire. Cristina loved vaudeville, although the singers performed more on Broadway than on the Orpheum Circuit these days.

Norman enjoyed the food and, his face in smooth lines and mouth relaxed, made small talk with Angelo about fishing on the Delaware. Every minute or so, he glanced over at Agnes, who discussed *The Great Gatsby* with Cristina. It pleased her he made an effort with Cristina's husband. Angelo needed no encouragement. He was an expert on fishing and held back nothing. Norman smiled and asked polite questions.

"Angelo, you've taken center stage," Cristina reprimanded. "Let Norman get a word in edge-ways."

Angelo pinched his nose and put his hands on the table. "Norman, what am I to do with a wife who scolds me in front of guests? Should I paddle her behind and carry her upstairs?"

He let out a roar of a laugh and slapped Norman on the back.

"Don't mind me. I just like to hear myself talk. Now what's it you do?"

"Nothing so interesting as fishing on the Delaware River."

Agnes heard a tinny strain in Norman's voice, but the others didn't seem to notice.

Cristina pointed her index finger in Norman's direction. "Knock it off, Norman Balmoral, you know full well you were the most talented architect at Smith and Weisskopf. Worst decision they ever made, letting you go. Angelo, this architect revolutionized the modern hospital, but they didn't understand—"

"I propose we talk about something other than Smith and Weisskopf," Norman said. He pressed his lips together and his jaw tightened. "Agnes, what is that?"

Agnes was tapping out the Bach B minor Invention on her knees, caught red-handed by her elders, just as always.

"Smith and Weisskopf will probably go out of business within the year, so you're right. There's no point in discussing them," Cristina said. "Let's talk about our weddings instead. You tell us about yours, and we'll tell you about ours."

Angelo took a stab at it. "It will be two years in July since our wedding. A beautyful affair, a procession down Christian Street from this house to my parents'. When the Cassatas reached our door, we welcomed them for a Champagne toast before our procession to St. Monica's where Father John Paul read the Mass. Uncles, aunts, and cousins all abounded—a lovely dinner, plenty of drinking and dancing. Cristina wore a white-laced dress with a long veil, and only one piece of jewelry, a silver necklace with a sapphire fleur-de-lis. And the band—a violin, cello, accordion, and clarinet. Beautyful!"

Norman flashed his eyes at Cristina. "Did he say a sapphire fleur-de-lis? Why Mrs. Rosamilia, how did you ever afford such an extravagance?"

Cristina dropped a serving fork on the floor. Why did Norman have such a sarcastic tone in his voice? He seemed to be glaring at Cristina, but why? And why did Cristina fuss so much about the fork?

"Dear me, that medallion was a family heirloom. It'd been in my mother's family for three generations. My great-grandfather gave it to my great-grandmother in Firenze. Agnes, have I shown you? Let's go into the dining room. I have some other heirlooms from Italy too."

They walked into the dining room, Cristina leading Agnes by the arm with Norman and Angelo following. Agnes looked back at Norman, silent with his eyes fixed on the floor, beads of sweat on his forehead. Funny, it wasn't the least bit warm.

As Cristina told the history of her family's china and the sixty-year-old daguerreotype of her Cassata grandparents in Modena, Angelo pulled out a chair for Agnes.

Norman began to breathe heavily. His face had gone gray, and his eyelids fluttered. "I'm feeling quite ill. I'm not sure I can remain inside."

Agnes rose. "Sweetheart—"

"Perfectly ill. I need to excuse myself for some fresh air. I want to be alone."

Norman made a beeline for the front door. Agnes ran to the front window and saw him sitting on the porch swing with his head in his hands.

Whatever happened? He'd been his usual robust self five minutes earlier. Had something offended him? She pored over the conversation of the past several minutes, but found nothing in Cristina's telling of her family history remotely bothersome. It must be a sudden spell of nausea. It'd probably pass as quickly as it came on, so she heeded Norman's words and went back to Angelo and Cristina.

He came back inside five minutes later. Even though his color had come back, he spoke in a heavy monotone.

"I'm sorry to say that didn't help. Agnes, I'd like to go home. Angelo, Cristina, I'm terribly sorry to spoil the evening."

Angelo suggested Norman lie down upstairs while they ate. Norman's jawline turned to stone, and his lips melded into a sliver. They made a hasty departure.

For someone feeling ill, Norman kept up a strong pace. When they turned the corner onto 5th Street, Agnes asked, "What was that about?"

He stopped in front of a row of juniper bushes. "I'm not feeling ill, but if we had stayed, I'd have been ill on their rugs. Angelo Rosamilia has no tact, and Cristina has no sensitivity. Did you hear how she talked about my career? I tried reminding her to change the topic, but no, she persisted and made me — her dinner guest — uncomfortable."

None of this made sense to Agnes. A simple faux pas at the beginning of a dinner party had mushroomed into a tempest.

"It reminds me of my first year in college when I failed the industrial design course. My professor humiliated me in front of my peers. I hated the attention then, and I hated it tonight. All I've ever wanted to do was my work, quietly and privately."

Agnes felt a headache take root behind her eyes. Somehow, she'd blundered again. "I'm sorry. I didn't know that. What would you like me to do?"

"I don't care for Cristina Rosamilia. I never have, to be honest. Tonight's fiasco simply cemented my view. I hate to ask this of you, darling, because I detest ultimatums," Norman said, though the tight pinching of skin surrounding his eyes made it clear that he was about to issue one. "I know you enjoy being Cristina's friend and spending time with her, but I'm not comfortable with you continuing that. I'd like you to keep your distance. Would you do that for me?"

The headache drilled deeper into Agnes's head. She'd heard words almost exactly like these several months ago when Mama had asked her to stop seeing Norman. She'd understood Mama's feelings, even if she hadn't agreed. But she found it difficult to understand why it mattered to Norman if she socialized with Cristina.

"Sweetheart, what was so unpleasant? She might've said too much, might've even been rude, but does it warrant ending our friendship?"

"I wish you'd try to understand my feelings, Agnes. I'm not planning on socializing with her again, and I don't want you doing so, either."

She felt a queer pang in her chest. She'd given up Mama, Uncle Collin, and probably even Granny to live with Norman. Now he wanted her to give up Cristina as well. What else would it be? The piano?

But she remembered how sweet it felt to lie by his side, to hear the gentle patter of his breath in sleep, to wake up beside him. She caressed her stomach. All for the baby.

"Norman, I will if I must. But I'd like to talk about this again when we're less upset."

Norman sighed and took her by the arm. "I guess we shall have to."

He walked so fast, Agnes thought he'd break into a run. Her ponytail swayed back and forth in the wind. Her hair would be an untidy mess by the time they reached home.

Her coughing and sneezing fits had subsided during the previous week, but they returned in full force by the next morning along with a vicious cycle of morning sickness. A dry cough, an itchy sneeze, morning sickness, banishment from her family, and now a feud between her friend and her husband. She wondered how much more of a test — or punishment, if Uncle Collin were to be believed — God had in mind for her.

10

AGNES, HER FEET WIDE APART, HER BACK ACHING from seven months of pregnancy, was slicing a cantaloupe when she heard the word *honeymoon* from Victoria at the table. She turned around to face the group but had to shield her eyes from the sun shining in the bay window behind Victoria—and the glare reflecting off the top of Cornelius's head.

"Norman, this young woman hasn't had her honeymoon, and she's only got two months before the baby comes," Victoria said, smiling at Agnes. "Goodness knows, there will be little chance to get away after the baby is born."

Cornelius nibbled on a cigar between yawns from his absurdly pink jowls, and Norman held a finger under his nose to avoid breathing in the smoke. They listened without a word.

"You should go to Charles's cabin. My cousin, Agnes," she explained as Agnes hurried back to the table. "Charles Tasker lives just outside Carthage near the Adirondacks. In September it's stunning. I had a letter from him just yesterday. My Aunt Victoria has contracted pleurisy, and he's with her in Syracuse. He undoubtedly will remain there through the fall."

Norman looked at his watch. He and Agnes were scheduled to stroll down to the Schuylkill River that evening—a stroll, Agnes had come to realize, only so far as Norman could relax. Every aspect of his life—the temperature in their room, his daily runs, his insistence that she walk every afternoon, his rigorous attention to a punctual schedule—seemed so regulated, she couldn't help but laugh.

"Norman, pay attention to your mother," Victoria commanded. "You have plenty of time to walk down to that park."

"I am paying attention, Mother. I've had so much work to do this month. You shouldn't have allowed Mr. Soltham to touch the books. I've been reorganizing them for months, and I want to finish the job."

"If only you would allow me," Agnes said for the umpteenth time. "Book-keeping was my job."

"My dear wife, we need you to take care of yourself."

"The books can wait," Cornelius said between puffs. "And they are our responsibility, not yours. Now then, that's settled."

"Dad, how will we pay for the train tickets and the meals? Money doesn't just fall out of the sky."

"This will be our wedding present. You may borrow the store's automobile, and we'll give you a gift of thirty-five dollars for your food and entertainment. That should be more than enough."

Victoria smiled. "Children, you can't very easily refuse. Son?"

All eyes turned to Norman, who gave them a frozen smile. He remained silent a moment. "That's very kind of you, Mother and Dad. I'll agree to it under one condition, and that's if I'm able to reorganize the books and the back office."

"Good. I'll inquire with Charles about using the cabin for a week in the middle of September. Will that be enough time for you, Norman?"

Victoria didn't wait for his answer. "Charles will be delighted, and if he isn't, Aunt Victoria will set him straight. I was named for her, you know. After three grandsons, I do hope for a granddaughter. Perhaps a third Victoria?" Her eyes became animated.

Agnes stepped back into her mind. Wasn't this for Norman and her to decide? She knew they wanted Cornelius or Victoria, but she wanted Martin or Katie. She didn't know what to say.

"If it's a girl, that goes without saying," Norman said. "I wonder who the baby will look like."

"No matter what," Victoria said, stifling a chuckle, "the baby will look like Cornelius."

"How would you know that, Victoria?" Agnes said, putting question marks in her eyes.

"All babies look like Cornelius."

They laughed, Cornelius — with his round, bald head and puffy cheeks — trumpeting loudest of all.

"Regardless of who the baby resembles, Norman," Agnes said, "we should discuss names in private."

"The child's right, Norman," agreed Victoria, her eyes and mouth softening. "Agnes, I must apologize. It's only that we are so excited about this child and hope for a granddaughter."

Cornelius harrumphed. "Speak for yourself, Victoria."

"If I had any control over that," Agnes said, still avoiding using her mother-in-law's Christian name, "I would love to present you with a granddaughter. But I'll be just as happy if he is a boy."

Norman's parents had gone out of their way to make her comfortable. Victoria cooked meals she'd never prepared, such as corned beef and boiled cabbage, because Agnes liked them. Cornelius sat down with her and discussed the Spanish-American War in a way that had her thinking he'd pushed Teddy Roosevelt up San Juan Hill himself.

But every week seemed to involve some new way she had to accommodate Norman's quirks. Or were they quirks? She knew so little about men, just Patrick, and he'd left home by the time she turned eleven. With Norman, there'd been the matters of open draperies (waking up to natural light, you see) and closed windows (mosquitoes in summer, you see). Agnes wasn't one to complain, but with the summer heat, she found it difficult to sleep as her pregnancy advanced. It didn't seem fair that she had to get circles under her eyes just to ward off mosquitoes, but didn't marriage involve compromise?

If she became pregnant again, it'd only be in wintertime, and her next husband had better like to close the drapes and open the windows. But of course, there'd never be another husband. This marriage was for life.

"Stop that tapping, Norman," Victoria said, irritation in her voice, "or I will make you sit on your hands. You always do that when you're bored. Both of you, start thinking about dates for traveling. Carthage is more than three hundred miles away. You'll have to allow for nine days: four to travel and five to stay."

Three hundred miles, Agnes marveled. Washington was the farthest she'd ever gone. "I've never traveled that far from home in my life. What if the baby comes early?"

"Don't worry," Norman said, "the baby couldn't possibly come that early. We'll have a splendid time driving there. It'll be just the two of us. We can leave on the fourteenth of September."

Agnes hoped being alone with Norman would restore some of the magic they'd experienced before this pregnancy had turned her into a tent and they'd begun abstaining. She missed that, she told him that same night before sleep. "Not half as much as I do," he said, laughing and turning over. "Nighty night, darling."

Victoria wrote Cousin Charles and heard back from him a week later. All would be ready for the young newlyweds on the fifteenth of September.

Norman finished reorganizing the store's back office by the tenth of September, so they left on the fourteenth at seven o'clock sharp, Agnes's foggy sleep-deprived head notwithstanding. They drove as far as Binghamton before stopping for the night. They arrived the following afternoon and Agnes breathed a little easier at the sight of the cabin nestled between rhododendrons and canopied by oak trees. She hadn't known whether to expect a dirt hovel or a large manor house. The cabin's main room was built around a stone fireplace, and Norman said he'd build a fire every evening. Perhaps they'd snuggle in the warmth, and she'd fall asleep in his arms.

They spent their afternoons on a blanket in the town's square enjoying the late summer sun. Norman was reading Hemingway's *The Sun Also Rises,* and Agnes was making her way through Virginia Woolf's *A Room of One's Own.* But she spent more time looking around the square than reading.

The square was bounded on four sides by a Congregational church, school, post office, and general store. Elm trees older than the town itself marked the square's corners. Like Philadelphia, its streets were named for trees: Chestnut,

Walnut, Spruce, and Pine. Agnes was grateful for the flat terrain that looked east to the Adirondacks. It made walking easier on swollen ankles.

Agnes felt very close to Norman on this trip. She walked next to him during the day, snuggled against him at night, and sat close to him at quiet meals, as comfortable remaining silent as talking. She enjoyed the sound of his voice, quiet on this trip, so different from his authoritative voice at home. She felt the warmth of his body, the hair on his chest tickling her as they lay together, her skin smooth, his gruff. Despite the abstinence, she felt closer to him than during their first lusty months. She'd lost count of the number of times they'd had intercourse since their wedding — about seventy or seventy-two, she guessed.

On the third evening, they walked across the small town for dinner at a French restaurant recommended by Cousin Charles because musicians played jazz on summer evenings. Norman secured a table in a cozy corner of the restaurant with French tapestries, dark-red rugs, and black tablecloths. They ate in solitude. The restaurant filled with people and a pleasant buzz during the next two hours. It seemed everyone knew each other, greeting one another by name and shifting between tables.

The musicians came out and began with Cole Porter, George Gershwin, and Samuel Barber. The small group consisted of an older violinist, two young men on the viola and cello, and a pianist. The pianist caught Agnes's attention.

She'd never expected to run into anyone she knew in a quiet village nestled in the woods of upstate New York, but there was Mr. Larney, her piano teacher. For the performance the manager had dimmed the lights, so she didn't expect Mr. Larney to recognize her. But she watched him, fascinated.

He looked so different from that day at the Reading Terminal Market when she pointed him out to Cristina. Mr. Larney dominated the restaurant from the moment he sat at the piano with his majestic posture, graceful arm swings, and his face's luminescent calmness, masterful in his technique, sure of his hold on the audience and even the musicians. He was the keystone of this group. All their music revolved around the piano. On the street, people might pass the pinkish balding man without noticing. But here in his tailored black suit and narrow black tie, he bent the audience to his will.

Agnes and Norman's small corner table sat fifteen feet from the musicians. Norman, while focusing on his fish, raised his eyes periodically to look at the quartet. Though he didn't give Mr. Larney his undivided attention, Norman tapped his foot to the music and occasionally stepped on Agnes's foot. Agnes fixated on the stage. This was a moment of transcendent beauty, her piano teacher in performance.

Their first set ended twenty minutes later. She'd been waiting for a pause to tell Norman. When the applause died down, she touched his forearm.

"That's Mr. Larney."

"Mr. Larney?" he asked. She'd forgotten they'd never met. Had she never mentioned her piano teacher? It seemed impossible that someone so central to her existence had gone unmentioned.

"He was my piano teacher for twelve years. He lives at 10th and Clinton Streets. You remember Mrs. O'Toole, whom you helped on the street back in January? She's his landlady." The musicians resumed with a medley of popular Cole Porter songs.

"Yes, of course. But why would he be in Carthage, New York, of all places?" Norman squinted as if he'd just developed a facial tic.

"I don't know. Let's listen. This is fascinating."

The musicians continued with Cole Porter. Norman finished his meal, and Agnes focused on the music. The man who had taught her to love the music of Beethoven and Mozart evinced a sturdy posture with rolling arms and liquid fingers, as if painting a Renaissance masterpiece. Agnes saw the same expression on every diner's face, as if to say, "What a genius."

What did she really know about Mr. Larney's life? She'd always thought it revolved around his piano students and the Church. But of course, Agnes had assumed everyone's life revolved around the Church. That's how it'd always been for her, until she'd met Norman.

A dull weight fell on her heart. It'd been six months since she'd played the piano. She hadn't planned to give it up when she married Norman, and she felt an empty void close in on her while listening to Mr. Larney. When the musicians finished, she swallowed this thought and stood to applaud with everyone else.

The lights came up, and Mr. Larney's eyes met Agnes's. He gave her a toothy smile from cheek to cheek, crossed his eyes, and walked over to them. She laughed.

"Miss Killer Thumbs! Such a pleasant surprise to see Agnes Limerick here." Mr. Larney opened his mouth in a big smile that exposed his teeth, and his round face went pink. He looked first at her, then at Norman.

Norman burst out laughing. "Killer thumbs? Do you have something to tell me, Agnes?"

"I'll explain later," Agnes said.

Norman rose from his chair. "She's Agnes Balmoral now, Mr. Larney. May I introduce myself? My name is Balmoral, but please call me Norman."

"And you may call me Brian."

The two men shifted away from one another to get a better view. What a contrast, Agnes noticed: her young husband, his jaw tight like piano wires, a formal baritone of seriousness in his voice, and her older teacher, laughing and smiling, his tenor speaking voice as playful as the "Minute Waltz."

"It is a pleasure to meet you, Mr. Larney. Please sit down with us a moment. Agnes and I were just finishing."

"Thank you, I will. Waiter!"

The nearby waiter peeked out from his blousy shirt and pleated apron to approach their table. Mr. Larney looked him up and down and whispered, "Bring us some white wine, please."

Norman and Agnes looked at each other. Perhaps at home, but never in a restaurant.

"Not on our account, Mr. Larney," Norman said. "I drink only small amounts at home, and Agnes, as you can see, is with child. Thank you, but no."

"Please forgive me. Alas, it's the force of habit coming over me. You're both far too young to remember the old days. Let's just hope Governor Roosevelt gets elected and puts an end to Prohibition."

"You realize that will happen," Norman said, "whether Roosevelt or Hoover is elected."

Mr. Larney didn't answer, and Agnes worried that Norman had offended him. But then Mr. Larney spoke up without any change in his voice. "Waiter, cancel my order. Soda water and lime."

Agnes wanted to know more about his musical group. "Tell us why you're here, Mr. Larney."

"I belong to a group of jazz musicians, and we travel throughout New York, New Jersey, and Pennsylvania every summer. We'll be here only until Monday. We end the tour every year with two weeks in Manhattan. That's next after here. The other boys live in Greenwich Village. I'm the only one from Philadelphia."

"But Mr. Larney, I never knew you played jazz piano. I always thought you performed classical only. Your Carnegie Hall recital was all German."

Mr. Larney giggled and sang out his response. "That was 1907, years before any of this was written. No, I'm simply keeping up with the times, my dear girl."

There was a pleasant buzz of conversation throughout the restaurant. It pleased Agnes to note that everyone seemed to be dining with someone, whether family, friends, or lovers. The music had elevated the mood.

"Enough about me. Congratulations on your wedding." He looked at her abdomen (her pouch, Norman called it). "Tell me all about it."

"I'm due in the middle of October, just four weeks from now. Norman and I have been married," she paused, "for some time. We're living in West Philadelphia on Hamilton Street with his parents while he looks for a job."

Norman's jaw tightened, but she ran interference by grasping his hand. "Norman is an architect. We met while we were working at his old architectural firm."

"I love architecture," Mr. Larney said. "One day you must tell me all about your craft. I'm very happy for you both. You've expanded your horizons, Agnes, just like I always hoped. Your father hoped the same too."

He motioned to Norman and gave them a happy laugh. "You went out into the world and got yourself a handsome husband. Mr. Balmoral, are you as smart as you are good looking?"

Norman's eyes bulged. "I don't quite know how to respond. I'd rather let the answer speak for itself."

"Please don't mistake me. I didn't mean to offend. Quite the contrary, I was complimenting your looks and your mind."

Agnes continued to hold Norman's hand. "Norman was the most talented architect at our firm. No one could hold a candle to him."

Norman gave a hollow laugh. "Agnes, you are exaggerating."

What did Mr. Larney know? Had Mama talked to Mrs. O'Toole? Did Mrs. O'Toole call out one day as he was walking down her staircase, "Brian, you'll never guess what the young Limerick lass has done." She detected nothing in Mr. Larney's demeanor, however. No, Mama wouldn't have revealed a word to anyone.

She had a quick worry. How would she ever tell the child?

Norman switched gears. "Mr. Larney, my wife and I are here for our belated honeymoon. We came quite at the last minute, and only my parents know we're here. We'd be very obliged if, when you get back to Philadelphia —"

"Oh, yes, I see," he interrupted. "You have nothing to worry about. Your honeymoon locale is a secret. I think it's quite romantic to have a getaway like this. And to have your old piano teacher burst your bubble and impose on your privacy —"

Norman smiled. "That wasn't my meaning at all. When you get back to Philadelphia, we'd be very obliged if you called on us in West Philadelphia. We live above Balmoral's General Store at 36ᵗʰ and Hamilton."

The cellist returned to the stage and waved at Mr. Larney.

"That's my cue to return. Please excuse me. Mr. Balmoral, it was a pleasure. Have you been walking the trails in the nearby woods? It is so beautiful here during the summer, as vibrant as the Highlands surrounding Queen Victoria's castle. Your castle, Mr. Balmoral."

Question marks formed in Norman's eyes, and he cocked his head. "What castle? I own no castle."

"Queen Victoria and Balmoral Castle. Only a light joke, I suppose."

Agnes laughed at his poetic humor. "That has been our plan. It's been so refreshing for me, especially having spent most of the spring and summer indoors. I already can feel the pressures of the city wearing off."

Mr. Larney locked eyes with her, and she felt a happy spark. Oh, how she missed him and the piano! "I know what you mean," Mr. Larney said. "I'm an altogether different person when I get out of Philadelphia."

Their remaining days passed like lightning. Before she knew it, the morning of their departure yawned. It had been a wondrous five days. She hadn't been aware so much tension could've accumulated in her bones and—despite the heaviness of pregnancy on her stomach, hips, knees, and ankles—could've been released by this wooded respite. The tall trees, their circuitous paths through the woods, the crisp air, all these things calmed her to a level of serenity she hadn't felt since before Limerick's Bricklayers had folded. She didn't want to leave this place, she thought as they packed their suitcases into the Model A's trunk. She said good-bye to Cousin Charles's cabin out the rear window as they drove away.

They spent much of that Monday in silence driving south on windy country roads. Goodness, it was beautiful, such lush oaks, elms, and pines dotting the rolling mountains and a sunny blue sky glistening. At first, the sun twinkled from the eastern horizon, and a cool breeze swirled through the car. As noon approached, the sun rose high and the day grew warmer. She noticed beads of sweat dripping down Norman's sideburns and a wet sheen glistening along his jawline. Somehow, she remained cool.

They chose a small restaurant on the south side of Munsons Corners for lunch. It was managed by a wrinkled married pair who worked in tandem to prepare the meals and serve the customers. "Just like us, Norman," Agnes said, giving him a chirpy peck on the cheek, "in forty years."

"Agnes, please. There are people in here."

She laughed at him. "No one noticed. It is our honeymoon, after all."

"Just barely," he answered.

They were back in the car two hours later heading south again. Norman took the lead. "I'd like us to play some word games. It will keep us occupied."

Why was it so important they be occupied? "How would Twenty Questions be?"

"Good idea. I'll pick the first one." He remained silent exactly one minute. "Okay. I'm ready for your questions, darling. I've chosen a person."

"Is it a man or a woman?"

He raised his brows so high at her, his forehead looked like an accordion. "Pay attention. This is Twenty Questions. A yes or no question."

"Norman, you pay attention to the road. All right, a yes or no question. Is this person a man?"

"That's better. Yes."

So this was a man, just like her husband sitting there, his jutting chin in profile, framed by collar and tie. Was this man as good looking as Norman? That wouldn't narrow it down enough, so she asked if he was presently living.

"No, ma'am."

Since when had she become a ma'am? Even Granny would've scoffed at that. Agnes might've gained thirty pounds and had fat ankles, but that didn't make her an old lady.

"Sir, did this dead man spend all his life in America?"

She squirmed in her seat. Pregnancy made sitting in a car more difficult. She looked out the window, admiring the scenery. Before he could answer —

"Norman, would you slow down a little? The roads are bumpy, and I'd like to enjoy the scenery rather than part with lunch."

"Yes to both your questions, and that counts as two." Was he serious or joking? She couldn't ask. He'd count that toward her twenty questions.

"For once be serious. My next question: Was this man famous?"

Norman lowered his voice by an octave, yes, this man most certainly was famous. She volleyed back.

"Famous throughout the world?"

"Why, yes."

Oh, what fun. She loved world history. She reviewed what she knew about him: a dead man, born in America, known throughout the world. But she didn't know why he'd been famous.

"Was this person in politics?"

"God forbid, no."

Norman despised all politicians. It might've been Governor Roosevelt, except that he still lived and breathed, unlike Norman's choice.

At the end of June, they'd listened to the radio all week long, riveted by Roosevelt accepting the Democrats' presidential nomination in Chicago. Victoria and Cornelius might be sticking with Herbert Hoover, but not Norman. Agnes had sided with him in their dinnertime debate. Grandpa Limerick might've joined the Party of Lincoln and cast his first vote for Ulysses S. Grant back in '76, but the Limericks and Dohertys had switched parties in '28 when the Democrats chose Al Smith, the first Catholic ever nominated.

She wasted five questions trying to narrow down the man's profession. No, he was not a vaudevillian, writer, musician, artist, or sculptor.

"Agnes, you're barking up the wrong tree."

She took a close look at Norman. What kind of man would he admire? Of course—

"Was he an architect?"

"Nope. Good guess, though."

"Was he a leader of industry?"

"Bingo!"

"Finally, though I don't know many of the robber barons."

"You've asked fourteen questions, my dear. You've got six left, and this one wasn't a robber baron," Norman said, his tone edging higher.

Didn't Norman know she could count? He'd offered the robber baron tidbit for free, no doubt annoyed by Agnes's political remark. Even after thirty years, talk of robber barons still could start fist fights. She knew where Norman stood—on the side of individual accomplishment, he'd say over and over again. His words had begun to grate on her nerves.

"So he's a world-famous industrialist who's dead. And, apparently, selfless. Did he found his company in the nineteenth century?"

"Most certainly."

"Did he die within the past twenty years?"

"Oh, yes."

She thought about John D. Rockefeller and Henry Flagler, but Rockefeller still snarled his business fangs occasionally. Flagler had been dead nearly twenty years. Aha. "Did he drill for oil?"

"No."

"A textile manufacturer?"

"No."

"Automobiles?"

"No. One more question, and then you have to guess."

She thought about Norman standing in front of the P.S.F.S. building, cranes lifting steel girders two hundred feet in the sky. "Was he in the steel industry?"

"Yes, and that's twenty questions. It's now either guess or lose."

She enumerated the steel magnates: Henry Clay Frick, Alfred Hunt, and Andrew Carnegie. Given Norman's answers, there could be only one possibility.

"It has to be Henry Clay Frick," she sputtered, a bad taste in her mouth at the name. Uncle Collin always had claimed Frick was possessed of the devil, at least where the Homestead Strike of 1892 was concerned.

"No, Agnes, you lose." Norman cocked his head toward her.

He had stumped her, probably with some rapacious steel baron no one except builders knew. "Who could it be?"

"Andrew Carnegie."

"But that's impossible. Andrew Carnegie was born in Scotland."

He had exclamation points on his eyebrows. "What do you mean?"

"I asked you if he was born in America, and you said yes. Carnegie was born in Scotland."

"No, you asked me if he spent his life in America. I answered correctly. Though born in Scotland, he was naturalized as a young man."

"Norman, you must've misheard me."

"I never mishear people, Agnes," he said with a staccato laugh. "It is you who don't remember. I heard you ask specifically, 'Did this man live in America?'"

Her soprano began to waver like the pendulum of a grandfather clock. "That wasn't it at all. I asked, 'Was this man, this dead man, born in America?'"

Norman began to stumble over his words as he picked up speed. Agnes looked out the window, the bushes and trees passed by them in a whirl, becoming a blur and dizzying her.

"Sweetie-heart, you are simply wrong. You lost the game. Don't act like a spoiled child."

"I'm not a child, Norman, I'm your wife. I didn't lose. You answered one of the questions wrong, and that's all there is to it."

She saw the speedometer rise above thirty miles per hour. Nobody ever drove that fast. Did he feel the accelerator beneath his foot?

He turned to look at her, one hand on the steering wheel and the other on her knee. "Sometimes you can be so stubborn. Do you want to persist with this?"

"I most certainly do." Norman opened the drapes at six in the morning, he closed the windows on hot nights, and he whistled any tune whenever he liked. In a world of stubborn people, Norman Balmoral took first prize.

"I won't have it, Agnes. Admit you asked the wrong question." Norman looked directly at her. The car swerved to the right. Agnes cried out.

"Norman, the tree."

He swerved back to the left. As he did, Agnes saw an orange tabby cat in her peripheral vision. Just as it came fully into view, the car ran over it.

"Oh, my God."

Norman's voice also rose. "What the hell was that?"

She looked out the back window. The cat's paws flailed about, its body seized up, then went limp.

"You ran over a cat. Stop the car. We need to go help the poor animal."

He looked in the rearview mirror, his profile as hard as bronze. "No, I won't. It's only a silly cat."

"Don't be cruel. I said stop right now, or I will make you stop." She grabbed his arm, and the car swayed from left to right.

Norman brought the car to a halt. "Are you crazy, woman?"

She got out of the car and walked over to the animal as her heart pulsed strong in her head. Dead. Not a trace of blood, but dead as a doornail. Agnes sat down next to the cat.

Her voice broke like glass on a cement floor. "Poor, innocent animal. I'm so sorry, little baby. We didn't mean to do this." She cradled the cat in her arms, and poured her heart out in a bath of tears.

She heard Norman approach, slow and steady. He spoke to her in velvet tones. "Darling, you're making too much of this. It's only a small farm cat."

Did that excuse their behavior? "It was a living, breathing animal. Can you really be that cruel?"

"Agnes, that's not fair. It's unfortunate, but it's probably a family pet they'll forget about as soon as they get another."

"How dare you? You murderer. You killed this poor cat, all because you had to be right about Twenty Questions."

His voice also rose. "For heaven's sake, it was only an accident."

She continued to cry. "You don't ever forget when you lose a family pet. Sometimes I hate you, Norman Balmoral."

"Agnes, you're beside yourself. Calm down or—"

But something was happening. "Be quiet," she ordered.

Her abdomen clutched her like a vise, and she lurched forward. For an eternity, her body tensed up in the spasm, but finally relaxed.

They stared at each other for a long time, silent and breathing hard. Then, just as Victoria had warned, she felt a warm liquid escape from between her legs.

"My God, a contraction, and the amniotic sac broke. The baby's coming."

Norman paced about, at a loss for once. "But it's not due for a month."

Agnes rocked back and forth again. "The baby isn't waiting. What shall we do?" And what would they do out here in the middle of nowhere?

He stopped in his tracks and tensed every muscle in his body. The veins in his forearms seemed almost to burst. "Maybe it was a false alarm, but let's drive into Endicott and get you to a hospital."

He helped her up. She felt more like herself—perhaps it had been a false contraction, after all. She lay the cat down at the base of a maple tree. As they drove away, she looked back and said a small prayer for him.

11

THE SOGGY HEAT MELTED THEM as they scoured the back woods of New York for any hospital they could find.

"This is like trying to find your way out of the woods wearing a blindfold," fumed Norman, sweating so profusely that Agnes could see the outline of chest muscles through his drenched shirt. He'd removed his tie and opened the top buttons of his shirt. The image did nothing to arouse her, and the suffocating heat inside the oven of the car worsened her mood.

Agnes was shaking from the throttle of her most recent contraction, and had no patience for his complaints after the fiasco with the cat. "We've been driving on this wild goose chase for two hours. Stop to ask for directions."

He glared at her. Twenty minutes later, Norman pulled up to a fueling station as another wave of contractions washed over her. The pain's reverberations speared her abdomen. She moaned an angry protest while Norman caressed her head. When the spell passed, he got out of the car.

Agnes panicked anew. She wasn't due until the end of October. Granny had taught her to squelch her fears, not to give in, but she hadn't prepared for this. Victoria had spoken about childbirth, but Agnes hadn't felt comfortable asking her mother-in-law for details. Squirming in the car while

Norman talked to an attendant, she tried to remember what childbirth would entail.

Dr. Altenhay, an old colleague of her father's who now treated her, had instructed that she go to the Pennsylvania Hospital when her time came, where he'd give her ether so she could enter "twilight sleep." She recalled Mama speaking about this in one of their rare conversations about childbirth, for she'd delivered her children — six, Agnes now knew — in twilight sleep. Granny had scoffed at that "silliness."

"Foolish girls too afraid of their own shadows," Agnes remembered Granny saying. "This habit of the young generation trying to ease the pain of childbirth with a little morphine here, a little ether there. Either you're awake and feeling it, or you're asleep. When my babies were born, I had chloroform and when I woke up, all over — except your father, Agnes. No money for a doctor back in County Meath. Siobhan, do you even remember your babies being born?"

"Yes, I do," Mama said. "I see nothing wrong with twilight sleep. It's the modern way of doing things, Agnes, just like using forceps. I didn't need them for you because you were so little, but I did need them for Patrick."

"Oh, poo," trumpeted Granny. "Those overgrown pliers do nothing but torture the poor child. It's a mother's job to deliver the baby, not the doctor's. No, my happiest birth was your father, Agnes. I just wish I'd done all nine without chloroform. Even with all the pain, I'll never forget the moment my first boy came into the world, if God lets me live to be a hundred. Which is any day now."

Agnes regained her breathing after the last contraction and caressed the locket around her neck. The picture of Daddy comforted her. She wished her grandmother were here, but Granny was in Philadelphia with Mama and Uncle Collin, and she hadn't seen them in months. Why couldn't she be home in the safety of her bedroom? Nothing bad could happen to her there, unlike here where the worst surely awaited her.

Agnes looked at Norman and the attendant, a leather-skinned old man whose straw hat was so wide, she couldn't make out his eyes. She observed them as she would've watched a silent movie, the old man gesturing, pointing down the road, drawing little routes on his hand, and pointing at the sky.

Norman scratched his head, then nodded and pointed down the road. He came back to the car.

"Hospital's eleven miles away. We have to hurry because a thunderstorm's on its way."

The drive took forever, and the air seemed as thick as hot soup. Just as predicted, gray clouds were gathering in the distance. A half hour later, they reached the hospital. Norman opened the gate and drove through, only to find a silent building surrounded by untamed grasses and wild shrubs. Ghosts inhabited the place, Agnes was certain, but he went exploring anyway just as yet another contraction hit Agnes. She clutched the seat and breathed hard.

She'd once dropped a bottle of soap in the girl's bathroom at St. Patrick's, which oozed out glass and a sticky liquid that caused a classmate to slip, cut her elbows, and break her ankle. Sister Kathryn James had spanked her seventeen times. Limping home to explain it to Mama, she'd thought that was the worst pain she ever could experience — until these pounding thrusts of agony made her plead for God to spare her this misery.

Writhing and shaking, she looked at the large building. No evidence of life, just the three-story white building with a dark slate roof. Its long line of tall windows on each floor stared back at Agnes, the windows broken and shutters half unhooked. The ghosts she envisioned mocked Agnes's pain.

"Norman!" she called out the window. He'd better hurry. She had no idea how quickly this baby would come, but she did know she needed a doctor.

Norman plopped down in the car and stated the obvious. "The place is deserted. We'll have to go back to the main road."

On they drove in search of help, in search of a doctor, in search of anything. It seemed her contractions were coming quicker now. Five minutes? Ten minutes? She had no idea, only the discomfort of riding over bumpy dirt roads in the noose of unyielding humidity. She could feel the baby shifting inside of her. What was happening in this godforsaken place?

"Stay here," Norman said as they pulled up to a house with a Victorian turret on one side and a surrounding porch. "I'm going to ask for help."

A large man with a pink face and long white hair came up to Agnes's side of the car. She flinched as he spoke through the window. "Ma'am, you lost? May I help you? My name's Lacey."

"Yes, sir," Norman interjected from his side of the car. "We're trying to find a hospital. My wife's in labor, and she'll be in trouble if we don't get help soon. We've been looking for a hospital for an hour."

Agnes gawked at Norman. "An hour? Is that all?"

"Sir, you're not going to find a hospital around here. Closest one is the Endicott hospital —"

"Already been there, sir. Closed —"

"Down, yes. Since winter. Hard times for everybody, you know. Then there's one on the other side of the Susquehanna from Binghamton. Fifteen, twenty miles east. Beautiful drive at least."

"Too far for my wife to manage. Do you know a doctor in this neighborhood who does deliveries?"

"Well, there was Dr. Wilson just down the road, but he up and left last spring after the bank took his house. Don't know where he went. Got to go to Binghamton, unless ..." The man scratched his head as he looked down the road. He nodded, as if debating with himself, then crossed his arms over his chest. "We got a midwife here in town just a mile up Sherman Road. But you probably don't want to go there."

"Why not? Isn't she any good?" Agnes said. Every possibility seemed blocked by obstacles or premonitions.

"Ma'am, she's the best. Hardly ever lost a baby. But she doesn't usually midwife for white folks. Colored, you know."

"I don't have a problem with that. Norman, let's be on our way. Sir, how do we find Sherman Road?"

"Let's think about this for a minute, Agnes," Norman said. He lowered his eyes and cast his mouth downward. "It's risky to have a negro woman deliver our baby. We need to talk about it."

"How is it risky, Norman? Negroes have delivered babies for thousands of years, and they seem to be doing pretty well. And Mr. Lacey," she said, pointing at him, "he says she's the best. Can you give me a reason why not?"

She got a whiff of Norman's body odor. The hours in this car hadn't agreed with him, and she felt nauseated by the stale smell of onions coming from his soaked armpits. She turned her head and gulped down the urge to gag.

Norman scratched his head, started to say something, and stopped. Finally, he addressed her. "Agnes, you misunderstand me."

If Norman were having this baby, perhaps he'd act less like a businessman and more like a human being. "All right. Give me a good reason, Norman, not a stupid one."

He cast her a stony look. "Look at it from her point of view. Anything goes wrong delivering a white woman's baby, she'll have trouble with the law. Last thing I want to do is bring a hard-working person trouble. Am I right, Lacey?"

"Reckon it could be difficult, but Miz Honeywalker, she's so good, she never has to worry. Been midwifing decades. Go on up that road, see for yourselves. Turn left and drive a mile. Can't miss the old Honeywalker place. Broken white fence, chickens, and goats in the front yard. Tell her old man Lacey sent you."

The wind picked up as their car rocked along the winding road and down the lane. They barely were able to drive faster than a few miles per hour. Agnes clenched her teeth at yet another contraction and bit down on her knuckles. When the pain subsided, she looked at the imprint on her fingers.

The car bounced along the uneven road. Agnes looked at the upholstered cloth seat beneath her, wet from perspiration. To make matters worse, the bumpy ride doused the car with a muddy grit and the windshield with slimy dirt. She shuddered as Norman dodged one puddle after another.

How could this only be a mile? It seemed like they'd crossed the Earth by the time the lane widened and the trees grew apart. They finally saw a broken white fence on the left side standing erect only at its center posts, falling down on either side onto overgrown grass. Agnes looked at the house beyond. "Can this be her home?"

The Victorian house taunted them, white with dark-green shutters hanging loosely by the windows, paint peeling off the walls, a broken swing on the front porch, a fallen tree bisecting the front yard. The reflection of the sky's glassy gray obscured Agnes's view through the windows into the house. Two goats ate grass in the yard, but Agnes didn't see any chickens. A rickety barn stood away from the house, its door open and blowing.

Agnes's imagination ran wild with visions of terrifying horrors here in the middle of absolutely nowhere. She couldn't help but recall a book she'd read years ago. The heroine had found a strange man hanging from the ceiling above the staircase. It might've been this very house.

Her mouth went dry. "Norman, let's get out of here *now*."

"No argument from me."

Norman put the car into reverse, but it balked. The rear wheel spun around and hobbled them into place. With the sounds of a sputtering engine and flying mud, a negro woman emerged from the barn and stared at them.

This must be Mrs. Honeywalker, Agnes realized as she looked at the petite figure. Wild white hair blew in the wind and framed her reddish-brown skin, brought even more into focus by her faded muslin dress. Aged bones protruded from the woman's wrists, elbows, and shoulders, and her jawline thrust forward into profile by a jutting chin, all out of proportion with sloping shoulders and a flat bosom. But her full lips, decorated by a spidery array of wrinkles, softened the picture.

Agnes's hopes deflated. "Oh, she can't be more than a hundred pounds. An old bag of bones, Norman. I can't imagine her delivering our baby."

The old woman took in the scene, and Agnes sensed annoyance in her lowered forehead. Norman continued his effort to force the car out of the ditch as she marched over. Agnes saw the chickens Mr. Lacey had mentioned fluttering behind the Honeywalker woman.

"Don't you be kicking up mud in my driveway, young man. You be stopping that car right now," she said with a wagging index finger. "What in the devil's name you doing here anyway? Who're you all?"

Norman leaned out the window. "I'm Balmoral, woman, and we're lost."

The old woman squinted. "No one ever lost out this far. You done come here for a reason."

Norman leaned out farther. "We're simply driving about. You've no place to question us, ma'am."

"You think I was a fool born yesterday? You done come to steal from me, I know it."

Agnes looked at the house, then at the woman. But for her predicament, she would've laughed.

"Well, you ain't getting nothing. I got me a rifle inside the house, and I'll use it if I need to. Your car's stuck in the mud. You might as well come on out from that contraption. We'll get old man Lacey's truck over here —"

Norman and Agnes got out of the car. An updraft blew his loose shirt tails up and Agnes's hair into her face.

"Old man Lacey," Norman echoed. "He's the one who sent us."

The old woman smiled at the mention of Lacey and looked at Agnes. Her smile widened. "Well, you having a baby. That's why you done come. Why didn't you say nothing?"

Norman towered over her. "You're our last hope. She's been having contractions two hours now. Can you deliver our child?"

Mrs. Honeywalker fixed her stare on Agnes. If she doubted the wisdom of delivering a white woman's baby, this would be the turning point. And maybe it'd be better if she did refuse.

"What're you talking about? Course I can, but ain't there no hospital for white folks?"

"No. We were driving south when my wife started having her contractions. Hospital's closed. We asked Mr. Lacey, and he sent us here."

Mrs. Honeywalker looked Agnes up and down. "Well, Lord Jesus, you come to the right place. Delivered me thousands of black babies—a number of white ones too. Upstairs you go. Ma'am, come on over here. Let me have a look-see."

Agnes squirmed under her gaze. She looked at the house, wondering how difficult it'd be to run back to the car and hide.

"Ah, don't you mind the house. It ain't so pretty, but it sure's the right place for you. Everything's gone to be okay."

"Ma'am, what's your name?"

"Honeywalker. Gracie Honeywalker's what they call me. Go on inside." She flailed her arms about in the direction of the house and looked at the rear of their car. "What you got in that there contraption?"

"Our suitcases. We're on our way home to Philadelphia. We just spent our honeymoon in the Adirondacks."

Gracie cocked her head. "Praise Jesus, must a been some honeymoon."

Norman laughed, but Agnes cringed. "Miss Honeywalker, we waited until we could afford the trip. My wife isn't due until October."

"Good. Smaller baby'll make the delivery easy as pie. Now you, sir, get those suitcases and bring them in the house. And it's Miz Honeywalker. Ain't been a miss since '71. You, ma'am, what's your name?"

"Mrs. Balmoral."

"I know that, silly. Ain't gone to deliver no baby to a Miz Balmoral. You got yourself a proper Christian name?"

"Agnes," she said as a clap of thunder coincided with another bolt from her abdomen, forcing her to bend down.

"Lord a mighty, a right-down contraction. How far apart?"

Norman looked at his watch and made counting gestures. "About fifteen minutes. She's had eight or nine. Isn't that right, sweetheart?"

It felt like a hundred but for once, Agnes hadn't counted. "Maybe it's eight *and* nine. That's seventeen. How would I know how many I've had?"

"Agnes, two weeks ago you woke up and told me you'd counted seventy-nine sheep before falling asleep. You tend to count."

Agnes frowned. "Which is more than I can say for you."

Norman closed his eyes and held his breath five seconds but didn't say a word. Something inside Agnes enjoyed bringing him down a level, and he seemed to be tolerating it rather well. Why on Earth had she been obeying him for the past six months as much as she had?

"Miz Agnes, if your contractions are at fifteen minutes, you listen to Miss Gracie and get yourself inside that house."

"Go on, sweetheart, you'd better listen."

Agnes gasped when they entered the house, dark like a catacomb. A long hallway cut it in half, and a narrow staircase led to a black void. The house smelled of rain and rueful neglect. The spare furniture in the living room sagged right down to the dirty floor. The dining room opposite had a small table, one leg broken, and two wooden chairs. A red-feathered chicken pecked at bird seed strewn about the floor beneath. Agnes's eyes rested on the portrait of a man with a broad, bearded black face. Defiance emanated from the painting.

Gracie spoke from behind Agnes. "I'll get my birthing stuff out back. You go on upstairs, bedroom's on the left, and get undressed."

The steps creaked under their unsteady feet. Norman followed Agnes up the staircase. If he hadn't been behind her prodding her forward, she'd have turned around and run screaming for Mama and Granny.

Norman led her into a dingy bedroom. An old four-poster bed with a round nightstand sat next to the door, on the far wall a large dresser topped by an oval mirror. The uneven floorboards squealed under their feet. The tan walls oozed varicose patterns of cracks and a single hanging—a large crucifix, the figure of Jesus watching over the room. Lurking shadows of the coming storm filtered in through the front window.

Agnes's clothes, wet from perspiration, stuck to her as she undressed. Norman folded his arms and surveyed the room doing nothing. What was the point in having a husband? She put on her white laced nightgown and climbed into the bed, pulling up a thin quilt and lying on her back. Her nerves got the better of her, and she trembled as she stared at the figure of Jesus. She felt for her father's locket and prayed for help. She had no idea what to expect of childbirth. Only that much was certain.

Gracie came into the room. "What're you doing in that bed already? I got to make it up right for you. Ain't safe to have no baby on dirty sheets. And you, Mr. Balmoral, you fetch me some more pillows from the room cross the hallway. She can't be lying on her back."

Agnes watched Gracie prepare the room like a dynamo, ordering Norman about, making the bed with white sheets that smelled of summer's air. A chicken might be wandering around and a grimy film of dirt might be stuck to the floors, but these sheets were clean. And soft, thought Agnes, as she lay down again.

Gracie placed a large tray of supplies on the nightstand next to Agnes. She rolled out a white towel across the dresser and laid out her equipment in military formation. Two small basins, a shiny pair of scissors, three bars of lye soap, a small rubber ball, a stack of towels, a pitcher of water, and a tall glass.

Agnes wondered if Gracie planned to deliver her baby in twilight sleep. "Do you have ether or chloroform? Morphine?"

"What you talking about? Ain't never used that stuff like those doctors done. No, you gone to have your baby right natural."

Agnes's nerves flashed a bolt into her stomach. If God put her to the task, she could accept death, but would he drag it out for hours?

"I can't do that. I'll die!"

"What're you talking about? It's the only way. I done never liked high-class ladies going under when their babies were born. If it was good enough for us slaves back in Kentucky, it's good enough for everyone. No, you'll be awake, Miz Agnes. You're gone to feel it all the way. Pain and joy, that's what I say. Got to have them both, that's what the good Lord Jesus tells me."

"My God, Norman, what're we going to do?"

"Gracie, please. Surely you can to do something, anything, to ease my wife's pain. Can't you see she's suffering?"

The three of them stared at each other—Agnes, dizzy from the room's swaying, Norman, shifting about on his feet, and Gracie, calm in the center of the storm. Agnes fixated on that calmness, their last hope.

"Never did see me a healthy woman couldn't push the baby out herself. You just leave it to me, Miz Agnes. I'll help you along."

Gracie poured a glass of water. "I'll come back with my other things. You just sit up in that bed. See my Jesus across the wall? He'll look over you, Miz Agnes. Between me and Jesus, we'll make sure you don't suffer none. Drink this. You ain't had no water, honey. Got to drink water, lots of it."

"Go on and drink, darling. Do what Miss Gracie tells you."

Norman went on his search for pillows. As Agnes gulped the glass down, she heard Gracie tiptoe down the stairs. Odd that a wrinkled old woman could make so little noise going down a rickety staircase. Agnes, alone but for the crucifix, looked around the room and got lost in a web of haunted fears.

What had she done, she thought as thunder jolted her back to reality, conceiving this child out of wedlock, marrying outside her faith? Would this be her day of judgment? Uncle Collin had been right; she shouldn't have been seeing Norman. She should've quit Smith and Weisskopf the very Monday after they took that first walk. Instead here she was, Agnes Balmoral, about to give birth at the hands of an ancient negro woman in the middle of a summer thunderstorm, the stinking man who'd done this her only witness. She tugged the sheets up to her chin, certain that unspeakable horrors awaited.

Norman returned with four pillows, and Gracie followed him in with two large basins. "This here's for bathing the child. Other one's for washing you down. You gone to sweat a lot, honey. Now you relax. Gone to be another five, six hours, I'd guess."

Every nerve in Agnes's body jumped, as if her blood had curdled. "Six hours? You can't hurry it along?"

"Can't hurry nature along, Miz Agnes."

Gracie directed Norman where to put the pillows — two under the knees, two more under the upper back — and she stood at the foot of the bed. "Now let me see how far long you are. You there, Mr. Balmoral, pull back that quilt."

"You're the boss. And call me Mr. Norman," he said, lifting the quilt off Agnes. She secured the nightgown with her hands. The sky lit up and thundered.

"Hmm. Storm's coming. Now, Miz Agnes, you got to lift your nightgown. I got to see how dilated you are."

She looked at Norman, his eyes soft and quiet. "Sweetheart, would you go in the other room?"

Norman looked at Gracie and shook his head.

"No, Miz Agnes, your husband ain't leaving. Don't be so gosh darn modest. He's your husband."

"What more can they do to me?" Agnes said to no one in particular as she lifted her nightgown, just a bit, and closed her eyes. A strange woman in a strange house in a strange town, the sky threatening to open up, and her husband, both of them watching her, a shapeless blob as attractive as a wet goat.

"Now there. One inch. Hmm."

"One inch? What does that mean?" Agnes dropped her nightgown back into place. "Will the baby make its way through the birth canal?"

"Don't you worry, Miz Agnes. One inch just mean it's gone to take a little longer is all."

Agnes moaned, but Gracie continued. "I'm gone to let you and Mr. Norman have some quiet time together. I'll tend to supper and then come sit by you while he eats. Mr. Norman, you have Miz Agnes walk about some. Ain't no good she stays in bed too long."

Right now, Agnes didn't especially want to spend time alone with Norman. "Norman needs to bathe. He smells like an outhouse."

Norman bit his lower lip and spoke in measured tones. "I can't help perspiring in the heat."

"Who cares, Mr. Norman? Well water's out back. Rinse yourself off out there. Miz Agnes, I'll bring you a touch of food. A nice chicken broth will calm your nerves."

Would it be broth from the chicken pattering about the dining-room floor below? She had no way of knowing what went on in this house.

"Where's the bathroom?" Agnes said. "I need to use the bathroom."

"Ain't no inside bathroom." She waved to the back of the house. "It's out yonder. And don't be asking for a light, ain't no electricity either. I'll get candles for when it's dark."

She handed a small basin to Norman. "Here, Mr. Norman, you have her pee in here and toss it out the side window. We got to leave the windows open, even with the storm brewing. Need the air. Trees won't mind her pee."

Another contraction ramped the pain a notch higher, and Agnes moaned. How did this old woman survive alone out here, no plumbing, no electricity? How could any human, male or female, exist through the biting winters and sizzling summers?

Norman sat on the side of the bed and held her hand while Gracie got Agnes a bowl of chicken broth. When she came back, he went downstairs to wash up.

"You drink this right down, Miz Agnes. This made it a whole lot better when I had my eleven right in this same bed."

Agnes couldn't believe any one woman had borne eleven children. One was enough for her. How could anyone go through this hell eleven times?

"You had eleven children?"

Gracie sat next to the bed and patted her hand. "Yes, ma'am. Took me almost fifteen years. So many children, never was sure did they all meet."

The gravelly tone in Gracie's voice calmed her a little. Even in her predicament, she couldn't help playing a little numbers game.

"Over the course of several years, they had to have all met. It'd be statistically impossible for eleven people under one roof to avoid each other for very long. Like atoms spinning around in a molecule, eventually they'd collide."

"Huh? You a witch or something?"

"Don't mind me, Gracie. I play games with numbers all the time."

"Then I got some more. Thirty-two grandchildren and a whole bunch of great-grandbabies too, but haven't counted them. Spread out all over God's creation. Got a few children in Poughkeepsie. Lucy, my favorite, she's been maiding for years way out west at Chautauqua Lake for some family of popeyed redheads named Ball. Liked her so much, they named their girl after her."

"What happened to your husband?"

"Died back in '90. Been a widow now more than forty years."

"Is that him in the painting downstairs?"

"That was my pa. He fought for Lincoln in the war. Died in '72, year after I married Mr. Honeywalker. We escaped from a Kentucky farm day after my eighth birthday back in '60 just before the war, come on up here through the Ohio underground. Done lived on this place since I was twenty and runned it all myself since my husband died."

The Ohio underground! Agnes never had met a former slave, let alone one who'd escaped and ended up running her own farm—and for decades too. No wonder Gracie thought midwifing was easy. "Well then, you must be —"

"Eighty. Done turned eighty last birthday. Can't complain. I might be old, but I can still do everything round here myself. Only thing I don't do anymore is men folk. I done had enough of them."

Agnes chuckled. "After eleven babies and thirty-two grandchildren, I can understand why."

Norman returned after another ten minutes and sat in the chair by the bed, his hair wet, but his body dry and smelling like Ivory soap. "How's my girl?"

He'd changed his shirt and looked less like a toiling laborer at the end of a summer day, and more like the dazzling architect she'd fallen in love with. "Gracie and I were talking."

"She's doing pretty fine, Mr. Norman, pretty fine. I got her laughing."

The skies grew dark, and the trees began to blow from side to side. The contractions arrived closer together—eleven minutes, nine minutes, then six minutes. They pulled her right back to agonized acceptance of God's revenge. *The wages of sin are death.*

Gracie lit candles in the room's corners. Norman started to close the windows, but Gracie stopped him.

"Miz Agnes needs fresh air more than we need dry floors."

Norman gave Agnes another glass of water before sitting down again. "Honey, your hands are all clammy and you're trembling. Are you nervous?"

She'd have smacked him if she hadn't been recovering from another unspeakable contraction.

"Are you joking? And what time is it?" She didn't want to have the baby in the dark. Too many ghosts and demons might be lurking about—

"About eight o'clock." They remained silent until Norman spoke up. "Sweetheart, I've been thinking. I'm sorry about the cat this afternoon, and I'm sorry about our game. I have no idea who was right, but it doesn't matter."

Agnes sat up and looked him in the eye. She'd forgotten about Twenty Questions. Even the cat had receded to the back of her mind. He hadn't admitted he'd made a mistake, but at least he'd apologized.

"Thank you for that. And you're right, it doesn't matter." Why couldn't he always be this agreeable? He'd made so many of their decisions, she'd come to feel she lived according to his rules. But all that seemed to be changing—

Another contraction. She threw her head back against the pillows and braced against his hand. "Oh, God, Norman, what in the name of Jesus are we doing?"

"Agnes, my hand—oh, that hurts." He pulled his twisted hand free and massaged it.

She glowered at him. "Let's not talk about your pain right now, Norman."

"Let me see if I can get something else for you to hold onto." He was back in a few minutes, tying a white sheet to the foot of the bed and knotting it for her to squeeze.

Gracie laughed. "White folks always do that when the pain gets bad. Don't figure it helps any."

Agnes breathed hard with the pains as they grew ever stronger. Darkness closed in, and the skies opened up in a deluge pockmarked by thunder and lightning. Agnes lost her sense of time. The only markers were the pains growing stronger and more frequent, thunder and lightning, Gracie entering the room every fifteen minutes to check on her, sitting up to urinate, walking in circles, and drinking glass after glass of water. At one point, she drank too much water and vomited a silky liquid into one of Gracie's basins.

Gracie continued to report slow progress in her dilation. Midnight approached, and Agnes grew restless. Gracie prodded her once again to get up and walk about. It felt good to be up and out of that sweaty bed that held nothing but torturous pain. She dreaded getting back in.

Between contractions, she thought about that one night in the spring before Daddy died. She'd caught influenza and her parents, fearful she'd succumb as had so many neighbors, sat with her while she vomited through the night. Then, just as now, a man and a woman had attended her, but now instead of Mama and Daddy, she had Norman with his triangular jaw and Gracie with the nasal twang and Jesus on her tongue, God registering his anger outside with the wind and rain. She gripped her father's locket in her palm.

In the hours that followed, Agnes receded behind a dim fog that consumed her. Sometimes the room expanded to huge proportions, and sometimes it smothered her with claustrophobia. The storm receded to a whimper, then blew into a maelstrom. The blackness of the night brought her to a state of panic. Jagged reflections of candlelight on the walls taunted her. She pleaded for mercy from Norman and Gracie, but little they did seemed to help. She sensed she and the baby were dying because the blackness in her mind told her so.

Behind her soggy delirium, she began to call for Granny. She wanted her grandmother now more than ever. She had a vision of Granny standing by the foot of the bed looking over her in one of her black lace dresses, bright red hair, high cheekbones, and pink wrinkles. Where was Granny, where was Daddy, and why had they forsaken her?

"Mama, I need you!" she cried out with useless tears, biting into the pillowcase at the next crest of pain. On that night so long ago, her mother had sat beside her bed placing a cool towel on her fevered forehead, singing a Brahms lullaby to get her to sleep. Now she saw her mother, slouching and as stout as ever, standing in the corner, shaking her head and weeping, "It's nothing Siobhan Limerick can be doing to save you now, Agnes Mary."

The other ghost in the room, her father, beckoned her with an outstretched arm. He waved her to join him on the other side. "Daddy!" she cried, "I'll be there soon enough."

She called his name again and again, reaching out with her hand. Instead of being soothed by her father's soft hands, the smile of his narrow face, she felt the rough ridges of Gracie's aged talon. The roughness brought her out of delirium, and she grasped only a distant whisper of Gracie's graveled alto.

"Ain't gone be long now, Mr. Norman. Good dilation. She'll be ready soon. Go bring the boiling pot from the stove."

Norman disappeared, and Daddy sat in his place. She looked at the pale, languid ghost, trying to penetrate her father's eyes, but the apparition turned foggy. She asked him where Granny was, but he didn't answer. When Norman came back and took his seat, her father vanished—as always when she needed him the most.

Daddy might've left her, but Norman had come back. She looked into her husband's clear eyes. Even in her delirium, she thanked God he sat next to her, patting her hand and stroking her head. He might boss her around, but at least she could count on him.

Her breathing became hurried, and her heart began to race. Through a blurry mist, she could see the storm had stopped and fresh light crept through the windows. The trees became visible again, and a quiet blue supplanted the thunderous black of the night.

She heard Norman and Gracie fussing about, but pain and delirium muffled their voices and figures into distant apparitions. Only a matter of time before God would release her soul from this protracted misery and send her back to her father.

Gracie's faraway voice called to her. "Okay, Miz Agnes, you're crowning now. You're ready. You reach down and touch the head. Go on, feel your baby's head."

Agnes struggled against Gracie's prodding hand.

"Okay, Mr. Norman," Gracie said. "You take her hand. She's fighting me."

Norman took Agnes's hand, but she struggled against him, too. She continued to moan. "Mama, I'm going to die ..."

"Look at me, Miz Agnes, you ain't gone to die. Look me in the eye, honey," Gracie said. "Look me in the eye. You ain't gone to die."

Agnes shifted her eyes from her husband to the midwife. From behind the cloud of pain, she gazed into Gracie's eyes, two black pools of kindness. Her head cleared, and she reached across her abdomen to feel her baby's head.

"My little baby!" She felt the wet, silky head of her child. She forgot the waves of pain during the past fourteen hours. She forgot the oppressive heat and humidity, the maelstrom outside, the humiliation of blood, feces, urine, and gas. She forgot the sweating, the discomfort, the nausea, the vomiting, drenched hair in her face and eyes, her lower back raging in protest, her moans of terror. She forgot the embarrassment of having a strange negro woman seeing her private parts. She forgot the wild throttling that left her writhing in agony. She forgot about crying out for her parents and grandmother. Her mind became consumed by the miracle that it was her body bringing forth this new life.

Suddenly, she knew with absolute clarity she could do it. She didn't need her mother, her father, or even her grandmother. They could witness this from afar. It would be she who brought this baby into the world, no one else. She didn't even need her husband. Only herself, Agnes Limerick.

Her eyes flashed to the crucifix of Christ, the Jesus she adored. Waves of love consumed her.

"I see, I know!"

Everything made sense all at once, all those disconnected pieces of her life. Her body, her soul, her God, this baby, what connected them all together, the continuity between one life and another, all framed by love. Her eyes dropped from the crucifix and met Gracie's.

Gracie smiled from ear to ear, and her black eyes sparkled. "Okay, honey. You got to breathe and push. Breathe and push! You birthing a little baby now, Miz Agnes. Just a few minutes longer. Breathe and push."

With innumerable deep breaths in and out, she pushed as hard as she could, each thrust more urgent than the last. Every part of her body breathed with the urgency of pushing this child out into the world. Yes, that was it, bringing her baby into this vibrant world. Her child! Breathe and push, she told herself, echoing Gracie's words, breathe and push.

"Child's head's coming out, Miz Agnes, Mr. Norman. You, sir, you talk to her now. You got to be the one, go on. Tell her what you see."

"Darling, breathe now and push. I can see our baby's head. He's beautiful, oh, sweetheart, he's beautiful. He's got brown hair."

It never had felt like a boy. "A boy, he's a boy?"

"Mr. Norman, you can't tell just yet. Ain't no penises on wet baby heads."

Agnes didn't understand. She pushed again. How long would this take? How many more pushes for this stubborn baby? And then she felt a small release from the pain—

Gracie guided the child out of the womb. "Head's out. You almost there, Miz Agnes, just a little more. Shoulders out now. Ease on out."

She breathed for the thousandth time and made a final push with an ecstatic cry.

"She's a girl, Miz Agnes. A fine baby girl," Gracie announced.

"A girl," Norman exclaimed, his voice crackling like a victrola. He reached down to kiss Agnes on her forehead, tears of joy streaming down his cheeks. "Our baby girl, Agnes, our baby girl!"

Agnes heard the same happiness in his voice she felt in her heart. He had wanted a girl, after all.

Her body was released from the pain that had grappled with her for hours. Agnes watched the deft hands of Gracie Honeywalker go to work. She patted the baby on the behind. She tied up and cut the umbilical cord, then placed the child on Agnes's stomach. Their daughter's first cries echoed all the way to those far corners where the silent spirits of Agnes's mother, her father, and Granny Limerick resided. Agnes hoped they could sense this moment somehow.

Gracie washed off the birth's blood and examined the infant, then swaddled her in a smooth towel and placed her in Agnes's arms. Norman gently edged his way onto the bed, their baby girl's peaceful mewling between them.

"Healthy as can be, ain't no worries over her being early," Gracie reassured them. "Ain't no different when the baby comes, ain't never no different, except this time I got the pa here. You be proud of yourself, Mr. Norman, you done seen your baby born. Miz Agnes, try to put the baby's head by your bosom. She's gone to need milk real soon, so get her used to it. And you gone to sleep real soon. I'm gone to get my own babies' crib now."

Agnes didn't remember the afterbirth, so captivated was she by this child in her arms — a pink jewel with brown curls and dark eyes. Agnes thought she recognized Norman's jawline and Mama's almond complexion, but too early to tell. She basked in the closeness of the child's serene eyes and her husband's warm strength. The three of them in this dear woman's bedroom, God only knew where, the light of a bright morning shining into the room.

"Norman, what day is it?"

"It's our little Victoria's birthday, the twentieth of September."

Agnes had forgotten they'd decided to name a girl after his mother.

"The twentieth of September, her birthday. From now on, every year the best day's going to be this day. Our little girl's birthday, Norman."

Gracie returned with the crib. "How're you all in here?"

Fatigue overwhelmed Agnes, and she fell asleep before she could turn her head to answer.

She awoke to the sound of the baby's crying. Norman lay beside her in his boxer shorts, purring away quiet hisses of sleep. The hair on his chest and legs nestled her with rough warmth. Gracie sat knitting in a chair near the bed.

"You stay there, child. I'll bring the baby to you. Mr. Norman done climbed into bed and fell to sleep just after you."

Agnes's lower back cried foul, but she sat up with relative ease. Odd, how light she felt, now that the baby was no longer inside. Having given birth, she supposed, she could move mountains if she wanted, without anyone's help — not Mama or Granny, Daddy, not even Norman.

She took the crying baby from Gracie and cradled her in her arms. She had the scent of spring air, with just a touch of saliva. Gracie prodded Agnes to feed the child, so she guided the baby's button mouth to her breast. The baby fiddled with it until she found the nipple and began to suckle.

"Ain't gone be much milk yet, Miz Agnes, but you feed her every few hours and there's gone be plenty right soon. Baby knows what to do better'n us."

"Gracie, what time is it? How much did I miss?"

"Getting on to noon. You done slept near three hours, Miz Agnes. Baby girl slept the whole time. Myself, I ain't tired. Birthing babies always livens me up."

Agnes looked again at the child, dark hair like Norman's, also his wide jaw and square chin. But she'd have brown eyes just like Mama. And long, thin fingers, maybe she'd be a pianist. Half Irish, half English, half Catholic, half Protestant — what a beautiful combination.

Trees filtered golden rays that bathed the room in sunlight, shone on Gracie's weathered furniture, reflected off the white basins, brought a satin sheen to Gracie's hair, and highlighted wall cracks in the wise old house. Agnes felt the first pleasant breeze since they'd left the cabin. Her eyes rested on Gracie.

"Go on, Miz Agnes. You get some time with your girl. I'll catch up on my sleep too. You just holler if you want anything. I'll be here in a jiffy."

Her baby finished suckling, cooed, and began crying. Panic seized Agnes in the throat, and she struggled to cry out —

"Oh, Gracie, come back. The baby's turning blue!"

Gracie barely had left the room and chuckled when she came back in. "Oh, Miz Agnes, you got to burp the baby after feeding."

Agnes lifted the infant to her shoulder and patted her back. "Mama has a lot to learn, little angel. Maybe you can teach me along the way."

She knew nothing about being a mother except what she'd observed from Mama and Granny. Suddenly, she wanted Mama to see her first grandchild, Granny to see her first great-grandchild. She wanted them to experience the same magic that consumed Agnes when she looked into the baby's dark eyes.

"I'm your own Mama, sweetheart. Welcome to the world, little precious."

Had Mama felt like this when she was born? Did all babies have the uncontested hold over their mothers' love that this one had right now?

Elgar's *Enigma Variations* came to mind. The melodic dissonance of his rhapsodic variations always had played beneath her most cherished memories. Feeling the priest's sign of the cross on her forehead at her first communion … Daddy carrying her on his shoulders through the streets of Philadelphia … playing with Racer in the square … mastering Beethoven's sonatas … listening to "Jesu, Joy of Man's Desiring" at Christmas … experiencing sex with Norman. And now this, the most cherished memory of all.

Nothing could've prepared Agnes for this peaceful absolution. Something like blissful calm descended from the heavens and wrapped itself around them. They'd found, in the most unlikely place, Gracie Honeywalker, the eighty-year-old enigma who'd brought this child into the world. *By the grace of God, Gracie Honeywalker.*

This child's true name came to her, decisive and clear. Norman wouldn't object, he couldn't, for the name wasn't theirs to choose. It came from God.

"And so, my little angel," she said to the music of Elgar playing in her head, caressing Daddy's locket around her neck, "you shall be our own Grace Martina Balmoral."

12

THE NEXT MORNING, AGNES FED THE BABY in a rocking chair by the window. A cool breeze flowed into the room. Gracie had brought the chair that morning before heading outside to do chores, telling her to rock the baby to sleep after the feeding.

She saw a large open truck approach the house. Twelve, maybe fifteen, negro boys got out of the back. Norman followed Gracie out of the barn, clad in black pants and undershirt, helping Gracie. The storm might've broken the heat and humidity, but the September sun still shone strong.

"You, Percy, out front with your brothers," Gracie said, parceling out orders in a booming voice that seemed to carry for miles. "Want you to pick the last of the green beans in the far field. Use my haversack, put them inside the barn. Mr. Norman done cleaned out the shelves. Stack them in there for the men come to get them.

"Seth, you take a few of the others out to the cornfields and bring the corn back in the cart. Need them by one today cause Lacey's coming to take them over to Endicott. Don't you be poking, either, cause I'll come out there and slap your hides. Lots a work to do today, so get cracking.

"Mr. Norman, we'll get the pumpkins and squashes. Junius and the rest of you grandsons, you come with us. Mr. Norman, you pull this cart."

Norman strained the muscles in his shoulders and biceps as he lifted the cart's handles. He dropped them, let out a moan, and massaged his shoulders.

"Heavy, ain't it? Can't handle it? Try giving birth like Miz Agnes done. If men gave birth, they'd pussyfoot a lot less. Let me show you how it's done."

Gracie marched over to the cart, leaned down, and used her body weight to pull the handles up from the ground—and dropped them.

"My eighty years can't be marching with this cart behind me, but something tells me you're strong enough. Got it, Mr. Norman?"

Agnes laughed. Norman had walked around in a velvety daze since Grace's birth, besotted by the baby, obeying any command Gracie sent his way. He'd registered only a *hmmph* when Agnes told him about Grace's name.

"We'll use Victoria for her middle name," he'd responded, and she'd agreed. Grace Victoria had a lovely ring to it, and they could save Martin for a son.

Today proved no different. He'd helped Agnes into the rocking chair, he'd held the baby in his arms, and he'd asked Gracie if he could help around the house. She said the barn needed fixing and cleaning. After a tender kiss on Agnes's forehead, Norman excused himself to help Gracie with her day's chores. She closed her eyes, content with her cooing baby and the thought that Norman was helping Gracie—and her.

Early that afternoon, Agnes awoke from a nap. Norman stood above her, out of breath, dirt covering his face, grimy sweat soaking his undershirt. She saw the hair on his chest and abdomen through the shirt, slithery like a wet snake.

"I've just had the most glorious morning. Gracie, the boys, and I picked over a hundred pumpkins and twenty bushels of fall squashes. We carted them over to the barn, ready for Lacey's truck. It'll fetch Gracie over two dollars, she says, if the wholesaler doesn't rob her. But Lacey always watches after her, that's what she says."

Agnes marveled at Norman's enthusiasm and wished they could stay here forever. It continued this way for nearly two weeks until Agnes finally told Norman she felt well enough to go back to Philadelphia. They'd best be getting home, he answered. Norman had sent telegrams to his parents and the Limericks the afternoon after Grace's birth. Victoria and Cornelius had replied right away, urging them to return as soon as Agnes could travel. They received a reply from the Limericks two days later. "First great-grandbaby. Knew she was a girl."

Norman packed the car on the morning of their departure. In the front hallway, Gracie handed Agnes a baby's dress, faded white lace.

"You take this, Miz Agnes. It was for my Lucy's christening back in '87. Jesus done watched over her real good. Maybe little Grace'll have the same luck."

Agnes thanked her and looked up at the portrait of Gracie's father. She'd seen defiance in his visage when they'd gotten here, but now she saw only incorruptible strength.

"Such determination to be free," Agnes said to Gracie, in a wistful tone. "You'd never know from the expression that he'd been enslaved."

"You one of the few to notice. Ain't nobody could ever keep Pa down. Maybe one day I'll give him to you."

The mud had dried since the storms, and Norman could put the car in reverse, but they got no farther than twenty feet before the car conked out like a dead mule.

Norman tried to restart the vehicle, but nothing worked. "Damn this car, anyway. I don't know anything about engines," he said.

Back to the house they went. Lacey came by later that day and took a look — "rusted out carburetor, can't go anywhere before it's replaced" — so they adjusted for another week away from home. Norman wired his parents for money. When the funds arrived a week later, Lacey drove him to Endicott to buy the carburetor. Norman installed it, and the car started right up.

"Shall we start back this afternoon, Agnes?"

"Got to stay this evening for dinner, Mr. Norman, Miz Agnes. Lacey's seventy years old today. He's coming over, and we're cooking venison. You got to stay, otherwise I'll have to get a chaperone. Can't have no white man over for dinner alone."

Norman scratched his forehead. "Lacey didn't say a word about it on the whole drive over to Endicott and back."

"Well, you just got to stay for dinner."

It was already after noon, Agnes said, so they might as well stay another night and get an early start in the morning. Lacey drove up to the house late that afternoon. Norman, Agnes, and Gracie were sitting in chairs on the front porch, admiring the October's low sunset. Agnes was holding the sleeping baby.

Lacey shuffled up the walkway as if gravity were pulling him into the ground. He stood in front of Agnes and pulled a yellow paper out of his shirt pocket. Agnes cringed.

"Miz Agnes, I got a telegram for you."

She handed the baby to Gracie and stood to read the telegram. She shrieked as soon as she read the first sentence. *A.K.L. had cerebral hemorrhage. Come quickly. C.D.* She dropped the paper on the floor as if it were poison.

Norman rose. "Agnes, what is it? You're white as a sheet."

"Granny had a stroke. Uncle Collin wants us to come home right away."

"So sorry, Miz Agnes. I reckon you'd best be going. Lucky we got the car fixed today. Jesus must've knowed something was up."

Norman addressed Agnes. "Darling, you need to sit down. You're going to faint." He supported her by the shoulders.

"Not now, Norman." She wriggled free and ran into the house.

Granny might be dying, and here they were, nearly two hundred miles away. It'd take a day to drive down to Philadelphia. Thank heavens they got the car fixed. She'd drive through the night, if need be, just to see Granny alive, at least one more time. She had to see her grandmother, to show her Grace Victoria, tell her about Gracie, the miraculous birth. To tell her about the farm, Norman harvesting pumpkins and squashes with Gracie's grandsons, collecting vegetables from the gardens once she'd recovered—oh, what wouldn't she tell her Granny! She had to see Granny's blue eyes once more, had to hear her say, "Oh, poo!" But what if the stroke had disabled her speech?

She barely could concentrate on what her body was doing—plopping suitcases on the bed, opening drawers, throwing clothing into the luggage—not caring whether Norman's undershorts mixed with her brassieres, whether the clothing lay flat. Agnes had a mind only on the road. Granny would be at the Pennsylvania Hospital, no doubt. Daddy had been the hospital's best doctor, and Granny was his mother.

Norman came into the room. Without a word, he helped her with the clothing. He gathered the baby's borrowed clothes and the old toys Gracie's sons had brought. They were leaving Gracie, Agnes thought, and a pang went through her. This was Baby Grace's first home, and now they were headed back to Philadelphia. And Granny, dear God, let Granny be alive.

They trudged down the stairs with the suitcases. They hadn't been that heavy when they'd arrived, had they? Out the front door, Gracie sat in the rocking chair with the baby, Lacey next to her holding Gracie's hand.

"Miz Agnes, Mr. Norman, you sure been good to me these last weeks. I sure appreciate all your help around here."

"Gracie, it's you who've done so much for us. We can't ever repay you. You brought our little Grace into the world."

Gracie kissed the baby on the forehead. Those kind hands, so caressing to anyone within reach. "Keep up with me, Miz Agnes. Don't you be forgetting old Gracie Honeywalker."

Gracie stood and handed the baby to Agnes. Lacey stood behind her.

"I'll write as soon as I get home, Gracie. You know I will." She leaned in to Gracie and gazed at her. She remembered the magic in Gracie's eyes just before the birth. She kissed Gracie on both cheeks. "I'll miss you, Gracie Honeywalker."

"Me too, Miz Agnes. You too, Mr. Norman. Maybe you can be a farmer down there in Philadelphia. You sure knew what you was doing here, Jesus knows it's true."

"Thank you, Miss Gracie. It's been an honor to work here." Norman gave her a firm handshake with both hands.

Gracie smiled. "Mr. Norman, you take care of your wife. You two best be gone. Your granny needs you. I don't. I got Mr. Lacey to look after me."

Agnes looked back as they drove away. She resisted the urge to wave. Gracie stood on the porch, Lacey behind her, his hand on her shoulder. She stifled her tears and looked forward.

They reached Philadelphia the following afternoon and parked at 10th Street in front of the Pennsylvania Hospital. Agnes bounded out of the car and darted in the hospital's front door. The tall steps and the sturdy Victorian building looked the same to her as the last time she'd been there fourteen years earlier when Daddy had died. Today, she turned in the opposite direction to the women's section.

"I've come to see Mrs. Limerick," she said to the first nurse she saw.

"I beg your pardon, ma'am?" the nurse said, rolling her eyes down Agnes's body. "Whom shall I say is inquiring?"

Agnes knew her wrinkled muslin print dress made for a motley appearance, but she didn't care. "Miss—Mrs. Balmoral, her granddaughter."

The nurse walked to the head station and scanned a list of patients once, twice, and a third time. "I'm sorry, ma'am, but there's no Mrs. Limerick here."

Agnes turned without a word and went back out just as Norman was coming in, with Grace in his arms. She motioned outside, and they headed back to the car.

"She's not here, must be at a different hospital. This doesn't make sense. Mama certainly would have brought Granny here. We'd better check at home before heading to Thomas Jefferson or to Penn."

"I don't think my parents will have heard anything. Let's go to the Limerick house instead."

"That's what I meant," she said as he opened the car door. "Leave the car here. Home is only three blocks away."

They walked down Spruce Street to 6th—how beautiful Old City appeared in October with red, gold, and brown leaves on the maples—but Agnes gasped when they turned onto 6th and headed down to Pine Street. She saw a dozen men in front of Mama's house, every one of them wearing black. She ran the last hundred feet to the house.

"No, Granny!"

When she reached the corner, she recognized Mr. Callahan, Tommy's father. "Mr. Callahan, please say it isn't true. She's still alive, isn't she?"

He looked at the other men, all dressed in black suits, all casting their eyes downward. Mr. Callahan spoke. "I'm very sorry for your trouble, Agnes. Blessed Mrs. Limerick passed on early this morning."

She sat on the front steps, her eyes swaying from one side of the sidewalk to the other. No tears came. Norman embraced her. "Darling girl, I'm so sorry. This is a terrible way to find out."

She heard her own voice in high-pitched vibrato. "I didn't have a chance to say good-bye."

He helped her up. "We'd better go inside. Your family will be there."

"We'll be inside after the women finish," Mr. Callahan said.

"What does that mean?" Norman asked, his mouth making a round *oh*.

"To prepare for the wake," Agnes answered, her voice so distant, she barely heard it herself. "Our older neighbors prepare the body. The women wash and dress Granny's body, and the men place it in the coffin."

The front door already had a bouquet of lilies and hydrangeas adorning it. Agnes opened the door. The house smelled like bleach. Of course, the women had cleaned from top to bottom. She looked in the parlor, where she saw the furniture moved aside and an open, empty coffin sitting near the front window, tall candles around its four corners. The front window was opened and uncovered, but the drapes were drawn everywhere else Agnes could see. The hall mirrors were covered in black linen. She looked at the grandfather clock, stopped at 6:15. Granny must've died just before sunrise.

Agnes heard the sound of voices upstairs from Granny's bedroom. She bounded up the stairs and saw Mrs. O'Toole at the entrance to the room. Eight women fussed about the bed. Agnes got a glimpse of her grandmother's white legs. A shiver sent icicles through her heart.

Mrs. O'Toole spoke from behind her. "Dear Agnes, I'm so sorry for your trouble."

"I must see her."

"Agnes, dear, a few minutes longer," Mrs. O'Toole said, shaking her head so much, her chins were jiggling up and down. "Wait until the men have brought her downstairs. We're dressing Annie Kate in her finest white Irish lace. She's going to look beautiful, Agnes."

The baby cried, and Agnes turned around. She'd forgotten that Norman had followed her into the house.

"Mrs. O'Toole, you remember my husband, and this is our daughter, Grace. Where is my family?"

"They're at St. Patrick's with your uncle planning tomorrow's funeral. Good afternoon, Mr. Balmoral. It is a pleasure to see you and this precious child."

Mrs. O'Toole offered to set up a crib for Grace so she could sleep during the wake. Agnes directed her to the third-floor storage room for the old crib, but first she wanted to know what had happened to Granny.

Mrs. O'Toole framed the story with gentle tones, endearments, and quiet words, but Agnes only wanted the bare facts. Granny had suffered a cerebral hemorrhage, the doctor said, so massive that the swelling had caused her brain to shift to one side of her head, leading to a final rupture in the brain stem that killed her fourteen hours after the stroke. She'd never regained consciousness.

"Did she say anything before she fainted?"

"She was sitting with your mother in the kitchen. I don't know."

Waddling old Mrs. Callahan came out of the bedroom and tugged Mrs. O'Toole on the arm. "Tell them she's ready."

"Agnes, dear, I think it would be best if you went downstairs to the kitchen while the men place your grandmother in the coffin. Mrs. Stein is there."

No sooner did they walk downstairs than the front door opened and in came the men, single file. They bowed as they passed Agnes and marched straight up the stairs. "Let's go into the kitchen," Agnes told Norman. "I don't want to see this."

"What are they going to do?" Norman asked.

"The men will carry Granny's body downstairs and place it in the coffin. Then the women will arrange everything just so."

They found Mrs. Stein in the kitchen, her squat figure nearly hidden by all the food and drink. Their neighbors had jumped right into action — and not just the Irish and Catholics. She saw platters of corned beef, cheeses, sandwiches, a large pot of Irish stew, spaghetti and meatballs, and a deli display of smoked salmon, onions, whitefish salad, and cream cheese. Mrs. Stein would've brought that from her restaurant, Famous's Deli 4th Street, Granny's favorite delicatessen.

Mrs. Stein came over to Agnes and held her arm. "I'm sorry for your trouble, Agnes Limerick."

Agnes introduced Norman and sent him to the car for her suitcase. She needed to change her dress. Mrs. Stein directed her attention to the baby. "What a beautiful baby, Agnes, and those soft eyes." But Agnes kept looking back toward the hallway. After a while, she saw the black shadows of six men carrying Granny's stiff body across the front hallway into the parlor.

Norman returned with her suitcase, and she went into the dining room to change her dress when he began chattering with Mrs. Stein about their marriage, honeymoon in New York, and Gracie Honeywalker. On her way back, Agnes saw the men leave the parlor and the women go inside, and after another eternity, the women left the parlor. Was Granny alone? That was forbidden at an Irish wake.

Agnes rushed into the parlor. She saw Mrs. O'Toole sitting on a chair in the distance. "Good, Agnes, you're here. I'll leave you alone with Annie Kate. Your family will be back soon, and you can have time with her before we close the front window."

Agnes knew she was dressed inappropriately. It was almost an insult to approach Granny's coffin in a blue wool dress, but she couldn't help it. She hadn't planned on attending a funeral during her honeymoon.

She stood by the coffin, feeling a shallow breeze from the window. Granny was dressed in white lace, holding red rosary beads with her hands, her gold crucifix around her neck — all white, like Granny's face, except for her red hair. She'd kept her hair red right up to the end. But the face shocked Agnes. Its right half seemed turned up at an angle — the chin, mouth, eyes, even the eyebrows, all of it. The hemorrhage must've occurred on that side. It pained Agnes to realize friends would see Granny with that frozen expression. All at once she hated the tradition of people viewing the body. She touched Granny's fingers and recoiled, guilt washing over her. She should've first kneeled to pray for Granny's soul.

She rose from her prayer two minutes later, and looked at Granny. She felt the tides shifting inside and knew she'd have to cry. Thank God. She wanted to sob until she could sob no more. She forced herself to touch Granny's hands and leaned down to kiss her on the cheek. Ah, Granny, what a lovely treasure you've been. But the tears didn't come.

The front door opened and startled Agnes. She turned to see Patrick. They all followed him inside one at a time. Patrick, wearing the same black suit he'd worn at Uncle Daniel's funeral, took her hands. "Thank you for coming, sister."

They greeted her, one at a time. Uncle James, Aunt Lucy, Aunt Josephine, Cousin Andrew, Cousin Kathleen, Aunt Julia, Uncle Paul, cousins—and then Mama, followed by Uncle Collin.

"Dear Agnes," Mama said, her black dress adorned only by Granny's pearls, "your poor sainted grandmother might've died, but you've come home."

Uncle Collin did not look her in the eye. "Agnes Mary, a blue dress for your sainted grandmother?" he said in a stale monotone. "Have you no respect?"

Of course, he'd be the one to point out her dress. She squirmed just as she'd done when she'd misbehaved in school, but she didn't apologize.

One by one, they lined up to pass by the coffin. It seemed to take an eternity. Her aunts, her uncles, her cousins, they all prayed, made signs of the cross, then kissed Granny. Patrick, Mama, and Uncle Collin stood last in line. When they reached the front, Norman came into the room with Grace and retreated to the back by Granny's piano.

The tears finally burst forth. She sobbed into Norman's shoulder, and the baby started to wail. All eyes turned to them, shocked at the sound of a baby's crying. No children were allowed at an Irish wake.

Patrick clutched his mother's arm, pointed at Grace, and said to Mama, "There is your granddaughter."

They approached Mama and Patrick at the coffin. Agnes took a deep breath and said, "Mama, we named her Grace—"

Patrick interrupted her. "Norman, welcome to our home. I am Agnes's brother." The two men shook hands, looking each other in the eye with clenched jaws. Norman's chin jutted out, just as Victoria's had done when she met Uncle Collin, and Patrick matched Uncle Collin's granite-carved face.

On seeing the baby, Mama's lips curled into a smile that spread across her cheeks and into her eyes, an expression Agnes hadn't seen since before Daddy had died. "She's a beautiful creature, so like my Martin. Let me hold her. Collin, look at this child. May I?" she asked Norman without looking at him.

He handed Grace to Mama, and she rocked the baby in her arms. Norman stepped backward as if to get out of the way and stood by the window. Before Agnes could tell him that he'd erred—

"Agnes, take care of this at once," Uncle Collin directed.

"Norman, you'd better come back from there. It's bad luck to stand between the coffin and an open window."

His mouth made the same round *oh* again. "I didn't know."

Agnes hung on Mama's expression through wet eyes. She looked as content as Agnes ever remembered, before Daddy had died, before the Depression, before Agnes had left home. A younger version of Siobhan Limerick rocked the baby as the child's wails subsided. Mama let the baby clasp her finger.

"Little graceful Grace, little graceful Grace."

One by one, the family came over from Granny's coffin to meet the child, but Uncle Collin remained on the opposite side of the room. Surely it was disrespectful for the deceased's family to pay more attention to an infant than to the dead?

"Oh, fiddlesticks," she could hear her grandmother saying, "the baby's alive, not me, and I look like a ghoul. She's my only great-grandchild, so they'd better mind her more than me."

She said this out loud to Norman, who arched his eyebrows. "You'd better get accustomed to this," she advised. "This is a wake. We cry first, and then we laugh and celebrate Granny's life. But first we have a few customary rituals in here."

Uncle Collin spoke first. "That's exactly right, Agnes Mary." She didn't think he was paying attention. "Now I'm going to close the window."

Norman asked why, and she explained the window remained open for two hours so Granny's soul could escape to heaven. They had to close it now to prevent her soul from coming back.

"What happens next?" Norman asked. She put two fingers to her lips.

Uncle Collin began singing in a monotone. "This is called keening." Agnes whispered to Norman. "He's mourning Granny's death in Gaelic. He's expressing the longing and love of an unhappy people for a matriarch who served them well for many years."

"It's lovely, sweetheart, but he sounds like a dying goose."

Uncle Collin yielded to Patrick, whose tenor picked up where their uncle's bass left off. Mama handed the baby back to Agnes and began her own keening. They followed, one by one, Granny's sons, her daughters, and her grandchildren. Finally, Agnes knew she needed to do the same. She looked sideways at Norman and handed Grace to him.

What did she want to say to this group of people, these relatives whom she'd deserted seven months ago? Granny had approved, no, Granny had almost pushed her into the marriage, telling her it was right to do. So that's what she keened. "Thank you, Granny," she wailed. "Thank you for giving me the courage and strength to marry the man I loved, to give a home to the child I bore, and to honor the sacrament of marital love." Several cousins turned their backs to her. Mama turned white and left the room.

Uncle Collin ignored Agnes's keening. "And now, it is five o'clock and time to receive our visitors. I'll wait outside."

Patrick intervened. "Thank you, Uncle Collin. With all due respect, I would like to take that responsibility. As you know, I've been head of Granny's family ever since my blessed father died in '18."

That was true, Agnes realized, proud of her brother, the first son of Granny's first son. Uncle Collin bowed to his nephew. Patrick walked outside to welcome the guests. She and Norman took the baby upstairs to the crib, and returned to find an endless line of people wearing black and gray.

The people entered, signed the guest book, prayed at Granny's coffin, and bowed to family members. "I'm so sorry for your trouble," this one said, that one whispered, the third one lamented. This one shook their hands, that one kissed them on their cheeks, the third one hugged them. "I'm so sorry for your trouble," Agnes heard a thousand times as these people from her youth filed into the parlor, made the same remarks and gestures, and filed out just as quickly. Their closest friends remained.

Few of her friends came to pay their respects. Mr. Larney, wearing the same black suit she'd seen him in just a short four weeks earlier, gave her a hasty peck before paying his respects to Granny. Cristina and the Cassatas didn't come, but they wouldn't have heard. The Irish grapevine wouldn't have meandered all the way to South Philadelphia. None of her schoolgirl friends from St. Patrick's came. Their parents did, but the girls did not—another sign, Agnes thought with a pang, that news of her marriage had reached everyone.

After nearly two hours, Patrick came inside, cheeks red from the brisk air, and announced the beginning of the second half. "We'll be going into the kitchen and dining room. Please join us to toast Annie Kate Limerick's life. Someone needs to hold *wog* over Granny, however. Mr. Shaughnessy—"

"Darling, what's that?" Norman whispered.

"*Wog* is the watch, someone standing guard over Granny's body. It's a sign of respect and an honor to be asked."

"I'd like to volunteer," Norman called out to Patrick.

"I'm sorry, Norman, but an Irishman and Catholic needs to stand guard," Patrick said, looking about the room, "Mr. Shaughnessy, would you be so kind?"

Poor Norman, trying to do his best and being thwarted at every turn. But then Mr. Larney spoke up.

"Allow me. It would be an honor to sit for Mrs. Limerick."

"Very well, Mr. Larney," Patrick said. "Now then, everyone, please follow me. Gentlemen, I've lit the pipe, and it's on the table in the hallway. I'd like to invite each of you to take one puff as a sign of respect for my grandmother."

They moved into the kitchen. Agnes and Norman followed, and she wondered what he'd do when they came to the pipe. He detested tobacco, saying it was bad for the lungs, ignoring medical arguments to the contrary. He ignored the pipe.

Mrs. Stein had made a herculean effort in assembling the buffet supper for fifty. People got their drinks first—Irish whiskey for the men, wine for the ladies, tea for those who wouldn't drink alcohol during Prohibition. Patrick walked around the room making certain everyone had a drink and then raised his glass of whiskey. "To the life of Annie Kate O'Grady Limerick!"

"And to the red hair she kept to her dying day and the blunt insults she hurled at the lot of us."

"And may her soul rest with God in heaven and keep the merry little angels from misbehaving."

"Our glasses to Annie Kate's blessed knitting needles and her black lace."

The tributes followed. Mrs. O'Toole spoke up, a little shaky and her mouth trembling after gulping down her first glass of wine. "All right, then. Annie Kate would've said, 'Enough, I'm starving,' so it's what I'm saying. Where's the food?"

They all filled their plates. Agnes took a sausage and red cabbage, smoked salmon with cucumbers, a slice of brisket, and roasted beets. Norman and she devoured their food. Her empty stomach purred. She hadn't realized how little they'd eaten since leaving Gracie's farm yesterday afternoon.

They sat on chairs in the dining room, alternating between eating their food and running up the stairs to check on the baby. Her aunts, uncles, cousins—they made polite conversation, but little more. Only Patrick and Aunt Julia spent much time sitting with them. Aunt Julia asked about Norman's family and showed interest in Agnes's tales about Gracie Honeywalker, until some of the ladies came into the room to start up a game of cards.

"Mercy, the ladies are starting a game of rummy, and I want to join them," Aunt Julia said, rising to sit with the women at a card table on the other side of the dining room. They'd set up the table especially for the wake. The women would play cards and by tradition deal an unplayed hand for Granny.

Agnes knew full well that election day was only three weeks from Tuesday, so it didn't surprise her when people began debating politics and sports—Governor Roosevelt, President Hoover, the New Deal, relief for the poor, the end of Prohibition, and the World Series. No one could believe the Yankees had shut out the Cubs, four games to none. She could hear it all. Norman joined a conversation next to him with the Finnegans and the Sweeneys. Both couples planned to vote for Roosevelt.

"Even if he is an Episcopalian, I'll vote for the governor," Mr. Sweeney droned. "Hoover's got starch on the brain."

"We've had more Episcopalian presidents than anything," Norman said.

"Which might explain the trouble we're in. If good Al Smith had been elected in '28, I can tell you, we'd be in better shape now."

"Unlikely," Norman said, his mouth forming its usual thin lines. "The forces that caused the Depression were already at work long before Hoover defeated Smith. We'd be in the same fix now, regardless of which man had been elected."

Mr. Finnegan sniffed. "I suppose you voted for Hoover back in '28 and you're going to vote for him again, young man?"

"Not at all. I did vote for Hoover in '28, but I plan to vote for Roosevelt this time. I like what he has to say about equal opportunity for all."

"Good for you, young man. And who are you?"

"I'm Balmoral, Agnes's husband. We have a three-week-old daughter sleeping upstairs."

Agnes felt as cozy as if covered by a warm blanket—Norman, here with their daughter, in her home, with her family.

"I heard about this. When is her baptism? I'll come to St. Patrick's to see your uncle baptize the blessed baby."

"We haven't yet decided. It surely will be at St. Mark's on Locust Street."

Why not St. Patrick's? Oh, yes—she'd agreed to become an Episcopalian, and Grace would be, too. The cozy, warm feeling evaporated, and she felt her heart sink.

The Finnegans and Sweeneys turned their attentions elsewhere. Norman and Agnes once again sat alone. Patrick came by occasionally, swaying from three whiskeys. Mama and Uncle Collin stayed in the kitchen. Agnes turned to Norman after a prolonged silence.

"Let's keep Mr. Larney company in the parlor."

They walked into the parlor. Mr. Larney sat at the piano fingering the keys but not playing. He'd closed the coffin after the keening, just as it had been closed for Daddy and Uncle Daniel.

"Mr. Larney," Norman said, "you're sitting there with nothing to drink."

"Mr. Balmoral, I seem to recall you don't drink alcohol," Mr. Larney said, nodding. "I'd hate to corrupt your principles."

Norman smiled. "That isn't the question. What would you like to drink? Whiskey, perhaps? This time I'll join you."

Mr. Larney flashed a broad smile below his moustache. "That would be just dandy, my handsome friend." Norman departed for the kitchen.

"He's delightful, Agnes. You really should hang onto him."

She sat in the chair next to Mr. Larney. He took her hands, fingering them one at a time. Agnes's scalp tingled at his touch, but guilt soon overtook her.

"These fingers haven't been playing the piano, young lady. Now you mind your teacher and start practicing every day."

"I would if I had a piano. But from now on, the baby will occupy most of my time."

"She'll take lessons herself one day, and she'll need your example."

Yes, of course, Grace would taken piano lessons, just as she had. Norman returned with two whiskeys in one hand and a cup of tea in the other. Had he worked as a waiter in Italy? He handed the whiskey to Mr. Larney and the tea to her.

"What was it you were saying about teaching our child, Mr. Larney?"

"I was noticing your wife's fingers. They look like they're out of practice."

"She plays them on her lap whenever she's bored."

Agnes frowned. Norman had upbraided her for this habit any number of times. He never let her get away with anything, like Uncle Collin and Mama, all wrapped up into one person. But a very attractive and funny person ...

"I only do it because the music sits in my head," Agnes said. "Whenever I had nothing to do here, I always came in this room and played. Now I'm living with Norman, and there's no piano. Here there's a piano, but no one to play it."

Mr. Larney tapped his foot. "The conclusion is inescapable. Piano and pianist clearly must be reunited. And for the baby's sake too.

"I understand from Mrs. O'Toole, your baby was born the twentieth of September on some farm in upstate New York. That was only a few days after we met at the restaurant."

She told Mr. Larney about Gracie and asked him about the time he spent in New York City. He'd been to a recital at Carnegie Hall and taken in *Show Boat* before boarding the train for Philadelphia. Then she asked him about piano students for this school year.

"Every year I have new pupils, but only the faces change. Otherwise, they're the same. Except you, of course."

"Sweetheart," Norman interrupted, "you told me a wake should celebrate life. Granny would've wanted you to play the piano tonight."

How kind of Norman to know this. "Mr. Larney, we can do our old favorite. What do you think?"

"Yes, Agnes, four-handed just as always. You take the *primo*. I'll take the *secondo*." The two of them squeezed onto the piano bench and began.

They played the music, but they didn't sing the words because Agnes always sang slightly off key and Mr. Larney never sang when playing. Norman recognized the song at once — "Londonderry Air," but she corrected him. "No, it's 'Danny Boy.' This is an Irish wake, not Princess Charlotte's funeral."

Playing the piano again, why — it'd been more than six months. It felt like waking up after a thunderstorm to a crystal-clear April day.

Before too long, people came into the parlor — Granny's friends, Uncle James, Aunt Julia, Patrick, her cousins, the friends who'd remained all evening. They sang when Agnes and Mr. Larney came back to the verse.

Everyone applauded when the song ended. Patrick raised his glass of whiskey in a toast. "May Granny's soul make its speedy way to heaven." Agnes scanned the room. Mama and Uncle Collin hadn't come in.

Mrs. Finnegan was the first to depart. "It's getting late, and it's going to bed I'll be doing before too long. Johnny, let's be on our way. Patrick, we'll be seeing you in the morning. Where is Siobhan?"

Thank the Lord, the exodus would begin and they could go to bed. It took more than an hour, but everyone left.

"Norman, you go to the car and get our luggage," Agnes said. "We'll sleep upstairs in my old bedroom. We might as well stay here for tomorrow's funeral."

Only Patrick and Agnes remained after Norman left. Mama and Uncle Collin were nowhere to be seen, but Agnes heard dishes in the kitchen. "I'm going to the kitchen to help Mama," Agnes said.

Patrick leaned toward her. "I'd like to have a word with you. I think it'd be best if you and Norman spent the night elsewhere. Mama is pleased you've come back, but I'm certain she doesn't want the two of you spending the night here. At least, not tonight."

She couldn't believe Mama would turn them out on the night before Granny's funeral. She rushed out of the parlor and into the kitchen. Uncle Collin sat at the table, and Mama stood at the sink with her back to them.

"Agnes, my child, please have a seat," Uncle Collin said, his pink face unmoving despite the whiskey.

She plopped down. "I'm exhausted, Uncle Collin. We're going upstairs to bed as soon as Norman comes back with our suitcases."

"Niece, I overheard your exchange with your brother. Please spend tonight at your husband's home and give us one night of peace. I suppose you know we cannot refuse you, but please do us this favor. Let us have some time at least to adjust to the new situation."

"I'm not allowed to sleep in my own bedroom? Why, Mama?"

Mama turned, her mouth open and a blank void in her eyes. She shook her head and went back to scrubbing dishes.

"It's not you that makes your mother uncomfortable, it's you and Norman together," Uncle Collin said. "So please respect her wishes. It's awkward enough with the terms in your grandmother's will."

"What do you mean, Granny's will? Mama, please say something."

Mama dropped the silver spoons into the sink and walked over. "Surely you know," she said, her eyes stormy and practically spitting out the words, "you come into your trust fund now that Mother Limerick has died."

The thought hadn't crossed her mind. How could it have?

"I suppose so, Mama, but why is that a problem?"

She sat down, her eyes red, her hands shaking, her voice trembling. "Your grandmother changed her will three months ago. She divided her money evenly between her grandchildren, but she left you all her earthly possessions."

Agnes thought about the piano. "I'm overwhelmed, but what was there? Just the piano, and she'd promised that to me already."

"You don't understand. Mother Limerick left you everything she owned. The piano, the silverware, the china, most of the furniture your father and I didn't bring with us when we moved here, and the house itself. She owned the house, Agnes, we didn't. This house now belongs to you. To you and your English Protestant husband. Now can you understand why I would be upset?"

13

SAD FATIGUE AND THANKFUL HOPE PULLED AGNES'S HEART in opposite directions late that night when she informed Norman of Granny's bequest. They were driving up Walnut Street to Balmoral's General Store as the baby slept in her arms. Norman fixed his eyes straight ahead and remained silent until parking in front of the apartment stairs. A trifecta of emotions numbed Agnes—despair over Granny's death, gratitude for the gift, emptiness for the isolation from Mama.

"Astounding," he said at last. "She didn't will the house to your brother. Shouldn't the eldest son inherit the family home?"

"Granny didn't care about conventions," Agnes said, a soft lilt soothing her voice. "Do you realize what this means? A house where we can raise Grace and enough money so we don't have to worry about hard times."

"What does your mother have to say about this?"

Agnes tried to scratch the scene of Mama throwing spoons into the sink from her mind but couldn't. "Mama is rather upset."

"I can well imagine. She wouldn't look me in the eye this evening. I doubt she'd remain if I moved in. Where would she go?"

The idea struck her as an unimaginable horror. "What do you mean?"

Norman spoke slowly. "I can hardly live with your mother if she's not speaking to me. I would imagine she feels the same."

Norman was choosing his words too carefully for that to be the real reason. "That may be, but I think you have another reason."

"If you insist, but you should know this already, dear wife. You have your own money and now, even real estate. I don't want to live in any house—Pine Street or elsewhere—until I can afford to pay for it myself. End of discussion."

Agnes looked up at the dimly lit apartment. All their disagreements seemed to conclude with Norman's "end of discussion." Her dream of going home might've lasted forty-five minutes, but yes, she would raise the subject again. It was ridiculous remaining cramped in small rooms above a jingling store with Norman's parents when they might live at George Taylor's mansion—no, her very own mansion—on Pine Street. She shut her eyes and held Grace close.

"Agreed, but only for now," Agnes said. "We'll talk about this again. Truth be told, it's vulgar to be discussing this when Granny hasn't been buried."

❧

After Granny's funeral, they settled back into life above the store. Grace delighted Victoria and Cornelius. They professed relief to Agnes that after three rowdy grandsons, they had a granddaughter. When Grace came down with colic, they took turns holding the screaming baby. Victoria told Agnes what to do when Grace contracted her first ear infection—dip a cotton swab in alcohol and gently pat inside the child's ear. After all, Norman had lots of ear infections as a baby. Agnes smiled. With Victoria around, the dark circles that had begun forming under her eyes began to recede.

After Grace's christening at St. Mark's (Mama attended—thank heavens), Agnes talked to Norman again about the Pine Street house. Despite pleading with him, he wouldn't consider it as long as Mama lived there and paid its expenses. And he insisted they wait until he found a job as an architect. Until then, they would live with his parents.

Grace's baby wrinkles had smoothed into lines that reflected Norman's triangular jawline and Mama's soft brown eyes, and she was crawling around the apartment by the time Agnes reassured Mama that everything would continue at the house as if nothing had changed when the lawyers settled Granny's will. Mama could have a life interest if she chose.

By the time Grace was walking and climbing the stairs up to the apartment, Agnes had resigned herself to living with Norman's family forever. Norman had done everything short of begging to get a job. Even with all the New Deal projects popping up, there were precious few opportunities for architects. Norman had been out of work for two years.

One day not long after Grace started speaking in sentences, Norman burst into the apartment, his eyes blazing and a wide smile dimpling his face, with news that spurred them to open a bottle of Cornelius's Champagne. "I've been hired by Howe and Lescaze. Do you remember the P.S.F.S. building? They're building a library on the Penn campus and need an architect to oversee the project. The models for my own library cinched the deal."

They were celebrating Grace's second birthday by the time the three of them moved into their own brownstone. Norman had pleaded for a fresh start, not the Pine Street house with Mama, which Agnes kept bringing up, but another house where they'd set down their own roots. They chose the maple-shaded neighborhood just south of Rittenhouse Square. Agnes fell in love with a three-storied brownstone on Spruce Street that had twelve-foot ceilings and windows that practically reached all the way up, plus a large music room in the back of the house where she could have Granny's Steinway. The street address spooked her — 1918, the year Daddy had died — but she decided to put superstitions aside.

Her trust fund had grown in the two years since Granny's death (thank you, President Roosevelt), and they had enough money to buy the property. Although Norman allowed her to pay for the house, he wouldn't let her pay for decorating it, even though her trust had plenty of money for the best walnuts and fabrics from Wanamaker's. And he trumped her decorating skills with frequent references to his credentials as an architect.

She tried to agree with Norman but couldn't help it when adjectives like ridiculous, pompous, egotistical, and selfish popped into her head.

Their kitchen ended up all white, as he specified, and the rest of the house was decorated in dark browns, reds, and greens. On the sly, she would buy one piece of furniture and one Oriental rug at a time, and the house was furnished to her cozy liking by the time she moved Granny's piano from the Pine Street house.

Within a week of occupying the new house, Agnes longed for a dog galloping up and down the stairs, barking when visitors came knocking, waiting for her to throw a ball across the hallway. So they went to Brookhaven and selected a breeder's golden retriever puppy. They named him Keaton after Norman's mentor at the Philadelphia School of Design. Agnes split her time between her toddler and their new dog for the next six months.

Keaton was housebroken and responding to sit, down, stay, and come, and Grace was lugging books across the parlor, insisting that Agnes read Kipling's *Rikki-Tikki-Tavi* when word came that Patrick, after a year's unemployment, had obtained a job in the Department of Labor as one of Madame Perkins's administrators. Now that Patrick could afford a larger flat, Mama would move there, and Agnes could do what she liked with the Pine Street house. Sell it, live there, rent it to out-of-work vaudevillians, it didn't matter to Mama.

Grace was playing blocks on the floor on the Sunday that Agnes hosted a triple celebration: Mother's Day, her twenty-fifth birthday three days earlier, and Mama's departure for Washington. Norman's parents declined, so it was just Mama and Uncle Collin, their first visit at the Spruce Street house.

While Grace played, Mama sat nearby on a peach-fabricked chair sipping sherry, smiling and laughing. Focus on Grace and all will be right, Agnes supposed her mother was telling herself. Uncle Collin and Norman sat in chairs near the front windows of the parlor, keeping their distance with formal topics such as politics. They debated the merits of legislation for old age insurance that President Roosevelt was steamrolling through Congress. Norman felt it would become law with huge Democratic majorities, but Uncle Collin thought Southern Democrats and Western Republicans would kill it. But only twenty-five Republicans remained in the Senate after the elections of '32 and '34.

Agnes agitated over possible fireworks between Norman and her family, so she spent as much time as possible in the parlor rather than watching over her beef stew. After a time, she announced, "Dinner is ready. Norman, would you take Grace upstairs for her nap?"

They seemed to have found common ground in Grace, but she wondered what topics they'd discuss now that the child was upstairs. Everyone seemed to be getting along, though Uncle Collin spoke quieter than usual. Agnes attributed it to sadness over Mama's leaving, though her uncle professed joy at Patrick's landing a job in the thick of the New Deal.

Agnes was pleased with the table she set. For the new house, Mama had given her Granny's Waterford crystal, Wedgewood china, and silver place settings adorned with the *L* insignia, as well as linen place mats and napkins. Agnes chose her dining room colors around the cherry-wood table — periwinkle blue for the walls, white for the ceiling and trim, dark blue below the chair rail.

"Uncle Collin, would you bless the food?" Agnes asked from the end of the table closest to the kitchen. It felt disrespectful to sit in Mama's place and for Norman to sit across from her in Uncle Collin's usual seat. Mama looked smaller than usual. She felt even more jitters with Uncle Collin sitting next to Norman.

"Agnes, this is your home," Uncle Collin said. "Your husband might like to have the honor."

Norman demurred. "Thank you, but I'll defer to you on this occasion."

Perhaps Norman might yet have a career as a diplomat. They served themselves, and Mama reminisced about Mother's Day dinners in the Doherty family. Agnes laughed when Mama reminded them what Granny had said — "In my day, we didn't have Mother's Day. About time society recognized the hardest working member of the family. Truth be told, it's the honest Labor Day."

Uncle Collin placed his hands on the table. He lowered his eyelids and his mouth, as if reading a sermon from the pulpit. "Old Mrs. Limerick puts me in mind of an amazing story I read just last month in *Harper's Magazine*. Now, mind you, I don't read the magazine," he said, lowering his tone. "I don't subscribe to it, I've never bought it, and I'd never, ever consider reading it on my own.

"Mrs. Kelly — Norman, she's one of my parishioners — insisted that I read this most inspiring story about a man who survived a fall down the slopes of Mt. Whitney. I was skeptical about its quality when she told me where she read it, for as we know, *Harper's Magazine* caters to the lowest sort of common man.

"To be kind, I agreed to read the article, despite my reservations."

Uncle Collin sniffed. He finished his sherry and replaced it with whiskey from a flask he pulled from his jacket. Agnes could smell the whiskey from six feet away. It didn't bother her especially, but Norman detested the smell of liquor. He stared at Uncle Collin, the whites in his eyes ablaze.

"To my utter surprise, I was riveted. The suspense was terrific as the man nursed his injuries, sewed up his wounds, and crawled his way down a treacherous terrain. A wonderful lesson about survival. I used it in my homily after reading Luke 16. It fit well with my theme of Lazarus rising from the dead.

"I have to admit that *Harper's Magazine* published a great story, even though it's a most ordinary periodical. Mind you, I don't read the magazine, I don't subscribe to it, and I've never paid for an issue. Mrs. Kelly lent me her own, and I gave it back. I don't want you to think less of me because I read the magazine."

Agnes felt the urge to read it, all the more for Uncle Collin's objections. She looked across the table at Norman. He'd gone back to his food, swallowing the last morsels of his beef stew. He always finished his plate like a drill sergeant.

But Norman's jaw had popped out on both sides under his ears. She'd lived with him long enough to know what that meant. Norman had no patience for intellectual pretensions. Before she could speak, however—

"We wouldn't think less of you, Father Collin, based on reading an article about survival," Norman said, his voice sharp. "But I must take exception on another matter. Must you bring a flask of whiskey to our table?"

Uncle Collin narrowed his eyes to slits. "What is your meaning?"

"You must be pleased that Prohibition has come to an end. It must make Friday night bingo vastly more entertaining."

Agnes froze, a half-chewed brussels sprout in her mouth. Norman loved them, but she hated them and called them cabbage garbage. Hearing this exchange she wanted to spit it out. She forced herself to swallow the bitter taste and chased it with a big gulp of wine.

"Norman, you are most impertinent," Uncle Collin said, tapping a finger on his plate. "Clearly, you never learned to respect your elders."

"With all due respect, Collin," Norman said, his voice silky but measured, "I don't believe it's respectful to bring your own liquor into your niece's home."

Agnes's heart nearly stopped. No one except Mama ever used her uncle's Christian name without preceding it with Uncle, Father, Pastor, or Monsignor. How could Norman be so reckless? She smelled a pungent animosity between them. Norman glared, and Uncle Collin tapped his fingers. Agnes wanted to hide.

"Siobhan, this proves my point about the Protestant English," Uncle Collin said, adding weight to his words.

"Collin, we must be careful," Mama warned.

Norman didn't shift his eyes from Uncle Collin. "What point is that?"

"The English have never shown any respect toward the Irish."

Norman lodged his tongue in one side of his cheek. "Sir, you misunderstand me. My objection has nothing to do with Catholic or Irish. The Irish are an essential part of the British empire. I respect their hard work and their devotion, which differs little from my own. They live in one of the most beautiful countries in the world. I hope to visit it with Agnes one day. What more would you like?"

Agnes still wanted to hide. She finished her wine and refilled her glass.

"What on Earth is your objection, Norman?" Uncle Collin asked.

"I object when anyone — even you, Collin Doherty — brings spirits into my home."

Mama laughed a bitter laugh. She lowered her chin and spoke from the right side of her mouth. "You mean your wife's own home, for as we all know, she bought this house with her Limerick inheritance."

"Siobhan, this time it is you who must be careful," Uncle Collin said.

Norman looked at Agnes. "Not going as you'd hoped, sweetheart."

"Mama, you're being unfair," Agnes said, her voice climbing to a high vibrato. She sounded like Mrs. Roosevelt every time she became upset.

Her mother's brows rushed together. "I don't see how, Agnes. Your father wouldn't have liked you using his bequest to buy a house with a Protestant."

"Mama, I don't think it's fair to bring up Daddy like that. You don't really know what he would've liked."

"When you live with a person as long as I lived with your father, you know their feelings without being told. But you haven't learned that yet."

Agnes glared at her mother. "It's rather convenient he isn't here to speak for himself. But I know Granny—"

Uncle Collin slapped his hand on the table. "Please, everyone. We do not need to conduct ourselves in this manner. I'd suggest we remain silent for a moment. We have much to be thankful for, not the least of which is this meal and this fine house. Norman, I apologize. I was wrong to pour whiskey at the table."

Norman spat out an unadorned *thank you* and rolled his eyes. She took a big gulp from her glass. The wine calmed her nerves. She promised herself she wouldn't lose her temper. Uncle Collin was right. They did have much to be thankful for, and they were a family even if they didn't agree.

"Mama, has Patrick decided where you'll live?" Agnes said.

Mama filled them in on the details. Patrick had found a flat near Dupont Circle two miles from his office on Constitution Avenue. He'd walk by the White House down Pennsylvania Avenue every day and past the Capitol on his way to the Labor Department. Agnes chuckled.

"I know what you're thinking," Mama said. "Your brother hated history, but that doesn't mean he can't work in the middle of it all. Isn't that right, Collin?"

"Positively ironic. Sometimes we resist what we end up loving the best."

Agnes asked her mother what she planned to do while Patrick worked. Would they join St. Patrick's parish in Washington? Mama shuffled her food around the plate before answering.

"Agnes, this is very hard on me. I'm fifty-seven and leaving Philadelphia for the first time in my life. I'm moving to a city I don't know. And I've watched you sell the Pine Street house to strangers at a greatly reduced price."

"Mama, we discussed this. Norman and I decided to continue living here. As painful as it was to sell the house, we had no choice. Remember, it's the Depression. We're lucky we found a buyer at all."

Mama grunted. "Did you have to sell to Presbyterians? The very idea, Presbyterians living in the house where your sainted father spent his last days."

Norman covered his head with his hands, and Uncle Collin fixed a stony glare on the candle centerpiece. Agnes could feel her temper rising again, but she drank more wine instead. It lightened her head, and its warmth relaxed her. She wouldn't lose her temper, and she'd keep quiet.

But Mama persisted. "Don't misunderstand me, daughter. I'm thankful you made no changes after Mother Limerick died. But I'm angry with her for putting me in that position. And I'm angry with you. You might've considered deeding the property to St. Patrick's. Collin barely can make ends meet."

Agnes told herself to remain calm and tried to envision a cool summer lake nestled in the Pennsylvania mountains where no one could find her.

"I did the best I could, Mama. It made no sense to keep Pine Street. I'm glad, because we can build our lives here rather than relive the past in the old house."

"It's a blessing your father isn't here to see how you've cut yourself off from us, daughter. Nothing good can come of this home when its foundation is based on a sin."

Agnes hesitated. As much as she'd wanted to avoid this topic, she'd known that Mama would bring it up one day. She looked at Norman, whose blue eyes blazed like two sapphires. She finished her glass of wine and spoke to a silent room.

"What do you mean, Mother?"

"You know exactly what I'm talking about." Mama pursed her lips and covered her mouth as if stifling a belch. "I can't say it. But I want to know, Agnes, before I move away, why didn't you come to me when you found out … that Grace was on the way?"

"It would've killed me, Mama, giving my child to an orphanage. I wanted Grace to have a mother and father, just like I did."

Mama stared at her cross-eyed as if she'd just spoken Greek. Gradually, though, the light went off in Mama's eyes, and tears then dimmed them.

Her mother choked on the tears. "Can you have thought so little of me?"

What other choice would Mama have had, Agnes asked herself, looking at Uncle Collin — and yet, his features had softened and almost become flabby.

Mama continued. "I'm disappointed in you, Agnes Mary. Yes, I would've been angry, but no, I wouldn't have done that. Grace is my granddaughter. I never would have wanted you to abandon your child, regardless of what others thought. I don't understand how you could forsake everything we taught you."

Agnes looked across the table at Norman, who rested his head in his hands like a teacher enduring a stubborn pupil. "I had to do what was right for my baby, Mama."

"You were always a challenge, Agnes Mary, determined to do your own thing in every way. I never had any difficulty with Patrick Sean. You were always so contrary, right from the time you climbed out of your crib. Not even a year old, and you already were escaping. And this," she said, tears falling, waving her hands at the walls, the windows, and the hallway, "is the final insult."

Norman's mouth popped open, and Agnes spilled her glass all over the tablecloth. But she ignored it. "The final insult? I don't need anyone to tell me how to live my life. Not you, not Uncle Collin, not even my husband."

"Agnes, don't raise your voice," Norman said. "Stay calm just as Collin suggested."

"Quite right, Norman," Uncle Collin echoed. He pointed his index finger at Agnes. "Niece, you must do a better job of controlling your temper. Siobhan, remember our promise. I spoke out of line, and I apologized. Now I expect the two of you to apologize. Please do as I say."

Yes, that's right. If we do as Uncle Collin commands, all will be calm and peaceful, but the very instant one of us does something he doesn't approve of, he threatens us with thunderbolts.

Life was so much better when Daddy was alive, she thought, her head swimming. Everyone laughed at his stories and his jokes, especially Mama. They took happy summer excursions up the Delaware, and Daddy brought friends home for Sunday dinner—interesting friends, writers, artists, and other physicians. All that ended when Uncle Collin took over. The jokes and excursions ended, the visits stopped. And Mama stopped laughing.

Agnes gave her uncle a look she hoped would turn him to stone.

"Mama, if I hadn't found Norman when I did, I'd have found another way to escape the prison Uncle Collin had created for us. A prison encased in stone, marble, stained glass, and a crucifix. Perhaps that's why Granny helped Norman and me. She wanted me to live my own life."

Yes, live her own life, just like Granny — and Gracie Honeywalker, eighty-two and still running the farm, spicing up life for Old Man Lacey.

"Granny encouraged Norman when I couldn't decide for myself. Did you know she prodded him to come to the house that day I left?"

Uncle Collin pronounced judgment. "Your grandmother didn't know what she was doing. She was a senile old fool."

"Not my observation," Norman said. "Mrs. Limerick was sharp as a tack."

Granny had braved the rough Atlantic seas, raised nine children, witnessed the rise and fall of her husband's business, and buried her husband and two of her sons. None of it had broken her spirit.

"She was no fool, Uncle Collin. You know as well as anyone how she fought tooth and nail for anyone she loved."

"Agnes, think about what you're saying," her uncle said. "You're making your mother cry."

God in heaven, he was right. She'd promised herself she wouldn't argue, but as hard as she tried to stop, she couldn't. And she had to defend herself. Uncle Collin's judgment carried the weight of ten battleships, and she'd had enough.

"If it's not my place, then whose is it?" All she'd ever wanted was to please her uncle, but nothing ever really satisfied him. She only could imagine the convent making him happy, but that would have felt like indentured servitude.

Mama's eyes flashed at Agnes, and her chin shook. "You repay your uncle after all he's done by saying he imprisoned you. An end to this argument, please. I don't want to leave Philadelphia like this."

Agnes gave her uncle a square look. "With all due respect, Uncle Collin, I know what you did for us. I'm grateful. But that life is not for me —"

"Your tone of voice, Agnes," Uncle Collin said. "I only did for you what I would've done for any of the boys and girls at St. Patrick's."

Agnes's mind came to a halt. Something about his inflection when he said *boys and girls* reminded her that her school friends had cowered before him — how he frightened them with his discipline, his stormy edicts, and his ruler. She glared at Uncle Collin sitting next to Norman, his fat hand pawing at the gold moldings on the table's corner.

"I have a few questions for you, Uncle Collin. I used to wonder why the children were so afraid, why they would cower when you entered a room. Did it have something to do with that ruler you carried around the school?"

Uncle Collin's face blanched, but it turned beet red when he spoke. "Stop this now, Agnes. You're tipsy from all that wine. You don't know yourself."

Mama agreed. "Agnes, take heed and be still. Remember, I am still your mother. Please obey me."

Agnes couldn't restrain herself. "No, you never beat me, Uncle Collin, but what about the others? Anthony Balfiglio let it slip one day. He said shivers went up and down his spine whenever he passed your office."

"I did nothing but teach them ethics and morals," he shouted.

"Daughter, your uncle has dedicated his life in service to others. Just like your father did, just as I'd always hoped you would do."

Agnes felt as if she were suffocating, just like she'd felt while living under Uncle Collin's watchful eye.

"I don't know, Mama. You mentioned my father. Did it occur to you that he might've set up our trust funds so we'd be free to make our own choices?"

"Your father and I never discussed money matters. He made all the decisions himself." Mama dried her face with her napkin. "Agnes, we *do not* talk about this sort of thing at the table. English Protestants might lay their troubles out for the world to see, but we do not discuss them because it is simply not suitable."

Norman ended his silence. "Oh, my Lord."

Uncle Collin pulled his chair back, and it screeched on Agnes's hardwood floors. "I never had to use that ruler, not once," he said, standing. "Siobhan, I refuse to remain in this house any longer. We're leaving at once."

"Good riddance," Norman muttered, but loud enough for them to hear.

"Norman, what you've done with this girl, I only can imagine. May the Lord strike you down for how you've changed her. You, young lady," Uncle Collin said, turning to Agnes, "I should advise you to repent and come back to the Church. You've placed your soul in jeopardy."

"In this house, you speak to my wife with respect," Norman said, his nostrils flaring. "It is I who must now ask you to leave."

Uncle Collin circled the dining room table slowly, towering over them.

"As far as what Anthony Balfiglio might've said, they're lies. That boy never told an honest tale in all his years at St. Patrick's. I did my best to drill discipline into him. Look at him now, a God-fearing man with a wife, a son, and a thriving business—when good men, even smart men, are starving."

"What could've possessed you to say such things, Agnes?" Mama implored. "You should be ashamed."

"I'm only asking questions, Mama. These questions have been gnawing at me for years, and I still don't have answers."

"It is a sin how you've disobeyed your mother," Uncle Collin said.

"It is a sin for me to dishonor her, Uncle Collin. The Ten Commandments tell us to honor our parents, not to obey them."

Uncle Collin shook his head. "Your father would be rolling in his grave to hear you speak like this. We're leaving."

"He's rolling in his grave at how you've judged me. Mama, Uncle Collin's poisoned you against me, just like he would with anyone who isn't Catholic and Irish. You act like it's the most natural thing in the world."

"Agnes, you will regret this," Uncle Collin thundered on his way to the foyer. "Siobhan, get your coat. Not another word. Do I make myself clear?"

Mama rose from her chair and wept anew. "I don't understand, Agnes. Why have you thrown us into this pit? My daughter is lost to me, Collin. She is gone!"

They left without another word. Uncle Collin slammed the front door.

The sharp bang pierced Agnes right to the heart. She wondered if the yelling had woken up Grace, but she heard no crying from upstairs. Norman stared across the table at her. All that remained of their dinner party were red stains from the wine, unfinished plates, half-drunk glasses, silverware everywhere, and soiled napkins on empty chairs.

Granny's piano sat in the music room, as yet unplayed. She'd wanted to perform a Chopin nocturne for Mama. Instead, she marched in there and banged out some Prokofiev.

14

APONDEROUS WEIGHT SAT LIKE A LODESTONE IN AGNES'S STOMACH that night. She lay beside Norman pretending to sleep so as not to disturb him, but she never managed to wander off to that neverland of dreams she so enjoyed. Sleep didn't come that night — or several thereafter.

Agnes spent a lot of time playing the piano in the bass clef those summer months of 1935. She played the Prokofiev C minor sonata every day, trying to get its driving refrain right and bring something fluid to the plodding pace, and it lodged itself in her brain. She lay awake night after night, replaying the opening bars in her head, feeling like a woman running in circles.

One afternoon, Norman stomped over to the piano and complained about her incessant practicing. "For heaven's sake, play something happier. You're making Grace cry. And I have a splitting headache."

She turned her head to their daughter, playing dress-up with her Patsy doll on the floor, no evidence of anything but bouncy pigtails, let alone crying. She'd never experienced heartburn, but something like a hot pain pinched her chest. Norman, eyes simmering like water about to boil over, did indeed look like his head would split in half.

After that, she practiced only when Norman was at work. On the nights she managed to fall asleep, she invariably woke up before six. A hummingbird had nested in the tree outside their bedroom window, and with the sunrise, he'd tweet out a high-pitched call that had Agnes hearing *Mama, Mama*, as if he were a lost chick wanting to suckle his mother.

When the bird stopped singing, Prokofiev's melody would wriggle its way back into her brain, and she'd lie helpless, tormented by its relentless darkness, like a catacomb inviting her inside for eternity. Norman snored out of beat with the music, but instead of snuffing out the noise in her head, the music's tempo raced ahead. When she couldn't fall asleep because of Prokofiev, a racing heartbeat, or four hours of nausea, she pretended to sleep so as not to disturb Norman. She'd lost more than ten pounds by the end of summer.

At first, she tried calling her mother daily, but Mama wouldn't answer. Two weeks after that terrible dinner, she'd walked down to Pine Street, pushing Grace in her stroller, but no one answered when she knocked. She visited again another two weeks later, just before turning the house over to the new owners and found the door unlocked, the house vacant.

She plodded through every room noticing every scratch on the molding, every scrape on the floor. A musty scent permeated the house, rodent droppings scattered the kitchen floor, sawdust lay below the cabinets, and the windows screeched when she opened them. It was as if Agnes's marriage, Granny's death, and Mama's departure had sapped all energy out of the house and it had given up. She felt sick, so she went outside for fresh air.

The new owners settled on the house and Agnes, at Norman's insistence, deposited the money into an account she opened at the Mechanic's Bank. Soon after and without Norman's knowledge, she wrote two drafts for $2,000 each and sent them to Uncle Collin, one for St. Patrick's and one to be forwarded to Mama in Washington. A week later, Mrs. Mallory, still Uncle Collin's secretary after all these years, returned the checks with a note that the gifts were appreciated but of no use to them.

Eventually, she lost interest in the Prokofiev sonata and went through something of a renaissance with Schubert. When she wasn't playing the piano, she buried herself in Shakespeare's plays. By the beginning of 1936, she'd read all thirty-seven of them. She craved companionship, but her childhood friends from St. Patrick's had vanished into their own lives. If the Depression hadn't forced them to migrate to other cities where their husbands obtained desperate work, they'd forgotten about Agnes after she'd run off with Norman. The only friend she saw on a regular basis was her neighbor from across the street, Mrs. Collingwood, a gossipy woman of gray hair, orthopedic oxfords, and tweed dresses, who declined to tell Agnes her first name. They'd remain Mrs. Collingwood and Mrs. Balmoral to each other, the fiftyish lady declared.

The silent afternoons when Grace slept upstairs and Norman worked in West Philadelphia had Agnes yearning for something to do and someone to do it with. There'd been Mr. Larney, but he traveled to New York every summer and busied himself with seven-year-old prodigies in winter. She thought often about Cristina, but she'd slipped through the cracks like the other girlfriends of her youth. In the four years since they'd last seen each other, Agnes often had wanted to share her anxieties with Cristina but couldn't. She'd wanted to call the Cassata household and find out if Cristina and Angelo still lived there, but she always stifled the impulse. Norman had never wavered in his position.

Then one Saturday in May, Agnes was reaching for tomatoes at Rigney's Market on South Street when another hand, bronzed and familiar, reached for the same fruits. "I saw these first," the alto voice said. Agnes looked up and saw Cristina's lantern-jawed face. They laughed and met in the aisle for an embrace.

"Stars above, if it isn't Agnes Limerick," Cristina said. She wore her dark hair shorter these days, her caterpillar eyebrows that much more noticeable above her glasses.

Agnes suggested they move toward the back near the storage room. They'd have more breathing space. Saturday morning always brought out a bevy of shoppers grabbing for fruits and vegetables in the narrow aisles. Agnes already had a basketful of produce, but Cristina had only tomatoes and olives. Agnes asked Cristina for a news update, and she wanted to hear it away from the nosy ears of shoppers.

"Now that you ask, Angelo's become a plumber," Cristina said in a tone Agnes might expect from Walter Winchell. "He got tired of listening to Ma sing Puccini over the stove. He decided on plumbing because people have clogged drains whether or not we're in a depression. Last year, we rented our own house a block away from Ma and Pop. Close enough for Sunday dinner but far enough away we can do whatever we like."

Agnes pictured Angelo and Cristina in the Cassatas' kitchen that steamy afternoon of 1931 and felt a wave of heat rise from her stomach. And then her own marital ritual, Saturday afternoons at four in the bedroom, came to mind.

"Does that still involve kitchen tables?"

"Agnes, your memory," Cristina said, the right side of her mouth curling up. "That would be awkward. I've got two boys now. Donald was born in November '33, and Ronald came last March. They're spending the day with Ma and Pop."

"Donald and Ronald?" Names that rhymed, could Cristina be serious? A giggle burbled up from her throat, but she swallowed it.

Cristina shrugged. "And whatever happened with your baby?" Cristina's lips came together into two pressed lines, and her words slowed. "That was four years ago. How time flies ..."

She hurried through the history, trying to ignore the frozen mask that had come over Cristina's face, depicting the happy tales of Granny's sharp tongue, Gracie's gnarly hands, and the Pine Street house. She overlooked painful topics such as the estrangement from Mama and Uncle Collin—and certainly not how Norman had quashed their friendship. He'd be angry with her, she scowled to herself, simply standing here talking with Cristina.

"Glad to hear Norman is working again. He always wanted to work for Howe and Lescaze, going all the way back to late in '29 when he came back from Italy."

"Whatever happened to Smith and Weisskopf?"

"I quit before Donald was born. I've become a librarian just like I always wanted. I'm working at a library on Penn's campus."

Working among all those books and getting paid for it? It sounded like heaven, almost like working at a music store surrounded by old music books, instruments, music lectures, and bow-tied piano teachers. She could just smell the musty scent of well-worn music books. How she'd love a job like that! "By any chance, Cristina, is this the new library that just opened?"

"Why, yes. It's a beautyful building, all glass and red brick."

"That's Norman's library," Agnes said, her heart expanding at the thought of Norman's dream achieved. "He designed it."

Cristina offered a throaty cliché about it being a small world. "Whatever happened that we lost touch, Agnes? I never understood why you disappeared. You went off on your honeymoon and after that, I never heard from you again."

Agnes tried to concoct a diplomatic answer. "So many things were going on back in '32 and '33. Grace was born, Granny died, Norman was looking for work, you know how it goes ..."

The lines between Cristina's eyebrows formed two crevices down the bridge toward her nose. "No, I'm afraid I don't. I called the store a number of times. Your mother-in-law took messages for me, but you never called back. What was the problem? Did I do something to offend you?"

Agnes hated to lie, especially to Cristina. "You spoke with Victoria? I never knew that."

"You could've called me on your own. I didn't understand the silence, Agnes. I asked myself time and again how I wronged you. Do you realize I've never even seen your daughter? We shared the most intimate secrets, and poof, you were gone." Cristina snapped her fingers.

"There was never anything, Cristina, honestly. I've missed you, really. I had the baby, Granny died, and Norman insisted I tend house with Victoria."

"I see. This is Norman's doing, isn't it?" Cristina said, the whites of her eyes boring a hole into Agnes. She looked away, certain her eyes would give her away—if the heat on her cheeks didn't.

"Nothing of the kind. And then my mother—"

"I always wondered how Mrs. Limerick adjusted to Norman. I always wonder how *anyone* adjusts to Norman, frankly. He's difficult enough without adding the Battle of the Boyne to the picture. What a doozy of a son-in-law he must be."

"I think you're very unfair about my husband," Agnes said, picking at the produce. Cristina's cross-examination agitated her, and she dropped a bunch of radishes. Then she told Cristina about Mama's move to Washington. "So there's no problem. I write to Mama every week."

"I'll just bet. Well, I hope Mrs. Limerick is happy in Washington. She was always real good to me and Angelo." Cristina's face settled into smoother lines.

Agnes had missed Cristina's velvety voice so much and now, though she needed to get home, she wanted to stay. Yes, she could talk with Cristina another time. Perhaps what Norman didn't know wouldn't hurt him.

"Cristina, I have to go home. Norman and I are dining out this evening and then going for a walk around Rittenhouse Square. Could we have lunch during the week? Our children could play while we catch up."

Cristina arched her brows and winked at Agnes. "Why don't we play and let them catch up? All things considered, I've missed our daily chats. How would Wednesday or Friday be? I'm off those days."

This Wednesday, Agnes had planned bridge with Victoria and her friends. And Fridays she lunched with Norman. But she weighed her options. "Wednesday, then. I'll call you Monday to pick a restaurant."

"Just remember, I work Mondays. Call me Wednesday morning. And what are you talking about? We'll eat at my house. Restaurants are high as cats' backs." Cristina rattled off her phone number and nodded at Agnes. "Don't you need to write that down?"

"I can remember Delaware 6226," Agnes said, giving Cristina a mock laugh. "I'm twenty-six years old, and 1962 is twenty-six years away. Sixty-two, twenty-six, you know."

Cristina groaned. "Gosh, it's nice to have the red-headed numbers magician back."

They hugged their good-byes on the street corner. Agnes started her walk home wondering how or even if she'd tell Norman. Well, phooey on him.

She thought about their old stove, which recently had broken down. Agnes had wanted to replace it with a new General Electric, but Norman had preferred having it repaired. She pleaded until he squeezed his mouth so hard, his jawbones nearly popped out. "No, we can't afford it," he boomed so loud, Agnes shrank back. Better to wait until he calmed down.

And the very next day, they reached an impasse on their summer vacation. Norman wanted to spend it with his family in the Adirondacks, but

Agnes preferred a week at Rehoboth Beach. Again, Norman wanted to save the money. She admitted it'd be an extravagance, but worth it for Grace to see the ocean.

"She can wait another year," Norman had said. "We already have the damned expense of that stove. We have to cut back somewhere."

"If we have the stove repaired, could we go to the beach this summer?" They struck a deal, and Norman consented to the vacation. Her new stove would wait.

Now as she entered the house with her groceries, she felt weighted down by her marriage, the demands to keep the house just as Norman wanted it, how he took for granted that she agreed with everything, the challenge of attending to his moods, amusing one moment and bossy the next. A price for everything, she told herself, and he did make her happy most of the time.

She found him on the parlor floor playing piggyback with Grace.

"All right, racy Gracie," Norman said with a laugh so hearty, Agnes could see his teeth and gums. "The ride is over. It's time for Mama to read you a story."

Grace climbed off Norman's back and darted her eyes at Agnes, her eyes and mouth wide open. "A story, Mama!"

Norman stood up. He'd stopped laughing, and his lips came together in two flat lines. "Where have you been? You've been gone two hours, and I've been itching to get back to work in the upstairs studio."

Now she'd have to tell him about Cristina. "If you only knew how much shopping I did—"

Grace ran over to her mother and hugged her legs. "Please, Mama, please read *Rikki!*" Agnes laughed. She'd been reading the same story to Grace for more than a year. Time for something else, perhaps *Grimm's Fairy Tales*? She'd love to start Grace on a second language before she got sidetracked by grammar and punctuation. The child would love *Schneewittchen*. What little girl wouldn't love a tale about a pretty girl and her seven dwarfs?

"Puddlecakes, Mama needs to put these groceries away, and then I'll read."

Her daughter pushed out her jawline and her forehead, just like Norman when he didn't get his way. She'd tell Norman about Cristina, but not yet. She pretended to laugh. "Now dear, if you make a pretty face, I'll be really quick and we can go upstairs to read. Your grandmother will read to you this evening while Daddy and I are out."

Grace smiled and clapped her hands. Agnes turned to Norman. "What time will your mother be here? After reading to Grace, I'll have just enough time to bathe and dress before we leave for dinner."

They allowed themselves one night each month to dine alone at a restaurant. Money matters had improved in the two years since Norman had started working, but he was strict. They dined out only twice a month, once with Grace and perhaps his parents, and the other time by themselves. Tonight would be special. Though she'd turned twenty-six two weeks ago, they hadn't yet celebrated her birthday. So Norman was taking her to the Bellevue-Stratford, a favorite with great views of Broad Street and the Academy of Music.

Norman reminded her that Victoria would be arriving at five, so Agnes needed to be quick in getting ready. And would she wear her white dress, so lovely for a spring evening?

The doorbell rang at five o'clock on the dot, and she heard Victoria speaking to Norman a minute later. She was always punctual, just like Norman. Agnes descended the stairs in the white dress ten minutes later. Norman, in his tan suit and dark-blue tie, sat in a hallway chair tapping his foot.

"Oh, be patient. You're always in a rush," she said to him. "Our reservation isn't until six o'clock. We've got forty-five minutes to walk seven blocks."

His eyes looked her up and down, and her body tingled. She'd worn the white dress trimmed with dark blue just as he'd asked. Instead of wearing her hair in its usual ponytail, she let it cascade onto her shoulders like young women were beginning to do. She liked the dress and was glad he noticed—hungrily, she thought, feeling his gaze on her breasts and hips. Well, she laughed, if he was a good boy, she'd take off her dress tonight and let him do what he wanted ... with her breasts and hips.

From their corner table on the top floor of the Bellevue-Stratford, Agnes and Norman could see the Academy of Music in one direction and City Hall in the other, so majestic, so dignified. Looking at the city from this vantage point during twilight made Agnes giddy. Two years ago, they were poor relations living with Norman's parents in three small rooms above a store. Now they had their own house and tonight were dining before the best views in town. They'd done it together, she with Daddy's inheritance and Norman with his resourcefulness. But she wanted to be resourceful too —

"Waiter, I'll have a martini," Norman ordered, as if overacting for the Hollywood cameras, "and my wife will have a glass of your best cabernet."

He sounded so much like William Powell, she responded in Myrna Loy style, "I'll have the whole bottle," though she felt light as a feather and hardly needed even a single glass. Norman's curvy smile, dimples, and dancing eyes were intoxicating enough.

He laughed. "Mrs. Balmoral, you'll do nothing of the kind. The wife of Philadelphia's finest architect can't be seen inebriated in public."

"Philadelphia's finest and most handsome. Just look at that tie, Mr. Balmoral, as dapper as Douglas Fairbanks Jr. Why don't you grow a thin moustache and become a swashbuckler?"

He frowned and jutted out his lower lip, but his eyes continued to dance. Then he laughed. "Why don't you become an aviator and fly around the world like Mrs. Earhart wants to do?"

"On no account would I leave you alone in Philadelphia with all these pretty girls chasing you."

"These days the only ones chasing after me are mousy librarians wanting me to build more bookcases at that infernal library—"

"Norman, dear," she started, feeling uneasy at the mention of librarians. "I had a thought on the way home from the market. How would you feel if I got a job? Not every day, but perhaps four or six hours, two or three days every week, perhaps at Longacre's Music and Instruments."

He patted her hand and smiled through glazed eyes. "Darling, you know how I feel about that. Your job is to take care of the house and Grace. Now back to my library—"

She sighed. "But I have a handle on the house, Norman. Just a few hours every—"

"Agnes, please, you interrupted me. I can't wait for the library extension to be completed. Next up will be stone houses in Bala Cynwyd. And before Grace is too grown up, we need to buy a house on the Main Line. It's where all the good families are going these days."

At the mention of moving, Agnes forgot about her dreams of working. She'd rather slit her wrists than leave the city.

"We could talk about that around the same time I go up in the sky for my round-the-world adventure and you go to Hollywood with a moustache."

"I'm serious. They've got the finest schools, and Grace would have a yard to play in. You'd make friends with other housewives, and I'd associate with other businessmen like me. It would be lovely living in the suburbs."

"I looked up *suburb* in the dictionary one day. It said, 'boring living arrangement for snooty Wasps who have nothing interesting to say.'"

"Laugh if you will, but mark my words. When times are better, people will escape the city and move out to the suburbs."

"Twaddle. Think of the museums, the parks, and the rivers. Who wouldn't want to live in this beautiful city and experience its history? Benjamin Franklin, Thomas Jefferson, John Adams, even George Washington walked these streets."

"They've been dead more than a hundred years."

They were saved from the argument by the arrival of their drinks. They toasted their evening out. Too good to be true. Disagreements about suburbs notwithstanding, they were getting along. She hadn't enjoyed herself with Norman this much since their cabin honeymoon. Perhaps a sign that more romantic evenings awaited them?

For dinner, Norman chose poached salmon and Agnes had roasted chicken. They left hand in hand two hours later after another martini and glass of wine, agreeing it'd been a terrific meal. So Agnes, feeling light on her feet, imagined the romance continuing on their walk, at home, and later on that evening—after they'd turned out the lights.

They meandered down Walnut Street, eventually onto Rittenhouse Square, and walked the perimeter with its long line of incandescent lights and leafy oaks. They passed an older woman—someone's grandmother, Agnes supposed—walking her floppy spaniel. Agnes would have to walk Keaton when they got home, though she didn't want to leave Norman for too long. He might fall asleep before she got back. She wanted him alert when they walked into their bedroom—together. They passed by Peterson's, and Agnes suggested Norman buy ice cream.

"If you insist, my love. Anything for my sunshine on this beautiful evening."

He gave her a jaunty kiss on the cheek. There was a jaunty dance in his step too. Like Agnes, he was in an amorous mood.

The main entrance to Peterson's on Locust Street overflowed with people, so they walked around to the side entrance on 18th. Agnes ordered chocolate-chip ice cream (her favorite), and Norman asked for strawberry sherbet.

"You always make me feel guilty, sweetheart, with how you eat. You've still got the same narrow waist and broad shoulders you had when I met you. Me, on the other hand ..." Agnes wanted him looking at her and admiring her. Could the light and airy feeling of this magical spring evening last forever?

"For having had a baby you have a lovely figure," Norman said, looking her up and down. "You've managed to keep that excess weight off — so far. But you do have to watch yourself." He chuckled as his eyes fastened to her figure. Breasts and hips again, she noticed.

"For chocolate-chip ice cream, I'll take that risk."

"Too much of that stuff, and one day you'll be as fat as Ida Collingwood."

Now how did Norman know that old busybody's first name and she didn't?

They found a bench in the middle of the park and sat down to eat. They weren't the only young couple spending the evening under the canopy of oak trees, being seduced by lilacs and rhododendrons. It seemed there were dozens of young men and women walking hand in hand smiling at each other. Everyone was finding love tonight. Ah, the magic of May ...

After finishing their ice cream, they continued to sit, enjoying the city's mid-evening restlessness, too late for a picture show but too early for bed. Agnes savored quiet moments like these with Norman, no need for chatter. With his career, her duties at home, and Grace, time alone came less often. She caught him looking at her, his eyelids lowered ever so slightly, and he ran his tongue over his lower lip. A wave of warmth rose from her midsection into her heart. "Shall we go home?" she said.

He crossed his legs. "I thought you'd never ask."

Agnes looked at his lap and giggled. "You wait here. I'll take these dishes back to Peterson's."

"All right, but don't be long."

"You'd better stay put. Mrs. Collingwood might walk by."

She turned on her heel and nearly pranced across the square to Peterson's. She felt on top of her world. May always brought out the best in Philadelphia, surrounding her with cool air and a green lushness. The spring impatiens intoxicated her, as did Norman waiting for her in Rittenhouse Square. She hurried into Peterson's through the side entrance, dropped off the bowls, and headed back to her husband.

But Norman was no longer on the bench. She walked slowly up to it, looking left, looking right. She'd been gone no more than five minutes.

"Where could he have gone?" she said, laughing at the incredulity of it. She looked back toward Peterson's and scanned the square from corner to corner, bench to bench, person to person. No sign of Norman, just happy couples holding hands as they walked by.

The blood in her veins seemed to freeze. "Have I gone crazy?"

She sat on the bench. Norman had the key to the house and, of course, his wallet. She had nothing but her twenty-six-year-old self alone in the dark—and her purse, though she'd brought neither money nor house key. Her pulse quickened. Don't panic. Home was only two blocks away.

But the minutes passed, and her anxiety grew as she sat alone. She had to do something, so she walked back to Peterson's. She looked inside for Norman, then outside at the 18th Street entrance and around the corner on Locust Street. No sign of him.

"I just can't believe it. Where is Norman?" she said, aloud again.

"Ma'am, may I help you?" a wisp of a man inquired. "You seem troubled."

"It's nothing, I'm just looking for someone."

She hoped no one else noticed her agitation. She didn't know whether she should be angry with Norman, concerned for his safety, or worried about his whereabouts. She walked back to the park, thinking he might've returned to the bench, but still no trace of him. She sat down again, looking at the same couples on neighboring benches, hearing the pleasant grumble of their conversations. They hadn't lost track of their spouses. She feigned a careless attitude, hoping they wouldn't notice her distress, praying no one would come over to her and ask, "Ma'am, what seems to be the problem? You look unhappy."

She'd give him another ten minutes, and then she'd go home. Victoria certainly would be there with Grace. Or would she be? Perhaps she, Grace, and Norman had abandoned her for places unknown—Ohio, Kansas, perhaps California. Mama and Daddy wouldn't have left her sitting alone on a dark Saturday evening, but what did she know, really, about the Balmorals? And did she really know Norman all that well? She never would have guessed he'd do this.

She heard laughter from the bench on the opposite end of the sidewalk. A miniature garden of Dutch tulips long past their bloom stood between her and a group of three young men. They were all younger than she. Was this how it'd be when she became old? Norman would be gone, Victoria and Cornelius would be dead, Grace would have grown up and moved away. She'd be an old lady with white hair sitting in Rittenhouse Square, listening to boys decades younger talking about Joe Louis and boxing. If they'd ever heard of him ...

Uncle Collin once had talked about how wonderful it was that Joe Louis was competing for the heavyweight title. He'd also admired Marian Anderson—great talents, he said, stymied by a hostile society, but somehow rising above the obstacles. That was the sermon he gave her when she told him about Gracie Honeywalker and her farm.

Perhaps Uncle Collin's curse had caught up with Norman. God had punished her by zapping him away with a thunderbolt. Nonsense, there had to be a logical reason. Norman was smart and strong. He must've gone home for some reason. Wasn't he always running on ahead of her? She sometimes thought Victoria and Cornelius hadn't taught him manners. A man should always walk next to a lady, never ahead of her, just as Daddy had escorted Mama. But Norman never did that.

She walked down 19th Street to Spruce and breathed a sigh of relief. Lights were on in their parlor and dining room. Victoria would be inside. Of course, they hadn't abandoned her. What had she been thinking?

It irked her to have to ring the bell at her own home. Agnes expected Victoria to answer, but Norman opened the door, already without jacket and tie. He held Grace, dressed in polka-dotted pajamas and resting her head against Norman's face. Grace reached for her mother. Victoria stood in the kitchen doorway. Agnes took in the scene, stunned.

"Where in the name of God were you?" Agnes demanded, her voice rising to a high pitch. Keaton ran up to her barking, his tail wagging, but she ignored him. "Why did you vanish?"

"I might ask the same of you, my dear," Norman said, his voice flat and his mouth two straight lines. "I waited forever and ever. You never came back. Finally, I went over to Peterson's and you were nowhere to be seen. So home I came, not even five minutes ago."

She stepped back, flustered by Norman's dead tone. And then she remembered her cold panic in the square and found her voice, red and hot.

"You couldn't have lost patience that quickly. I practically ran across the square to Peterson's and back again so you wouldn't be alone too long. I wasn't gone more than three minutes, maybe five. What happened to you, Norman?"

"Nothing happened to me," he said, his voice tinny and his face white. "You lost track of yourself. Why must you poke? If you'd be more conscientious of people's time, you'd have fewer problems. I waited in front of that ice-cream shop for ten minutes. Sometimes, my dear wife, I just don't understand you."

Victoria stepped into the foyer, hands on her hips. "It would be better if my granddaughter didn't hear this disagreement. Norman, give her to me." She took Grace and headed up the stairs to the nursery.

Agnes exchanged an angry glance with Norman, but they remained silent until Victoria closed the door upstairs. She waited for him to explain himself. When he didn't, she barged ahead. How dared he mock her as if his behavior held no consequence?

"You couldn't possibly have lost patience that quickly," she repeated, this time louder. "If I didn't know Victoria and Cornelius better, I'd swear they never taught you manners. As it is, you're a rude, selfish —"

"Shut up," he said, raising his voice. "I've only been home five minutes."

This was an outrageous lie. Norman was acting like a man possessed, just as Uncle Collin had described, a man not in control of his mental faculties. She'd waited on that bench twenty, perhaps thirty minutes after coming back from Peterson's. He hadn't come looking for her. And she'd scanned the square for him like a hungry hawk.

"I waited and waited for you," he said. "You're always running late. Changing your dress, puttering after Grace, fixing your hair. Why don't you cut it off and wear it short like all the other wives? It's embarrassing that my wife has a ponytail, as if I were married to a child, which is how you behave most of the time."

"If I'm ever running late, it's because you stand around doing nothing but tapping your foot and breathing through your teeth. And rearranging the books, opening the drapes, closing the windows, turning off the lights. What idiotic nonsense you go through every day. Like nothing can be perfect enough." She felt her blood pressure rise. "And I was only gone three minutes. You ran off, only God knows why, and you're lying—"

"If you're going to persist with this stubborn obtuseness, I shall be only too glad to spend the night elsewhere."

His arrogance! Nothing appealed more to her right now than a night alone in her bedroom. She could sleep as late as she pleased and with the draperies closed for the first time in more than four years. She wouldn't have to deal with being ordered about or slaving over his fussy habits. She longed to be rid of him, free to do as she liked.

"You can leave right now if you wish, and take this with you." She loosened her wedding band and threw it at his feet. She turned toward the stairs, preparing to ascend to their bedroom — her bedroom tonight, alone and free of his smothering demands. He caught her by the arm. She cried out from a sharp pain in her wrist and tried to wrestle away, but he held on like an asp.

Norman's eyes bulged, and the veins on his temples flared out. "Don't you ever throw your wedding ring at my feet. That's disrespectful."

"Ouch! That hurts. Let go of me, you self-centered, you egotistical ... blah!" Why couldn't she ever think of a good insult when she needed one?

"Enough of this nonsense," he said and pulled her body into his. She pushed against him and broke free, but he rushed in a second time, clutching her head and forcing a deep kiss that made her gag. He revolted her, this vampire who wanted every last drop of her blood. She broke free and slapped him.

His face reddened, and he massaged where she struck him. The veins on his temples no longer bulged. "No one's ever slapped me like that, not even Dad."

What had become of her, resorting to violence like a common criminal? Norman didn't deserve it. "I can't believe I did that. I'm so sorry."

She reached for him but pulled back, afraid he'd retaliate. Instead, he gave her two soft blue eyes and quivering eyelids, like a child who'd smashed an antique vase and wanted his mother to forgive him.

"I'm sorry too," he said. Their stare stretched into an endless minute.

He pulled her into him a third time, and she melted in his arms. She smelled stale vodka on his breath and felt heat from his skin. She felt the muscles in his chest and arms, tense as the rocks along a cold river. And she succumbed, weakening in his grasp, submitting to his kisses. The hardness of his body enveloped her. The texture of his tongue made the center of her body ache, and she wanted him again, just like she'd wanted him earlier in the evening. Perhaps the argument didn't really matter, after all. Only once before had she needed him in this way, and when that had happened—

Norman led her up the stairs to their bedroom. He banged the door shut. Somewhere between the door and the bed, the lights went out.

Agnes woke up early the next morning. Norman lay naked and snoring beside her. It was the first time she'd awoken before he did, and she rather liked the pensive solitude. She put on her robe and tiptoed down the stairs to start breakfast. She found a note next to her ring on the hall table.

She recognized Victoria's elegant slants in the note, so different from her scratchy hand pecks. "Your ring. I trust everything is settled between the two of you, certainly for Grace's benefit if not your own. After Grace finally fell asleep, I walked Keaton, but he didn't relieve himself, even after two times around the block. I hope this hasn't created a problem."

Odd. She walked Keaton four times a day, and he never failed to urinate. The dog had followed her into the kitchen, stretching and yawning before lying down. She leaned down to him, and he rolled onto his back for a pet. He wasn't acting like he'd missed his evening walk. If he had, he'd be nudging her with his wet nose. Victoria must've been mistaken, unless Norman had walked him last night. But that couldn't be, because Norman had come home only five minutes before she. Unless he'd been lying, of course—

She banished that thought and walked to the kitchen to make bacon and eggs. They had to be ready for church in less than two hours.

15

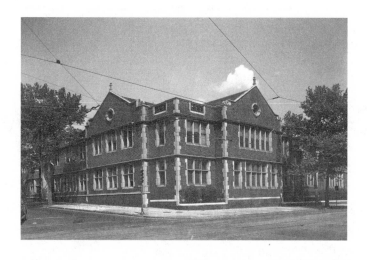

Harold dressed as Mickey from *Our Gang* for Halloween 1940—his first. Agnes had sewn a Munchkin costume for their cowlick-headed three-year-old, but Norman didn't want their son dressing as a dwarf. With his slender and fair tow-headed blond looks, Norman said, he'd do better as Mickey. And then Grace had wanted her mother to make a Scarlett O'Hara dress, but Agnes wouldn't have her eight-year old wandering about town with exposed shoulders. So she made her a Glinda the Good Witch costume to assuage the girl's tears. Besides, Agnes far preferred *The Wizard of Oz* to *Gone With the Wind*. Better to deal with a green-faced witch who tried to steal red slippers than a green-eyed flirt who tried to steal other women's husbands.

Norman didn't go trick-or-treating with her and their two chipmunks. He worked late, citing a deadline on his latest project. He'd spent too many evenings away from home this past month. She complained, but he only shrugged his shoulders and said, "Hard work yields great dividends."

The following evening, she basked in a rainy evening home alone—yet again. She could just smell Thanksgiving coming. Keaton lay at her feet, the children were fast asleep, Norman dined with a client at Bookbinder's on 2nd and Walnut, and she had the cozy green walls and mahoganies of the parlor all to herself. She snuggled in her robe and propped her feet on an ottoman. Norman had invited her to join him for the evening, but she'd declined. She never liked his business dinners and Norman knew that, so they both got what they wanted—he got his evening away from home, she got her quiet evening reading.

She finished an old article in *Harper's* about the impending demise of English royalty. Edward VIII had so sullied the House of Windsor by his affair with the twice-divorced Mrs. Simpson, the article titled "Queen Victoria Is Dead" opined, that even reliable George VI and young Princess Elizabeth could do nothing to save the monarchy. But Agnes agreed with Norman that Edward VIII's choice of a middle-aged Betty Boop over the royal throne was the best thing that could have happened to England. Had the Duke of Windsor stayed on the throne, England would've succumbed to Hitler, Norman said.

She finished reading the *Harper's* article and went back to knitting Norman a sweater. She turned on the radio, buried herself under one of Victoria's quilts, and listened to political news. If President Roosevelt won the election, he'd be the first president to serve a third term. She understood that he'd decided to break George Washington's tradition of the two-term limit because Germany and Japan loomed across the globe. Like many others (but not Norman), Agnes believed America shouldn't take on the risk of a new president.

She'd followed Norman's lead four years ago, and cast her first vote for Alf Landon. Norman would heat up like a furnace if she told him how she planned to vote this year. In the eight years since he'd cast his vote for Roosevelt, he'd come to despise the president for "smothering the poor with handouts." He also complained that Mrs. Roosevelt, to him a sinister combination of Madame de Farge and Lady Macbeth, lorded it over her husband—and the government.

No doubt he assumed she'd vote for Wendell Willkie on Tuesday, but she liked Franklin and admired Eleanor. When Norman wasn't looking, she read "My Day" and reveled in the first lady's opinions about racial bigotry, persecution of Jews, the marital woes of young people, and knitting. But not without envy. Eleanor had her daily column, trips down coal mines, and Teddy Roosevelt for an uncle. She had laundry, cleaning, and Uncle Collin, who still hadn't broken his wall of silence even after five long years of sad regret for Agnes.

Roosevelt and Willkie had held rallies in Philadelphia this past week. Agnes had taken the chipmunks to see the president wave from his Ford convertible, his little Scottie dog, Fala, perched atop his lap, no doubt fetching more votes than bones for his master. When the clock chimed ten, her own pistol puppy jumped up and nudged her with his nose.

"What is it, Keaton, do you want a treat?"

He just looked at her and wagged his tail, not the least bit excited by the magic word. That meant one thing only.

"Keaton, not now. It's raining cats and you."

He nudged her thigh again and ran to the door. She really didn't want to walk Keaton in the cold rain. Oh, why did Norman seem to have business on rainy evenings? Walking Keaton evenings was his job, not hers. In eight years of marriage, it was the one household chore she'd persuaded him to do.

"All right, doggy dog," she said after putting her coat on and leashing him. "We're going for our walk. Now you be a good boy and —"

The telephone rang just as she reached for the door. Her nerves jumped. Who could that be at this hour? No one ever called this late on a Friday evening.

"Hold on, Keaton. Mummy has to answer the phone. You sit and stay."

She dropped the umbrella and tossed her hat onto the foyer table. The phone rang half a dozen times before she reached it in the kitchen.

"Good evening?"

"Is this Mrs. Balmoral?"

"This is she. Who is calling?"

"Officer Gerald Sullivan from the West Philadelphia police."

A hollow pain seized Agnes's stomach. She grabbed the kitchen desk and sat in the chair. "Something's happened to Norman. Is he dead?"

"No, ma'am, but there has been a fight. Mr. Balmoral is being treated for injuries at the University of Pennsylvania Hospital. I don't have much more to tell you just yet."

Her hands began to shake. "But he was spending the evening on 2nd Street. Why didn't they take him to the Pennsylvania Hospital?"

"Mrs. Balmoral, we don't have those details. The incident occurred between two buildings at Sansom and 39th. The other man was killed, and your husband sustained wounds. We'd suggest you go without delay to the emergency room. An officer will meet you there. We will need a statement from your husband."

The receiver clicked. What had Norman been doing in West Philadelphia? And how'd he get into a fight? And—most horrible—what would happen to Norman if they charged him in the man's death? She had to get to the hospital fast, but not on foot in this rain. For once, she wished they owned a car. So she called his parents. Cornelius told her over Victoria's background moans that they'd pick her up in twenty minutes.

Keaton nudged her thigh again. She leaned down to kiss his forehead. "Keaton, you'll have to wait." He could go to the bathroom in the house tonight, she thought as she galloped up the stairs to change. She'd put on a black dress to walk the dog—bad luck to wear to a hospital—so she quickly changed into her tartan plaid skirt and white blouse. Then she called the Collingwoods to see if they could sit with the children. A breathless Mrs. Collingwood appeared at the same time Cornelius and Victoria pulled up in their Hudson.

"Do let us know what happened to Mr. Balmoral," Mrs. Collingwood said, a somber expression on her plump face. "We are so very concerned."

Agnes pulled on her heavy tweed coat and ran out to Cornelius's car. Very concerned, indeed. Ida Collingwood would be planning how to add this to her gossip repertoire.

They made their way to the hospital without a word from Victoria. Cornelius kept up a steady chatter about the rain, darkness, and the interminable streetlights. Why did they have to put these contraptions at intersections, he said, when people could see the crossing cars?

Agnes wished her father-in-law would shut up. She barely could think with all the chatter. So she stared out the window, biting her fingers and tapping her feet. Norman should've been taken to the Pennsylvania Hospital, so much closer than the two miles to this one—miles that were taking forever to drive. They eventually passed Penn's track field and came to the hospital on University Avenue, but found themselves at a one-way street going the wrong way.

Agnes groaned. "Stop the car and let me out," she said. Cornelius braked the car to a screeching halt. Agnes popped out and ran across the block to the emergency entrance.

Inside, she was blinded by white light as she entered—white everywhere, as if the hallway to the emergency room were lit by the heavens above.

"Where is he?" she said to the first person she saw, a woman in a white lab coat sitting behind a small desk. "I'm Mrs. Balmoral. Where's my husband?"

The receptionist jumped out of her chair and nearly ran into an orderly steering a wheelchair with a patient down the hallway. "You're the wife," she said. "Come this way, Mrs. Balmoral. Please be mindful of the patients."

Being treated with courtesy like this portended bad news. Her hands shook, and she felt an edge in her every movement. She followed the lady down two hallways to a larger room that was an even brighter white—the emergency department's reception area, where a cluster of people dressed in grays, blacks, and tans sat—and felt a sharp pain behind her eyes.

"Mary," the receptionist said to a rotund figure in white sitting at the nurses' station, "this is Mr. Balmoral's wife."

The entire room broke into applause.

"What the dickens is going on?" she asked, barely breathing, her hands no longer shaking. "The police said my husband was in a fight, and you're all applauding."

The head nurse lumbered out from around the nurses' station and led Agnes by the arm. "Mrs. Balmoral, come this way. We're so proud of your husband this evening," she said, nodding and smiling, "the way he rescued that young girl—"

"My God, he's dead!" She clutched her chest and stepped back. Now she knew why they were treating her like fine crystal in a tornado.

"Not at all," the head nurse reassured her. "His condition is stable."

Agnes breathed a little easier, but her mind raced forward. "Then what are you talking about? I was told he was injured in a fight. The police said the other man died. What does a young girl have to do with this?"

"Your husband saw a man assault a college girl and charged him. It's very likely he saved her life."

Cornelius and Victoria rushed into the room, their heavy coats hanging off their shoulders. Thank goodness, she wouldn't have to face this without them. Agnes hadn't noticed until now that Victoria's gray hair flowed loose down her back instead of pinned to her head in its usual chignon.

"These are Mr. Balmoral's parents. Please, all we want is to know how he is."

The nurse addressed Cornelius. "Mr. Balmoral is presently being prepared for surgery. He was stabbed in the stomach and has various cuts and bruises elsewhere. He's lost a significant amount of blood but is in stable condition. You can wait in here." She motioned them to a smaller private room. "I'll have one of the emergency room doctors come to you presently."

Yet another white room that had steel chairs. Agnes shivered as she sat down. What had Norman been doing, getting in the middle of a street fight in West Philadelphia? He was supposed to have been at Bookbinder's.

"Cornelius, our son must be in terrific pain," Victoria said. She clutched her neck and fell into a chair opposite Agnes.

"Nonsense. You heard the nurse say he's going to be okay."

Cornelius wiped his forehead and sat next to his wife. He'd gained a lot of weight recently, now as bald and fat as Winston Churchill. How unlike Norman, fit and muscular. Well, that strength would help Norman now.

Agnes wanted to explode. Norman could be dying, and she hadn't seen him yet. She might be a widow already. Mama ... even through the lens of her terror, she could remember the horrified blankness on Mama's face all those years ago when the nurse had told her Daddy had passed away. *Passed away.* She hated the expression, as if someone had made a casual choice to return a chicken entrée at a mediocre restaurant.

A few minutes later, a big-eared resident popped into the room and introduced himself. "Nurse Gertler tells me you're the Balmoral family. You must be very proud of him. He saved a young woman's life."

The resident could have been no older than Agnes, barely old enough to shave, let alone operate on a knife wound.

"Please, doctor. We'll be proud of him later. What is my husband's condition?"

The young man lowered his eyelids, pushed out his chest, and stepped back. Thinks he's important, Agnes thought, wanting to slap him. "Your husband was brought into the emergency room unconscious with multiple wounds, mostly superficial to the face and arms, but one major wound to his lower abdomen. He's being prepared for surgery to close the wound.

"The abdominal gash hit no major internal organs. We are lucky in that regard. But he has lost quite a lot of blood. We believe his chances are very good, particularly because he is in otherwise excellent physical condition."

Surgery? Loss of blood? Agnes put her thumb in her mouth and chomped down on it, but felt no pain. How could his chances possibly be good?

"How did this happen?" Agnes said.

"A police officer is interviewing the young woman right now."

"I'd like to speak with him, but first I want to see my husband."

"You can't see Mr. Balmoral for a while, ma'am. He's just now gone into surgery. Get me Gertler," the doctor said as he walked away, "I need Gertler."

Agnes looked at her blank-faced parents-in-law. If they were going to find out anything, she'd have to be the one to do it. She went after the resident.

"Doctor! I'm not simply sitting here and waiting."

He turned around. "Ma'am, you need to be patient. The detective in charge is with the young woman, and she, well, you see ..." he stammered *sotto voce*, "she doesn't want to be disturbed. You see, she was being assaulted when Mr. Balmoral rescued her."

Agnes's chest felt hollow once she understood. "How dreadful!"

"It's bad enough for the young girl that she has talk about it to a detective. Please go back to the waiting room. I'll see if I can find someone else."

"If you insist," she said. "But please hurry! I'm going crazy, wondering what happened to my husband."

Agnes watched the big-eared resident walk down the hallway. The mystery of Norman's evening rattled her, and she walked down the corridor to calm her nerves. She pretended to look at paintings of Philadelphia's rivers. How had Norman had come upon the young woman and her attacker? And what had made him jump to the rescue? She couldn't know what went through his mind — and what happened when the knife entered his abdomen. She cringed over his pain. But what had taken him to West Philadelphia in the first place?

She simply stared at the paintings, but finally went back to the waiting room. Cornelius was nodding off. How could he fall asleep? Victoria kept sighing, so much that Agnes couldn't stand it and left again. Better to stare at cheap paintings.

She wandered the hallways and ended up sitting at a table in the empty cafeteria. What would her life become if Norman were to die, and how would she raise Grace and Harold alone? She felt sharp daggers of superstition in even contemplating this and said a quick prayer for forgiveness. Of course, Norman would survive. She diverted her attention to the marble-tiled floor, a black-and-white checkerboard. Sometimes life felt like a game of chess, and she had no idea whether she was a pawn, a queen, or a player moving the pieces.

She looked up at the clock. Norman had been in surgery for more than two hours. She went back to check on Victoria and Cornelius. She found a stick figure of a woman with a flat head and enormous glasses sitting with them, writing on a notepad like a demon. Cornelius was speaking when she walked in.

"... and he studied architecture in Florence back in '29, just after the crash. Here's his wife, Agnes," Cornelius said, exposing his teeth and gums. "They were married in—"

"Here in Philadelphia," Victoria said, frowning at her husband. "Miss Ellis, this is my daughter-in-law. Agnes, she is a reporter for the *Inquirer*."

The reporter rose from her chair. "Yes, Mrs. Balmoral."

Agnes felt fatigue at the thought of going through this story with yet another complete stranger. "May I ask what brings you here?"

"We had a report from the police that your husband was involved in a fight with a man who was assaulting a college girl. I'm writing an article about the story. Given the attention this case is bound to get, perhaps now would be a good time for us to gather some background information on your husband."

From anxiety over Norman's condition to curiosity about the story, Agnes's mind was a confused jumble of thoughts. "I'm afraid we can't help you very much. You see, we only just found out about the incident. The police have ignored us since we got here almost three hours ago."

"The detective is still with the young woman. If you'd be so kind as to answer my questions, I can give you some information. Unofficially, of course."

"You know a lot more than we do. What have you learned?"

Agnes's mind became numb as Miss Ellis recited Norman's biography and then gave details of the attack. Norman charged a large man in an alley between 38th and 39th Streets at Sansom, allegedly because the man was assaulting a young woman who screamed for help. The man purportedly turned on Norman and stabbed him in the stomach, at which point Norman became enraged, grabbed the knife, and stabbed him in the heart, killing him instantly.

Agnes jumped when Miss Ellis told them the girl's name. Edith McAdoo, the youngest daughter of William Gibbs McAdoo of California.

"That name sounds familiar," Cornelius said, "some polecat from years ago."

"He retired from the U.S. Senate in '39," Miss Ellis said. "More than twenty years ago, he was President Wilson's Secretary of the Treasury."

Agnes looked at her parents-in-law. Victoria's eyes were wide, and Cornelius rubbed his face. No recognition, so she clarified it for them. "This means the girl is Woodrow Wilson's granddaughter."

Miss Ellis informed them that Mrs. McAdoo was coming from Washington, but that Senator McAdoo wouldn't be coming from California where he lived. It seemed likely that Mrs. McAdoo would bring along her stepmother—Edith Wilson, the former first lady.

This astounded Agnes. "This is all quite amazing, Miss Ellis, but I'm more concerned about my husband's health at the moment." The doctor could come in at any time and pass a sentence of widowhood on her—a life sentence without parole.

"Indeed. I thought you should know about the young woman."

"Another question. Do you know when this happened?"

"Approximately 9:15 this evening."

That wouldn't have been possible. Norman had dined at Bookbinder's until about that time. His dinner reservation had been for 8:00. He couldn't have been walking in West Philadelphia so soon afterward. The mystery deepened. The edgy feeling came back to Agnes's arms and legs.

They were spared further discussion with the reporter when the resident came back into the room, smiling and as eager as a young puppy wagging its tail for approval.

"I have good news, Mrs. Balmoral. Your husband has come through the surgery like a winner and is in recovery. The surgeon will be coming here shortly to discuss his condition."

"How long before we can see him, Doctor?" Victoria asked.

"A few hours, ma'am. We need to monitor him carefully. He's sedated and needs to wake up before you see him. He's going to be fine."

"What a relief," Agnes said and relaxed. She must've been clenching her hands, because her fingers ached. "Victoria, he's going to be all right."

Yet another doctor wearing a white lab coat came into the room. Agnes could see blood on the smock. He must be Norman's surgeon. And that had to be Norman's blood. She recoiled from the sight and tried looking him in the face, but had difficulty keeping her eyes from the red splotches.

The surgeon dismissed the resident and introduced himself as Dr. Rosenthal, explaining—in a brusque manner, but courteous in a gentleman's way—he had sutured and closed a three-inch gash on the right side of Norman's abdomen. No damage to his organs, the doctor reassured them, but there had been superficial wounds to his face, arms, and neck.

Miss Ellis took notes feverishly. Agnes frowned at her. "When may I see my husband, Dr. Rosenthal?"

"He won't be transferred to a private room until later on. I'd suggest you go home and get some rest. Come back in the morning when he's awake."

Agnes looked at the clock, nearly three. How had the hours gone by so quickly? "I don't want my husband to wake up without me by his side."

"Very unlikely. His body has gone through a terrible ordeal, and he's going to need a lot of sleep to recover. You too should have rest. Judging from the reporters outside, you're going to need it."

"What do you mean?"

"I've been told news reporters and photographers are outside the hospital. Apparently, they got wind of the fact that the girl was Roosevelt's daughter."

"No, Woodrow Wilson's granddaughter," corrected Miss Ellis.

"One Democrat's just like any other," said the doctor. "But the news folks have to report something. Mrs. Balmoral, if you're ready to leave, I'll have an orderly escort the three of you out the back exit."

"Thank you, Dr. Rosenthal," Agnes said, looking at Miss Ellis, "but we're not afraid of the news people. We have nothing to hide."

"Suit yourselves, but I warn you it's a mob scene."

She should have heeded his advice. A sea of faces, notepads, cameras, and flashes confronted them when they stepped outside the hospital. Blinded by flashes, Agnes squinted and covered her eyes. A cacophony of questions assaulted her.

"Mrs. Balmoral, can you tell us how your husband saved Miss McAdoo?"

"Mrs. Balmoral, what's it like to have a husband who's so brave?"

"Mrs. Balmoral, what is your husband's prognosis?"

"Mrs. Balmoral, is your husband the P.S.F.S. architect?"

"Mrs. Balmoral, is it true that your uncle is the pastor of St. Patrick's?"

Endless questions. She had no idea how they would've known her name or her background. What about her marriage license? Had they gotten that too?

Apparently this was too much for Victoria, who begged Cornelius and Agnes to help her make her way to the car. Together the three of them crossed the street, and the reporters followed them like hungry dogs. But at last, they were safe and drove away.

"Thank heavens no reporters came here," Agnes said as they approached the house. "Victoria, Cornelius, go on in and upstairs to the third-floor room to sleep tonight. I'll let Mrs. Collingwood know we're home."

She found the old lady sleeping in the parlor, her head resting on the back of the chair and her mouth open, snoring like a rusty furnace. But for the crisis, she would've laughed.

She nudged Mrs. Collingwood on the shoulder and whispered, "Mrs. Collingwood, it's Agnes. You can wake up now. It's time to go home."

The woman awoke with a little snort and looked at Agnes, her eyes blank. Then she opened them wide and spoke in a clear, hurried voice. "How is your husband?"

"He's resting at the hospital. He'll be fine. But let's save the questions for tomorrow. I'm sorry it took us so long to come home. Thank you, dear, for staying with Grace and Harold. You've been an enormous help."

The old lady submitted as Agnes escorted her to the door. Agnes was dead tired, but happy to be home. Poor Keaton whined and wagged his tail at her.

Agnes laughed at her forgotten dog. She grabbed her coat from the hallway chair and his leash from the table. "Keaton, now we can go for your walk."

The next morning, Agnes awoke early to a sunny Saturday. She put on her robe and went downstairs to start a pot of coffee for Cornelius and boil water for Victoria's and her morning tea. And then she opened the front door for the newspaper. As she reached down to pick it up, she heard unfamiliar voices approach from 19th Street.

"There she is!"

"Mrs. Balmoral, we have some questions for you about your husband."

"That's the hero's wife."

Horrified, she realized she was standing there in her bathrobe, her hair a wild red mess. Perhaps they'd write about that? She banged the door shut, peeked out the parlor window, and counted six — no, seven — reporters. All this attention was absurd. And then she saw the *Inquirer's* headline.

Norman Balmoral, Local Architect, Rescues Late President's Granddaughter

Norman's picture was on the cover page, the one he'd submitted for his American Institute of Architects membership. Movie-star handsome, she marveled, with that jawline and square chin. "Grace, Harold, come see Daddy's picture in the newspaper," she hollered up the stairs.

The children scampered down, followed by Victoria and Cornelius.

"Children, look, your father's picture is in the newspaper."

They examined the picture, and Grace cocked her head. "Sweetheart, last night he saved a young woman's life, and she turned out to be President Wilson's granddaughter," Agnes said. "But when he did that, he got hurt just a little bit, and now he's in the hospital getting better. We can visit him after breakfast."

Grace frowned and made saucer eyes at her mother. Harold walked over and pulled on her robe. "Why can't he be at home, Mama?" he said. "We wanted to play with him this morning."

"He'll come home in a few days, darling. Now, you go —"

The telephone clanged. Agnes answered it, expecting the nuisance of yet another reporter. Instead, she heard Cristina's throaty voice.

"What's this about Norman I'm reading in the newspaper? I didn't know you were married to Sir Lancelot of the Lake."

Agnes groaned. She wanted to get to the hospital and here was Cristina poking fun.

"Very funny. We've all had something of a shock. The police called last night at ten. Norman was in a fight —"

"I can read the paper. But tell me all the important stuff. Did you meet Wilson's granddaughter? Has the president's family contacted you?"

"Cristina, no to those questions." Agnes brought her up to date.

"Sweetie, is there anything I can do for you?" Cristina said, a raspy tone coming into her alto voice.

"Well, yes. There are a bunch of reporters out front. Can you get rid of them? Come over here and flash your white teeth and a smile at them —"

Cristina laughed. "Are you asking me to flirt them away, Agnes Balmoral?"

"I don't want to be interviewed." She checked the foyer for the children. They'd gone into the parlor with Victoria and Cornelius, but she lowered her voice anyway.

"Someone's bound to ask when we were married. Grace is too young to absorb that," Agnes said. And then she had a different thought. "I do want you to come over here, but not to flirt with reporters. Would you take the dog for a few days? Use the back entrance. Key's under the chrysanthemum pot. I doubt the reporters will be a bother after we leave for the hospital."

"Glad to help. Donnie and Ronnie will love Keaton. So will Angelo."

After hanging up, she realized Cristina hadn't asked about Norman's condition. Not long after Agnes had become pregnant with Harold, Norman had come home early and caught her laughing with Cristina in the kitchen. He'd upbraided her for concealing the visits, but they eventually reached a compromise. Agnes could be friends with Cristina, but they wouldn't socialize with the Rosamilias. So it came as no surprise that Cristina avoided Norman too.

Agnes put on her blue tweed dress. Norman would be awake and she wanted him to see her in one of his favorites. It wasn't even eight o'clock when the five of them left the house, but the group of reporters outside had swelled from seven to twenty. She gasped—she'd rather flee Paris with the Nazis chasing her than face reporters again. Didn't they have anything more important to cover, such as Tuesday's presidential election? They held close together, turned their heads away, and crossed the street to the car.

The hospital was even more brutally white than it had been last night. The morning's head nurse, her face as long and thin as the Tin Man, scowled at her. "We do not permit children in the hospital rooms, but since you're Mr. Balmoral's family, I guess we'll allow it. After this, no children."

When they arrived at Norman's room, they found an orderly guarding the entrance. He stood six feet tall with perfect posture and shoulders practically as wide as the doorway. He looked more like a bodyguard than a hospital orderly.

"Nothing to worry about, Mrs. Balmoral," the orderly said. "Doctor's orders that no one outside his family should disturb Mr. Balmoral. He's become quite popular. The story started spreading like fire as soon as patients started waking up this morning. They all started coming around looking for him."

A nurse stood over Norman, taking his pulse. His complexion seemed even milkier than usual. But perhaps that was only in comparison to his nurse. If she hadn't known better, she could've sworn it was Cristina holding Norman's wrist. She had the same figure, olive skin, and wavy hair.

"Daddy!" Harold exclaimed.

"Norman, my son," Victoria said, her hand on her neck. "You're awake!"

"Just a half hour now," the nurse said, "so please be quiet."

"Good morning, darling." Agnes kissed his forehead. No fever, she was glad to feel, but he already had a thick stubble. Norman would want to shave. He never missed a day.

"Not so quickly, ma'am," the nurse said. "We don't want to risk infection."

"Oh, she'll be fine," Norman said.

"Not her," the nurse said. "You!"

Agnes ignored her. "Norman, tell me how you're feeling. Are the nurses treating you all right?"

"Well, I'd say, 'All in all, I'd rather be in Philadelphia,' but I am in Philadelphia."

They laughed, but Norman's face contracted, and he groaned in pain. "Don't tell any jokes, whatever you do. It hurts when I laugh."

"At least he's kept his sense of humor," Agnes said, smiling at Victoria. They set their coats and purses down on a bureau. Victoria sat in a chair next to his bed, but the rest of them stood. "Norman, have you seen the newspaper?"

"No, Agnes. Why do you ask?"

She ran her fingers through his hair and rubbed his head. "Your picture is on the front page of the *Inquirer*. You're being proclaimed a hero for what you did last night."

"What I did last night?" His face turned white. He looked confused, even afraid.

"You don't remember? Well, last night —"

"Agnes, let me tell the story," Cornelius interrupted. "Son, you were in a fight with a man who was attacking a young woman and —"

"But why would I be on the front page of the paper?"

"Because the woman you saved is the granddaughter of President Woodrow Wilson." Cornelius beamed as if he'd accomplished the deed himself.

Norman lowered his voice, but it came out scratchy. "Nurse Gertler, would you excuse us? I'd like to have some time with my family."

The nurse frowned. "All right, Mr. Balmoral. I'll be back in ten minutes."

Once she'd left, he said, "If I was going to save the life of a politician's granddaughter, why couldn't it have been a Republican?"

Victoria leaned forward in her chair. "Norman, are you in a lot of pain?"

"I've had better days. My abdomen is very sore, and it hurts when I laugh." He looked up at Agnes with soft eyes. "Please don't say anything funny, Agnes."

Her heart twinged at her husband, still a little boy despite his heroic rescue. "Darling, you need to get lots of rest."

"Why does everyone say that? The doctor came in fifteen minutes ago. He says I need to stay in the hospital until Tuesday or Wednesday. It had better be Tuesday, so I can vote for Wendell Willkie."

"No, Daddy," Harold said. He rushed over to Norman's bed, his blue eyes blinking fast. "Come home today."

"It's all right, son. I have to rest so I can get real strong to play horsey with you next Saturday."

Victoria sighed. "That will be too soon, Norman."

"Nonsense, Mother," he said. "I'll be up and back to normal before you know it. Why, only yesterday I—" and then he stopped.

"That reminds me," Agnes said, pausing a little, "why were you in West Philadelphia? You were having dinner at Bookbinder's all the way down in Old City, three miles from where the attack took place."

Norman's mouth fell, and he turned his head to look out the window. "I met with my client for dinner, and he invited me back to his house at 41st and Chestnut. The attack must've happened when I was walking back home."

She folded her arms and observed Norman. He didn't usually avoid eye contact when they spoke. "I think I understand, but perhaps I'm wrong."

He gave her a penetrating look, and a thin glaze veiled his eyes.

"Son, you're so brave," Victoria said, stroking his leg under the sheet. "Not to mention, famous. You can't imagine how many newspeople are outside waiting to interview you."

Norman turned his head away again and heaved a heavy sigh.

"I don't want to talk. What you're saying confuses me."

"Quite right, and here we are badgering you when you should be resting." Cornelius said. "Victoria, Agnes, let's go to the waiting room for a bit."

Norman looked toward them, but averted his gaze yet again. He began to cry. The sight of Norman crying hit Agnes like a punch in the stomach. Something had to be very wrong. "Norman, I'll stay until you settle down. Cornelius, Victoria, would you take the children to the cafeteria?"

They left without a word, Victoria holding Grace's hand and Cornelius holding Harold's. Agnes sat down in Victoria's chair.

She reached for Norman's hand. His crying escalated. "Norman, I know you're tired, but why on Earth are you crying?"

"I'm not proud. I'm a-a-ashamed," he stammered, his cheeks flush. "Embarrassed, ashamed, and afraid."

"Whatever for?" she asked. He averted his eyes once again.

"It's all over, Agnes. Everyone's going to find out now that newspaper people are asking questions."

"What do you mean?"

He didn't look like he was suffering. The surgeon had said he'd recover fully, so what was upsetting him? Her mouth went dry, and her heart thumped a heavy beat in her head.

"I've wronged you so. You've been such a good wife and I've been—"

"You're not making sense, Norman. You've been a wonderful husband."

What did he mean? Had he stolen money, been unfaithful, embezzled from Howe and Lescaze? Did he have another wife somewhere she'd never known about? Was he involved with sordid people? Not Norman, not the architect with perfect posture, six o'clock morning runs, and a one-martini limit.

"I can't bear to tell you this."

Whatever Norman needed to confess, it had to be very bad. Agnes's blood rushed from every part of her body into her stomach. She didn't feel her arms bracing the steel chair, her feet resting on the floor, her spine pressing against the back of the chair.

"The way you're talking," she said, "it sounds like you attacked that young girl rather than the other man."

"I knew when it happened, I knew I'd have to tell you about it someday, but I didn't expect it'd happen like this. It's bound to come out now. It won't be long before the newspapers talk to the restaurant—"

He was choking on his words. He clearly regretted something he'd done, and it must have been something truly horrific. Her nerves broke and she blurted out, "Stop this and tell me now."

Norman waited until his sobbing subsided.

"I lied to you. I wasn't having dinner with a client last night. I was having dinner at the Richmond Club." He scrunched his face and broke into tears again, but he continued like a man jumping off an ocean cliff.

"With ... with a woman and it wasn't you. I had an affair."

A thunderbolt hit her in the heart. She squeezed her hands into the arms of the chair while images assaulted her brain—Norman over there in his bed, the Richmond Club, a furtive dinner with another woman, an affair. Rage flooded into her brain. She jumped out of the chair and kicked it with all her power. It crashed to the floor. She kicked it a second time, then a third ...

"I don't believe this! I knew there was something fishy about last night, but I never thought anything like this. You've been with another woman? You took her to the Richmond Club? You took her to our restaurant where we had our first date?"

She visualized what he'd done. He'd taken off his clothes with another woman and done things with her that were theirs alone to do. Did he kiss that woman in the same way that always took Agnes to a place of smooth contentment? Did he rub his hands through this woman's hair just as he always did with Agnes? Did he wrap his chest and legs around her in that way that always made Agnes feel like they'd become one human being? She let out a dry moan. The refrain kept repeating in her head, *He's been with another woman.*

"Agnes, I can see you're upset. I'm so sorry, but we need to remain calm. If the newspapers get hold of this, I'll be ruined. And to think of my parents finding out—"

Agnes paced the room, looking for something to strike. She couldn't hit Norman in this hospital room. But she had to do something, so she took dead aim for the chair and kicked it again, full force. It slid across the floor and banged against the wall. But it did nothing to mitigate her anger. It boiled within her, and all she wanted was to find the most hurtful words he'd ever heard. And she wanted to be rid of him—for good.

"You care more about your idiot parents than you do about our marriage. Oh, don't you worry, everyone who matters to you will find out what low-class trash you are. I'm calling the editor of the *Inquirer* and telling him to run a new headline. *Norman Balmoral is a lying son of a bitch.* To hell with your family and to hell with you."

"Son of a bitch?" Norman said as if not recognizing the words. "Please, Agnes, I promise I'll never see that woman again—"

"Who is it? What the hell is her name?" She glared at him.

Nurse Gertler knocked on the door. "Is anything wrong in here?"

"No," Norman answered in a high pitch. "My wife and I are just having a discussion."

"Mr. Balmoral, I'm sorry to interrupt you, but I have two pieces of news,"

Nurse Gertler said. "First, your brother and his family are on their way. Second, Mrs. Woodrow Wilson is on the telephone for you. May I transfer the call?"

Norman murmured something, but Agnes blocked him out. She couldn't bear the idea of making small talk with Norman's brother and sister-in-in-law or their boxy-headed brats. So she grabbed her coat and purse and left the room. She had no idea where she was headed, but her feet led her down the white corridor. She had to get out of this hospital. She had to leave. She needed fresh air.

She marched out the front doors of the hospital. A swarm of men — and some women too, she noticed — wearing hats and holding cameras stood outside. She did her best to ignore the maelstrom of questions coming at her.

"Mrs. Balmoral, a word, please, about your heroic husband!"

"Mrs. Balmoral, how is your husband this morning?"

"Mrs. Balmoral, have you been contacted by Senator McAdoo yet?"

"Mrs. Balmoral, what does it feel like to be the wife of a public hero?"

She kept her eyes forward, her feet planted firmly in front of her. Thank goodness, no one followed her. Home, that's where she wanted to go, directly home and as fast as possible. By the time she walked the two miles to her block, the cool November air felt as sweltering as July.

Yet more reporters stood outside her front stoop. She plunged through this second wave of adulations for Norman and lowered her head to enter the house. The silence inside surprised her. Keaton didn't race to the front door with a boisterous greeting. She found a note from Cristina on the front table.

I took Keaton. Call me with news about Norman. I trust he and the McAdoo girl will recover. I did my best to discourage the reporters from remaining. I even gave them my best smile, but they couldn't be dissuaded.

At the mention of Cristina's smile, Agnes wondered what the other woman looked like. Did Norman want some other woman because her own hips had grown too fat, or were her breasts too small? Was she too old at thirty? Had he lost interest in her now that she'd given him two children? None of it made any sense. His interest in having sex with her had not dwindled in the least. She intended to find out everything. She had to know why he'd done it.

The telephone's jingle broke the silence. She ignored it, but it wouldn't stop. "What is it?" she answered. "What do you want?"

"CBS Radio from New York, Mrs. Balmoral. We'd like to send one of our reporters to interview you and your husband."

She banged the receiver against the wall and left it dangling on its cord. Removing her coat and dropping her purse on the table, she sat down and looked around her. White everywhere, just as Norman had wanted. Everything in this kitchen was white.

She wanted to play solitaire, enough games so that she'd win at least once by the luck of the draw. So she stood up to go into the parlor. She looked around the room. "It's time to remodel this damned kitchen. I'm sick of all this white."

16

INFECTION SET IN, AND NORMAN WAS UNABLE TO CAST HIS VOTE for Wendell Willkie. President Roosevelt got his third term — with the help of a fifty-five percent majority, Pennsylvania's thirty-six electoral votes, and Agnes. She envisioned Norman fuming in his hospital bed when she voted at the Ethical Society, so she gave the Roosevelt-Wallace lever an extra-special oomph.

Norman came home a week later (far too soon) and established convalescent territory in their bedroom. Victoria nearly wore a groove in Agnes's Oriental rug from the door to the bed, nursing her "baby boy" by serving chicken soup, dressing and bandaging his wounds, and reading to him. After an insufferable week, Agnes prodded her back to Cornelius and the store's ledgers.

Agnes kept her distance from the baby boy, but he kept ringing the bell for her. She responded with snake's venom.

"I'll get your lunch when I'm good and ready, Norman."

"That bandage doesn't look like it needs replacing until tomorrow, Norman."

"No one besides your parents has called to ask about you, Norman."

"You're capable of going to the bathroom yourself, Norman."

She allowed herself the luxury of guillotining his name. *Philadelphia Magazine* might've featured him in a cover story, *The Washington Post* might've written an article about Mrs. Wilson's donation in his honor to the American Institute of Architects, Mayor Lamberton and Senator Davis might've visited him in the hospital, but helpless in bed at home, he held his tongue — until the Saturday before Thanksgiving when he dressed himself for the first time and moved about on his own.

He sat at the kitchen table that morning staring at Agnes and placed his hands on the tablecloth. "You and I need to make peace."

Agnes stood at the sink, scrubbing dried egg from an iron skillet. Victoria had departed with Grace and Harold for a day at the zoo. Grace wanted to see giraffes, and Harold wanted to see the lions, tigers, and bears that had scared Dorothy on her way to Emerald City. A cold day in hell when she would make peace with the infidel, unless he agreed to her terms. If she hadn't spent the recent nights weeping over the loss of their commitment and the days stewing in anger over his betrayal, she might've decided what that meant ...

Agnes turned to face him when she finished cleaning. She clenched the skillet and let it dangle by her side.

"First of all, I want no divorce," he said, his voice even and not a single line on his face. "I ended that relationship the evening I was stabbed. The woman meant nothing to me. You do."

Agnes's chapped lips cracked open. "The knight in shining armor doesn't want a divorce. But if you want to make peace, you must tell me everything. Leave out nothing, and I mean *nothing.*"

"Is there any purpose in giving you the unhappy details?" He still kept the smooth poker face, as if negotiating the price for a new house.

She bored her eyes into him as if they were tiny drills. "You're in no position to argue, Norman. What is her name?"

Norman blistered under her gaze. "If you must know, her name is ... is Mary Alden — was, at least, before she got married."

Agnes recognized the name but couldn't place it.

"I knew her before you and I met, before she got married. She worked at Smith and Weisskopf. Her husband died last year."

Now she remembered. Mary Alden was the young woman Cristina had told her about, the one whom Norman had dropped all those years ago. She'd gotten married and moved to Pottstown.

"She lives in Doylestown but has been visiting her sister in town. I ran into her quite by accident one Saturday morning this fall when I was running."

"You're lying. Years ago, Cristina told me she lived in Pottstown."

"Wrong as usual. Mary's lived in Doylestown since she got married."

Cristina had told her Pottstown in no uncertain terms, yet Norman insisted she'd lived in Doylestown. The two locations were too far apart for both of them to be correct. But perhaps Mary and her husband had moved from one to the other during the intervening ten years.

Norman fixed his eyes on the sterile white table as he revealed the details. He'd had dinner with Mary twice and was "close with her" just once. The second dinner was the night of the attack.

The attack in West Philadelphia. For an instant, Agnes wished Norman had been stabbed in the heart instead of the stomach. Then he might know how she felt. She paced with the heavy skillet.

She stared him down. "You haven't told me what you did with that trollop."

Norman popped his mouth open and scowled. "Calling her names won't accomplish anything, Agnes."

She wanted to do a lot more damage than foul names. "Sticks and stones, Norman. Tell me."

He sighed and hesitated but enumerated what they'd done. Intercourse, no birth control. The reality screamed in her head, Mary might be pregnant. Grace and Harold might have a bastard sibling by July, and she'd have no choice but to divorce Norman. How would she ever explain that to her children, not to mention Mama and Uncle Collin? She could hear them now: "We told you so." And then Norman would marry that woman and build a new family with her, Mary's three girls, and their child. Would he kidnap Grace and Harold into his new lair?

"Why didn't you use birth control?" Agnes said, her voice a squeaky clarinet.

"Mary's a Catholic and doesn't believe in birth control. Unnatural, she said."

Agnes felt dizzy and steadied herself on a chair. "I suppose she thinks adultery is natural. And this isn't the first time you've ... how is it they say ... screwed an unmarried Catholic girl."

"Put that skillet down, Agnes. You're about to faint."

She threw the skillet onto the floor, and it boomed like a gong. "Happy now? And why are you staring at the table instead of looking me in the eye? Be a man, Norman. Did you have sex on this table when I wasn't at home?"

Norman flinched, but he did look up. She saw the first true flashes of pain in his eyes. Good.

"How dare you insinuate," he said, his voice tight as piano wire. "I would never insult you or the children by bringing that into our home. Why are you asking these questions? What do you hope to gain?"

Her voice began to quiver. Nothing made sense to her now, not this house, his straying, even why she'd married him. If she were to make any sense of anything, she had to know everything. "I want to know —"

"What? What more do you want to know?"

Norman had divulged the sordid details of his affair. She knew what he had done, with whom, how many times, and when. But she couldn't squelch the nagging doubt that kept poking her in the side. It reminded her of reading a letter from a long-lost friend who hadn't dotted the *i*'s and crossed the *t*'s.

"More?" he repeated. "I've told you everything."

She struggled to figure it out though her ankles felt weak, her heart torn in two, and her head numb. "I want to know if I can ever trust you again."

"Is that all? If that's the reassurance you need, of course, you can trust me. Surely I've done enough in the past eight years to command your trust?"

Eight years as husband and wife, all brought to naught in the blink of an affair. A pack of thoughts circled in her head like wolves waiting to attack — their bedroom, their house. Grace reading books with Harold, playing blocks at her feet. Mama and Uncle Collin gone forever because of Norman. Gracie Honeywalker still puttering about her farm up in New York, watching sunsets with Old Man Lacey. Granny Limerick dead and gone, the only one who had approved of Norman. Perhaps Daddy would've shot Norman, saying his daughter deserved better. But Martin Limerick treasured life too much.

The thought of gunfire electrified Agnes, and her mind cleared. "I want to know why. Why did you cheat? Why, Norman, why?"

"What can I say? I'm sorry. It will never happen again."

She was crying now, so words required effort. "But why did you have an affair, Norman? If you don't tell me, I'll tell your parents — and the neighbors."

"Remember my position in society. Remember Howe and Lescaze."

His career? His position in society? He'd breached their marriage vows, and he cared more about his job and the neighbors? The tears flowed freely now. She struggled to use words that echoed the refrain in her head —

"You won't tell me why, you're not going to tell me why."

She leaned over the sink. Harold's plastic cup, with its picture of Pluto the Pup on it, dried grape juice stains on it. Harold, her boy, lanky and fair, not yet four. Agnes surrendered to her sobs. The tension in her stomach drained away, her arms and legs began to relax, the strain in her back began to loosen, and the sharp pain in her head began to soften. She allowed herself to moan, and the floodgates opened.

"You want to know why? All right, then. I did it because I wanted to do it," Norman said, his baritone echoing throughout the room. Agnes glanced back at him. He had a sharp flash in the whites of his eyes that reminded her of a cornered wolf. "No other reason. I felt the temptation, and I gave into it. I love you, Agnes. I love our life together, and I love our children — and I love having sex with you. But that doesn't mean I don't want other women. In our eight years together, this is the first and only time I've strayed. Please forgive me. Let's put this terrible episode behind us, sweetheart. Right now."

She heard his words but kept her focus on Harold's cup. Her sobs quieted. She straightened from the sink, turned, and looked at Norman, knowing she must look like a cross between a madwoman and a drowned hen, like Bette Davis in *Of Human Bondage*. But to hell with it.

"I have no idea if I can forgive you. And put this behind us? I don't know. Right now, I've had enough." She headed for the front of the house.

"Agnes, please don't leave me. We shouldn't end our marriage over a single indiscretion."

He was acting like a seven-year-old boy caught with his fingers in the cake. "For heaven's sake, I'm not leaving you. I'm going for a walk."

She grabbed her purse and Loden coat from the hook in the foyer and looked in the mirror. Just red eyes and a splotchy face. A walk in the cold air would do her good. Keaton bolted into the hallway, triggered by the signs of an impending walk. But Norman could walk him. He needed the exercise. She'd walk alone today.

❧

The bracing cold soothed Agnes's face, and she smelled snow in the air. She walked the perimeter of Rittenhouse Square, not caring a whit about cracks in the pavement. When she was a little girl, she and Daddy had tried to walk on as many stones as possible without stepping on the cracks. She'd even played that game with Norman in the winter of their romance. But never since.

When had she become her mother's age? She never took walks anymore like she'd done only a few years ago. She never took a book and a blanket to Washington Square, nor set out on a lazy afternoon without a known destination or return time. She never saw all four squares in a single day anymore—Washington for the sun, Rittenhouse for the shade—nor did she view Renoirs at the Art Museum and see ships on the Delaware River in one afternoon.

Whenever she walked now, it would be to the market, to the children's schools, to church, occasionally to a performance at the Walnut Street Theatre. She had schedules, appointments, ballet lessons for Grace, playground afternoons for Harold, obligations to society acquaintances whose prejudices and opinions she didn't share. Her strides reminded her, *You've got to be somewhere, so hurry.*

The purse on her arm sagged, and her shoes felt heavy. She always carried a purse upright on one arm because she liked to swing the other. It held handkerchiefs, pictures of her children, shopping lists, pens and pencils, a checkbook, aspirin—and a feminine napkin, but even the days she needed those were numbered.

Would she remain married to Norman? The children would never have happy lives if she cut Norman out of their lives, if she boarded the train for Washington with Grace and Harold and cried for forgiveness on Mama's shoulder. Harold might be all right, because he'd be too young to remember his father. But Grace? She thought about her quiet daughter, the constant reader. Grace never would again lift her head from the safe world of fiction.

No, she and Norman must remain together, but nothing could be the same. She would be civil, even affectionate, supportive of his career and their home together. He would work, she would cook dinner, and yes, they would have sex—when they both wanted it rather than on Norman's weekly regimen. But she didn't want to have any more children.

When had Mama first felt old? Did it happen when Daddy died? Mama had been only a few years older than Agnes was now. Did it happen when Agnes ran away from home to marry Norman? Perhaps it happened that terrible Mother's Day before Mama moved to Washington. Agnes remembered her last words: "My daughter is lost to me." But her mother still lived, and those words didn't have to be the last Agnes ever heard from her. She might reconnect with Mama and even Uncle Collin, who still served at St. Patrick's.

She yearned for them, her soul cried out for the comfort of laying her head in the nest of her mother's soft bosom, of sitting in the parlor with her mother and uncle and feeling their cocoon of love, conditional though it may have been, knowing their blood was her blood. And knowing they would raise battle flags if someone tried to harm Agnes. How she wanted to see Mama clutching a tear-stained handkerchief to her breast, Uncle Collin looking down at his feet deep in thought, reaching for words of solace and prayer.

Noon on Saturday, he'd be eating lunch before preparing the final draft of his homily. She pictured him in a flannel checked shirt, savoring Mrs. Mallory's corned beef and sauerkraut and making a mess on his chin. Uncle Collin ... that Mother's Day, she'd surrendered to anger and wine. She'd blurted out terrible things, and because of that, she'd lost her mother and her uncle—all for a husband she now wanted to vomit out of her life.

What could she say to Uncle Collin? How could she frame an apology after five years of silence from both sides of Rittenhouse Square? She
needed time to phrase her words, and she wanted to see him before going
back to Norman. So she turned up 19th Street, rather than walking in the
direction of St. Patrick's, and headed toward Longacre's Music and Instruments. She'd lose herself in the piano music at the store, imagine herself
in a Vienna salon witnessing the masters performing for noblemen. That
would clear her head.

"Hello, Mr. Longacre," she said on entering the store. The owner, his
wrinkled shirts and loose ties as familiar to her as the shelves stocked with
ancient German music, greeted her like a long-lost child. Agnes tried to
remember when she'd last come into the store, probably just after Harold
had been born. With two children, a husband, and a house, she'd become
too preoccupied to play Granny's piano, let alone buy music.

Someone was playing one of the pianos in the back room. She wouldn't
be able to monopolize the pianos in the back like she'd done in past years,
so she browsed the shelves instead. But she recognized the sounds from
the back. Of course, she knew the music, Schubert's posthumous sonata
in B flat, but familiarity came from the technique as much as the musical
poetry of the simple melody. She recognized the nuances, the phrasing,
and the manner of performance—exactly as she'd been taught herself.
With no doubt whose fingers were on that keyboard, she headed back to
say hello to Mr. Larney.

A hush fell on Agnes's heart when she entered the room. No wonder she
couldn't make any sense of her life. She had allowed music, the thing she
loved best, to fade into the background.

Mr. Larney faced her from the piano, his eyes on the keyboard, mas-
saging the first movement's lengthy development. She'd never thought he
could look so young and relaxed. How old was he? She did the math, a
few years shy of sixty, almost the same age as Victoria. Observing him at
the piano in a purple-green striped bow tie and blue jacket, he looked far
younger than sixty. He sat there, every wrinkle smoothed out, the lines in
his forehead invisible as if all the troubles of the past ten years had never
occurred. To look at him at the piano, Agnes could forget about the De-

pression, the soup lines of gray-clad men, women, and children winding their way from Lombard onto Broad, the silence at the banks because so few people dared tread there. She could forget about England at war with Germany, Japan terrorizing the Pacific, and most heartbreaking of all, the plight of the Jews.

During a pause, Mr. Larney looked up. His eyes jumped, and he flashed a wide grin.

"My student with the killer thumbs! How long have you been there?"

She'd been mesmerized for minutes. "Long enough to enjoy the performance. I recognized your technique when I walked in the door."

"Agnes Mary, exactly the same as when I saw you last. Even your hair's still in a ponytail. I'm trying out the pianos. It's time I brought a real instrument into my studio. The damper broke on my old Wurlitzer."

"I love the sound of this one, very smooth. It brings a tingle to my scalp."

"That's a good sign, but the touch on this one isn't right for me. Come, child, help me pick a different piano."

She looked left, then right. "I don't see any children in this room, do you?"

He cupped his hand over his mouth. "You have me there. All right, young lady, let's have two adults select a piano."

"Don't give up on this one just yet. Let me have a go, but not with Schubert."

She edged him off the piano and started into Barber's *Excursions*. He took his glasses off, pushed his tongue into his cheek, and crossed his eyes as if she'd just scratched her nails on a chalkboard.

"Come now, Mr. Larney. You don't have to make faces."

He put his glasses back on. "I can hear your fingernails clicking from over here. A good pianist trims her nails every week, young lady, and she practices her scales every day. You can't fool old Mr. Larney."

She stuck her tongue out at him and laughed — for the first time since Halloween, she realized. "You're right, this piano's not right. Another one?"

He sat down at another long Steinway and launched into the Schubert. "These days I'm just gaga over Schubert," he said, making his way through the singing melody. "He really is full of wonderful surprises, isn't he?"

"As long as you play him as written. That's what you always told me. Unlike Beethoven, whom you always nuanced to death."

Mr. Larney talked over his playing. "Beethoven might've been deaf, silly girl, but he was the master. He left room for interpretation, hence the nuancing. Schubert, on the other hand, you have to get out of the way and let the music play itself."

He stopped at the puncture of an F sharp minor chord. "Case in point, a B flat sonata with the development section in F sharp minor. This Steinway is too brassy. Not for me at all. What's next? Let's try that one."

She sat at the third piano and played the *Pathetique*'s slow movement, a safe choice not likely to garner theatrics from Mr. Larney. She played the whole thing and launched into Debussy's *Arabesque*. How she enjoyed this! It made her feel ten years younger, even with her rusty, clicking fingers.

"Allow me. I think this Steinway has the right texture," Mr. Larney said, nudging her aside in the middle of the Debussy. He continued the *Arabesque* from where she left off. "Perfect. It flows like cool water on Appalachian stones."

She looked inside the piano at the strings and the velocity of Mr. Larney's hammer strikes, remembering her lessons from so long ago. Being back at the piano excited her so much, she wanted to remain all day.

He played piece after piece — Debussy, more Beethoven, Scriabin, a little Bach, a few Mozarts, ending with the E flat Schubert *Impromptu*. Agnes looked at her watch, just past 2:30 p.m. She'd have to visit Uncle Collin another time. More than five years had passed, after all. She could wait another day or two.

"This is the one," he exclaimed. "Now let's juggle some numbers and figure out how on God's Earth I'm going to pay for it. Mr. Longacre!"

Agnes heard the owner's clunky soles approaching on the wood floors. "Yes, Mr. Larney, what may I do for you?"

"Eureka, I have found it." A wide smile zigzagged up his pink face. "How much do you want for this Steinway?"

Mr. Longacre clucked his tongue on his teeth, looked at the ceiling, and tapped an index finger on his cheek. He projected from his teddy-bearish face an appearance of adding a complex line of figures in his head. Mr.

Longacre knew what he was doing. The longer he took, the more likely Mr. Larney would drop to his knees and beg for mercy.

"Hmm," he said at last. "Ordinarily, I would ask eleven hundred. This is a Steinway grand, and a large one at that. But for you, Mr. Larney, considering all the students you've sent here over the years, I'll sell it for nine hundred."

"Eight hundred sounds better?" Mr. Larney ended on a question mark.

"Eight hundred fifty. Final offer, Mr. Larney."

"It's a bargain."

"Good, I'll put the papers together. How much do you have for a deposit?"

Mr. Larney retrieved a wallet from his jacket's pocket. A used candy bar wrapper—Snickers, Agnes noticed—fell onto the floor. "Twenty dollars."

"That will do for a deposit." Mr. Longacre left them in the music room.

Agnes clapped her hands. "Congratulations, Mr. Larney! You've just bought the best piano in here."

"Yes, I know, dear," he said, his voice distant. His smile had evaporated, and he dropped his eyes to the piano's keys.

Agnes walked over. "What's troubling you?"

"I'm doing calculations, Agnes. Four hundred fifty from my mother's inheritance, Two hundred thirty from my savings. How much is that?"

"Six hundred eighty," Agnes said, like an automaton.

His face fell—his eyes, his cheeks, his mouth, his jawline. "I don't have enough cash. Whatever will Mr. Longacre say now? Let me think, I need to remind myself of something your father told me, Agnes. Every problem has a solution."

Mr. Longacre returned. "In all the excitement, Mr. Larney, I neglected to ask if you had an instrument to trade in."

"I do indeed. A forty-year-old Wurlitzer grand, but the damper pedal needs replacing. How much can you give me for it?"

"Sixty. Drexel's been after me for a used grand. It'll suit their dance studio perfectly. That's seven hundred ninety, Mr. Larney. I'll finish the paperwork."

Mr. Larney's wrinkles emerged, and his forehead creased into canyons. "How much am I short, Agnes? I never could subtract."

"One hundred ten dollars," Agnes said.

Mr. Larney lived in the third-floor apartment at Mrs. O'Toole's house, the same apartment where Granny and Grandpa Limerick had lived sixty years ago. He'd been there more than thirty years, teaching piano lessons on the old Wurlitzer. He could have that magnificent Steinway in its place, the instrument that suited him best, but for one hundred ten lousy dollars.

There would be hell to pay for what she was about to do, but Norman had done nothing but give her headaches and grief during the past month. In the past two hours alone, Mr. Larney had made her laugh and feel like a feather-light girl of sixteen again with just piano music and silly faces.

"You don't have to worry, Mr. Larney," she heard herself saying. This seemed just right. She stifled the thought of how Norman would react. He could turn cartwheels naked on Spruce Street. She didn't care.

"What do you mean? The price is seven hundred ninety. I've only got six hundred eighty. Even I know that's a problem."

"You don't understand," she said, almost singing the words. "I'm going to pay the extra one hundred ten."

He raised an eyebrow. "I wouldn't consider taking a gift from you."

"It's not a gift. I expect you to repay me. Over time."

"That might take a long time to repay."

"You said I hadn't been practicing my scales. I always did best when I had a teacher, Mr. Larney. If I took piano lessons again, I'd practice. And I'd learn the Schubert B flat sonata. Would you do that for an old lady like me?"

He flashed a broad smile. "An old lady? You're as young as the flowers of spring. But I think I'm beginning to understand."

"Look at the money as an advance. I think that's about a year of lessons?"

"For you, Agnes Limerick, it pays for a lifetime of lessons."

Her heart jumped. She'd always be Agnes Limerick to Mr. Larney. No matter what Norman did or said, no matter how long Mama and Uncle Collin kept their distance, she could depend on him — and music — to lift her spirits.

"It's a deal," she said. "Let's sign the papers before Norman throws a fit."

Mr. Longacre came back with a stack of papers and, after explaining the business of selling the new piano and buying the Wurlitzer, handed them over to Mr. Larney to sign, which he did—with his left hand. In all these years, Agnes never had known he was left-handed.

17

Later that afternoon, Agnes learned Mr. Larney had no plans for Thanksgiving. "Yes, you positively, absolutely, certainly, definitively, most assuredly must come for Thanksgiving."

She told her family she had a surprise for Thanksgiving, and *voilá*, Mr. Larney showed up with a smile and a red parka that snowy Thursday. He delighted Harold with his polka-dotted bow tie and by building a three-story house from Lincoln logs on the parlor floor. Agnes laughed, but Norman sat stone-faced in the presence of Mr. Larney's giggly tenor. Cornelius and Victoria proffered formal courtesy, arched brows, and good grammar.

At dinner, Norman seemed to lighten up a bit, unclenching his jaws and even letting a small laugh escape when Mr. Larney broke from his conversation with Harold to profess thanks that the presidential election was over. "God knows what 1941 will bring, so let's hope we all make it through the next four years in one piece." After dinner, they had a concert in the music room.

"I remember this piano at Mrs. Limerick's wake," Mr. Larney said over a medley of Gershwin songs. Harold sat next to him on the bench, as still as one of Victoria's figurines, his eyes fixed on the piano. He was a good boy and didn't bang on the keys, as Agnes had worried.

Granny's wake, a yearning pull at her heart. She still hadn't gone to clear the air with Uncle Collin. But she would before Christmas ...

"Agnes, some Beethoven," Mr. Larney said, finishing up "I Got Rhythm." She gave them a quiet rendition of the *Moonlight Sonata*, easy enough to get by Mr. Larney's twitching nose. "Excellent, my dear. You'll perform even better after a year of weekly lessons and daily scales."

"This is news," Norman said, a clip in his voice.

What if Mr. Larney mentioned the money? Agnes hadn't breathed a word about it, and though she still detested the sight of Norman, she didn't want to lose the advantage she enjoyed over him—making food decisions, playing the piano when he worked upstairs, where they took the children to play.

"It's the least I can do for Agnes—"

"Enough of that, Mr. Larney," she said. "Shall we go to the dining room? I made a pumpkin pie for dessert."

The children made a beeline for the table, followed closely by Cornelius and Victoria. "Norman, you help me with dessert. Mr. Larney, would you join the rest in the dining room?"

Norman cross-examined her in the kitchen about the piano lessons, trying his best to recreate the scene at Longacre's and what had led to the proposition. Had Mr. Larney persuaded her, or had she volunteered? She answered him in a short staccato that it'd been her idea, at which point he threw up his arms and went back to the dining room.

Thanksgiving passed into Christmas, and Christmas passed into 1941 with Agnes becoming stronger every day on the keyboard, more settled about her life, more eager to wake up and make breakfast early, just so she could sit at the piano the very minute Norman left for work. More happy, she had to admit, than at any time since Mama had left Philadelphia, but for the nagging torment that she still hadn't gone to see Uncle Collin. Every week, she promised herself she'd walk over to St. Patrick's, but at the end of each week, she still hadn't done it. She'd do it in January, she told herself, but when she didn't, she decided on February ... and she still hadn't set foot on the marble floors of St. Patrick's when summer arrived. What had seemed an urgent need in the winter had shrunk to a distant whimsy.

By the end of summer, she could feel the piano bending to her will. She practiced forty-five minutes of scales, arpeggios, and drills every day. At last, she returned to the level she'd been when Mama ended her piano lessons, as if the thirteen years since had passed in a single day.

In September, Mr. Larney proposed she take her music to the next level and compete in the Pennsylvania Piano Competition. She would have until the end of January to prepare.

"I'll tell you the hard truth," he said after one Thursday's lesson. "You have to know what you're up against. Professionals who practice six to eight hours every day. Thirteen-year-old prodigies. Harsh judges who'll criticize everything you do. You'll be practicing the same five seconds of music hours at a time until you get it right. Even with all that practice, your nerves might turn your fingers into jelly in the performance.

"But despite all this work," he said, breathless, "there's no better way to improve your technique and your musicianship—and to discover the true potential of your talent. Are you prepared for this kind of work?"

With the possible exception of her darling chipmunks, nothing compared to the joy she felt when she sat at the piano—Mozart's agility, Beethoven's power, Brahms's fantasies, Chopin's nocturnes. "Yes, Mr. Larney, I am prepared."

They chose music for the competition that showcased her skills, including her favorite, Beethoven's *Les Adieux* sonata, plus Mozart's A-major sonata with its famous Turkish march. But those pieces were ten minutes short of the required forty-five minutes. They settled on a new one, Chopin's *Fantasie* in F minor. Long ago, she'd heard Mr. Larney perform this panorama of longing in his recital at the Academy of Music. She'd fallen in love with it but never studied it. Now, Mr. Larney agreed to the *Fantasie* on the strength of Agnes's familiarity with Chopin's ballades.

They decided to start the program with Mozart. Its lyrical first movement of variations started with a serene theme everyone knew. Norman generally ignored what she practiced, but even he ended up whistling the melody around the house. Mr. Larney had told her she had to start with something easy, though Mozart was never simple. The first movement would give Agnes an opportunity to warm up her fingers and calm her nerves.

Mr. Larney hesitated about following the Mozart with the Chopin *Fantasie* because it created minefields if Agnes's nerves took over. Two sequences of four arpeggios in octaves, especially, could detonate a bomb. The left and right hands moved away from the keyboard's middle in opposite directions at a ferocious tempo. The arpeggios would require hours of practice. Even if she mastered them in the privacy of her music room, Agnes might get nervous and hit the wrong notes in front of guests at practice recitals or for him.

Agnes shook her head. "I've wanted to do this piece ever since I heard you at the Academy. I'll master those arpeggios if it's the last thing I do."

Les Adieux would be her reward for mastering the Chopin. The sad theme of lovers saying good-bye suited her. She wanted to believe Beethoven's lovers reunited at the end, even though the same unhappy three-note *mi, re, do* sequence told a different story all the way through the sonata.

But Norman hated this Beethoven sonata. One Sunday afternoon in October, he shouted to her from the hallway, "Agnes, stifle that awhile. My head's about to split open."

"I'm almost finished. Two more pages."

"Now, Agnes. You've been practicing two—"

The phone rang. "—hours. Be quiet while I answer that."

She stopped and heard Norman's footsteps retreat to the kitchen. She hadn't told him about the competition, but she hadn't told him much of anything in eleven months of piano lessons. They had less and less to say to one another these days. She knew nothing about his job, what projects he worked on, with whom he ate lunch. All they talked about were Grace and Harold's latest activities and fascinations, usually after they'd gone upstairs for bed. And when they had sex, Agnes found herself staring at swirl patterns on the ceiling, trying not to tap out piano music on Norman's back while he squirmed on top of her, doing the same things he'd been doing since '32. But at least, they did still do it—

"My God, no!" Norman's anguished shout interrupted her thoughts. She ran out to him.

She found him sitting on the kitchen floor. He looked up, his eyes blazing and face crimson, and chomped out the words. "My father ... massive stroke ... thirty minutes ago ... gone."

Three days later, six compatriots from the Spanish-American War in full military garb served as pallbearers at Cornelius's funeral. Father Thomas eulogized Cornelius in a communion Mass at St. Mark's. After a long procession to Villanova in teeming rain, they buried him in the Balmoral plot. The gusty rainstorm soaked their black suits and dresses.

Since Cornelius's death, Agnes had caught Norman crying alone in the bedroom, bathroom, or kitchen. And then he'd conceal his grief. "Balmoral men don't cry and we don't show our grief in public," he told her. She had a hard time evincing grief for her father-in-law. He'd been kind to her and the children through the years, and she'd liked him. But she couldn't recall having had a deep conversation with him in nine years, with the possible exception of his battle tales from the Spanish-American War. But she did console Norman with as many hugs, kisses, and kind words as she could muster, for she knew, better than anyone, what it meant to lose a father.

"I'm glad Victoria decided to have the casket closed," Agnes said when she walked into their bedroom the evening of the funeral after playing the piano for a half hour. Norman was getting ready for bed. She opened the closet to get undressed and put on her white-and-blue nightgown, Norman's favorite.

"You never listen to me, Agnes, and this proves it. I told you two days ago, we don't believe in open coffins. Death is a mystery between the soul and God. From the moment of death, the body belongs to God. My father didn't want anyone to see his body after death. Mother saw him, but only at the hospital right after the stroke."

Norman's words made Agnes's stomach grumble. She remembered Uncle Collin saying much the same after Uncle Daniel died in '30, but with a different conclusion — that viewings were an opportunity to attain a state of grace, though Agnes, who struggled not to gag at the sight of a corpse, had never agreed. A year had passed since she'd resolved to see Uncle Collin, yet nothing had come of it. Perhaps she'd reconnect with Mama first . . .

"I'm glad, really. I'd rather remember him alive. To this day, I can still remember what Daddy and Granny looked like lying in their coffins. I wish I didn't have those memories."

"I do wish you'd pay attention when I'm speaking to you. Lately, all that interests you is that damned piano, even right after my father's funeral. Your piano this, Mr. Larney that. If you showered us with even a fraction of the attention you gave to music, our lives would be far better."

Perhaps one day she might go on strike, and he'd finally see how much she did for him, with or without practicing the piano. But not yet, not until Grace and Harold were in school . . .

"What are you talking about? I haven't let anything slip. Grace and Harold are happier now than they've been in years. Have you noticed how well Grace is doing with her own piano lessons?"

Norman looked at the ceiling and shook his head, his mouth a downward crescent. "But things have changed. You have to give up your lessons for the time being. Mother will need your help with settling affairs at the store. Between the house, the children, and that, you won't have time for Mr. Larney."

"But I thought you never wanted me to work at the store." The irony soured her mood. She'd practically begged him years ago for something to do at the store, and he'd refused. She swallowed her urge to snap at him.

"May I repeat myself, darling," he said, climbing into his side of the bed. "Life has changed."

"Don't you worry, Norman Balmoral. I'll help your mother as much as she needs. It's hardly necessary that I give up piano lessons. Mr. Larney has been working so diligently with me this past year."

"Mr. Larney can live with a little disappointment. It should be enough that Grace is now his pupil."

She slipped into her side of the bed but stayed far away from him and turned her head away. They might've buried his father that day, but he didn't have the right to squash her dreams.

"All right, Agnes, if this means so much to you. As long as it doesn't interfere with your responsibilities at home. That includes me, my mother, and most of all, Grace and Harold. I don't approve of my wife letting anything interfere with her obligations to the family."

What a hypocrite! If they hadn't buried Cornelius that day, she'd have reminded him about Mary Alden and his disregard for obligations to the family. It boiled her blood—and he dared lecture her on obligations?

"No need to make a fuss, Norman. I'm going to be a great pianist." She pulled the covers up to her chin. "Let's get to sleep. It's been an exhausting day."

In the next month, Agnes juggled her obligations and her joys. She rushed to get Grace and Harold off to school every morning—Grace in the third grade now and Harold in kindergarten. She picked up after the children and kept the house clean. She washed, dried, folded, and ironed the laundry. She went to the market, washed breakfast plates, prepared dinner every afternoon, making sure she served it fifteen minutes after Norman arrived home. She kept her social schedule with the Rittenhouse Society, the Episcopal Women's Bridge Club, and kept track of invitations and thank-you notes.

As it turned out, Victoria didn't need Agnes's help. She bounced back like a jack-in-the-box. One week after Cornelius's funeral, she returned to the store and announced to Mr. Soltham and the employees that she'd manage the place herself. Within two weeks, she'd completed an inventory, spoken with the store's suppliers, reorganized the stock room, and reviewed the monthly ledger.

So Agnes attended to her own household chores, to Grace and Harold, and tiptoed around Norman's persnickety demands. *Could we have this for dinner, darling, and please dust the cobwebs on the chandelier.* And she practiced the piano three to four hours daily, so long as Norman didn't catch wind of it.

When Norman thought she was attending bridge club in Mrs. Collingwood's salon, she was working on the *Fantasie's* arpeggios. When he thought she was walking around Rittenhouse Square with society ladies, she was busy clarifying nuances of expression in the slow middle movement of *Les Adieux*. When Norman thought she was helping Victoria with the store, she was laboring over the racing tempo of Mozart's "Turkish March."

One weekday afternoon in November, Agnes fell off the piano bench when Victoria walked into the music room unannounced. She must've let herself in with her own key. Victoria laughed.

"Why the guilty expression? I'm not here to punish you," Victoria said.

Agnes clutched the side of the piano, sure that her shaky legs wouldn't hold her up. "You surprised me, that's all."

"I've been standing here five minutes. You were off in another world playing that beautiful music. Brahms?"

"Chopin."

"You play the piano, Agnes, like Romeo seduced Juliet," Victoria said, pulling up a chair and sitting next to her in much the same way Mr. Larney did. "You deserve it. We women have to keep our children happy, our houses in order, and our men thinking they rule the world. I know my son wants you helping me at the store, but between Mr. Soltham and me, we've got the place humming. You stay here and make magic with your fingers."

Victoria had gotten rid of the chignon since Cornelius died, and now wore her white hair pulled tight behind her head—less Eleanor Roosevelt, more Greta Garbo. With her gray dresses, white lace collars, and pearls, the new style accentuated her aristocratic lines and articulated her diction.

"It might surprise my son, but I don't need anyone's help. He's treating me like a helpless woman, just like Cornelius did. In forty years of marriage, I said, 'Yes, Cornelius,' and 'No, Cornelius,' but went off and managed the house my way. And the business."

At least Cornelius had paid attention to Victoria. Norman rarely noticed what she was doing unless it collided with his idiosyncrasies—those damned chandelier cobwebs, for example.

Agnes let out a sharp laugh. "It would appear I'm already doing that. Victoria, I'm studying for a music competition at the end of January. Norman wants me to give up piano lessons and spend more time with you, but I haven't even told him I committed to the competition."

"Nonsense. There's no reason you can't do both."

"Exactly my thoughts."

"Don't you worry about Norman. Let's face it, men are vain and fragile. If he thinks he's in charge, he'll be happy. Let him give you advice about managing Grace and Harold and running the house, but do it however you see fit."

Did Agnes really know her mother-in-law? She'd always seemed to defer to her husband's and sons' wishes. Yet, Victoria had managed to survive the worst years of the Depression, keeping her family happy and well fed, the store running when so many others had failed. She'd made it all look so effortless, unlike the torment Agnes endured trying to keep Norman on an even keel.

"You sound as radical as Mrs. Roosevelt."

Victoria laid a hand on Agnes's thigh. "There's nothing Mrs. Roosevelt says that hasn't been God's truth for hundreds of years. Women have to be stronger than men. They have no idea what real strength is. We give birth, after all. Don't ever doubt yourself, Agnes, or any woman who's gone through childbirth."

She recalled these words with waves of affection for Victoria throughout that autumn of 1941, and she whistled her way through household chores instead of groaning. Walking the dog, seeing the children off to school and Norman to work, writing thank-you notes and organizing dinners, hosting Thanksgiving for all the Balmorals, decorating the house for the holidays, buying Christmas gifts, she accomplished all these tasks like a breeze swirling through Rittenhouse Square.

Grace and Harold were thriving at the Friends' School in Germantown. Grace absorbed any book she could get her hands on and read well beyond her nine years. She'd also started to learn German, a language that still perplexed Agnes. But Norman had done well with German in school and practiced with Grace at the dinner table, taunting Agnes with phrases that made no sense at all.

And Harold! Her son had made all sorts of friends at kindergarten, boys and girls alike, and had become the class's good samaritan, just like her father, she thought with pride. One day that November, she had learned from his teacher, Harold saw Sara Tiller looking out the exit door window at children playing in the courtyard and exclaiming, "I have no coat and it's too cold." He didn't mind the cold, he said, so he loaned her his coat.

She secretly blessed her mother-in-law when, on the first Sunday in December, Victoria told Norman at dinner that Agnes had been a great help at the store, even though Agnes hadn't lifted a finger at Balmoral's.

"Norman," she said, her voice as matter-of-fact as if discussing plans for St. Mark's Advent bazaar, "you have no idea how helpful our Agnes has been. I couldn't have survived without her, son. After your father died, I had no idea how to straighten out the books. Cornelius kept money matters to himself, as you well know. When I looked into the books, I was overwhelmed. If it weren't for Agnes and Mr. Soltham, the store would've gone under by now."

"I don't deserve the credit, Victoria," Agnes said. She marveled at her mother-in-law's ability to tell a harmless lie without trembling. "Mr. Soltham is really the one who's helped you the most."

Norman dropped his chin and opened his mouth so far, Agnes could see the back of his throat. "Are we talking about the same Mr. Soltham?"

"He doesn't blow his own horn because he doesn't need to," Victoria said. "Why do you think he's been with us since '24? He's been with us almost eighteen years because he's so reliable."

"He seems so unsure of himself, Mother."

"I would rethink that, Norman. It's not right to judge someone hastily without considering the facts."

Agnes knew her mother-in-law appreciated Mr. Soltham's work, but she didn't entrust him with much in the way of responsibility. And yet, here was Victoria, extolling his virtues for Norman's benefit. If only she were capable of managing Norman like this. She'd always just blurted out her opinions. He'd seemed to like that during their courtship, but since then ...

Nevertheless, she decided to follow Victoria's example, so long as she could.

After dinner, the family adjourned to the parlor. Agnes read fairy tales to Harold, Victoria busied herself with a crossword puzzle, Norman balanced their monthly accounts at the desk in the corner, Grace became immersed in *Little Women*, and the radio played in the corner. But Agnes and Victoria looked at each other, tiny pinpricks in their eyes, when CBS announced that Japanese forces under Emperor Hirohito had attacked Pearl Harbor, killing hundreds of Navy men and crippling the Pacific fleet.

Life became a still photograph — their grandfather clock not ticking, Grace and her book immobile, Keaton's tail flat on the floor, no aroma from Victoria's tea, Harold not pressed up against her hip and no longer eager for her to read. And then the moment crashed when Norman cried out and rushed over to the radio. Agnes's eyes burned, and she felt her teeth against her cheeks, so dry had her mouth become.

The following day, Norman stayed home from work. Friends' cancelled school for Grace and kindergarten for Harold. Victoria closed the store for the day and joined them in the parlor to wait for more news. Late that afternoon, they listened to President Roosevelt address a joint session of Congress and ask for a declaration of war against the Empire of Japan.

Norman had moved the radio to the middle of the room between the two high-backed chairs he and his mother used during cocktail hour. This particular hour, the adults were drinking gin martinis. Agnes sat on the sofa opposite the chairs trying to focus on a game of Parcheesi with the children, nursing her own martini with dread rather than olives. She couldn't help thinking back to '17 when President Wilson had asked Congress to declare war against the German-Austrian alliance. She'd been a little girl, frightened by the ugly pictures in the newspaper, listening to Mama, Daddy, and Uncle Collin talking about war.

"President Roosevelt has my full support," Norman said, surprising Agnes, as he regularly denounced Roosevelt as a Bolshevik. "Thank goodness he was re-elected. Mother, Agnes, you need to put your personal feelings aside and support the president. I expect we will all need to serve the war effort."

Agnes wondered why she'd married a man whose grandstanding made her want to giggle, but she snuffed out the thought.

"Let's have the dust settle and see how Japan responds," Victoria said. "They stand no chance against the United States. This may all blow over."

This made sense to Agnes, but apparently not to Norman.

"I think you're mistaken, Mother. And I'm going to volunteer when the president calls. Dad was in the Navy, and so shall I be."

Agnes looked again at Victoria, hoping her mother-in-law would dissuade Norman. But all she saw in the deepening lines around Victoria's mouth was the worry of a mother whose son might go to war — the same lines, she supposed, forming around her own mouth. As difficult as living with Norman could be, as much as she looked forward to peace and quiet when he worked, she didn't want him ten thousand miles away in the middle of the Pacific Ocean facing enemy fire and God only knew what other mortal dangers.

"You'll be thirty-six in July," Agnes said. "You're too old for active duty."

"If I can't go on active duty, I'll do something else for the Navy. I won't fail my country in its time of need."

Victoria drank down her martini with a quick turn of her wrist. "Prepare us another round of martinis, son, and make mine neat."

18

THEY USHERED IN 1942 WITH RAISED GLASSES toasting America's men in uniform. There was talk of rationing rubber, gasoline, clothing materials, even food. Agnes had no qualms about doing without—she'd managed to survive the Depression—except where piano was concerned. That first Sunday in January while the children played and she lay in bed with Norman after an afternoon siesta, she told him about the competition.

He sat up and glared at her, his forehead rigid and his eyes bulging. "Just when will this competition take place?"

"The last day of January." She felt the rush of Norman's *no* coming. Ironic but typical, right after she'd given him a *yes* only an hour ago. The afterglow seeped out of the bedroom.

"Not possible. That's my boss's sixtieth birthday party, may I remind you, and we must organize it. You can hardly expect me to do the planning, so you'll need to help. Just where is the competition, and how long will it take?"

She didn't understand why he needed her to assist him with his boss's party, but she answered his questions nonetheless. "Bethlehem, at Lehigh

University. Mr. Larney and I will take the train in the morning and return
in the evening."

"No, Agnes, I forbid it." He gulped down a glass of water on his nightstand. "And don't pout. You look like a guinea pig."

She'd pout if she felt like it. Norman had opened the window, and the
room was freezing. Agnes put on her robe, sat by the fireplace, and stoked
the logs.

"I'm not a servant, Norman. You can't expect me to obey orders."

"Be reasonable, Agnes. Let's talk about this like adults. Think of your
family and your children. I need you to oversee arranging the birthday party."

"You prepare the dinner. What's your boss ever done for me? He barely
knows my name."

He walked over to her, naked and flopping around. "It's not my job to
cook meals, it's yours."

If only Norman's body, still alluring after a decade, were occupied by a
less obnoxious man. "Put something on, Norman. It's January. I cook your
meals, I clean the house, I do your laundry, I do the shopping, I take care of
the children—all so you can go to work and do nothing but design stupid
buildings no one likes."

"If I didn't go to work, Agnes, we'd have no roof over our heads."

She fumed. He would never acknowledge Granny's bequest. "I bought
this house with my own—"

"We'll talk about this another time. For now, no piano competition." He
turned and headed to the closet. She noticed his rear end was starting to sag.
He dressed while she smirked. What would Norman look like when he was
forty-five? She'd enjoy it when he began to wrinkle around the edges of his
eyes and get misshapen brown spots in odd places. Then perhaps his ego
would come down to Earth.

Done dressing, Norman headed for the door but stopped. He turned his
head slowly back to her. "Is this why you've been playing the same hideous
music for three months?"

"Of course not. I only found out—" He slammed the door on his way out.
Moments later, she heard the front door bang. She looked out the window
and saw him stomping down the block, head down and hands in his coat

pockets. A few hours later while practicing the Chopin *Fantasie*, she heard him come back and march up the stairs to his third-floor studio.

For dinner, she made a meatless macaroni and cheese to serve with a green salad. Agnes wanted to be among the first to ration. "Dinner is ready!" she yelled up the stairs. Grace and Harold came running, but not Norman. She climbed the stairs up to the third floor and knocked on his door.

"I heard you," he said without opening the door. "I'll be there in a minute."

Agnes and the children were halfway through their meal when Norman wobbled into the dining room, dragging along the odor of gin. His eyes were bloodshot, and he swayed like a pendulum.

"How lovely of you to prepare dinner. Macaroni and cheese, my favorite."

Even drunk, he managed to cut her down. Grace and Harold never had seen either of them drunk, so she didn't want to fan Norman's flame by taking the bait. "Take a seat, Norman, and eat your dinner. It's getting cold."

When he sat down and took his napkin, his hand brushed his water goblet, and it fell over. Water spilled onto Harold's dinner plate and into his lap. Their son let out a little scream, his eyes melted, his chin started to tremble, and his cheeks turned red. The boy's four-year-old floodgates opened.

"Water cold, Daddy, water cold!" Harold exclaimed between cries, turning his head from one parent to the other. "Mama, he ruined my macaroni."

"It's all right, sweetheart," Agnes said, casting Norman a glance she hoped carried daggers. But, no argument in front of the children. "I'll give you my serving."

Norman shot her a curved frown and mumbled to Harold, "My mistake, son."

After dinner, he managed to navigate his way up to bed. He was snoring when she joined him two hours later. Uncle Collin frequently had overdrunk, but she'd never seen him teeter on his feet, nor heard him snore like a saw on rotten plywood.

The next evening, Norman walked into the kitchen after work cold as stone. He informed her that, oddly enough, his boss had rescheduled the party to the following weekend.

"I don't know what witch's spell you cast to make that happen, but you still don't have my leave to go to Bethlehem."

She turned to look at him and opened her mouth to speak, but he raised his hand. "You clearly deceived me. All this time after my father died, after Halloween, all through Thanksgiving, Pearl Harbor, and Christmas. Every time we sat down to dinner, every time we made love, you lied to me. You and your Mr. Larney."

Was he jealous of Mr. Larney? She went back to stirring the tomato sauce — spaghetti for dinner, their usual on Mondays. Harold called it *pisketti*, but it was really Cristina's recipe — linguini in marinara.

"I didn't deceive you. This opportunity came to me … just after Pearl Harbor. I didn't mention it because we had the holidays."

"There are a lot more important things than your cute little hobby."

She sharpened her green eyes. "Music is the thing I love best in this world. How dare you belittle it."

"Why not? You did the same thing about architecture yesterday, and that's the most important thing in my life."

"I don't recall that."

"You said I designed stupid buildings no one liked. How soon we forget."

Good Lord, he was right. Melting waves of guilt flooded her heart and then her mind. Norman deserved better. "Just a moment," she said as he turned to leave the room. "Let's discuss this like grown-ups. I think we should both apologize."

"What have I to apologize for?" The lines in his forehead reminded Agnes of the cinnamon danish she prepared for Christmas breakfast every year. So, yes, he was aging. Good.

"Yesterday I dismissed your career as stupid. I'm sorry about that. Today you belittled my work on the piano. Apologizing is the right thing to do."

"You can hardly compare your keyboard tinkering with my profession. I spent five years of my life earning a degree. You're a housewife who's dabbled in piano lessons with a poof teacher."

How could she respond to his piggishness? In their early days, he had applauded Jews and negroes for working hard, encouraged her to break free from Uncle Collin's iron hand, and admired Gracie Honeywalker for running a farm. Now he acted like a constipated patriarch. She'd have thought they lived in the Middle Ages rather than 1942. Even though she had no idea how he'd changed, she wanted to smack him.

Agnes thought about her own parents, Victoria and Cornelius, Granny and Grandpa. Had they fought similar arguments? Did they play furtive tricks on each other? When she displayed knickknacks and books on the shelves, she always found them rearranged the next day. When Norman opened the windows, she closed them, only to find them reopened at bedtime. When Norman sorted the closets and turned hanging clothes to face left, she reversed them to face right. And so on ... for years.

She couldn't imagine her elders facing similar challenges. What might life be like if something took Norman away? What if he died young, like Daddy? She certainly wouldn't bury her grief in blacks and grays like Mama had—but no, she didn't want Grace and Harold to grow up without their father. They deserved more.

"This is where you cross the line, Norman. I'm entitled to my dreams just the same as you. Whether you like it or not, music is my dream. What kind of example would I set for Grace and Harold if I gave up on my dreams?"

Norman sat down. She resumed stirring the sauce. "You're making a mountain out of a molehill," he said. "How can a silly piano competition have anything to do with dreams?"

"I love music, Norman," she said, sensing his resistance wearing thin. "Better than anything except our family. I can't be a good wife and mother unless I'm doing something that makes me happy. I might add, Grace and Harold are happier too since I've started playing again."

He paused while silence filled the room, the hard lines of his mouth softening into the hint of a smile betrayed only by his dimple. "They do seem to be doing rather well."

"It's more than that. Look at Harold giving his coat to Sara Tiller so she'd be warm during recess."

"Who's Sara Tiller, and what's she got to do with your dreams?"

"Our five-year-old is a little gentleman. He wouldn't be that way if we weren't raising him to believe in his dreams. Let me have my own."

"All right," Norman said after a stern minute. "I'll consider it, but I warn you, I've made no decision. I don't like you disobeying me. A man deserves loyalty from his wife, but I do see how much this means to you."

She opened her mouth to speak, but he raised his hand. "End of discussion. I'll call the children down for dinner."

Agnes wondered whether they'd discuss it again. The competition was three weeks away. During that time, she continued practicing, performing the program for friends, to rousing applause from Cristina and even Mrs. Collingwood—but never Norman—until nine days before the competition when Mr. Larney declared she was ready. Norman didn't raise the topic once, but he grew ominously silent during the final week—and absent. Every day, he left for work early and returned late.

That Saturday morning, she woke up early, resolved to go, no matter what. Let Norman be damned. She banished the thought of the temper tantrum she'd come home to at the end of the day. Who cared what he thought?

Norman was sleeping (or pretending to sleep) when Victoria arrived to take Grace and Harold for the day. A light snow was falling, so Agnes departed for Reading Terminal in her Loden coat and matching hat, only to be greeted at the station by a cackle of laughter from Mr. Larney, who also wore a coat and hat in Loden green. Practically twins, he said.

"I've been to this competition oodles of times," he said after the train reached Bethlehem and they made their way through the snow to Grace Hall at Lehigh. "But this is the most exciting of all because it's your first, and I suppose because you've been around the longest. How long is it? Twenty years?"

"Twenty-five years, eight months. I started lessons on my sixth birthday." It seemed like yesterday.

"When we arrive, you'll register in the lobby. There will be half a dozen small music rooms with pianos for warming up your hands. Play a few scales and arpeggios, some light music, but do not play any part of your program. You have to think this will be the easiest thing in the world to do, like walking in Philadelphia neighborhoods. Just relax. You know the music inside and out," Mr. Larney said, his cheeks pink from the cold, but his voice warming Agnes with its tenor vibrato, the same tone that had calmed Agnes's nerves before her childhood recitals.

She registered, and they gave her the number nine—a good sign, the day of her birthday in May. She walked down to the basement to practice and saw two of her competitors through door windows. Both were teenagers wearing thick glasses, not a middle-aged housewife with children and a belligerent husband.

She practiced for two hours as Mr. Larney had urged. Finally, an escort called. Butterflies rose in her stomach and tormented her when Agnes entered the hall and pictured herself facing the judges and daring to approach the piano. With gold moldings surrounding the stage, red-velvet carpeting down the aisles, hundreds of matching chairs, and marble floors, she felt like she'd entered the Palace of Versailles. A nine-foot grand in Louis XIV mahogany trim stood at center stage.

Only thirty or forty people sat in the cavernous hall — Mr. Larney included, thank God, alone in the back. She approached the piano and took note of the three judges in the front row, each with a notebook. The man closest to the aisle rose. He looked like Santa Claus but with spectacles and a black suit.

"Good afternoon, Miss Balmoral," he said in the voice of a choir's lead bass.

"Mrs. Balmoral." Her spirits fell. Off to a bad start.

"Indeed. We don't usually have married ladies. Welcome to our competition. We would like to hear you start with the Mozart. Ladies and gentlemen, Mrs. Balmoral, a student of Mr. Brian Larney in Philadelphia."

The audience clapped. She curtsied and sighed in relief. The butterflies in her stomach began to settle. Mozart would be easy.

But something was wrong. Her fingers felt weak, even arthritic. Settle down, this was the easiest segment. It was difficult knowing all eyes in the audience were boring in, eager for even the slightest mistake. So she cast the audience out of her mind, and allowed the beauty of the Mozart in, first to her heart and then to her head. By the time the segment ended, the smooth legato had returned to her fingers, and she could feel her body breathing in the music's flowing rhythm.

When she finished, the judge stood, but no one applauded. "Thank you very much," he said. "Play the Chopin *Fantasie* from the beginning, but only up to the first march."

Five minutes of music. She began and felt a sense of calm descend. This Steinway had deep tones even richer than Granny's. The slow introduction yielded to the romantic allegro that kept building in power. She had mastered the music—it was hers to give the audience. She could feel the suspense growing inside her as she approached the climax—those four massive broken arpeggios. Her hands would be moving across the piano in opposite directions. She felt those arpeggios marching on like a military guard on a wartime mission.

She played the first two arpeggios perfectly. Oh, how she wished her family were here to witness this. Norman finally would understand what this meant to her. Mama and Uncle Collin, they'd be proud. And Daddy, if only—

She missed a few octaves in the middle of the third arpeggio but ended on the right notes. And then she missed the ending notes in the fourth. Damn Norman, why did he have to sabotage her at the worst possible moment, even when he was nowhere in sight?

She tried to forget about that final thud but knew it was over as she limped toward the end and felt sharp pains prick at her chest. She'd have to put on her best face, smile when the audience clapped (if they did), and accept their hollow compliments with good grace. But every compliment would be tinged with embarrassment.

She stopped at the march and rose from the bench. The Santa Claus judge said, "Thank you again, Mrs. Balmoral. One more, please. Would you play the first movement of *Les Adieux*?"

She played the Beethoven well but knew that when the judge's letter arrived in the mail next week, she would've lost. She'd also sacrificed peace with Norman, only to lose here as well, just as she'd sacrificed Mama and Uncle Collin to be with Norman. A triple loss.

When she finished, fifteen minutes had elapsed on stage, fifteen minutes for which she'd spent countless hours practicing. She curtsied to purse-lipped applause. Mr. Larney beamed a pink-faced smile at her.

Those damned arpeggios. Why did Chopin have to make the piece so impossible? The *Fantasie* was supposed to have been a dream, not a nightmare. She said as much to Mr. Larney after they boarded the train to Philadelphia.

"Don't place too much emphasis on the technical glitches. You mastered the music like a lion tamer. No one cared about your mistakes. Being a perfectionist just isn't in your nature. When you play, you care more about the heart of the music than whether it's perfect. For an artist, that gives you a great advantage."

"But Mr. Larney, you always insist on perfection in our lessons."

"Yes, but never in a live performance. I insist on perfection so that your technique is solid. That's merely the basis. Do you think anyone wants to listen to a trained monkey on the keyboard? No, they want someone like you, someone who isn't even aware she's pouring her heart into the music."

"Have I always been like that?" Perhaps she had been, and no one but Mr. Larney had grasped it. He sat up in his seat, his arms folded across his chest, his heavy Loden coat making him seem larger, more authoritative.

"No, but you're older now. Whatever's happened in your life has made you stronger and wiser. I had to ask myself when I heard the opening bars of *Les Adieux*, when did Agnes make a sad good-bye in her young life? Then when I heard the chorus, I knew you'd overcome that loss."

The last of winter's light receded as the train made its way south that late afternoon. It reminded her of a train ride with her parents at the end of a day's visit to Princeton when she was perhaps five. She'd sat on Daddy's lap.

"I suppose you're right. I have been unaware of it," she finally said, her voice so quiet, he asked her to repeat it.

She reached her house two hours later and opened the door. Darkness greeted her — no children, no Keaton, nothing. She turned on the lights, ran up the stairs and back down to the kitchen. A note lay on the table for her.

I had hoped that you would come to your senses about this unpleasant business, but I see that I am to be disappointed. I've taken the dog and joined the children at Mother's. We hope to see you there tomorrow for breakfast.

She sat at the table, a strangling sensation forming in her throat. She remembered Mr. Larney's last words and walked into the music room to "pour her heart out." She gave a flawless performance of the *Fantasie* for no one but herself.

No telephone call congratulating her on making the final round came, but a letter did arrive six days later. It contained her musical program with handwritten remarks, probably from the Santa Claus judge. "Your technique is masterful, and will only improve with time," the scripted hand read. "Your performance lacked sufficient depth in the Chopin, but the Beethoven proved your potential. We look forward to hearing from you again."

"What of it," Cristina said the next afternoon when Agnes took Grace and Harold over to play with Cristina's boys. Agnes unburdened her disappointment on Cristina. They sat in the kitchen sharing a bottle of chianti and opera music on the radio while Cristina roasted a chicken in the oven and the children played upstairs. Several toys crashed on the upstairs hardwood floor, and the noise carried as if through a tunnel in the Rosamilias' Queen Village row house, where they'd moved after Angelo's plumbing business took off.

Cristina marched to the foot of the staircase and bellowed up, "Pipe down, we're trying to hear ourselves think!" She scowled and came back to Agnes. "Look on the bright side. The letter encouraged you to return."

"Norman's acting like a hornet disturbed from its nest."

"He should be proud, you doing something with your life other than cooking and cleaning. If he could think of anyone besides himself, he might get along better in life. As it is—"

"I wish I could work in a library like you, Cristina. How do you manage your boys and work at the same time?"

Agnes began to think of what she'd do next. Another competition? No, not for at least a year. A job? Norman would never permit it.

"Their grandmothers. When the boys aren't in school, the two of them bicker over who gets to babysit. Angelo's mother is a militant disciplinarian—she slaps those boys when they get out of line. But they walk all over my mother."

A loud bang upstairs jolted them out of their skin.

"Knock it off up there," Cristina yelled. "Those children are driving me crazy with that game of Sardines. With the heat in this kitchen and this heavy sweater, I can barely breathe, let alone hear."

"Cristina, they're just enjoying themselves. No harm's been done."

"I'm with Angelo's mother on this. You have to keep them in line, or they run all over you. It's the only point where I agree with the Germans. Discipline. My boys can use all they get. Angelo's just their playmate, so the job falls to me."

"That's a problem I don't have with Norman. Sometimes I wonder how much Grace and Harold play with him. He's all discipline, order, and exercise. You should see him, still as wound up as the day I met him. Just as thin, too."

Cristina took the roasted chicken out of the oven and placed it on the counter to rest. "I can only imagine. Angelo's put ten pounds on his stomach since we got married."

Cristina's chicken smelled delectable. Agnes looked at the bird covered with rosemary, garlic, and olive oil. No wonder Angelo had gained weight. She gulped down the last of her glass and refilled it with more Chianti.

"Norman tells them, 'there's a place for everything, and everything in its place.' And my personal favorite, 'children are meant to be seen and not heard.'"

Cristina dropped her lantern jaw and groaned. "Nothing but clichés and platitudes. What a dictator! Does he still turn off the heat at night and open the windows, like you've told me?"

"It's February, and the children and I freeze to death at night. At least he leaves the fire going in our bedroom and in the nursery. 'I'm paying the gas bill, Agnes, I get to turn the heat on and off.' When I complain about the cold nights, he says, 'Discipline, Agnes, discipline.'"

Cristina rolled her eyes. "What about 'Dying, Agnes, dying?'"

"He's threatening to run off to Europe. Pearl Harbor has convinced him that he's essential to the war effort. He doesn't feel all that strongly about the Japanese, but he wants to crush the Nazis."

"Whacky as ever. Men, how do we live with them? Angelo wants to hide in the basement whenever I ask him if he's going to join up."

Agnes giggled but supposed she'd rather have a coward than a fool for a husband. "Can we trade? You get Norman and I get Angelo."

"Not in a million years. I would claw Norman Balmoral's eyes out in fifteen minutes. But that Mr. Larney of yours, he's a ball of fire—"

"Be serious, Cristina. Mr. Larney isn't that sort of man—"

"Perhaps because he's a homosexual."

"Shh, don't say that."

She hated the word, so dirty and ugly. What it described didn't bother Agnes, despite what Uncle Collin and the nuns of St. Patrick's had lectured. When she considered Mr. Larney, she could only think that his innocence and creativity led him down a different path—something beautiful. The fact was, Agnes had never known anyone quite so alive. She couldn't grasp what he felt when he was with a man, perhaps something like she felt with Norman. But his freedom and independence added to his charm.

"Your Mr. Larney would be a lot more fun than Norman to live with. What a charmer he is, those plaid jackets and bow ties. He can wear color even at fifty."

Agnes did the arithmetic in her head. "He's fifty-eight."

"He doesn't look a day over forty-five."

A wave of affection swept over Agnes. "Norman doesn't like it, but I think Mr. Larney's a wonderful influence on my children. Imagine if you'd grown up with someone who liberated you from all the rules the nuns drilled into us—"

"Speak for yourself. I ignored most of the rules," Cristina said, laughing from her throat and talking from the right side of her mouth. "Like the one about skirt length—"

"Grace has been flourishing since she started taking piano lessons. Better grades, more friends, eating and sleeping better."

"Send Mr. Larney over here to do something about my little hellions." A heavy object hit the floor above them. Cristina left the room, and Agnes heard her voice through the floors, followed by an "ouch" and crying boys.

She came back, shaking her head. "A stiff dose of discipline. See how it works with my boys? And speaking of naughty boys, how's Norman behaved since the piano competition?"

"Cold as fish, but civil. He's been very quiet, and I haven't wanted to upset the applecart," Agnes said. "Victoria advises me to ignore his moods and go my own merry way, but I've always found that difficult to do."

Cristina laughed. "She's become a modern woman just like Mrs. Roosevelt."

"Somehow I don't see Victoria Balmoral going down into a coal mine, writing a newspaper column, and zooming around the country like an electron."

The children came running down the stairs and fell into a rambunctious pile in the foyer, laughing at the game's messy conclusion.

"Three strikes," Cristina said, crouching to the position of umpire. "You're out."

"That's my cue to make an exit. Thank you for the talk," Agnes said, standing and finishing off her wine. "It's dinnertime for the children. And Norman."

Agnes and the children trudged back home in a flurry of snow. When they turned the corner onto Spruce Street, she saw the third floor lights were on. Norman would be upstairs working in his studio. Her heart melted. Why did they always seem to be at cross purposes? Surely they could find a way to breach their differences.

She picked up a pile of mail from the postal box, and the children ran up to their rooms. After throwing the mail down on the foyer table, she went into the kitchen to put a roast in the oven. She walked back to the hallway and looked up the stairs. She decided to talk to Norman then, rather than in front of the children at dinner.

Norman sat with his back to her when she knocked and entered. She placed her hands on his shoulders, unsure of how he'd respond. When he didn't push them off, she kissed the right side of his head.

"Can't you see I'm working on these blueprints?" he said.

She was determined to break through his steel wall. "I suggest we change our plans. I'm sure Victoria wouldn't mind keeping Grace and Harold overnight. I've already put a roast in the oven. It'll be ready in ninety minutes. It's probably the last filet we'll have in a while. We'll be rationing soon. And I think you and I would benefit from an evening alone."

He patted her hand and spoke in a soft voice. "If you leave me to my drawings, I'll agree to it."

As she expected, Victoria jumped at the opportunity to host the children overnight and fetched them an hour later. In the kitchen, Agnes hummed the Puccini "Che Gelida" she'd heard that afternoon at Cristina's. She made a Waldorf salad and simmered asparagus on top of the stove. Then she reduced the asparagus to low heat and went upstairs to change into a plaid frock, a dress she remembered Norman remarking on.

Coming back downstairs, Agnes passed Keaton in the foyer and saw the pile of mail. "Heavens, I didn't even open the mail," she said to her dog.

In the kitchen, a letter fell from the bottom of the pile. Agnes leaned down to pick it up. It was addressed to Norman from the U.S. Navy. A shudder of dread ran down her spine. Without a second's thought, she opened it.

> *February 2, 1942. Washington, DC.*
>
> *We received your application dated January 12, 1942, to volunteer for active duty with the U.S. Navy. Based on your age, your request is denied.*
>
> *We reviewed your qualifications, however, and wish to consider you for the position of Architect in Naval Construction Services, to be based in England. Please report to your regional office at 1215 Washington Avenue, Philadelphia, PA, on Wednesday, March 4, 1942, for a physical examination and interview.*
>
> *Please confirm both receipt of this letter and your appointment.*

Agnes dropped the letter onto the table and plopped into a chair. She became utterly unaware of her surroundings, not even the roast and sizzling asparagus. She stared through the void of the kitchen windows into February's darkness.

"This is how it ends," she said aloud, seeing the abyss she'd dreaded for so long. Norman intended to leave her. Did he also want a divorce? Was this his way of punishing her for the competition? How would she manage expenses with him abroad? When had he planned to tell her about this? What about Grace and Harold? The chipmunks had been so happy even though the world was falling apart. Their father leaving would devastate them.

February was turning into a dead month. Drained of energy, she laid her head in her hands and cried weak tears.

And then Norman rushed into the kitchen. "Agnes, our dinner!"

He grabbed the oven mitts, snatched the roast out of the oven, and extinguished the flame under the asparagus. He glared from the eyes downward, and his mouth quivered.

"You idiot, look what you've done! You've ruined our meal."

Her tears tasted like vinegar. She raised the letter in her hand. "When were you planning on telling me about this?"

He sat down opposite her and read the letter, his expression reminding Agnes of the lawyer who had read Granny's will—all business and no warmth, like someone who only cared about signing a contract. *On the dotted line, please. Then leave me alone.*

"In due course," he answered. Agnes knew him well enough. He had no intention of apologizing for his deceit. And he had no plan to comfort her. Her face hardened, and her tears dried up.

Agnes's gaze matched his exactly, like two duelers staring each other down. "You volunteered for the war without discussing it with me. You can't keep that information from me, Norman. It isn't right. Abandonment is grounds for divorce in Pennsylvania."

He sighed like a horse. "When you went to that piano competition against my wishes, you're the one who abandoned our marriage. So I decided to do what I wanted. If you're unhappy about that, you have no one to blame but yourself."

She had deceived him about the piano competition, she had to admit. But did that entitle him to treat her this badly?

Norman revolted her. He'd lied to her about his past with Mary Alden. He'd alienated her from her family. He treated her needs with reckless abandon, he belittled her accomplishments, and he hated her friends. She'd sold herself to the Faustian devil, and for what? A love affair with a handsome dictator.

She felt like the revolutionaries of '76 when they sat down only a mile from here and drafted their complaints against George III. She needed to write her own declaration of independence from the tyranny of Norman.

"How can you equate my one-day piano competition with your leaving home and crossing the ocean to fight in England for who knows how long?" she asked, underlining her words. "I didn't think you could be so stupid, Norman."

"Are you calling me stupid, wife?"

"You haven't treated me like a wife, you've treated me like property. This isn't the Middle Ages, Norman. It's 1942. I'm a modern, independent woman. If you recall, I bought this house myself. I have my own mind, I have talent, and I can do as I please. Without worrying how my every action affects Mr. Norman A. Balmoral."

Every muscle fiber in his face bulged against the skin. "There's a price you'll have to pay for your freedom."

"A price to be paid? Let's talk about consequences. I didn't commit adultery, you did. Did you think I could ever trust you again?"

"I regret that relationship," Norman said, his voice straining. "I know I hurt you, so despite my misgivings, I permitted you to dabble with the piano for a time. But you've changed since then. That Mr. Larney has poisoned you against me."

She snorted. What condescension. "Hogwash."

"If he had the proper respect for my position as head of this household, he wouldn't have suggested you enter that competition."

They bickered for an eternity. They had been fighting like this more and more, and the battles always droned on in unendurable monotony. She wanted them to end, and she wanted peace. But this time, the battle differed. He wanted to go to Europe. She thought about Hitler's blitzkrieg and got the shivers, imagining Norman in the path of those bombs. War had real consequences. He could be killed.

She turned away from him and looked out the kitchen door. Wait a minute, if she didn't care what happened to him, why would she get the shivers? Of course, she cared, she was his wife. But no matter how much she cared, they couldn't continue fighting like this.

"Norman," she said, looking at him. "What's the real problem between us? Enough of these battles over the piano and Mr. Larney. It isn't the war, and it isn't a piano competition. I think it's something much more serious than that. Why are you so angry?"

He looked up, down, and to the side — everywhere but at Agnes. "You know why I'm angry. You disobeyed me."

"You're a smart man, Norman Balmoral, a very smart man. You know a wife doesn't have to obey a husband."

He fidgeted, refused to look at her, and mumbled, "I don't know what you mean."

"I think you do." Her voice came out as flat and even, not the usual shrill vibrato when she confronted problems. "I think it explains why you went back to Mary Alden."

They remained silent except for the white noise of his strained breathing. "The truth will tear you apart," he finally said.

Her heart pressed into her breastbone. "I promise I'll listen to what you have to say."

He turned his head and covered his eyes.

"Norman, are you crying?"

"No, I'm not crying," he whimpered.

Her head began to clear and she saw the truth, clear as spring water. She understood at last, but instead of tearing her up inside, it sewed everything back together. She knew why he objected to the competition, why he objected to her family, why he buried himself in work and exercise, why he had an affair. She knew what drove his insatiable need to control everything—the heat, the lights, the children's activities, their food, their sex life—and she knew why he always had to have something to do.

His chest was heaving, but he continued covering his eyes. The house's absolute quiet petrified Agnes. Victoria had the children, but where was the dog? Was Keaton bearing witness to this exchange between master and mistress? She looked out the kitchen into the hallway. Keaton rested on his side. He saw her and wagged his tail. She was grateful for the sheer normalcy of his thumping tail. It stifled her fears.

Her blood flowed smooth in her veins, and all those fighting yearnings—her music, her marriage, her children, her mother—fell into place. The reason for it all stared her in the face. She felt no fear of the future, no regret for the past as she gave it words, one syllable at a time.

"Would it help, Norman, if I told you I know? It's obvious just to look at you. You want your freedom. You've never really wanted to be married to me—or to anyone, I believe."

He faced her, ghostly white, his eyes an electric blue, and broke into a chaos of sobs. "Yes, it's true. I never wanted the obligation. I accepted the responsibility, but nothing about it has made me happy. I don't want to be obligated to anyone but myself. And I hate myself for it."

She thought about their decade together. There'd never been a real moment of security in their marriage, any sense of permanency and continuity that had defined her parents, her grandparents, and Norman's parents—the knowledge that they'd be together to the end of time, no matter what. That would not be the case for Norman and her. She must've always known it deep down but had never acknowledged that he'd leave one day for one reason or the other, whether for a job, another woman, or a war. That's why she'd hesitated for so long before marrying him. And she'd gone back to Mr. Larney to prepare for this day and to become the woman she'd always wanted to be.

The more calm she became, the wilder he sobbed. "I wanted to be a good husband to you, but I couldn't. Please forgive me, Agnes, please forgive me."

"You can't help being who you are."

"What I am is despicable."

"No, you're a fine man. You've provided very well for us. It's not your fault you never loved me."

The last tears ran down his splotchy face. His beard was heavy. He hadn't shaved since yesterday. "What do you mean?"

"You don't want to be married to me, Norman, and you've never been in love with me."

"That's not true," he said, a heavy urgency in his voice. "I've loved you since the first moment I saw you. Do you remember the bathroom at Smith and Weisskopf? You were so charming, and you didn't know it. You entranced me right from the start. You had spirit, just like your grandmother and Gracie Honeywalker. All the other girls bored me, but you challenged me. No, I don't want to be married, but I do love you. And I love my children. Our children."

"Where do we go from here? Shall we separate?" She couldn't bring herself to say the *D* word, but she knew … one day that would happen, too. But neither of them said it.

"Yes, after my assignment with the Navy is completed," he said after a long pause. "Until then, I see no reason to change anything."

"You don't have to go to war, Norman, just to leave me. You have my blessing to leave."

"You don't understand. I want to go. You talk about your dreams with the piano, but I have dreams too. I've always wanted to serve my country."

In all the years she'd known Norman Balmoral, he'd never wanted to serve anyone but himself. Agnes opened her mouth to object, but instead took a long, hard look at her husband—the symmetry of his physique, the square chin, the alabaster skin, those piercing blue eyes. What did she know about his dreams? And what did she really know about him at all? She closed her mouth. What would that serve now?

"When you put it like that, I can understand. But Norman, how are the children and I to survive while you're gone? What if you don't come back home alive?"

"Have faith, Agnes. We'll find a way. I won't be at the front as a soldier, I'll be working in an office as an architect."

It felt wonderful to talk and be heard, to listen and hear, even if they stared the end of their marriage in the face.

"Why didn't you talk to me sooner about the war? I'm not unreasonable, Norman. I would've seen your point of view."

"Yes, but I didn't believe that. So I'm sorry."

Except for his affair, it was the first time he'd been the first to apologize. And for the first time she felt as though she could see the world through his eyes.

"I'm sorry too, sorry most of all that we didn't talk sooner."

He caressed her hand, which still held the letter. They looked at each other for a long moment. They rose for a hug and held it. She began to feel the spark and seized it. Norman's beard nudged the side of her neck. She ran her hands through his hair, stroking his jaw. Whether driven by defeat, an instinctive fear of being abandoned, or desperate nostalgia, she still felt that jolt and wanted his body, against her better judgment.

"Agnes, my lover, we'll always have this."

"Norman Balmoral, come upstairs with me," she said, pulling him to her.

He pulled her back into him. "Not so fast. You always wanted to do this on the kitchen table. Now's your chance."

When they were finished, their clothes scattered on the floor, they drank a bottle of wine and scavenged through the remains of their dinner. With disregard for the mess, she looked outside of herself at the scene—Agnes and Norman Balmoral ending their marriage with sex on the kitchen table. Was there a better way to end a marriage?

The details of Norman's commission became known soon enough. He was to depart in May for officer training in northern Virginia and leave for

London and the U.S. Naval Construction Services afterward. Agnes occupied herself with the piano, the household, Grace and Harold, too busy to think about their impending separation—and the permanent one to follow.

She and Norman stayed out of each other's way. They said nothing to anyone about their plan to separate when Norman returned from the war. She had no idea what lay ahead for her family, but she knew she'd have to work. So many women were going to work now that men were departing for Europe and the Pacific.

One woman in particular did stop working. Victoria sold Balmoral's General Store to Norman's brother and gave Mr. Soltham a hefty retirement payment. She informed them, very casually over tea and with absolute authority, she'd be moving into the Spruce Street house to live with Agnes.

In April, Agnes had her hands full moving Harold to the third floor—an easy decision, since Harold loved the playroom across from his new bedroom—settling Victoria in his second-floor bedroom, and getting ready for Norman's departure.

As luck would have it, Agnes's birthday fell on the day before Mother's Day. Norman would depart that Monday for officer training. They had a family dinner on Mother's Day to mark the occasions. The next morning, Agnes gave Norman her father's locket as a parting gift just before they all waved good-bye at the station. Norman's train rolled out of Philadelphia and vanished.

19

AGNES PRANCED A HAPPY MINUET DOWN THE FRONT STEPS to Spruce Street that first Monday in October 1943. She reveled in Philadelphia's Indian summer, satisfied by Victoria's tea and blueberry scones and the joy of Grace and Harold departing for another week of school. Her step anticipated the weekly routine of her new job — her own, she pinched herself, where she'd been working a year.

What fun to be going to work on such a glorious morning! She hummed *Eine Kleine Nachtmusik* to the crystal blue sky and breathed in the morning's oaky scents. Fall might be on its way, but summer was performing quite the finale.

She'd planned her outfit the previous evening, a Sunday routine that filled her with anticipation for the coming week. She'd chosen a tartan plaid skirt, laced blouse, double-breasted jacket with matching hat and white gloves. Agnes had forgotten the gloves and hurried back inside to fetch them. But she never forgot about her hair. Veronica Lake's "peekaboo" was all the rage, but she couldn't hide half her face with her straight hair. So she settled on a more practical updo. She had the ponytail for it, after all. Twirling and pinning it onto her head cemented her businesslike appeal. Above all, she wanted to work hard and give the appearance of it.

She always wore oxfords for the mile-long walk to work, her feet the one place where comfort overruled fashion. Her office lay at the corner of 5th and Arch, an imposing building constructed by the Works Progress Administration during the '30s. How different from now, those Depression days when desperate eyes, shaky hands, and sickly stomachs begged on every corner. Though two wars killing thousands—perhaps millions—bookended the country, and all too many households wore gold stars for fallen sons, Philadelphians brimmed with real hope for the first time since Lindbergh had crossed the Atlantic. Everyone worked, everyone did something for the war, and everyone purchased bonds to defeat Hitler and Hirohito. Children collected cans, women labored at factories, the men fought overseas. And although the president's rationing of gas and rubber kept most cars off the streets, a ceaseless energy had seized the city of Ben Franklin, its citizens united in a common effort to defeat the Third Reich and the Empire of the Sun. Agnes and her household did their part—war bonds for Agnes, meatless Tuesdays for Victoria, tin cans for the children, and a victory garden in their small backyard.

She gave everyone she passed on the street a snappy hello, every businessman attired in a dark suit with a red, white, and blue tie, every doctor on his way to the hospital, every banker heading for a day of savings and loans, every lawyer off to courtly bickering. The men tipped their hats, the women smiled. If the women were not on their way to work, they were taking crabby children to school or walking their dogs. Agnes walked Keaton around the square every morning while Victoria prepared breakfast.

She hopped over the alleyway at Camac Street and contemplated her new project with Dr. Friedman, the mathematician with the rumpled suits and wild gray hair who entranced everyone when he came up from Washington to discuss problems he asked them to solve for the War Department. She didn't know why he drew complex formulas on the chalkboard, asked them to solve differential equations, posed questions of mathematical logic, creating a puzzle that never quite seemed to fit together. The eleven young men she worked with—she was the only woman who'd passed his examination to become a research assistant—knew no more than she. But Dr. Friedman just twitched his bushy eyebrows and moustache at them and shook his head. *Loose lips sink ships.*

Dr. Friedman divided his time between Philadelphia and Washington with occasional visits to Princeton, where he held an adjunct position at Einstein's Institute for Advanced Study. Agnes had thought he was Einstein himself, so much did he resemble the mad scientist with his froggy cheeks and sloping shoulders. But unlike Einstein, her new boss had a full head of hair.

Bored with her first job at the War Department as secretary to a bean counter who'd never addressed her by name, Agnes had jumped at the chance to take the examination. She'd scribbled out her answers with a half hour to spare and ended up scoring second highest among the thirty-two applicants.

Dr. Friedman snatched her up from the secretarial pool. "Her mind works like a mousetrap," he noted when introducing her to his administrator, Dr. Goldberg. "I can imagine no better choice than this red-headed *balabusta.*"

She had no idea what *balabusta* meant, but the doctor's smile reassured her. "Anything I know about mathematics comes from Sister Kathryn James. She drilled differentials into our heads during my final year at St. Patrick's."

"My dear Mrs. Balmoral," he said, laughing. "A bespectacled *mensch* like me wouldn't know a *bissel* about Catholic drills. As long as you can solve the problems I give you, I don't care if your education came from nuns, Buddhist monks, or a sacred Hindu cow. You report directly to me."

"Why me? I have no college education."

"It is that you ask the questions. You have a curious mind, and to me that is a thing of great importance. No college degree can give you that. Mrs. Balmoral, I have no college degree myself, only an honorary doctorate I received after publishing my first paper. Perhaps one day you will publish papers and receive useless degrees too."

In the three months she'd been working for him, he'd encouraged her through any number of mistakes and taken time to answer her questions about calculus and mathematical logic. Every week, he gave her a list of mathematical equations to solve, usually with some mind-bending twist in the discussions he included with the problems. She'd sit at her desk working through them as if she were trying to solve one of the puzzles her father had given her as a child, but the answers to these never came as easily. Somehow, she usually derived solutions before the doctor returned the next week.

Dr. Friedman even opened her eyes to Einstein's theory of relativity. What this had to do with her work, she had no idea, but she did grasp its broad outline. If she sat in the front pew, Father Thomas's sermon seemed louder than if she sat in the back. If she stood under a maple tree in Washington Square — just like now on her way to work — it seemed taller here than from the other side of Independence Mall. And today's twinge of sadness when she thought about separating from Norman, ending the marriage that had produced Grace, Harold, and their Spruce Street home, paled in comparison to the torment she felt after they'd made that decision.

This Monday morning, she sat at her desk and put some distance between herself and her marriage. The thought of being without Norman would have killed her a few years ago, but she'd managed to survive the past year just fine. Agnes organized her desk — her notebook, a stack of papers to be read, and problems to be solved on the left side, last week's work and her colleagues' workbooks for review on the right, a clean desk blotter in front of her — and began her day's work.

And yet, without understanding why, her mind kept coming back to Norman while she tried to solve one of Dr. Goldberg's induction problems. After Norman left, she'd written him three cordial letters, mostly about Victoria's adjustment to life on Spruce Street and the children's summer programs at St. Mark's. Though he always included her in his letters' salutations to the children, he never replied directly. So she'd stopped writing. Why suffer ink smudges on the side of her left hand for his benefit?

She had longed for his departure, believing she'd sleep late and keep the windows closed at night. Without him, she spread out in bed like an octopus and no longer worried about sarcastic "keep to your half of the bed" remarks. But she found herself rising earlier, savoring her mornings alone before walking downstairs to Victoria's breakfast, licks from Keaton, and hugs from the children. Then she started walking the dog before breakfast, even before combing her hair, and enjoyed her Rittenhouse Square promenades with the other dog walkers. Hello, Mr. Levine, good morning, Mrs. Barlow — this from a woman who in thirty-three years rarely had arisen before eight without a thick fog in her head. What a beautiful world of asters, marigolds, and chrysanthemums these mornings beheld, and all she'd had to do to discover it was declare independence from Norman.

Even now, no one knew that Agnes and Norman's separation would be permanent. Not Grace and Harold, who pitter-patted around the house with happy smiles, not Cristina, wrapped up in her boys and Angelo's surprise commission to the Pacific fleet, and not Mr. Larney, who continued to teach them piano. But Agnes occasionally sensed from Victoria's eyes that she knew.

Norman's situation in England preoccupied Victoria. Her head twitched at every unexpected knock on the door, afraid the U.S. Navy was delivering a telegram announcing Norman's injury or worse. For herself, Agnes no longer worried. If Queen Elizabeth thought London was safe enough for the princesses and King George, then Norman would be safe in the Navy's fortress. Judging from the letters he wrote the children, he seemed content with life in London and didn't worry much about getting killed.

Dr. Friedman came over to her desk, his walk somewhere between a shuffle and a bounce. "Come up for air. Your head is buried in those equations."

Agnes must've been daydreaming. "Good morning, Dr. Friedman." She cast a furtive glance at her desk—so organized, it looked as though she hadn't done any work. She looked down the long aisle at her colleagues' desks, every one of them stacked with a mess of papers that advertised productivity. She knew Dr. Friedman had come to expect more discipline from her than the others, the reason why he'd given her the desk closest to his blackboard where they met for discussions. His private meeting room lay just beyond.

Dr. Friedman proceeded to tell her about his weekend—something about Rodgers and Hart at the Bucks County Playhouse and pretty Miss Kitty Carlisle—but Agnes's heart jumped when he asked her to come to his office after lunch.

"Nothing to worry about, Mrs. Balmoral, only a very special project."

Later that morning, she completed a long series of calculations for a trigonometric proof she'd started Thursday. She typed up her report, including a problem statement, a discussion of methodology (new vocabulary for Agnes), a summary of her results, the details of her calculations, proof of her results, and a discussion of her findings.

Agnes handed the report to Dr. Friedman, who flipped through its six pages. "The *balabusta* strikes again. Mr. Lincoln said you can't please all of the people all of the time, but I think you are the exception."

If only he knew she hadn't pleased anyone in recent years, she thought on her way to Morris House for lunch. What did he have in mind for her special project? Dr. Goldberg had mentioned a problem to optimize train travel with a variety of complications — total weight, speed, distance traveled, number of passengers, available routes. Dr. Friedman had presented a similar problem, a mathematical puzzle with strange numbers, some extremely small but others extremely large, requiring her to measure the speed of teeny-tiny objects, their weight at various gravitational pulls and their force when traveling at lightning-fast speed. Agnes had tried solving the problem, but failed. She derived outrageous numbers for force far larger than anything she'd ever fathomed and just knew they had to be wrong.

She decided she'd prefer Dr. Goldberg's train problem if Dr. Friedman gave her a choice. At least she understood trains. When she returned from lunch, she found him standing near her desk.

She hung her jacket and dropped her purse into a drawer. "Am I late?"

Wrinkles creased all over his face. "The plan has changed. Our own meeting will have to wait. Someone special is here. He's waiting in the conference room, Agnes."

He never called her Agnes, nor did he ever cross that line of familiarity with the others. This must be something very important if a special visitor wanted to see her. Perhaps she'd be going to Washington or Princeton? She'd enjoy a trip out of town, except for leaving Grace and Harold —

He opened the door to the conference room, and she saw her priest, Father Thomas, sitting at the table. Except for his white beard and hair, he was dressed in black. What was he doing at the War Department? She knew at once this meeting had nothing to do with work.

"Agnes," he said, coming over to her, taking her hands in his, and pulling a chair out. Dr. Friedman closed the door and sat down with her. Her mouth went dry, her stomach lurched, and her heart raced from moderato to allegro to presto in nothing flat. She could hear her pulse in her ears.

"Father Thomas," she said in an uneven tone, wanting to stall his words as long as possible. "I don't understand—the Navy should've sent—I don't have a clear picture of this."

"Agnes, I have very unhappy news to report."

She rose, her back to the men, and peeked out the window at people walking on the opposite side of Arch Street. "A few moments, please, before you say it."

In a frozen eternity, a thousand memories swirled through her head. Mr. Balmoral, the brash architect, rushing into the bathroom when they first met at Smith and Weisskopf. Norman, the man who kissed her for the first time outside Mrs. O'Toole's house. Her lover, the man who made impetuous love to her in the back office of his parents' store. Norman, who flirted with Granny. The father of her children, carrying them on his back in Rittenhouse Square. The architect whose passion for buildings and structure enlightened their city walks. The commissioned naval officer who bid Agnes good-bye with a smile as she placed her father's locket in the palm of his hand. The husband who took responsibility for his mistakes, even when they ended the marriage. And the man whose milky-white body she could taste even now. Agnes stretched the final seconds of her marriage as long as she possibly could.

"Dear girl, Norman was killed on Saturday in an air raid. He'd been working in the secure area of the basement. After the first bombs hit, he went upstairs to assist the injured. It was then that the second wave hit the building and killed the remaining survivors, including him. He was identified yesterday evening."

The formality in Father Thomas's words struck her like an iceberg. Her eyes remained fixed on the street scene. A man was selling pretzels and hot dogs on the street. Wasn't it past the lunch hour? She had no idea of the time.

"The U.S. Navy sent a condolence telegram to the house on behalf of President and Mrs. Roosevelt, followed by a longer telegram with the details. For myself, I can only offer you a prayer."

Shock plunged like a boulder into her stomach, and she became dizzy.

Her stomach lurched, and vicious cramps seized her abdomen. She buried her head in the closest wastepaper can and vomited. A profuse stream came out her mouth and nose.

She felt Dr. Friedman's calloused hand running through her hair, stroking her head. He didn't say a word but continued patting her head and rubbing her temples. His hands' rough warmth soothed her convulsing mind.

She couldn't bear to look up. The putrid taste in her mouth and nose compared as nothing to her embarrassment. She saw the blueberry bits from Victoria's scones in the basket. Victoria—how would she react?

"Victoria, oh my God ... a mother's loss ..."

Dr. Friedman brought her a wet towel. She wiped her face and dried her tears. She was grateful when he took away the soiled can and left her with Father Thomas.

"Victoria received the telegram and sent me here. I've sent Mrs. Collingwood to escort Grace and Harold home from school."

"Grace and Harold," she repeated—then panic set in. But Father Thomas put his hand on her shoulder and recited the Lord's Prayer. It comforted Agnes to hear the familiar words, and she recited it with him. When they finished, she lifted herself from the floor, sat down at the table, and covered her face with her hands.

She waited for more tears, but anger bubbled to the surface instead. How dare Father Thomas intrude on her, how dare he give her this information at work for her boss and co-workers to hear, and how dare Norman go off to London where bombs fell daily, and how dare he orphan their children? She knew Father Thomas was being kind, but she blamed him, Norman, the U.S. Navy, and Dr. Friedman for the news and for her vomiting. She detested throwing up.

"Norman and I decided to end our marriage just before he left. A moot point now, don't you think?"

"I wish there were something more than a prayer I could offer you," Father Thomas said, his white beard turning down in a sad frown as he clasped his hands. "Norman was a brave man, and now you must be very brave in his place."

"Admirable sentiments, Father Thomas. How many times have you said that to widows in the last year?"

Widow. She was now a widow, just like Victoria, just like Mama, just like Granny had been. Was this the curse of marriage, that you ended up burying the man and raising his children alone? But she had wanted Norman to leave, and she'd been relieved, even happy. Her hands, her head, even her chest began to shake. *Dear God, I wanted him gone and now he's dead.*

Father Thomas continued, but she barely listened. "Sixteen times, I'm afraid. You're the seventeenth. Agnes, please let me escort you home so I can pray with your family. I have a car waiting outside. Norman's brother must be notified. And your own family, Mrs. Limerick and Monsignor Doherty?"

She came back at the mention of Uncle Collin and Mama. How would they react? After eight years, she had no idea whether they'd offer condolences or cheer.

"I will tell them myself. And I appreciate your offer of a ride home, but I would prefer to give this news to my mother-in-law and children myself."

"Let me remind you, Victoria knows. It was she who received the telegram. She called me, wanting me to come here and tell you personally."

Would it ruin Victoria to bury her younger son? She had buried Cornelius two years ago and had survived that loss. Victoria had real strength. But how would this affect the chipmunks? Grace at eleven and Harold nearly seven, both happy and growing by leaps and bounds — at least until now. The thought hit Agnes with the impact of a gunshot. Her tears gushed like summer rain.

"How do I to tell my children?" she asked, blowing her nose into a handkerchief. "No child should ever have to lose a father."

Her memory flashed back to that day in 1918 when Uncle Collin told her she'd have to be a very brave little girl now that Martin Limerick "was gone to heaven." Why did priests always want you to be brave? She would not ask her children to be brave. Let them be as frightened as they liked. Then perhaps they might recover from their father's death one day.

On the Saturday after three weeks of the family's tears, sympathy and covered dishes from neighbors, and finally dead silence in the house, Agnes woke up to walk Keaton in Rittenhouse Square. But her empty stomach cried foul, and her head throbbed. The furniture, paintings, and porcelain figurines in her bedroom loomed from small to large and back to small again, but she willed herself to rise. She opened the heavy draperies, and the morning sun pierced her headache. No matter what the day portended, she was thankful for good weather. The funeral procession would be undisturbed by rain.

She wished she could hide in her bedroom for all eternity, but she had no choice but to go through with the day. Victoria depended on her, Grace and Harold depended on her. After walking Keaton around the neighborhood, she labored over her grooming, putting on her only black dress, knee-length and narrow-waisted. Then she gasped in the mirror. The dress hung too loosely on her frame. Had she really lost so much weight in three weeks?

She hated this dress, and her wobbly mind made it all the more depressing. As if guided by an external force, she rummaged through the closet for a dress that would fit—and found her white dress, which she'd last worn before Harold was born when she weighed less. It had been Norman's favorite with its blue trim and smart, crisp lines. The neighbors would talk for weeks about the shocking behavior of a new widow wearing white to her husband's funeral, but what did that matter?

She found the chipmunks at the table in the kitchen. Grace, dressed in a blue skirt and white blouse, her brown hair in a shoulder-length bob, was reading a book. And Harold, who was drawing in a coloring book, was still in his knickers and would have to change into his Sunday best after breakfast. To look at the children, she wouldn't have known they were burying their father today. Agnes had difficulty gauging the effect of Norman's death on them. Harold had cried for several hours that Monday afternoon after coming home, but Agnes doubted his six-year old mind really understood it. Grace had stood rooted in place as if bracing for an attack. Since then, she'd buried herself in books and dolls.

Victoria, her face an ashen gray when Agnes and Father Thomas had come back that first afternoon, had hugged Agnes with a limp body and walked up to her bedroom, her face a mask. Since then, she'd left the room only to bathe and eat the few morsels Agnes pushed at her. This morning, Agnes prepared oatmeal and ladled it into bowls.

"Grace, Harold, eat your breakfast. We need energy for the long walk." She forced down a good portion, knowing that otherwise she'd faint in the warm October sun. After breakfast, she knocked on Victoria's door.

"Victoria, we'll be leaving for the train station in thirty minutes."

"Yes, my dear," she heard through door. "I'll be on time."

The U.S. Navy had arranged for a military escort to drive them to 30th Street Station shortly before eleven. It felt like entering a cave when they got into the black limousine, and she was thankful when they were able to climb out and walk into the station's hall of marble, glass, and eighty-foot ceilings. They quickly found the others. Norman's brother, huddled in conversation with his boys, Cristina, dressed in black and conversing with Mr. and Mrs. Cassata. And Mr. Soltham, chatting up Mr. Larney.

She felt certain Mr. Soltham gave her white dress a disapproving look, but no one else seemed to take notice. Like Victoria, she'd worn a dark veil and hat, but Victoria was hiding her puffy cheeks and splotchy complexion. Agnes wanted to protect her skin from the sun.

A man in naval uniform approached. "Mrs. Balmoral? Please come with me, all of you." They followed him to the upper track level where six uniformed men awaited the train. Agnes shook their hands and thanked them for granting her special request that men from the Pennsylvania Guard serve as Norman's pallbearers.

At eleven o'clock sharp, Norman's train crawled into the station. Agnes could hear her heart beating to the rhythm of the final approach. Passengers disembarked from each car, going about their business without noticing the officers and mourners in black — or the new widow in white.

It seemed an eternity before the last passengers left the station. The lead officer called the others to attention, and they marched to the caboose. Five minutes later, three officers on either side emerged carrying Norman's flag-draped coffin on their shoulders.

A thick lump filled her throat when Agnes saw the coffin. Victoria wept uncontrollably behind her, but Agnes swallowed her tears.

Harold leaned into Agnes and looked up at her with Norman's blue eyes. "Mama, is Daddy inside that box?"

Victoria moaned at this question, but Agnes leaned down and kissed his head. The officers carried Norman's coffin to a nearby gurney and began the procession to the horse-drawn caisson waiting outside. A small crowd had gathered around it, and Agnes resented the gawkers' intrusion. Why did people delight in others' misery? She watched the officers set the coffin onto the caisson. One officer took the horse's lead, and the remaining six marched on either side. Agnes followed close with Grace and Harold, the others behind them as they started their procession toward Chestnut Street.

Over the objections of Norman's brother, she'd insisted on a horse-drawn caisson they'd follow on foot to St. Mark's, whether in rain or sun, whether by herself or with the others. Norman and she never had had a car in the city, and she saw no reason to depend on one now. Agnes knew funeral processions didn't take place on foot any longer, but when Mayor Samuel called to pay his respects and informed her that, in honor of Norman's bravery when saving Woodrow Wilson's granddaughter, Senator Davis and Mrs. Wilson would be accompanying him to the funeral, she took the opportunity to ask him to intervene.

She saw the Philadelphia police diverting traffic from Chestnut around the post office and onto 30th Street. It was good of Mayor Samuel, though closing the streets hardly seemed necessary. Hardly anyone drove a car these days with gas rationing. They crossed the bridge over the Schuylkill River, its muddy waters flowing toward the Delaware, and into Center City. She looked back toward West Philadelphia with Drexel University in the distance and noticed onlookers joining their procession in the rear. To her astonishment, more and more joined. She had no idea who these people were. They were dressed in ordinary Saturday wear—from dungarees and overalls to suits and ties, house dresses to Sunday best.

People waited on both sides of the street beyond the bridge and down the hill. They must've read yesterday's headline in the *Inquirer* about the funeral. People had long memories. The attack on Edith McAdoo had occurred nearly three years ago, and it touched Agnes that Philadelphians had come to pay their respects. Norman had been a brave and honorable man for his city—and his country.

They would soon pass St. Patrick's, the brown stones of the church, the gray façade of the school. Why had she not thought to shift the procession to Walnut or even Locust? This would be awkward. Uncle Collin was parish priest and principal of the school, her only family member still in Philadelphia. She'd neither seen nor heard from him since that distant Mother's Day. She'd wanted to make amends but had procrastinated too long. Agnes knew Uncle Collin would've read the newspaper and would know about the funeral. But today wasn't the day to face him.

She tried to keep her gaze ahead as they passed the long block, the church on her left. In spite of herself, she peeked to the side. No sign of life. A ghostly stillness pervaded the gray-brown exterior of the church, parish house, and school. No white-haired man looked out from the office, and no pink fingers pulled back the curtains of any school windows.

Five times these past weeks, she'd sat at the telephone and reached to dial the Washington phone number she'd extracted from Aunt Julia, but each time she hesitated. On the sixth try, she let it ring as her hands shook and her heart pounded in her ears. When no one answered, she went upstairs to calm her nerves, climbed into bed, and cried into her pillow. She hadn't heard from any of them, not her brother, not Mama, and most of all, not Uncle Collin.

The procession made its way down Chestnut Street, now crowded by tall, narrow buildings and an even narrower street. If people didn't salute the caisson, they wept. Agnes again felt a lump in her throat at what the tribute meant — Norman's death. She leaned down to Grace and Harold. "Children, remember how your city paid its respects to your daddy."

Just before they turned onto 19th Street to make their way to Rittenhouse Square, Agnes heard a din of rustling noise behind her.

She saw an endless panorama of Philadelphians behind her, perhaps three hundred people, extending nearly all the way back to St. Patrick's almost two blocks back. The crowd that had watched the procession from the sidewalks had continued joining it in the rear. Norman might lie dead in the coffin, but his city had come out in full force. Agnes raised her chin and resumed the march to St. Mark's.

Once again, Rittenhouse Square's quiet beauty struck her as they came upon its diagonal sidewalk. The noon sun shone through the trees' leaves, which had started to turn orange and gold only in the past two weeks. Agnes closed her eyes and breathed in the city's oak-scented air. She loved this square in a way Norman really had never appreciated. The majestic oaks along the diagonal enclosed their procession like raised swords at a military wedding. Agnes smiled for the first time that day. She was glad Rittenhouse Square, where they'd spent so much time with Keaton and the children, would bear witness to Norman's funeral.

In the center of the square, they passed the bench she and Norman had sat on that spring evening of '36. She remembered her anxiety as she searched the square for her elusive husband. How utterly insignificant her anger that night seemed now.

They turned onto Locust Street, the church only a block away. It had been an hour's walk, the officers, mourners, and people of Philadelphia following the caisson. Agnes was glad they were all a part of this. This was her city, this was her home, and these were her people.

The caisson stopped at St. Mark's, its broad red doors already open. Agnes faced the people who had joined their procession and bowed her head. They stood silently, many with tears in their eyes.

Father Thomas carried the cross of St. Mark's outside, three acolytes behind him. The officers shifted the coffin onto their shoulders and marched in unison up the stairs. Father Thomas turned back inside, followed by the guard and the coffin. They laid the coffin on a small stand. Agnes and the mourners gathered behind it.

"Our Lord said, 'I am the resurrection and the life,'" Father Thomas said at the entrance. "'He who believes in me shall live, though yet he dies; and whoever lives and believes in me shall never die.' We come here today to celebrate the life of God's servant, Norman Aloysius Balmoral."

The officers lifted Norman's coffin once again and began the procession down the center aisle toward the altar. Agnes willed herself to focus on the beauty of the Gothic columns, the stained-glass windows, the dark wood trim. It was the only way she could fight off her body's urge to weep, to shake, to lie prostrate, and to surrender to the reality of saying good-bye to Norman. Her throat constricted as the organ began "A Mighty Fortress Is Our God," her favorite.

She remembered walking down St. Patrick's aisle in a similar procession twenty-five years earlier on a Saturday much like this. She'd forgotten Mama had chosen this hymn for her father's funeral. Martin Limerick, her daddy, gone too soon, just like Grace and Harold's father. Without lowering her head, holding her lips firmly in place, she surrendered to tears.

The dark veil began to smother her as she cried. She hadn't worn a veil for her wedding, so why should she wear one for Norman's funeral? She didn't like the custom, so she handed her hat and veil and to the closest person, a stranger. "Please take this. I don't need it."

She looked at the left and right aisles. The church was packed. Many were church members, many were Victoria's friends, and she recognized a number of architects. She saw the Collingwoods, the Whitlingers, the Curreys, women from the Rittenhouse Society. She saw Dr. Friedman, who had come alone, his tender hazel eyes nodding encouragement. As they neared the front, she saw Mayor Samuel and his wife bow their heads ostentatiously as the coffin passed their pew. Senator Davis and Mrs. Wilson stood beside them. Politicians were insincere, but this was real.

She stopped crying when she saw who occupied the fourth pew on the right, the first behind the three reserved for her. Mama stood on the end looking at her, one hand on the pew for support and the other holding a handkerchief pressed to her lips. Uncle Collin stood beside her.

Astonishment momentarily flooded out grief. What was Uncle Collin doing in a Protestant church? Had he changed his views since he'd damned them to hell's fires? The music ended just as Agnes drew alongside their pew.

Her mother had aged since that Mother's Day. The stout-faced woman with salt-and-pepper hair had been replaced by a woman with wrinkles and thinning white hair. Only the word fat could describe her now — no one would accept stout any longer. She wore black-framed glasses just like Uncle Collin's. Agnes tried to remember Mama's age. She'd be sixty-seven in July, old enough to be at the end of life without being elderly.

She wanted to break free from a thousand eyes and lay her head on Mama's shoulder. She wanted to hide in her mother's embrace, and she wanted everything to be right again with the world. Of all the people she knew, Mama was the only one who possibly could make things right again, the only one with whom she could be the child, not the one who made the decisions. But she kept tight reins on herself.

"Hello, Mother," Agnes said, lifting each of the children's hands in her own. "Here are your grandchildren. Grace Victoria you know. She was a toddler when you left for Washington. This little boy is Harold Norman. Grace turned eleven last month, and my baby turned six in February."

Harold pulled at her dress. "Mama, I'm not a baby. Who is she?"

"I'm your Grandmother Limerick," Mama stammered. "I've come to see your mother."

Harold glanced at Victoria. "But I have a grandmother."

The corners of Mama's mouth curled into a little smile, and she patted her handkerchief on her bosom. "Well, you've got two now."

Harold looked at Agnes. "Yes, you have two," she said. "This is my mother, just like Nana was Daddy's."

Her son turned his head from Mama to Victoria, then looked up at Agnes. "Does that mean she scolds you for going outside without your hat too?"

Mama laughed a little while Agnes observed Uncle Collin in his clerical collar. He cast his eyes away. Like Mama, he'd aged and gained weight, but something more had changed. Perhaps his complexion, a deeper shade of red, or the purple spider veins on his nose? Had they always been there?

Beyond Mama's exchange with Harold, Agnes remembered none of their small talk in the aisle. She only could stand there, amazed they'd actually come without an invitation, without any pleading, and feel at least a little less grief. She looked in Mama's eyes and saw a sliver of gray dullness. How sad those eyes looked, and yet—

The officers rested Norman's coffin on the catafalque in front of the altar, and Father Thomas stood above it ready to begin. Agnes stammered something to Mama and stepped into the front pew with Victoria and the children. Norman's brother and his family filled the second pew. Cristina, the Cassatas, Mr. Soltham, and Mr. Larney filed in behind them.

Even though she knew the funeral service well, Agnes found it difficult to concentrate on Father Thomas's words. Her mind wandered back to her first piano recital at St. Monica's four months after Daddy died. Mama had gone to New York to nurse Aunt Julia after a fall, despite Agnes's angry protests, and Granny had escorted her to the event. But just as she sat on a thick stack of books Mr. Larney had placed on the piano bench so she could reach the keyboard, Mama had rushed inside and sat next to Granny. Today she felt the same relief, and it extinguished the pain in her heart, at least for a moment.

Surely this was a beginning. She wanted the funeral to end, she wanted to rush to Mama after the burial, she wanted to ask so many questions. But only one really mattered. Uncle Collin — where did he stand with her? Something in her mind sensed his avenging eyes on her back. Or was it her imagination? She had no way of knowing, unless she interrupted the ceremony and interrogated him in front of all these mourners.

She considered how Dr. Friedman might approach the problem.

Excuse me, Father Thomas, a pause in the service while I investigate the problems with my uncle.

Uncle Collin, did you not damn the deceased for all eternity, as well as myself, just a short eight years ago?

But she believed Uncle Collin would refuse to answer her questions, so she decided he would remain *in silencio.*

And if you did, then do you recognize the inconsistency in attending the funeral of one of the aforementioned damned?

In the scene she played out, Uncle Collin only would give her a confused look of regret and apology.

So, in consideration of the previous damnation and your attendance, Uncle Collin, may I conclude that you have reached a point of forgiveness? Father Thomas, I have concluded my investigation. You may resume.

Satisfied by her mental pantomime, she redirected her attention to the service. She'd lost track, for Father Thomas had delivered the eulogy and moved on to breaking the bread and offering communion. Agnes approached the altar with Grace, Harold, and Victoria. They knelt in front of the center post. Agnes took a communion wafer and the wine challis. As always, she felt the peace of Christ descend into her soul when Father Thomas's fingers traced the sign of the cross on her forehead.

A little different from our communion, Mama and Uncle Collin, but just as magical, isn't it?

They returned to the front row, and the other mourners lined up for communion. Agnes kneeled, as usual, and prayed after receiving the sacrament. When she looked up, she saw her mother approach the altar alone and receive the sacrament, then turn around and look at Agnes. Mama made a sign of the cross and passed by Agnes's pew.

Agnes returned to her prayer. She'd almost forgotten about Norman, but this was his funeral, after all, so she prayed for him, for his soul, for their children, and gave thanks for giving himself to her, at least what he'd been able to give. Norman Balmoral, odd to think he'd been her husband, that she represented him and his family at this funeral. A funeral attended by Philadelphia's mayor, a senator, even a former first lady. And Mama and Uncle Collin.

She sat back in her seat and looked at the young children beside her. She held them close and smiled. They deserved to know their mother had a family different from Norman's, that more than one color of blood flowed through their veins — Catholic and Irish, Episcopalian and English. She breathed in the scents of oak, marble, stone, and wine — the same here as at St. Patrick's. The architects who designed these churches didn't draft anything different between them. The stones of St. Mark's held the same reverence for God as the stones of St. Patrick's. Agnes, a happy tear in her eye, turned to look for Mama and Uncle Collin.

When she did, she saw they had gone.

20

AGNES WRAPPED HER BATHROBE ABOUT HER and knocked on her mother-in-law's door. "Victoria, I know you're inside. Please come to the door." Still no answer, she turned the handle and peeked in. "May I come in?"

Agnes tiptoed in and gasped. But for a few rays of morning sunlight forcing their way through closed draperies, Agnes would've seen nothing. The bed was unmade. Victoria's funeral dress lay in a pile on the floor with her shoes, hat, and veil. A tray from yesterday's reception sat on the nightstand, a smorgasbord of chicken breast, crusty mashed potatoes, brussels sprouts gone to mush, and gravy glued onto Granny's Wedgewood. A broken martini glass had scattered on the floor near her bed.

Her mother-in-law sat curled in the high-backed chair by the window, blanketed by an old shawl, her bare toes peeking out the bottom. After Agnes's eyes adjusted, she noticed tissues on the floor surrounding the chair, like rose petals strewn on a bride's red carpet. Victoria rested her head on the side of the chair, her hair tangled and untidy out of its bun.

Victoria pointed at a wooden carving on her dresser. "My boy gave me that rhinoceros for Christmas back in '21."

Agnes's heart contracted. Norman's death had turned Victoria's life upside down in a way that Cornelius's had not. Agnes couldn't bear to see Victoria succumb to grief. She remembered how Granny had survived her father's death — and Uncle Daniel's. *You do what you have to do.*

"You haven't eaten for days, Victoria. Come downstairs for breakfast. I've made bacon and eggs. After breakfast, we're going to church. We'd like you to come."

Victoria covered her eyes with her hands. "If only I'd been an affectionate mother, maybe God wouldn't have punished me. If I'd known God would take him away from me, I'd have held my baby closer when he cried out for me."

Agnes grabbed the wastepaper can and started dropping the tissues into the basket. Victoria sat upright.

"Don't do that," Victoria said. "Those are my tears for Norman. I'm saving them. Put those tissues back down."

Agnes looked in the wastepaper can, then at Victoria. "All right, but I insist you come downstairs today. Let me clean the room for you. It would be good for you to have communion, talk to friends afterward, go for a walk this afternoon. It's much cooler today than yesterday. Wouldn't that be nice?"

"It would be nice if my son weren't lying under six feet of dirt next to his father."

Agnes kneeled on the floor in front of Victoria and took her hands. "I know how trying this has been for you."

"Trying?" Victoria said, her puffy cheeks becoming taut, her eyebrows arching, and horizontal lines twitching on her forehead. "I'll notice you didn't join me for the viewing. I never felt so alone as looking at my son's dead face, not even his wife there to share it."

Agnes hadn't wanted to see Norman's corpse, cold and devoid of life, before the long drive to the cemetery. She couldn't bear looking at him, knowing how she'd behaved. And she refused to allow her children to see their father's body, despite Victoria's pleading. She still could remember the empty feeling of seeing Daddy dead when Mama had prodded her to kiss him good-bye, knowing he'd never smile for her again. She didn't want that for Grace and Harold.

"I couldn't have borne it, Victoria. I don't want to think about … yesterday. I just want to make it through today. I need your help raising Grace and Harold. If you're going to come downstairs, do it for your grandchildren. They need us."

Victoria looked across the room and sighed. "I'll think about it."

Agnes kissed her mother-in-law on the forehead and left. She now knew how difficult it was to bury a husband, and she could remember what it had been like when Daddy died. But she had no idea how Victoria felt, what pain she endured. She thought about the pain Mama must've felt over her lost babies, a pain so deep that she'd never spoken about it.

Since seeing Mama at the funeral, she longed for the sound of her voice, even if it came with a reproach. But perhaps Mama had gone back to Washington, and she'd never see her again. She had no way of knowing other than to call the rectory. But Uncle Collin would be in church on Sunday morning.

Victoria didn't join them at St. Mark's. That afternoon while collecting the family's laundry, Agnes knocked on Victoria's door but got no answer. She peeked in and found her mother-in-law asleep. She went down to the kitchen and dropped the basket on the washing machine. Thank heavens, she'd bought it and the spin dryer before the Japanese attacked Pearl Harbor and manufacturers stopped making them for civilians. Otherwise, she'd be washing clothes by hand.

She put the dirty clothes in the washer and went back to last night's dishes — a daunting stack of plates, crystal goblets, and teacups. Agnes sighed. She hated cleaning up after visitors, especially unwelcome ones like yesterday's.

That damned Mrs. Collingwood. She and her chinless husband had stayed long after the others, claiming some absurd privilege that permitted a neighbor to monopolize an exhausted widow on the evening of her husband's funeral. Agnes lost her patience when Mrs. Collingwood asked how this had affected her sleeping habits.

"Indeed, Mrs. Collingwood, ever since I found out that a bomb blew Norman to smithereens, I've been unable to sleep. I prowl the house all night long. Right now I'm so exhausted, I barely know what I'm going to say next. You might remember that when Mr. Collingwood kicks the bucket."

Mrs. Collingwood popped open her mouth, stared at her husband, and sniffed. "I think we should be going, Agnes. I'll check in on you tomorrow or the next day."

Poor hen-pecked Mr. Collingwood, following his wife out the door, whispered into Agnes's ear, "Don't mind Ida. She means well enough. If you need anything, you have only to ask."

Agnes replayed the scene as she finished up the last of the dishes, wondering why she'd insulted Ida Collingwood. She knew the old lady meant well, but she couldn't tolerate her fussing about. The doorbell rang not long after Agnes had dried the last of the goblets and headed to the music room for an hour of solitude at the piano.

"Oh, poo!" she said, wanting to play some Mozart. "Who can that be?"

She looked in the hall mirror before opening the door—a dark-blue dress was good enough for a Sunday afternoon caller, sober enough for a widow without being as morose as black. She checked her hair—again good enough, pretty without being garish. Her red updo went well with a blue dress. She opened the door.

Thank heavens, it was Mr. Larney. She could be herself and not worry about gossip. "Oh, Mr. Larney, I'm so happy to see you."

"Agnes Mary, I had no chance to talk with you yesterday," he said. "All those fat matrons buzzed around you like clucking chickens."

She took his jacket and pointed him to the parlor sofa. "They meant well. Hold on a moment, Mr. Larney, I just finished a load in the washing machine."

After she transferred the clothes to the spin dryer, she sat down next to him.

"I came because I knew you'd be lonely on the second day," he said. "It's always worse after friends and relatives depart, and you're left with the silence."

"After yesterday, I was looking forward to being left alone. I just finished cleaning up and was about to sit at the piano. I'm practicing Mozart's C major variations for our next lesson."

"Twinkle, twinkle, little star! So what's stopping you?"

"I have a caller, a very important caller."

"It is only I, dear pupil, your fairy piano teacher. Play away, shall we? Let's have a contest. You play as many wrong notes as you can tolerate, and I'll try to make a different daffy face each time you miss a note."

She laughed at him on their way back to the music room. They were like lovers, not two minutes in the parlor before heading to the back room — lovers of the piano.

"Miss Killer Thumbs, I would like to hear the variations, but not as your teacher, as your very old and very devoted friend." A broad smile stretched across his face.

"Yes, indeed." She sat at the piano and started into the variations but played the repeats only for the main theme. She wanted to cover as much music as possible with Mr. Larney, and she didn't have patience for repeats.

Mr. Larney stood by the piano, rolled his eyes, and oinked like a pig. "You're skipping the repeats. Mozart wrote them out in long hand. The least you can do is respect the cramps he got doing it."

She slapped her hands on her thighs. "I'm the widow today, Mr. Larney. No repeats. Tomorrow you can be the widow and do as many repeats as you like. I even have a black dress you may wear."

He laughed so much, his chins jiggled up and down. "I'll forgo the black dress. It's simply not my color. Play on then and skip the repeats. Mozart will be forced to forgive you."

When she finished, he clapped like a hummingbird's wings. "Brava! *Encore une fois, s'il-vous plait!*"

His French was correct, but his accent resembled nothing like the actors in *Casablanca*. His half-Irish, half-Philadelphia brogue would've convinced the French Resistance to abandon the Allies for the Germans.

"I've got an idea, let's do a duet. Mozart Symphony No. 40, four-handed. You know, ta-de-da, ta-de-da, ta-de-da, da!" Agnes hummed.

"Like a hummingbird in heat."

"You dirty old man, Mr. Larney, you're speaking with a new widow. Kindly remember yourself in front of your elders."

"I see no one older than I in this room, Mrs. Balmoral."

"My widowhood outranks your age, which by my calculation is sixty any day now. Just when is your birthday, Mr. Larney? November 24?" Agnes arched her left eyebrow, a trick she'd learned from Vivien Leigh in *Gone with the Wind*.

"This year it's November 31."

She relaxed her face. A little Scarlett O'Hara went a long way. "Very funny. You take the *primo*, and I'll take the *secondo*."

They started into the symphony. How she enjoyed this, despite the pain of the past month. But for Mozart and Mr. Larney, her mind would travel back to when Norman's coffin had been lowered into place, and she'd hear the grinding noise of those gears once again. The lightness of this music and Mr. Larney's laughter helped her squelch the memory.

"So light and airy, these Mozart duets," she said when they finished. "We should do one of these for my next recital."

When would she ever have the time for anything other than work and raising children? That raised another question. She wouldn't even have work when the war ended and the men came home. How would she send Grace and Harold to college?

"You should do as many recitals as you like. There are no obstacles now."

Norman, an obstacle — her heart pinched her. "There's no money in recitals. I have two children to raise."

"Teaching music would suit you," he said, and then in his best Tallulah Bankhead voice, "You'd be *simply fabulous*."

He was kind, he was sincere, and he meant the best for her. But she'd need to earn a lot more money than he did if she wanted to send her children to college. After all, at sixty he was still renting a room from Mrs. O'Toole for twenty-five dollars every month. And then an idea electrified her.

"Perhaps next year. For now, I have my job with Dr. Friedman. I'm returning to work a week from Monday, but there is a way you could help."

They'd planned to convert the extra bedroom on the third floor into a sewing room for Victoria, but this would be much more entertaining. "Why don't you move out of Mrs. O'Toole's house and come live with us? You can bring your piano, and we'll put it right here alongside my own. Think of our duets, how much easier it'll be to teach students without a nagging landlady."

He frowned. "It would offend Mrs. O'Toole."

"I'll charge you the same rent for room and board without any premium for students like she charges. Oh, please consider it, just for me! And if not for me, think of Grace and Harold." She gave him her own version of Tallulah, "They *simply adore* you. You'll have the third-floor bedroom across from Harold."

Mr. Larney walked around the room. He kept his back to her. "I sleep late, I play the piano well into the night, my younger students bang the hell out of the instrument, and your neighbors will gossip more than crickets in summer. Are you sure you want to consider this?"

"We'll manage. Please, Mr. Larney, I need the income."

"All right, my dear. I'll consider it, as long as you stop with the 'Yes, Mr. Larney' nonsense. My name is Brian."

"That's a bargain, Mr.—Brian. We'll plan it for December—"

The doorbell rang. Agnes looked down the front hallway. Three o'clock on the grandfather clock. How quickly her time with him always passed.

"That's my cue to leave," he said. "If I am to leave the estimable Mrs. O'Toole, I need to inform her right away. I'll bet she bursts a blood vessel."

Agnes opened the door to find Cristina juggling her hat and compact mirror in one hand while rearranging her hair with the other.

"This wind, Agnes. What's a girl to do with her hair? Good afternoon, Mr. Larney."

Agnes felt no strong wind. "It's Cristina Rosamilia, the woman with a million roses in her eyes," Brian said. "Take good care of our Agnes."

"Brian is just leaving. We were playing Mozart duets."

"Perfect timing, Agnes," Cristina said. "Mozart bores me to tears."

"Saints preserve us, it isn't Mozart who's boring." Brian kissed Cristina's cheek. "Good-bye, Agnes. I will let you know about the third floor in a couple of days."

Cristina hung her coat and adjusted her dress in the mirror. After Agnes brewed a pot of tea and plated some cookies left over from the reception, they settled into the sofa in the parlor.

"What did Brian Larney mean by his last remark?" Christina asked.

"He means you're boring because you don't like Mozart."

"Not that, Miss Smarty Pants. The third floor."

"I've invited him to live here."

"Very interesting," Cristina said after a long pause which saw her go from a twist of the head, to a tap of the index finger on her mouth, and finally to a low giggle that burst into a full-throated laugh. "From little Caesar to the court jester. What does Caesar's mother think about this?"

Agnes resented Cristina's insult, but she'd long ago become accustomed to such outrageous remarks. She would've said something, but the reference to Victoria caught her. Brian's bubbly quirks might coax Victoria out of that bedroom, or she might barricade the door and hide forever. She'd always extended courtesy to him, but living with him under this roof could ignite fireworks. Agnes would have to take that risk.

"I'm certain she'll understand. Victoria always surprises me. Norman's death has hit her hard, but perhaps the diversion of Mr. Larney will bring her out into the world again."

"When does the Pied Piper move in?"

"Cristina, he hasn't agreed yet. He's worried about Mrs. O'Toole's reaction."

"I'd jump ship at the chance. How long has that witch of a landlady been lording over him? Didn't you tell me she won't even allow him to open the drapes when he's teaching?"

"All the more reason he should come live with us. I don't think he'd ever be afraid of me. No one's afraid of me. Perhaps I might do better if people were."

"You forget the grand dragon of St. Patrick's. He looked like your mother dragged him to that funeral in shackles and chains."

Agnes froze all the way through. "That is my uncle, Cristina. Remember that, if nothing else. He is a very, very good man."

She wanted to smack Cristina. Grand dragon? How dare she! Agnes ran to the kitchen and paced, biting her knuckles. After a minute, she remembered the laundry. She grabbed the clothes and brought them into the parlor to fold. Why not? Cristina always fidgeted with chores when Agnes visited her.

"If Uncle Collin's afraid of me, it's because he raised me, and I rejected his teachings," Agnes said, her voice shaking like an ill-trained opera soprano. "He has a legitimate point of view. But I don't have the time to talk about it."

Cristina cleared her throat, and her voice seemed far away when she spoke. "What will Mrs. Balmoral do now that she doesn't have to answer to her uncle or her husband? What will you do for money?"

Agnes wished Cristina had stayed home this afternoon. Her finances were not Cristina's business. She knew very well how much money they had at Mechanics Bank—$2,152.45, plus her income at the War Department and Victoria's pension check from the government. The income wasn't nearly enough to live on with tuition to Friends' School and the household expenses, and the savings would evaporate in three years. What if Victoria took ill? She was sixty-two. Medical costs had skyrocketed with the war.

"I think we'll manage just fine," she said, her voice sharp and cutting — she hoped. She looked at the clock, nearly four, thank goodness. Cristina would have to go home soon to cook dinner.

"Agnes, this is Cristina. You can tell me if there's a problem. I might be able to help you out. You could work behind the counter at Cassatas'."

Not for all Queen Elizabeth's jewels would she work all day on her feet. "There's no problem. Let's talk about something else."

"If you need money, you could always sell this house and move back to the general store. Or, you could marry an old widower from Chestnut Hill."

Agnes gasped. "I'd rather become a cloistered nun and wear a hair shirt."

Cristina burst out laughing. "You're only thirty-three. Can you honestly tell me you won't be with a man ever again?"

She gave Cristina an icy stare and let silence fill the room, wondering what had gotten into her. The grandfather clock chimed four. Agnes rose.

"I don't want to be rude, Cristina, but it's time for you to go."

Cristina's head jumped back. "Why the sudden change in your mood? Whatever did I say?"

"You know very well why I'm upset."

"Oh, my goodness, you —" Cristina said, standing up. "What did I say?"

Agnes rolled her eyes. "I've been listening to you for the last half hour. You called Norman 'the little Caesar,' you've been prying into my financial affairs, and you can't wait to gossip about my romantic life."

Cristina's eyes grew as large as two eggs. "I'd never presume to gossip, sweetheart. You mean too much to me."

Agnes felt that familiar lump in her throat and lost control of her voice. "Even though we bungled our marriage, I still miss Norman. May will be two years since the train carried him away from me forever."

"I know. I can picture him standing on the platform, blinking his blue eyes at you, waving good-bye ..."

Agnes heard Cristina's words, but the image of saying good-bye to Norman pushed Cristina out of her mind, and a sad, dull feeling seeped from her head, into her heart, and right through to her bones. "I wish we'd never decided to end our marriage."

"Mercy, I never knew that."

She turned around and released her sobs. Cristina embraced her. "Ah, sweet girl, I thought my sense of humor would lift your spirits, but it backfired. I'm sorry."

Five minutes later, the doorbell rang as Agnes was settling down. Cristina straightened. "The good Mr. Larney left when I came in, and now it's my turn. Donnie and Ronnie will be wanting dinner."

Agnes wiped her face with a handkerchief from the pile of laundry. "If it's another battle-ax like Mrs. Collingwood, please don't leave."

Cristina shook her head. "No, I have to go. But you need to straighten your hair before answering the door."

Agnes inspected herself in the mirror on the way to the door. She couldn't do much about her face, but she did pat her hair back into place. She opened the door, and there stood her mother in a raggedy gray coat.

Agnes's jaw dropped. Mama seemed to appear and disappear out of nowhere these days. "Mother, my goodness ... I wasn't expecting you this afternoon. I don't know what to say. Oh, my stars."

She looked at Mama, she looked at Cristina, and then looked at the sky—because little on the ground seemed to make sense to Agnes. Her stomach gurgled as if in unison with her mind.

"Mrs. Limerick, do you remember me? I'm Cristina Rosamilia."

"Of course, I remember. Agnes, would you care to invite your mother into the house?"

"I'm sorry, Mother. Please come in. Cristina was just leaving."

"No, I'm not!" Cristina barked. Mama's visit would furnish just the kind of drama that would amuse Cristina for days, and Agnes found her voice at last.

"Cristina, you just told me you needed to prepare dinner for your boys. Has anything changed in the past two minutes?" Agnes nodded toward the sidewalk. "My mother and I will want to have our own visit."

Cristina rolled her eyes. "Where are my manners? I'm sorry we can't have a longer visit. Do give my regards to Monsignor Doherty."

"Thank you, Cristina," Mama said. Cristina donned her hat and coat and left. Agnes took her mother's coat and recognized her dark-red dress underneath. Mama had worn it all through the Depression years. She sighed. If only she'd known, she'd have bought Mama a new dress and coat, money matters be damned.

Agnes escorted Mama into the parlor. "Mother, would you have a seat?" She pointed at the sofa, but Mama sat in the high-backed chair and plopped her purse onto her lap. The chair's peach fabric made Mama look like a plump strawberry.

Agnes sat down on the sofa. Apparently, Mama didn't intend to stay long, otherwise she'd have made herself comfortable on the sofa. Agnes reserved those chairs for visitors like Mrs. Collingwood, people she wanted to get rid of as soon as the requisite twenty minutes had passed. But the sight of Mama sitting in her parlor warmed Agnes's heart, and she wanted her mother to remain longer.

"Your Aunt Julia asked to be remembered to you," Mama said. She didn't smile, and she spoke in a monotone—but not unfriendly—so different from the tremulous voice Agnes remembered. "She could not come from New York because her arthritis is acting up. The doctor says it's probably her hip, though no one in our family has ever had bad hips. My own belief, it's something in New York City's water." Mama eyed Agnes's pile of laundry. "What's this?"

"Just some laundry I was folding before Cristina left," Agnes said, picking up one of Victoria's blouses.

She wondered how Mama liked Washington. Mama lived with Patrick in his rented rooms on the top floor of a house on Massachusetts Avenue. "It suits me well enough," Mama said when Agnes asked about it.

She reached into her purse for a set of pictures and handed them to Agnes. Agnes examined a photo of a large Victorian house, Mama and Uncle Collin standing on the front steps, and another one, a raised view of the city looking toward the Washington Monument.

"Is this view from your living room? It's quite magnificent, but it looks too high for the third floor."

"Thank you, daughter. We have a large bay window. The apartment is on the fourth floor, not the third."

She pictured Mama, sixty-six and climbing three flights of stairs. Funny how living on the third floor seemed majestic, whereas living on the fourth floor seemed penurious. But something in Mama's wrinkles prevented Agnes from asking more questions about Washington, much less about Uncle Collin.

Mama talked a little about Washington, her friends at church, the places she walked, how much it differed from Philadelphia, how things had changed in the bunkered city since the war began with soldiers stationed throughout and Red Cross-uniformed men and women patrolling the streets. Even Mrs. Roosevelt, whom Mama would see riding her horse in Rock Creek Park, was known to wear a Red Cross uniform when touring Washington's hospitals. Agnes continued folding laundry and made polite replies to her mother's trail of conversation.

After a while, though, the trail dwindled to an end. Agnes felt an uncomfortable pause. Mama looked around the room and made small talk about the furnishings, wall hangings, even the draperies — anything except Agnes herself. The warmth in her heart began to chill.

"Mother, it meant a lot to me that you and Uncle Collin came to the funeral. You made quite an impact on the chipmunks — I mean, Grace and Harold. They asked a lot of questions on the way to the graveyard."

"They did?" Mama asked, her voice rising, and Agnes felt an excited warmth rush into her heart.

"Yes, indeed, Harold especially," Agnes hurried on. "He doesn't quite understand the idea of having two grandmothers. Norman's father died two years ago, and he was too young to remember Cornelius, so for him it's always been just Nana. Victoria moved here when Norman went to England."

"I know."

"May I ask, Mother, how did you know?"

"Your Uncle Collin keeps me informed of the events in your life."

But how would he know anything? Mama had pressed her lips together and widened her eyes, as if daring Agnes to ask more questions. She complied. Their visit had been going well, and Agnes didn't want to bring Uncle Collin — or that Mother's Day dinner — into it.

"And Grace? How is my granddaughter?"

"She's become very quiet since Norman died. I'm worried about her. Even before that, she spent a lot of time reading, but she's barely lifted her head from her books in the last month. She's reading *Gone With the Wind* again."

"A fine book," Mama said, a deep crease between her eyebrows. "Wonderful story about an Irish family, even if the stubborn lass forsakes her upbringing and falls in love with two English Protestants."

Agnes stood and straightened her dress. "Mother, please. We buried my husband only yesterday. Must we fight the same battles even now?"

Mama gave her an expression that looked like she'd swallowed a grapefruit. "It was reflecting on the book I was doing, child. I didn't come here to argue, I came to pay my respects. And I wanted to make sure all was right with my daughter. You know very well I never approved of Norman Balmoral. Despite that, you are still my child, and I care about what happens to you."

"But I'm not a child, Mother. I am a grown woman, thirty-three years old. Half your age, I might add."

Mama let out a little yelp, and her eyes shone like glass, but she didn't cry.

Agnes wanted to hold her ground, so she changed the subject. "I'm all right. Widowhood is odd. Some time you must tell me how you did it. When Norman went to England, I worried about him dying, but I didn't worry about me surviving. Now that it's happened, the only thing I worry about is my children. How did you ever do it, Mother? How'd you raise us after Daddy died?"

Mama's eyes crinkled ever so slightly around the edges, and her mouth pulled down. She remained silent and then said, "I had my faith, I suppose, and your uncle was always so helpful. And your father left us with quite a lot of money. It's the money you used to buy this very house."

Mama clenched her teeth and released them. "The hardest part, the most difficult was wondering how it would affect you. I worry still about Patrick. He works day and night just to keep us in that fourth-floor apartment, when he should find a wife and raise a family. I hear nothing but disappointment from Collin, who says it's unnatural for the boy to be unmarried at forty-three."

Blood rushed to Agnes's face. "Our family would do well with less meddling from Monsignor Doherty."

"Mind your tongue, young lady," Mama said, her voice choppy. "You don't want to cut this family in two once again, now do you? I'd like to sew it back together. Your uncle has always had your best interests at heart."

Agnes could feel the temperature rising. She wished they were out for a walk with Keaton rather than interviewing each other here on the parlor furniture.

She breathed and tried to keep her temper from percolating. Mama had traveled all the way from Washington to attend the funeral of a son-in-law whom she'd detested. That meant something, and she'd be doubly outraged if she knew how Norman had behaved in the marriage.

"I'm sorry about everything, Mother." She hesitated, then decided to elaborate. "I'm sorry it hurt you when I left home to marry Norman. I'm sorry we couldn't get along properly. And I'm sorry you haven't seen Grace and Harold in eight years. But as Granny said, you do what you have to do."

Mama didn't say anything, but what more could be said? Agnes finished folding the laundry and laid the children's underclothes on the coffee table. How odd, Harold's underwear on top of *The Architecture of Frank Furness*. Architecture, the love of Norman's life, something she'd belittled him about more than once. Her heart ached. If only ...

"Your grandchildren are playing upstairs, Mother. Shall I fetch them?"

"Of course." Mama gave Agnes her first real smile of the visit. "That is one of the reasons I came to Philadelphia, to attend to my grandchildren who've just lost their father."

"And for what other reasons?" Agnes said, a staccato at the edge of every syllable.

"To see my only daughter. The time for us to reconcile is long past, child."

"Thank you," Agnes said, this time with soft edges. "I'll go fetch the chipmunks, but only if you promise to stay here. As a matter of fact, it surprised me that you left the service right after communion."

"Don't say clichés like 'as a matter of fact,' daughter. It's a waste of time. I know it was rude. I left because I couldn't bear what I saw."

"A Protestant funeral? Much like a Catholic one."

"Not that, daughter. I couldn't bear seeing my daughter, a young widow at her husband's funeral with two children, sitting in the front pew with her mother-in-law. It reminded me too much of myself. You should remember. You were there."

Agnes slapped a hand over her mouth. Why hadn't she realized what the funeral would've meant to Mama? She'd been too focused on her own shock, never considering what Mama might've been feeling. She looked at her mother, a round strawberry with apple cheeks sitting in a peach chair. Life had passed Mama by, and she'd never complained once, not even about losing four babies. Agnes wished she could think more about others than herself, and there was no better time to start than now.

"I'm going upstairs to fetch Grace and Harold. They'll be excited to see you. I'm also going to bring Victoria, if I can snatch her out of her grief. Someone needs to help her, and I think you're just the one to do it."

"I know nothing about Victoria Balmoral. How could I possibly help?"

"Something tells me, Mother," Agnes said — and corrected herself. "Mama. Mama, something tells me you could help a grieving mother move past the loss of a child better than anyone."

21

HAROLD, ALWAYS ENAMORED WITH TRAINS, had begged her for two years to ride the Broadway Limited. She finally gave him his wish — at Brian's suggestion, to spend a weekend in New York two weeks before Christmas. It was a snowy Saturday when they boarded the Broadway Limited at Zoo Junction for Manhattan. The diversion pleased Agnes, and she was thankful they weren't departing from 30ᵗʰ Street, where she'd have to relive Norman's funeral and the terrible emptiness of that day.

Agnes got on the train with Brian and the children, a bevy of red, blue, and green coats, scarves, hats, and gloves, all prepared for a snowy weekend. She'd thought Victoria would accompany them when she'd made their reservations at the Paramount Hotel and had written away for tickets to *Oklahoma!*, and even had held high hopes that Mama would come up from Washington. But Mama came down with a head cold before the trip, and her mother-in-law declined. Victoria had emerged from her bedroom and even had gone to church a handful of times, but she wouldn't leave town. She might sink into her grief, Victoria explained, and there'd be nowhere familiar to go if she weren't in Philadelphia. So it would be just the four of them, off to New York for a weekend of Christmas festivities at Times Square, Fifth Avenue, and Macy's.

"What fun, children! Brian, you and Harold sit by the window," she said as they slid into their compartment. She'd dressed in a blue-gray suit with pleated skirt and jacket, a fashionable but modest choice for Philadelphia's newest widow.

Brian started up a game of *Notes and Songs*. He'd hum the notes of a well-known song (his first choice, "The Little Drummer Boy"), and the children would guess it in as few notes as possible (seven notes for Harold). Since Brian had moved into the room across from Harold, the two had become best buddies. Harold would stand at the door to the music room and listen to Brian drill scales into his students' heads. Later, Brian would help Harold set up houses with blocks and laugh when he tore them down.

Somewhere north of Princeton, their game morphed into *Categories*, books being their first. They found a book for every letter except Q and X. Agnes demurred from the second round — movies, of course. She wanted to write a letter to Mama before reaching New York.

Agnes wrote letters Friday evenings after dinner but recently hadn't had the time. Victoria still failed to rouse energy for cooking, even though Mama had remained in Philadelphia an extra week, taking Victoria for walks around the park, to St. Mark's for early morning communion, to the zoo and movies with Grace and Harold. And Brian had moved in and given them concerts every evening before dinner and games every Sunday afternoon. Preparing all the family's meals now fell to Agnes. Victoria finally had begun joining them at the dinner table and, just this past week, had started knitting Christmas sweaters for Grace and Harold.

So Agnes was only half finished with the letter she'd started Friday, thanking Mama for the package of Christmas gifts, when she saw the snowy majesty of the Empire State Building across the river. They'd soon pass under the Hudson River. She'd wanted to tell Mama about her job, about the condolence letter she'd received from President and Mrs. Roosevelt, about the U.S. Navy notifying her that she'd receive a widow's lump sum payment of $27,000. But the tunnel's darkness enveloped the train, so her news would have to wait.

Penn Station took Agnes's breath away, a million busy people rushing in a million directions like atoms colliding in a molecule. And the noise and the lights! Agnes had considered 30th Street a beehive of activity, but now it seemed like a deserted depot in an Appalachian village. Brian quickly led them up to street level in a fizz of conversation about what to expect when they emerged onto 33rd Street.

"The first thing we'll do is walk over to the Empire State Building, the tallest building in the world," he told them, tipping a porter to take their suitcases to the Paramount. "Harold, when was it built?"

Harold stood to attention, pursed his lips, and opened his eyes wide. "1931, just like the P.S.F.S."

"Excellent, an architect like his father."

A whisper of pain squeezed Agnes's heart. Harold, just like his father? The four emerged outside to a city covered in white. Thank heavens, they'd dressed warmly and worn snow boots. "Perhaps we should take a taxicab," Agnes said.

"Poppycock," Brian said. "It's only two blocks away. Everything we're doing in New York is a short walk, except perhaps the Carnegie Deli. I thought we'd have lunch there after attending Mass at St. Patrick's Cathedral."

She'd wanted to take the children to the Cathedral of St. John the Divine, but Brian told her Morningside Heights was too far away and they'd have time for nothing else on Sunday. And Harold counted on seeing Santa Claus at Macy's, so they'd attend services at the Catholic cathedral rather than the Episcopal one.

She kept a tight hold on the children's hands as they walked down 33rd toward Herald Square. Grace and Harold, their red and blue coats bright against the snow, stared with wide eyes and opened mouths as if it were none other than Emerald City. Agnes had thought Philadelphia had as much as any city needed to offer, but Manhattan's size overwhelmed her. She felt as though her own city had been multiplied by sixteen.

Brian chatted up a blue streak about New York. "Lunch at Bernie's Kosher Deli after the Empire State Building. And then *Oklahoma!*, the most popular show on Broadway since *Show Boat*."

Jewish delis — Agnes salivated at the thought of Mrs. Stein's lachs, knishes, and blintzes. She hadn't wanted a kosher pickle this much since being pregnant with Harold. "Is Bernie's anything like Famous?"

Brian laughed. "It's more like Famous than Famous is."

"Won't that be fun, Grace?"

Grace turned her head to Agnes, and her hair flopped in front of her face. "I suppose so," she said into Agnes's Loden coat.

Agnes had been unable to predict Grace's moods since Norman died. The child had resisted the trip, pretending she had too much homework, even pleading with Victoria to intercede, but Agnes had said no.

"Darling, look at the buildings and all the people," Agnes said to her daughter. "Always make the most of new experiences like this one, sweetheart."

They walked by the Empire State Building and looked up. It seemed to reach for the heavens. So many throngs of people walking past them just like swimming upstream, Agnes remarked. Brian explained they were businessmen with their briefcases, wearing black derbies, and fur-clad women, carrying packages from Gimbels and Macy's, all racing to Penn Station on their way back to Westchester County. It seemed the only ones heading their direction were young couples holding hands, most of the men in uniform. Norman came to Agnes's mind once again, and she felt yet another twinge of pain. If only ...

On their way to the St. James Theatre for *Oklahoma!* after their lunch of corned beef sandwiches, cole slaw, and cheese blintzes at the noisy diner, Grace smiled and laughed more, brightening with the day. The sun had emerged, and the sky had turned blue, bringing the city into white magnificence. Agnes cried out when they reached Times Square. Norman and she often had talked about visiting New York.

"I don't see how anyone could not love New York," she said, Gershwin's melodies running through her head, yearning to breathe in all the city had to offer. "If only we could have a month rather than just a weekend."

"Mama, I have to go to the bathroom," Grace said, her words hurried.

"We'll be at the theater soon."

"I mean now."

"Grace, you can wait. We're only ten minutes from the theater."

"Mama, why did we have to rush out of the restaurant? You never do anything right."

"That's enough. Look, here's a restaurant on the corner."

But the host refused them. "Only paying customers, lady."

"I beg your pardon?" Agnes said.

"There's the sign, ma'am, restroom for customers only."

"We'll use the bathroom at the St. James," Brian said. "This man's a rude son of a bitch."

"Watch it, pal," the man said. But Agnes scored a point for Brian, even if he was teaching her children bad words. The man deserved it.

"What's the St. James, Uncle Brian?" Harold said on their way out the door. "Will the show be performed at church?"

"No, this is a theater, and *Oklahoma!* is the only thing playing. We were lucky to get tickets at all, let alone orchestra center."

The rousing excitement of "Oh, What a Beautiful Morning" and "The Surrey with the Fringe on Top," a succulent dinner at Le Petit Forts, elegant mattresses in their three-room suite at the Paramount Hotel, a carriage ride through Central Park on Sunday morning, the majesty of St. Patrick's Cathedral, snowballs in Herald Square, all made the weekend a joy. And when Grace finally started laughing at the snowball fight, Agnes decided the trip had been worth the money. Well worth it, seeing her children laugh and frolic in the snow, chasing each other and Brian around Herald Square, falling down, laughing some more, getting back up and dusting the snow off their coats.

"Children," Agnes called out to them. "One more stop to make before we board the train. Do you still want to see Santa Claus?"

"Ten more minutes," Harold cried and went back to making snowballs.

"Five minutes!" she countered.

She'd be a lucky woman if she had half Brian's energy at sixty. She was pleased he'd agreed to live with them and that he'd come on this trip, despite the stares she got from the Rittenhouse Square matrons, Mrs. Collingwood included, when she mentioned her "boarder." A scandalous thought, young Mrs. Balmoral traveling with an unmarried man, even if he had a pug nose, was overweight, bald, and sixty. She knew they disapproved, but didn't care.

When they entered the grand foyer of Macy's on 34th Street, Agnes gasped and covered her mouth. She hadn't imagined how grand it would be. Yes, Wanamaker's in Philadelphia had a special charm with its organ concerts in the central rotunda, but it paled in comparison to Macy's opulence.

The store was covered in lavish greens and reds, its deep-red carpets atop swirled marble floors, sixteen marble columns supporting the structure, twenty-foot ceilings adorned in gold, crystal chandeliers above the sales booths, ornate wooden consoles where saleswomen marketed fine colognes, jewels, clothing, and a grand staircase curving up from the first-floor literature department to the children's department above.

Macy's splendor impressed out-of-towners year-round. But at Christmas, festooned with elegant gold-bowed wreaths, draped together by loose evergreens, twelve-foot-tall trees decorated with white lights, doves, and angels, and silver banners celebrating the holiday, Macy's harkened back to the Gilded Age before depression and war had changed everything.

Agnes wondered how the store could afford the extravagance. The Depression might have ended only a few years back, and the government now rationed everything from cotton to butter, but no one would notice anything like scarcity here. Nor would anyone imagine that suffering existed in the world. The atrocities in Europe and oppression in the Far East seemed too distant from this vantage point.

"I've never seen such bright gold and silver," Agnes said. She and Brian walked toward the grand staircase. Grace and Harold's mood rose even higher than snowballs in the park, and they pranced ahead, hand in hand.

Brian smirked. "Unless possibly around Cristina's neck."

"You're incorrigible. The jewelry is so attractive on her."

"What is she doing for herself now that Angelo's been sent to the Pacific?"

"Work, I suppose, and taking care of Donnie and Ronnie." Agnes turned to face Brian at the base of the staircase as the children started up. "I haven't seen her in two weeks. She seemed down that day. I think Angelo worries her. Perhaps she thinks Norman's death is contagious."

Brian clucked his tongue and shook his head. Agnes thought he'd stick his tongue out the side of his mouth and cross his eyes like he'd done so often in piano lessons, but he kept a straight face. "Pure superstition. Norman was ten thousand miles from the South Pacific."

Piano music floated toward them from the back of the store. "Brian, I think someone's performing a concert for us. Shall we listen?"

"If you ask me, what puts Cristina on edge is having her husband that far away. Behind those bushy eyebrows and eyeglasses lies a wild woman."

How could he tell? "Brian Larney, shame on you. Grace and Harold, come down those stairs. We're going to listen to the music before visiting Santa."

They came upon a small group of people listening to a young woman, a redhead who reminded Agnes of herself ten years ago. She played Christmas carols at the piano. Grace and Harold squirmed in front of Agnes, and Grace pulled her skirt a minute later and said, "We're going upstairs to see Santa."

"Sweetheart, wait until the music is done."

"Agnes, I think it's all right for them to visit Santa while we're down here."

"All right, Grace," she said, taking a compact mirror out of her purse to smooth her hair. "You may go, but you hold onto Harold's hand."

They were off in an instant. She smiled and looked after them, telling herself not to worry. Grace was growing up faster than Agnes could grasp.

"Look at that couple over there," Brian said, nodding at a middle-aged couple. "I'd guess they haven't had sex in ten years. I was watching them when we walked in. No touching, no conversation, no real connection."

"What about that couple?" Agnes asked, looking at a woman in a cheap fur and her mate in sailor's dark blue. "What does your crystal ball reveal there?"

"They haven't had sex yet. He wants to, but she wants to wait until they get married."

"How do you know?"

"She's holding his hand, but she's clutching that coat close to her throat. It's not that cold in here. Clearly, she's keeping something to herself."

Agnes thought for a minute while the pianist played "Hark, the Herald Angels Sing" and "Do You Hear What I Hear?"

"Did you ever think about Norman and—" but she stopped. She wasn't ready to confide in him, least of all in the middle of a New York City department store. "Never mind, forget I said anything."

Agnes couldn't believe Brian's boldness. Only Cristina matched it. Curious, her two closest friends exercised no restraint in talking about sex. She'd hardly have expected a librarian and a piano teacher to speak so frankly, but she did enjoy it. She'd certainly never heard it from anyone else.

"We need to get upstairs before they talk to Santa," Agnes said. "Harold's already rattled off a long list of toys he wants for Christmas, so I know what he wants. But I have no idea what Grace wants Santa to bring this year."

Agnes wished Grace would snap out of her moods. Her daughter always had jumped for joy at Christmas, but not this year. The pianist started into *The Nutcracker Suite*. Agnes always had found the music tiresome and stupid.

"Isn't Grace getting a little old for Santa Claus?" Brian said.

"She told Norman two years ago she wanted to continue it for Harold's sake," Agnes said. "Let's go upstairs, Brian. Perhaps they'll make it through the line and we can come back here before the pianist gets to the 'Waltz of the Flowers.' That's Grace's favorite."

They walked up to the second floor, the toy department on one side and children's clothing on the other. Starting with a harried mother and her two sons, one sucking his thumb and the other crying loudly, they saw a long line of children—just like the first two—bisecting the floor.

"Quite the line of hooligans," Brian said. "And there's Santa. Ho, ho, ho. Do you see the children in this line?"

Agnes balanced on tippy-toes just like the *Nutcracker* ballerinas. "It's like finding needles in a haystack. Let me see."

Scanning the line forward and backward, she saw neither Grace nor Harold. Perhaps she and Brian had lost track of time and they'd advanced to the front?

Agnes walked up and down the line, searching for Grace's red coat and Harold's blue, her brown hair and his blond. But she reached the front of the line without seeing them. She walked up and down again, Brian ten feet behind.

"Pardon me," she said to a father with three young girls holding lollipops. "I'm looking for my children, a boy and a girl. He's six and she's eleven. Have you seen them?"

The man scrunched his face into curly wrinkles and rolled his eyes. "Lady, there are a hundred children matching that description here."

Agnes rushed to Santa. No sign of Grace and Harold, not even on Santa's lap. Nowhere they'd looked, nowhere they could see, nowhere Agnes could imagine. She turned to Brian.

Every nerve ending in Agnes's body zapped. "Where in the hell are my chipmunks?"

She scanned her left, her right, behind her, in front of her. She focused on the people in her range of vision, the line of children waiting for Santa, their mothers and the few fathers. She looked toward the front of the store, her views obstructed by pine trees and evergreens displayed on book cases, shelves, and around the columns. Christmas reds and greens played out in front of her darting eyes and dared her to find what was missing.

"I've got to find them," she cried, dashing toward the front of the store.

"Stay calm, Agnes. Let's ask Santa first," Brian said, his face pink and his mouth open and shaking. She ran back toward Santa.

"My children are missing," she blurted at the fat man who had a five-year-old pouting boy on his lap. "I need your help. Grace and Harold are their names. She's eleven, has long brown hair and brown eyes. He's six, blond hair, blue eyes, fair and freckled. Grace is wearing a blue coat. He's wearing a red."

"Ah, yes," Santa said. "Perhaps ten minutes ago. They sat together on my lap. They got this odd look on their faces when I asked what they wanted Santa to bring them. The girl said, 'Geronimo.' They jumped off my lap and vanished."

Grace never spoke like that at home. "Thank you. Brian, you stay put in case they come back. I'm going to look for them."

"But Agnes—"

She ran to her left and disappeared behind a curtain of Christmas trees. Ah, the toy department, surely they'd be there.

She darted to the counter, scanning the displays of cars, choo-choo sets, all the toys Harold loved best. Why wasn't he here? But very few people and no children resembling her own meandered among the toys. She asked a stout lady with pointy glasses behind the counter. With a lift of her eyebrows and a shake of her head, the lady told her she hadn't seen any stray children running around. If she had, she'd have turned them in to the security guard.

Agnes looked beyond the toy department. There was a passageway to another department in the front. Ah, dolls! Yes, Grace would want dolls for Christmas. Yet, there were no children in this department, empty but for another woman at the counter, her nose buried in a stack of receipts and orders.

She glanced up as Agnes approached and inquired, then said, "Sorry, ma'am, not a soul's been here for a half hour. You'd think we were fighting a war."

Agnes would've made a sarcastic reply but didn't have the time. Beyond the doll department was an elaborate display of model airplanes. The model kit department! Surely Harold would be playing there. He loved flying and told her he wanted to be a Navy pilot just like his daddy. When Agnes corrected him, Harold shook his head and said no, Daddy was a pilot just like all the other boys' fathers.

But there was no trace of Harold and Grace in there either. She'd circled all the way to the front of the store, certain her children would be ogling toys, dolls, or model airplanes. But no Grace and Harold.

Her heart picked up a beat, her mouth went dry, and she felt a queasy weight in the pit of her stomach. She circled the front of the store to the other side, looking down a long passageway. Children's clothing. Perhaps Grace wanted clothing for Christmas. She checked the boys department — nothing. She ran on to the girls department — nothing. She sped up and scanned the toddlers department — again, nothing. Finally, the babies department before circling back to Santa. Grasping at straws, yes — Grace and Harold, no.

She sprinted two steps at a time up the staircase to the third floor. They could be no place other than here. She and Brian had stood near the staircase on the first floor, and she'd just scoured the second. The third floor was the only other one open to customers.

It was getting hot in the damned store. At the top of the stairs, she reached an open foyer with a marble hallway leading to the back where an organ sat. Music, that was the reason she'd lost her children. If she and Brian hadn't been so focused on listening to the damned pianist and talking about sex, she wouldn't have lost track of Grace and Harold. They were all that remained from Norman. Was God punishing her for having pushed Norman away, by snatching their children back? Was he punishing her for loving music more than Norman, for laughing with Brian at the piano on the day after the funeral?

The heat under her Loden coat became unbearable. She tore it off and threw it over an artificial bush, but dropped her purse on the floor, so she bent down to pick it up. On both sides were more displays of Christmas trees, evergreens, and festooned columns. Why did the store have to conceal so much? Damn the decorations. She needed a clear field of vision to find her babies. She ran to the left side. The trees yielded to linens, fine china, silver, and crystal, but no one had seen any unaccompanied children. She raced around the corner, but the bath, kitchen, and housewares departments all reported the same thing. No children and very few adults. But would she like to inspect their finest Wedgewood? To hell with the Wedgewood, she replied.

"I need to find my children!" she added, her voice high and tremulous.

"Mind you, pipe down," the salesman said. "There are other shoppers here."

She didn't care if she made a spectacle. After all, she'd never see these strangers again. So she ran to the marble foyer and back down the stairs to the Santa line.

Now Brian was gone. Her children gone, Brian gone. She was alone. Mama had gone to Washington to live with Patrick. Victoria had receded under a cloud of grief. And Norman had died just like Granny and Daddy. Oh, Norman, not our children too …

She raced again to the front of the store, and headed back into the children's department. She ignored some sort of yellow sign and slipped on a patch of shiny flooring. She twisted her ankle and landed on her elbow. Her ankle throbbed, and flashes of pain shot down her forearm.

She burst into tears, not sure whether her ankle or elbow hurt more. No one would help her. Where were her children? They needed her, and she needed them.

A white-haired guard came up to her. "Ma'am, are you hurt? Let me help you into a chair."

"I'm not hurt. Leave me be. I can't find my children. They're lost somewhere here in this furnace of a store. I've got to find them."

"Oh, we'll find them. Where did you last see them?"

They passed a long mirror, and Agnes got a look at herself—limping, sobbing, hair fallen onto her shoulders, her suit disheveled. Who cared?

"First floor by the stairs. I've looked everywhere on the second and third floors."

"Hold on, hadn't you better look on the first floor again?"

"That's where we last saw them. They ran up the stairs to visit Santa while

I listened to the music. I stood right near the staircase. I would've seen them come back. It couldn't have been more than five minutes."

The guard escorted her by the arm. She limped, ignoring the screaming pain from her ankle and elbow. But she didn't care about the pain.

They walked down to the first floor to the guard's back office. She sat down beside the desk, retrieved a handkerchief, and blew her nose. The guard asked her for pictures of Grace and Harold, and she fetched snapshots from her purse.

The guard alerted the front desk. "If these children are still in the store, we're going to find them. Now I need to talk to the head guard. Just a moment." He looked outside the office's door. "What have we here?"

Agnes turned and saw a heavy-set man in a dull-blue suit leading Brian to the back office.

"Agnes," Brian said, "I've never been so glad to see you. I flagged down this security guard and we've been trying to locate the children. We went up to the third floor. The guard thought they might've smuggled themselves up the stairs to the fourth floor, but they're not there, either. Why—"

Another woman with pointy glasses — this one much older and wearing a heavy gray tailored suit– stomped toward them, pulling Grace and Harold in her wake.

The floodgates of relief stilled Agnes's throbbing mind and aching heart. "Thank you, God!" She forgot her ankle pain and jumped up as the children broke free and ran to her. Agnes kneeled on the floor and hugged them.

"I found these children snooping around for heaven knows what in the music department, rifling through antique music books and banging on the piano," the woman said. "I suppose you're the mother —"

"Darlings, don't ever leave Mama again. I was worried to death."

"Why, Mama?" Harold said. "Everybody was really nice except for this mean old wicked witch."

"You should be ashamed, losing track of your children. The store has its rules—" the woman said.

"Never mind, Mrs. Needlemaier," the guard said. "Thank you. You've given a lot of us peace of mind."

"Now hold on—" she said, but scowled and left in a cackle of noisy heels.

Agnes breathed easier. "I didn't know where you'd gone, chipmunks. Neither did Uncle Brian. Please don't ever do that again. Don't go anywhere without letting Mama know. Too many bad things happen to little boys and girls these days. Promise me?"

Grace and Harold fell silent. Agnes looked up at Brian, hoping he'd add a point or two, but he simply rested his face in his palm. She'd have to be the one to discipline the children.

"Grace, why did you disappear from Santa's lap? Why didn't you just wait for Uncle Brian and me after seeing Santa?"

"We weren't done visiting Santa, Mama."

"What do you mean, little Gracie?"

Her daughter dropped her chin, rolled her eyes up, and shook her head. "Don't call me 'little Gracie,' Mama. I'm eleven."

"All right. Tell me about Santa."

"Well, Mama," she said, leaning back from Agnes to look at her. "Santa asked us what we wanted for Christmas."

"Of course, he did. That's what Santas do."

"I took one look at Harold, and we both knew right away what we wanted. So we ran back downstairs to the music department."

"What a mystery children are! Why'd you do that? There are no toys or books in that department."

"We wanted to get something for you, Mama. The only time we've seen you smile since Daddy died has been when you're playing the piano. And when you and Uncle Brian were listening to that piano player. We wanted Santa to bring us some piano music so you'd be smiling all next year."

Agnes's heart glowed at the thought of her chipmunks and their undeceptive wisdom. They were looking after her, it turned out, and saw things about her that even she hadn't noticed. Funny how they noticed she smiled only when she played the piano, as if an escape from grief for their father. Why, Norman had said nearly the same thing. *You're using music to escape from me.* What a ridiculous notion, and yet ...

22

S EVEN WEEKS AFTER D-DAY AS THE ALLIES BATTLED toward Paris, Agnes announced on a sunny Saturday in Rittenhouse Square that she'd be traveling with Dr. Friedman to Washington. The five of them sat on a blanket with Keaton. To celebrate the war's progress, they made the warm afternoon a festive occasion—Agnes and Grace in jumper dresses with white blouses, Brian in a red-and-blue short-sleeved shirt and white slacks, Harold in his favorite blue knickers. Only Victoria, in her gray cotton dress, wore muted colors.

"Whatever for, my dear, and for how long?" Victoria said. "What needs to be done in Washington that can't be accomplished here?"

Agnes looked at her mother-in-law, the high cheekbones and square chin that she'd had given Norman and Grace still dominating her thin face. She hadn't regained the weight she'd lost after Norman died, but at least she smiled more often, as she did now, and joined them for outings such as this.

"Never you mind, I know nothing, only that he's chosen me to accompany him for a War Department briefing. Dr. Friedman has been very secretive. I don't think anyone in our office knows why."

"Can I come with you, Mama, pretty please? The Pentagon is bigger than anything in Philadelphia, and it's brand new," Harold said, trying to shade his eyes with his hand. His blue eyes seemed more sensitive to the sun than Grace's brown. And Agnes observed the sun reflecting a brilliant glare off his face and blond hair, cowlicks shooting in different directions, his face whiter than either she or Norman ever had been.

"*May* you come with your mother, Harold," Brian corrected. "Something tells me, Agnes, you know more about this project than you're telling us. Despite that blank stare, I think you know everything, but you're sworn to secrecy."

Agnes sighed. "I would appreciate it if you didn't correct my children's grammar. That's my prerogative. Harold, we say *may* when we're asking for permission and *can* when we're talking about our capability."

Harold rolled his eyes. Brian laughed so hard, he snorted. "You're avoiding my question," he said.

Brian's snort sounded like a pig, and he looked like one with that pug nose and pink head. And once in a while, he *might* try to read between the lines, but she wondered if he really *could*, being Brian.

"You'll never know, because now that you've asked, my lips are sealed in perpetuity."

"What's purple tooty, Mama?" Harold said.

"Mama, I need your help with ballet practice," Grace said. She scrunched up her mouth and nose, and pulled at Agnes's sleeve. Her hair bobbed side to side. Since Grace was nearly twelve, Agnes allowed her to forsake the ponytail and wear her hair loose, something her own mother had waited too long to do.

"It's July, Grace. I didn't think you would have any serious assignments until September."

Had she lost track of what her children were doing? Although Victoria and Brian took turns taking Grace to ballet rehearsals and Harold to summer school during the workday, that didn't excuse her. Education was the most important thing she could provide for the chipmunks.

"Grace, I can help you," Brian said, clutching imaginary pearls. "I am your piano teacher."

"I'll help you with ballet, Grace," Victoria said, clutching authentic pearls. "I am your grandmother."

How should she handle this skirmish? Sometimes she wondered if she'd made the right decision, inviting Brian to live with them. But he did so much for the children, even if Victoria resented it, and he infused a happy mood to the house.

"I'll be gone two days next week. We leave Wednesday morning and return Thursday evening. Victoria, will you take care of the children and the house?"

"Dadgummit, two days." Grace said, moaning.

"That's enough, Grace," said Agnes, "and I'd like to know where you learned that word, young lady."

Grace's eyes turned into two brown saucers, and she looked at Brian.

Agnes frowned. "You're teaching my children good grammar and bad words."

"Mercy, me," Brian said. "Growing pains — my own, I expect. She probably heard me say it in the middle of a piano lesson. I'm sorry, Agnes. Grace, I made a mistake when I said that word."

Grace's reservoir of tears almost spilled over. "I'm sorry, Mama."

Agnes felt a wave of sympathy for her darling girl. She could remember suffering similar rebukes from Uncle Collin, and not that long ago, either.

Brian rose from the blanket. "It won't happen again. Would you excuse me? Miss Barlow is coming for her lesson at four o'clock, and that's in twenty minutes. Thank you for a lovely afternoon in the park, Agnes," he said, bowing to them. "And you, Victoria."

Her mother-in-law lowered her eyes but bowed her head. Her eyelids wrinkled in a way Agnes never had noticed. Victoria waited until Brian had left before raising her eyes, the blues shining at Agnes and her mouth razor-thin. "On a Saturday afternoon? I thought we agreed, no students on weekends."

"We did, but this is Betty Barlow. She rescheduled just this once. Her family is going to New York next week to meet their father on leave."

"It's always 'just this once,'" Victoria said. "I wish we could have one solid day of peace and quiet."

"It irritates me too, but we agreed to music lessons when he moved in."

Agnes felt a throb of guilt. She'd lost track of the piano in recent months, dabbling no more than two or three times a week. Between her job, Grace and Harold, and keeping Victoria and Brian on an even keel, she had no time to herself. So she yielded the instrument to Grace, who'd progressed from beginner to advanced just since January.

And then something popped into her head. Norman had made every argument to discourage her from playing but hadn't succeeded. But now that he was dead, she no longer felt the urge to play. Was it more than just being too busy with raising the children, managing the house, and going to work? Could it be she'd buried herself in music to avoid Norman and now that he was gone, she no longer needed, or even wanted, to play?

Victoria shifted on the blanket. "The music lessons don't bother me, but young children banging on the piano does. Would you do something about it?"

Something told Agnes that noise wasn't Victoria's real objection. "Victoria, I wish you liked Brian better. I know his teaching is an inconvenience, but he does lighten the mood around the house. Isn't that right, Grace? Harold?"

"Yes, Mama," they answered in perfect unison.

Victoria sighed, looking her daughter-in-law squarely in the eye. "He hardly seems the proper role model for my grand—"

"Nevertheless," Agnes said. "He's a member of our family, and we need to accommodate him. And his students."

"Oh, all right. Brian Larney is a likeable sort. If it makes you happy. But he does try my patience on a daily basis."

If Victoria ever decided she'd had enough of Brian and moved in with Norman's brother, how would Agnes manage? But no, Victoria detested her other daughter-in-law's social climbing. Agnes bargained she'd rather live with Brian than try to outdo Main Line society matrons. But what about Brian? Perhaps he just didn't fit in with her family.

"Mama, if you're going to Washington, will you see Grandma Siobhan?" Harold asked.

"Yes, I'll be seeing Grandma." Of course, she'd visit Mama. Agnes smiled inside and out. She hadn't seen Mama since she'd come to Philadelphia for her birthday in May. A golden opportunity to see Mama's home in Washington.

"Shall we buy her a gift?" Agnes said. "Her birthday is this month. She'll be sixty-seven."

Keaton jumped up and ran after a squirrel. But the squirrel scurried up a tree and left Keaton barking at the trunk, his record at catching squirrels still zero. He came back, nudged Agnes in the side, and whimpered.

"What is it, Keaton?" she asked, petting his forehead and nudging him back. "Do you want to go for … a walk?" The dog jumped up and barked at the sky. "Okay, chipmunks. Enough baking in the sun. We're going for a walk to the art museum to see the children's exhibit. You too, Victoria."

The following Wednesday morning, Agnes stood on the platform at 30th Street Station, dressed in a dark-blue skirt and jacket, carrying a satchel. The train waited for the passengers to board, impatient to be on its way, she supposed, wondering where Dr. Friedman might be. At last, the good doctor sprinted down the stairs, an odd sight for a man nearly sixty in an ill-fitting suit and floppy hat. Once aboard, Agnes and Dr. Friedman walked from car to car looking for seats, balancing in the aisles as the train rocked out of Center City. They found seats by the time the Schuylkill River came into view. Dr. Friedman buried his head in a scientific journal while Agnes enjoyed the view. She didn't want to read in the moving train.

After they passed Wilmington and headed into Maryland, he lowered the journal to his lap, folded his hands, and looked at her before speaking. "Please forgive me for asking a personal question, Agnes. It's been nine months since … since October. May I ask how you've managed this job and your household? Is there anything we can do to help?"

Agnes looked at the Maryland farmlands and tried to shut everything else out. How had she managed? After Norman died, she thought she'd retreat into the shadows of mourning and cloak her grief by raising his children. But the waves of real grief never had really come, perhaps because they'd agreed to a separation, perhaps because she'd gotten accustomed to his absence, or — terrible thought — perhaps because she'd even liked it.

Thank goodness she'd returned to work only a month after Norman died and didn't have to brood over it. From the new year on, work had proceeded at a furious pace. Agnes understood more and more about Dr. Friedman's project of nuclear fusion. He would say nothing of the project's larger purpose and seemed to enjoy deflecting his proteges' questions with evasive answers. He darted back and forth from this place to that — Princeton, Washington, even New Mexico. Agnes had heard a rumor from a pink intern with thick glasses and matted hair that their project was at the center of an effort to build a "super bomb" to use against Germany.

Agnes didn't believe this. Dr. Friedman hated war, he raved against violence, and he lamented the state of the "world on fire," as he called it. He told Agnes that he hated the Germans for enslaving and mistreating the Jews en masse when the International Red Cross wasn't looking, and he deplored the daily casualty counts, which he felt would surpass fifty million. Agnes couldn't believe the number. And despite all the horrors she'd heard in the news since Kristallnacht, she prayed the nation that had given them Bach, Brahms, and Beethoven wasn't murdering kind and generous people such as Dr. Friedman, Mrs. Stein, or Mrs. Weisskopf. Deep down, however, she admitted the truth ... without wanting to.

She spoke up after a minute. "I'm managing well enough, Dr. Friedman. The children keep me busy, and I have help. My mother-in-law lives with us and so does our piano teacher. He's an old family friend."

Her heart jumped into her throat. She hadn't yet called Mama, but she would when they reached the hotel. "When do you think I could visit my mother, Dr. Friedman?"

"Tomorrow evening. Then we can return to Philadelphia on Friday morning. We dine with War Department officials tonight."

"I'll call when we register at the hotel. The Mayflower, you said?"

"Yes," he said, tilting his head and body forward, and whispering. "The government is treating us with only a little less grandeur than they treated King George and Queen Elizabeth."

"Why are we receiving royal treatment?"

"First things first. We're not going to the Mayflower until evening. You can call your mother when we get to ..."

"Get to where, Dr. Friedman?"

"I'm going to finish my reading. Why don't you read something too?"

He had an uncanny knack for avoiding her questions by asking questions himself. So she rummaged for her latest book, an Agatha Christie mystery, *The ABC Murders*. The killer was obvious — D must've done it — so Agnes put the book down, unmotivated.

A military attaché Dr. Friedman knew greeted them in the grand hallway at Union Station and took them to a black Packard. It looked like something Al Capone would've driven. Despite a heavy rain, the attaché donned black sunglasses as he drove down Louisiana Avenue and sped onto Constitution Avenue. They drove alongside the Capitol. Agnes hadn't seen it since Mama and Uncle Collin had brought them here in the mid '20s. It still made Agnes dizzy to look at the round dome. She remembered the Coolidge years and especially Mrs. Coolidge — named Grace, just like her own girl.

The driver turned onto Pennsylvania Avenue, and Agnes saw the White House in the distance. She noted the landmarks they passed — the National Gallery, John Marshall Park, the National Archives. They made a sweeping turn toward the White House. She remembered the mansion being pure white, but it looked gray, as if thirteen years of depression and war had taken a heavy toll.

"Before we get to the Pentagon, would you ask the driver to stop on this side of the bridge?" Agnes asked Dr. Friedman. "I'd like to photograph it for my son."

His moustache twitched a little. "We're not going to the Pentagon." The driver made a sharp turn onto 15th Street on the left side of the White House. Dr. Friedman pointed at the building. "That is where our meeting is."

The White House? Agnes would be stepping foot in the executive mansion? That's what Dr. Friedman had meant on the train. Why, she'd make her call to Mama from the White House. *Hello, Mrs. Limerick, this is the White House calling. We have your daughter on the line.*

The driver rolled down his window at the entrance gate and spoke to the guard. "Dr. Friedman and Mrs. Balmoral, an appointment with the president."

Agnes felt like she'd swallowed a frog. President Roosevelt, F.D.R., the only thing we have to fear is fear itself, "Happy Days Are Here Again," a rendez-vous with destiny, and Fala the Scottie—that president. She couldn't believe it.

"Oh, my stars! Why'd you bring me with you on this trip, Dr. Friedman?"

Dr. Friedman laughed. "Calm yourself, Agnes. You'll find out soon enough. And you're as rigid as a statue. It's only a meeting with the boss."

The boss! All of Washington called Roosevelt *the boss*, except perhaps Mrs. Roosevelt. He'd been president for so long, few people remembered another boss. "What on Earth is this all about? If I'd known I was going to meet Roosevelt, I'd have worn my best dress—"

"Thank goodness you're wearing dark colors. Anything else would've been inappropriate. Everyone will be wearing dark suits."

"But I might've worn something prettier for the President—"

"He's already married, Agnes, and old enough to be your father. He's hardly interested in what young women wear—"

"That's not what I hear. What about that pretty Norwegian princess who's been living on the third floor of the White House?"

He puckered a frown. "Pay attention. We've only got a minute before we enter the fishbowl. Above all, be calm. Roosevelt hates it when visitors get fidgety, and he's likely to comment if you do. We'll be escorted to the Map Room after the others arrive. By custom, Roosevelt already will be seated at the conference table with his head buried in a stack of papers. Don't be fooled. You can be droning through the details of some bureaucratic minutiae, and he'll have his head buried in a communiqué from Churchill. Then he'll regurgitate what you said word for word, and it'll sound better coming from him.

"Mind you, don't be overflattered if he pays you too much attention. Aside from his secretary, you'll be the only woman there."

Flirting with the President? Her nerves played up their usual symptoms, but she paid them no heed. "I won't know what to say."

"Then don't say anything, not a single word. Unless, of course, he asks you to speak. Then you must."

"Oh, dear Lord, if only my father could see me now." She could picture just how his eyes would light up his long face. But no use hoping for things that could not be.

"Well, at least we can have the receptionist dial your mother."

Agnes craned her neck to view the colonnade on the building's south side. A faceless guard marched them to a waiting room where all the dark suits and military uniforms sat. Dr. Friedman greeted them by name and turned to Agnes. "We'd better speak with the receptionist."

Agnes gave Mama's number to the receptionist, whose rapid sighs as she dialed instilled guilt for using government property on family business. After a few moments, the receptionist said, "Hello, Mrs. Limerick. This is the White House calling. I have your daughter here," and handed Agnes the receiver. She felt butterflies, and her hands shook as she put it to her ear.

"What on Earth—"Mama said in beflummoxed tones.

"Hello, Mama. I'm at the White House for a meeting with—" but the receptionist shook her head a loud no, "— Dr. Friedman, my supervisor."

"May the saints witness it, my daughter is calling from President Roosevelt's White House."

"How are you, Mama?" she asked, giggling. "I've only got a few minutes."

After watching fireworks on the Mall, Mama had fallen and sprained her ankle, but was getting along fine now. Patrick had transferred to the Social Security Administration and spent long hours at his new job. "But how are my grandchildren," Mama asked, "and the lovely Victoria—"

"To the purpose of my call, Mama," she said, an eye on her watch. "I'm here for two days and would like to visit you tomorrow after work."

"Oh, dear. Your brother is taking me to Pittsburgh for a long weekend. We're visiting his friend."

"Late this afternoon, then?" A little balloon inside Agnes's heart began to lose its air. Would this visit run away from her?

"We're leaving on the five o'clock train," Mama said, her voice fading. Why did that voice still incite so much guilt? She hadn't lived with Mama for years.

"This is my fault," she heard herself admitting. "I should've called you last week when I found out about the trip. Will you forgive me?"

"Of course, dear," Mama said, in a formal tone. "Perhaps I might come to Philadelphia for Grace's birthday in September."

That reminded Agnes. "I brought you a birthday gift. May I leave it with someone?"

"That's very kind of you, daughter. Mrs. Gallagher lives on the first floor. She'll be at home tomorrow afternoon."

After she hung up, the receptionist asked her to complete a form. Her name, home address, age, marital status, her family's ethnic and religious background. Where did her family live? Did anyone else work in government? Agnes didn't understand why they needed this information, but this was the White House, after all. When she mentioned Norman's death in England, they asked more detailed questions. Had she noticed anyone unusual at the funeral? Had a stranger contacted her afterward?

It certainly had seemed unusual to find Mama and Uncle Collin at Norman's funeral, but she answered otherwise. "The only unusual person was the mayor of Philadelphia."

The receptionist cracked a smile. "He's a Republican, isn't he?"

"Just like my late husband. But I became a Democrat in '42."

Agnes returned to the waiting room. A sturdy blonde woman entered the room and introduced herself as Miss Tully, the President's secretary. "The President and Secretary Stimson are conferring in the Map Room and would like you to join them. Have you all been given a protocol sheet?"

Agnes looked at the doctor. He clarified it for her. "What we're allowed to say and when we may say it. Don't worry. Call him Mr. President, and the rest will follow."

"Please follow me," Miss Tully said.

The clacking of soles on the basement's marble floors kept Agnes's heart from jumping out of her chest, but it didn't stop butterflies from ricocheting in her stomach. Franklin Delano Roosevelt, President of the United States. Elected three times, each a landslide. Dr. New Deal and now Dr. Win the War. What was Agnes Balmoral of Philadelphia doing here? She wanted to turn around and run all the way to Mama's house on Dupont Circle.

Her hair? Ah, yes, the red updo. Good. Very professional, very intellectual. Surely he liked smart women, or did he prefer pretty ones? Mrs. Roosevelt was smart, but she had those enormous buck teeth. Agnes remembered Norman's joke. *Eleanor can bite an apple through a picket fence.*

They filed into the Map Room, Agnes after Dr. Friedman. In hindsight, Agnes had difficulty remembering the room, focused as she was on the white-haired patrician sitting at the conference table, his pince-nez low on his nose. He was whispering to Secretary Stimson. The President's gray suit seemed too large for his bony frame, far thinner than the man Agnes saw in news-reels. His pink complexion was splotched in purple and brown. He signed a document and handed it to Miss Tully, but his hands and mouth shook — a man far older than his sixty-two years. What didn't she know about the man who led the fight against Nazi tyranny and Japanese aggression?

And then he flashed the Roosevelt grin and cast his magic spell. "Wel-come, gentlemen and you, madame," he said bowing to her. Henry, have you briefed these people on why they're here?"

President Roosevelt had bowed his head at her, but only because she was a woman. She might as well have been Rita Hayworth.

"Just the principles, Mr. President," Secretary Stimson said. "They know they're here to answer your questions about the project."

"Fine. Let's start at once. We'll save pleasantries for the children's hour."

Children's hour? Oh, yes — martinis at five.

"Ladies and gentlemen, thank you for doing this work at my request. Some of you know, but most do not, that you're working on a project of international significance. My friends, we hope to build the bomb theorized by the studies of Professor Einstein at Princeton. You have more than one hundred thousand colleagues working on this effort. Secretary Stimson, would you give these fine people some background?"

"Certainly, Mr. President," the old Republican with a gray moustache said. "Dr. Friedman has been leading three simulation studies, one in Washington, one in Princeton, and another in Philadelphia. We've brought key scientists from each of these groups today to discuss the findings. Dr. Friedman, if you please."

Agnes gawked at her boss, sitting there with a tiger's grin, and began to tap out Mozart's 40th Symphony on her lap. So the old pacifist was at the epicenter of a major new weapons program — and not just any new weapons program, if the rumors were to be believed, but the super bomb that would kill thousands and level Berlin and Tokyo in just minutes. Agnes wasn't sure how she felt about working on such a project, even if it meant winning the war, even if it meant fewer people died in combat. But she listened to what they had to say.

"Absolutely, Secretary Stimson," Dr. Friedman said, looking out the corner of his eye at Agnes. "We have resolved many of the calculations regarding its destructive power, the force of energy unleashed by the explosion, and the scope of its effect on its surroundings." He lowered his voice. "Ladies and gentlemen, this bomb has the capacity to level the city of Berlin in less than fifteen minutes, perhaps less than ten."

"Give me the details, Dr. Friedman," the President said.

The good doctor answered Roosevelt's questions for thirty minutes, as the President probed the doctor's theories, played devil's advocate, and did his prosecutorial best to poke holes in the arguments. On and on they droned until finally the President laughed. "You've won the duel, doctor. A bully job explaining it . . . And what's that tapping noise? Has someone got the fidgets?"

Agnes stopped dead. She didn't think anyone would hear her pretend piano. Roosevelt sat ten feet from her. How'd he hear it?

"It seems to have stopped. Back to the weapon. We now know its destructive power," Roosevelt said. "Secretary Stimson, what is the progress in building it? Bring us up to date on Oak Ridge."

"By the end of the year, we plan to begin trials at a site some distance from Los Alamos. The bomb we're building for this demonstration will have one-tenth the power of the bomb we ultimately expect to make in the war against Germany."

"Be mindful of Japan, Henry," the President said. "They are the greater foe. Dr. Friedman, how do your findings apply to this?"

"We came close to writing the specifications for a trial bomb that would have leveled most of northeastern New Mexico. It would've created an ash cloud of dust that would've darkened most of the country for three or four days. But thanks to my assistant's relentless attention to detail," he said, motioning at Agnes, "we corrected these errors and are on track for a trial explosion by December, January at the latest."

What was he talking about?

"Mr. President," Dr. Friedman continued, "may I introduce my assistant,

Mrs. Balmoral from Philadelphia. It was she who corrected my calculations and identified an error of magnitude of two hundred fifty-six. We old scientists have much to learn from the young ones."

The men laughed, but Agnes blushed. So this is what he was talking about, the package of equations she'd recently completed, delicately informing him of the errors she'd found—off by a factor of two raised to the eighth power.

"Mrs. Balmoral, quite obviously we owe you a debt of gratitude," the President said, the jaunty tone of campaign speeches in his voice. "We shall make you honorary governor of New Mexico. I shall inform Governor Dempsey myself."

"Th-th-thank you," she stuttered. "I was only doing the job Dr. Friedman asked me to do."

"My dear Mrs. Balmoral, you did so much more," he said, a bright twinkle in his eyes. "You saved countless lives. Developing this weapon may help us defeat the Germans, perhaps even the Japanese, and bring our boys home from the front even sooner. Is your husband serving?"

Her chin jutted out. He didn't remember his own condolence letter, but why should he? He'd signed thousands in the past two years. "My husband was killed last October in London. A bomb raid leveled offices of the U.S. Navy."

The President reflected a moment. "I'm afraid we suffer far too many casualties for me to remember them all. But you have jogged my memory. Balmoral, his name was Norman, I believe."

So he did remember! She nodded.

"I remember because of the name and a story my wife told me."

What could Mrs. Roosevelt have had to say about Norman's death in London?

"Listen, everyone, a history lesson," he said, turning to Agnes. "As you know, my wife met your husband in the fall of '42. Queen Elizabeth took her on a tour of U.S. installations in London, including the one where your husband was stationed, which was—"

"U.S. Naval Construction Services," Agnes said. She gulped at the President's revelation. She'd had no idea.

"Correct. Our son, Elliott, who's serving in the Marines, escorted his mother and the Queen to your husband's facility. They met your husband, a lieutenant, an architect, I believe?"

She wondered if her face betrayed surprise, but she did her best to play an even hand. "Yes, Mr. President."

"I have a lifelong interest in architecture, especially naval architecture. I designed my summer house in Hyde Park and one for my missus too. And I was Secretary of the Navy during the Great War—"

Secretary Stimson cleared his throat.

"All right, Henry, *Assistant* Secretary of the Navy." The President laughed. "Secretary Stimson is the only one here who outranks me. He was Secretary of War for Taft back when I was a mere state assemblyman from Dutchess County."

The President's tone became serious again. "When we received the report of your husband's death, my wife, who reads casualty lists carefully, remembered the name and told me the story. 'A gentleman with a clear head on his shoulders,' she said. How lucky the two of you were to have each other."

A sad ache pulled at Agnes's heart. Everyone who spoke about Norman said the same thing—how lucky they'd been. She had felt the impulse to flaunt the truth, and now she just wanted to flee the room. But she didn't have that option with Franklin Delano Roosevelt looking at her with an audience of twenty stone-faced men wearing black.

"Thank you, Mr. President, and for your condolence letter."

"My missus does that when she knows a person. It's a wonder she hasn't popped up on your doorstep in Philadelphia. Henry," he added, turning to Stimson, "find something permanent for Mrs. Balmoral in Washington. We can't afford to give up someone as smart as she. Do you agree, Dr. Friedman?"

Dr. Friedman nodded. "Absolutely, Mr. President. The war effort depends on sharp people like Mrs. Balmoral."

"We're concluded, gentlemen—and Mrs. Balmoral. Thank you for your good counsel. Secretary Stimson, Dr. Friedman, proceed immediately with the test in New Mexico."

Agnes waited for the President to rise. To her shock the men rose but the President remained seated. Surely they should wait for him to rise first? But she followed their lead. The President poured over the papers in front of him. His pince-nez drooped down his nose, and his hands shook again. The whole weight of the world resting on the shoulders of this frail man.

She'd never believed the rumors that he couldn't walk, but now she knew they were true. Even so, she rejected the idea of Franklin Roosevelt as an invalid who relied on servants for basic needs. This man with the magical charm and the twinkly wisdom, somehow he'd fought paralysis to become the most powerful man in the world — ever.

She tugged at Dr. Friedman's sleeve. "I'll be just a moment."

"No, Agnes —" but she'd already walked back to the President.

"Mr. President, please excuse me a moment," she said, fearing she'd lose the courage if she didn't persist. "You flatter me to say I'm doing much at all for the war effort, but it is you who've done so much for us. You might be in Hyde Park right now with Mrs. Roosevelt and your family if you weren't making this sacrifice for us."

The President listened and smiled, that twinkle back in his eye. "You are very kind, child. When you return to Washington, please contact my wife's secretary, Miss Thompson. We welcome newcomers into our circle all the time. She'll schedule you for dinner in the private residence. My daughter, Anna, will be there too. She's a few years older than you. Her husband's overseas, just like my four sons. I can only imagine your pain …" He grew somber, then brightened. "Please come see us. Eleanor would love to meet you."

Eleanor would want to meet her? She hesitated but wanted to say something, so she blurted, "I was also married on St. Patrick's Day, Mr. President."

"That's a bully coincidence. Uncle Ted would've said that — I expect you know, he gave Eleanor away at our wedding. He proceeded to make himself center of attention the whole afternoon. I hope your father didn't do the same."

"My father died when I was eight. Norman's father gave me away."

"Just like Eleanor, a young girl when her father died. Teddy Roosevelt's younger brother, Elliott. She still talks about him."

She bowed. "Thank you, Mr. President. I'd be delighted to accept your invitation. My mother lives here, and I plan to visit very soon."

"It is I who must thank you, child. You've brightened my day."

She felt his eyes on her back as she left. President Roosevelt, sixty-two and unable to walk, but leading the world to freedom.

Agnes felt like she was walking on clouds during the remainder of their stay in Washington, so much had Roosevelt's endorsement overwhelmed her. And she could barely sense the tracks under the train on the ride back to Philadelphia. Maybe she could do anything Dr. Friedman asked of her. But the mid-afternoon storm that soaked Agnes on her walk from 30th Street Station brought her back down to Earth.

She entered her house and found it crackling with electric animosity. When she peeked a hello into the music room, Brian nodded, tossed his head off to the side, and resumed playing Debussy. Agnes turned the corner into the kitchen and inquired with Victoria. She'd lost patience, Victoria said after Agnes put her purse down, when Brian's least talented heathen had banged on the piano for an unendurable forty-five minutes. So she'd reciprocated by stomping up to her room and banging the door shut. At lunch, Brian retaliated with the first movement of Brahms's F minor piano sonata. A fate worse than death, listening to that dark music while trying to digest tuna salad.

"I've had enough," Victoria said. "I've finally managed to accept my son's death, but I don't have to live with this. It's either him or me. I'd rather deal with your sister-in-law's sewing circles than his little monsters."

With that, Victoria marched up the stairs. Agnes looked up the staircase at the receding figure of her mother-in-law. She had no choice, really. Victoria was her mother-in-law, her children's grandmother. Brian was a friend. She turned her eyes to the music room and began a slow walk down the hallway.

"Brian, we need to talk," she said, interrupting a "Claire de Lune" far more pleasing to the ears than the Brahms first movement.

No one ever said these words without planning some kind of confrontation, and no one ever heard them without expecting the worst. Brian stopped in the middle of a broken arpeggio. D flat was such a lovely key for arpeggios, but Agnes wanted to keep her focus. He squinted and cocked his head, then rose and smirked on one side of his mouth. His shirt tails were loose, his bow tie missing, and the sleeves rolled up. He'd obviously been playing a long time.

"Mrs. Balmoral must be complaining about my music," Brian said, as if reading her mind. "Well, my work is art, my work is a thing of beauty! My work transcends daily worries like laundry, wastebaskets, fingernail clippings —"

"As melodramatic as Bette Davis in *Dark Victory*," Agnes said, laughing in spite of herself. "No Academy Award nomination for you."

"Agnes, dear, there is a method to my madness," he said with a dramatic flourish of arms and shoulders in silent movie gestures.

"We need to talk about Victoria—"

"That is precisely my purpose," he said.

"Now you're making Bette Davis seem as restrained as Greta Garbo in *Ninotchka*. Back to my point, Brian. Please sit down and be quiet—"

"No, Agnes, I'm the teacher, you're the child! I played the Brahms at lunch and allowed Miss Rice to bang away this morning—"

"That's the problem. Victoria's at her wit's end, and I need to make some changes—"

"Ah, then my plan is working."

Agnes's eyes popped. "I beg your pardon?"

"She very well needs to be at her wit's end. When I moved in here, she moped about her bedroom, feeling sorry for herself and never saying a damned thing. Remember the queen of the realm I first met at Thanksgiving in '40? Now that I've gotten her all riled up, she's come back."

Agnes cracked a smile. Maybe Brian knew a thing or two about human nature that she didn't. "How much longer are you going to persist in this?"

"Not until she threatens to leave you for Norman's brother. By the way, I never can recall his name."

"Well, she threatened," Agnes said, patting him on the shoulders. "And the brother's name doesn't matter."

They laughed, and laughed, and laughed some more. Victoria had come back to herself, no longer holed up in her bedroom mourning Norman. Agnes had to admit that Brian could take most of the credit. She knew full well she'd never ask Brian to leave. This bald, fat man was just too cute and sweet to give up. And Victoria, maybe her threat was just a threat. Hopefully, at least.

"Are you going to start being a good boy, Brian Larney?" She kept her hands on his shoulders and gave him a squeaky soprano.

"Why yes, Agnes Balmoral," he answered, bouncing his sapphire eyes at her. "I'm always on my best behavior."

"No, you're not. You've got the Irish devil in you, but not the devil Uncle Collin talks about." She kissed him on the forehead and looked him in the eye. In that fraction of time, she asked herself, why not? So she kissed him on the lips, a tender kiss that reminded her of one of Cristina's vanilla profiteroles. Lips that yielded to hers, without pulling back, without pushing forward and taking charge, so unlike Norman. And without flooding her with passion. They were softer than Norman's lips and definitely kinder.

23

THE FOLLOWING MORNING, AGNES WALKED by the parlor with a sack of dinner vegetables from the market and found Grace in her bathrobe on the sofa, her knees bent in front of her and with her nose in *National Velvet*. But her nose was too far into the book.

"Some distance, Grace," she said, putting down her bag and feeling her lower back tightening. Was she aging? "You're reading too close to your eyes."

Grace complied but complained. "Too blurry, Mama." That ignited a monthlong quest for eyeglasses. Agnes welcomed the diversion, even if it meant visits to the pediatrician, opthalmologist, and optician that culminated in a pair of spectacles. Grace chose round lenses and wire frames.

It gave Agnes time to figure out Brian. What had she done, feeling the heavy air between them every time they passed each other in the kitchen, on the stairs, or in the music room. It felt like she'd disrobed in front of the Pope. Every time he opened his mouth at dinner, she was afraid he'd say something funny that would trap her in cozy happiness, or make some elaborate reactive gesture that would trigger giggles around the table.

Brian behaved like his usual chameleon self. He cracked jokes that had

Victoria scowling (but squelching her own laughter), and he played with Harold and his Lincoln Logs. But he did stop evening practices and weekend students. So Victoria stopped complaining.

And then a letter arrived from a Brent Lacey, Esq., Endicott, New York—Old Man Lacey's son, Agnes recalled. She knew immediately that Gracie Honeywalker had died, and the letter confirmed this. Agnes plodded into the kitchen, sat down, and stared at the splotchy patterns in their linoleum floor, remembering Gracie's smile when Grace was born.

The letter also mentioned that Gracie had willed her the painting of her father. Did Agnes want it, the lawyer asked, and would she send ten dollars to cover shipping costs? Agnes thought about the portrait with its defiant sneer—and wired the money. Two weeks later, it hung in her entryway.

Late in August, Harold asked Agnes for a second dog. No, she said, Keaton would be jealous. Brian took up the cause with a dramatic whimper, laying his head on Agnes's shoulder and crying like a dog. Why couldn't she relax like he did? He seemed as untroubled by their kiss as a toddler spilling milk. But even after confiding in Cristina, who took the news with a mild laugh, she couldn't shake the feeling she'd done something wrong, as though she'd sinned with Brian in the same way she had with Norman. Ah, Norman ...

In early September, Dr. Friedman presented her with the formal papers of her commission, her new position with the War Department at the Pentagon. She'd be required to move to the nation's capital, he said, and would have the security of a staff position at project headquarters. He believed she'd thrive, and he felt relieved for her. The work in Philadelphia for the research project would end after the nuclear test was completed before the new year, and the group would disband.

"Don't tell anyone about this last point, or I'll deny it," he said.

The decision rested with her, and her old anxieties, *should she or shouldn't she*, shifted into overdrive. At least she had until the 22nd to decide and would report on the first of November, if she accepted.

Grace's birthday fell on the Wednesday before the deadline. Agnes planned a surprise party after services the Sunday beforehand. Mama would arrive by train at noon, and Brian would have corralled the guests into the music room by the time they returned from church. On Saturday, Victoria took Grace and Harold to the library to read, leaving Agnes alone to prepare for the party, except for Keaton and his barking at passing neighbors, Brian snoring upstairs, and a pounding humidity.

A scorching heat wave had been baking Pennsylvania and New Jersey since Labor Day, Philadelphia most of all with its matrix of concrete-paved streets, office buildings, row homes, and honking cars. Townies claimed they could see sweat dripping from the William Penn statue atop City Hall. Like her neighbors, Agnes braced for yet another dripping hot day.

So Agnes took this opportunity to clean house, barefoot and clad only in the lightest calico she could find, her red hair back again in a ponytail. She'd begin tackling the boxes demanding her attention at the far end of the dining room beyond her cherry table, just on the other side of the matching credenza. After Norman died, she'd packed his clothing into boxes to donate to the poor. But like everything else lately, she'd procrastinated. When the U.S. Navy sent a red box containing his personal effects, she added it to the stack, unopened. Victoria couldn't bear to look at it, and Agnes didn't want to. Since then, the boxes had taken a nomadic tour throughout the house—the third floor, Agnes's closet, the cellar, and finally the dining room. Back to the cellar they'd go, at least for Grace's party.

Cleaning and the boxes notwithstanding, she could procrastinate only a few more days. Gray-skinned, disorganized Dr. Friedman expected an answer—an affirmative answer. Unlike most decisions in her life, she couldn't wriggle her way out of this deadline. Six days, one hundred forty-four hours until the deadline. And then she dusted the grandfather clock—no, one hundred forty-three hours. No amount of cleaning or practicing the piano could delay the inevitable. *Yes or no, Agnes, which is it?* Would she end up tossing a coin yet again?

Her old anxieties rumbled in her stomach like a bad oyster. Should she accept the job in Washington for the financial security she sought for Grace and Harold? Victoria and Brian wouldn't leave Philadelphia. Her mother-in-law would move in with Norman's brother. And Brian—she'd convinced him to leave thirty years of bickering safety at Mrs. O'Toole's, and not even a year later she contemplated forcing him to move again, without even acknowledging their kiss or what he meant to her. She owed him so much more.

Agnes was humming Mozart when she started cleaning the parlor. She'd freshened up the room in lighter colors that spring. Pale yellow against the drapes, rugs, and the mahogany furniture made for a nice contrast. But the air remained stagnant and dusty despite the house's open windows and prayers that a cool breeze would sweep down Spruce Street.

She started dusting the bookcase and came across *The Fountainhead*, a novel Victoria had bought and read a few months before Norman died. She'd raved about it, but Agnes had no wish to read about a self-involved architect who thought he was better than everyone else. She picked up the book, wondering if she might understand Norman a little better, but she detested everything she'd ever heard about Ayn Rand's philistine politics. When she put the book down, she tore her left index fingernail on a bare hook. She pulled the loose end off and drew blood. Her finger throbbed.

Why hadn't she trimmed these last week? No self-respecting pianist ever forgot to trim her nails. She'd been preoccupied with work, Brian, and the household, of course. She washed her hands and resumed dusting.

The telephone rang, and her nerves jumped. A quiet moment gone, an opportunity wasted to reach some sort of decision about Brian, her money predicament, her job, Philadelphia, her house, Victoria, the children, Mama and Uncle Collin—too much to resolve, really. These days her brain was a jumble of mixed emotions. Nothing organized, nothing added up, nothing made sense.

"What is it?" she answered at the kitchen desk. "What do you want?"

Cristina's scratchy alto ricocheted from the other end. "Has someone kidnapped Agnes? She doesn't answer the telephone like that."

"Thank heavens, it's you, Cristina." Her nerves stopped poking at her skin. "I've got too much to do to deal with anyone else."

"Would you like me to help set up tomorrow morning?"

"Brian will be organizing the guests tomorrow, but could you come over this afternoon instead of early tomorrow? I'm swamped."

Cristina groaned. "Sorry, honey, Ma is coming for lunch and an afternoon with the boys."

"Oh, that's too bad. Are you staying cool over there?"

"If you consider ninety degrees and soupy air cool, then yes."

"How I'd love a day with you on the town. Remember walks and lunch? Two married ladies ..."

"Beautyful! But now I've got three children and you've got four."

"In that case, Brian and Victoria are the oldest children in Pennsylvania."

"You know better than I. As to why I called, what's your decision? Are you going to marry Sister Brian or move to Rooseveltland?"

Agnes usually appreciated Cristina's directness, but this wasn't one of those times. She felt as put on the spot as if singing the *Messiah* off key in front of a thousand disapproving nuns. Hallelujah, indeed.

"I'm not ready to make a decision, Cristina."

"Huh? You've been avoiding the situation with Brian for weeks, and Stimson wants your answer Friday. The Allies will march into Berlin and string up Hitler before you're ready."

"It's bad enough, having to make a decision without barbs from you."

"I apologize, but that doesn't make the deadline go away. I know this is difficult, honey. Every time you reach a crossroads and have to pick the left side or the right, you freeze up like an ice cube."

Agnes sat at her desk and looked around. She was glad she'd changed the kitchen back in '41, and replaced all that white with periwinkle blue and pale yellow. "It's not that easy. None of my family wants to move to Washington. Victoria won't leave, and the children depend on her. And Brian's life is here too, and I—"

She looked at a neat stack of bills that soon would have to be paid. Real estate taxes, the children's tuitions, doctor bills, so many obligations. Could she pay the bills if she declined the Washington offer and lost her job? How far would her $27,000 widow's benefit go? No, she must go. What about Victoria, Brian, her house, her city ... and everything she loved?

"Sweetheart, I know you. Brian is a homosexual. He's almost thirty years older than you. He's affectionate, he's considerate, and he's helpful. He's everything Norman never was."

Agnes felt the pressure in her head rise again. "Why must you always demean Norman? He was a good man. Yes, he hogged the bed at night, he groomed himself an hour every morning while I crossed my legs, he had trouble digesting fruit at night and fanned the blanket whenever he did. And the damned fool cheated on me. But he was a good man."

"And all of Philadelphia thought he was a hero. There aren't many people who'd take on a Goliath of a man like he did, his gold watch smashed into a million pieces, being stabbed in the abdomen. How'd you ever manage? When it happened, I wanted to give you a place to hide ..."

Agnes was about to ask what she meant, but Cristina giggled. "Passing gas and fanning the blanket? I don't know which is worse, that or the affair."

"Don't be silly. You have no idea what it felt like. I had to pretend I was happy with the newspapers, Norman's parents, my children, when all the time my stomach was churning like a volcano ... a place to hide from what?"

"You need to focus on the present, meaning Grace and Harold. All you have left of Norman are his personal effects from England."

"And I haven't even opened that box. I couldn't bear it, knowing that I'd pushed him—"

"Didn't you tell me you gave him your father's locket? I suppose he wore it every day."

"Did I mention that? I suppose it's in there if he wasn't wearing it the day he died." Good God, the only memento she had from her father, and she'd given it to Norman. Her pulse grew quick, thinking about that unopened box, and she became silent. Agnes inhaled a deep breath, but it didn't help.

Cristina broke the silence. "I suppose he wore the locket every day—"

"What did you mean, you wanted to find me a place to hide? I didn't tell you about Norman's affair until long after it happened."

Cristina paused, then said, "I knew before you even mentioned anything. I could tell from your high-pitched voice. I could tell from how you stood away from him. I could tell from the blank look in your eyes. I knew because that's what I felt like when it happened to me."

Agnes looked about her kitchen, so peaceful that morning despite the heat, the scene of so many happy moments. Why did men cheat? Even sweet-natured Angelo had violated his vows. So what did these happy kitchens matter?

"Cristina, I'm sorry," she said, lowering her voice. "I never knew Angelo—"

"On second thought, I don't want to talk about it. Not now."

"May I call you later in the day?" Agnes said, but she heard a click.

A thousand thoughts usually darted through her mind when she attended to boring chores such as cleaning, but she focused on the details for Grace's birthday party when she resumed. She'd clean the living room, dining room, and kitchen now. Later, she'd stow the boxes in the cellar, shop at the market, and pick up the cake.

But her left hand stopped in midair above the credenza as she finished dusting the dining room. A tiny little disturbance took root in the back of her head. It was crazy, this gray cloud forming in her brain, but something about Cristina and the conversation unsettled her. The images of her father's locket, Norman's gold watch, and the attack in West Philadelphia merged into a single horrifying thought. Cristina knew too much, but how? No, her mind was playing tricks on her. Cristina detested Norman, but knowing about the gold watch, her father's locket? Had she been spying on them? She resumed her dusting.

Her mind slowly reeled backward in time — Cristina, quiet and flanked by her parents at Norman's funeral. The first to call the morning after Norman's accident, soliciting details. Running into Cristina at the market after so long a silence, afraid to tell Norman later that day. Norman forbidding her from seeing Cristina after becoming ill the only time she and Angelo entertained them for dinner. Cristina's unforgettable reaction when Agnes told her she was pregnant. *Are you insane.* How Cristina dismissed Norman when Agnes first inquired about him — rudeness, contempt, enormous dislike.

No one would believe her husband and best friend had an affair, like a bad cliché in a dime-store novel. No, it was with Mary Alden. Her best friend would have never done that. Or had she?

Agnes wrestled her demons inside, but they kept picking at her brain. Ridiculous suspecting her best friend of betraying her while happily married to Angelo Rosamilia, the mother of two boys, a librarian in West Philadelphia. But wait, Norman had designed that library, his first project at Howe and Lescaze. Cristina had gone to work there when it opened.

A terrible certainty exploded in her head. Cristina had been the woman with Norman the evening of the attack. But if she confronted Cristina, her certainty would be reduced to fantastical imaginings — unless she had proof.

Buried in the stack of boxes on the other side of the room, Norman's red box still sat unopened. He'd been a free agent in the year before his death. What if Cristina had gone to see him? Not during wartime, of course. But they might've corresponded, letters between London and Philadelphia.

She fought the stack of boxes for the red one in the middle. Before she knew it, she found herself sitting on the floor with a time capsule of Norman's life arrayed in front of her on the Oriental rug.

Agnes recognized scattered clothing. She'd laundered that underwear, ironed those shirts, and caressed them to her cheeks before their marriage had begun its long slide to collapse.

Cornelius's medal from the Spanish-American War, Norman's confirmation cross. Papers from his naval commission, his passport. A tied stack of photographs. Architects' pencils and tools. She opened a thin folio titled *For Agnes*, and discovered sketches of their house, a renovation Norman never had mentioned but obviously planned. The sketches were dated March 1943.

A crumpled white-laced handkerchief with the initials *A. K. L.* — Granny's very own, Daddy's locket wrapped inside. Agnes opened the locket, a photograph of her on one side, Grace and Harold on the other.

She felt pulsing waves gnawing at her from her abdomen, into her throat, into her mouth, orchestrated by her heart leading a symphony of discordant nerves. Norman was dead. She never would gaze at his face again. It didn't exist, nor did his velvet baritone, his oblique jawline, the dimple on his right cheek. And she never would lay her head in his arms again, never feel the warmth of his body next to hers. And she'd never be able to say *I'm sorry* to him, to apologize for pushing him away, being glad he'd gone to Europe, enjoying her time alone with the children, Brian, Victoria, the house — their life.

After all these months, she surrendered to her grief and allowed her body to shake, her voice to moan, and her eyes to shed waterfalls of tears for her husband. Norman had intended to come back, even though they'd agreed to end their marriage, all while she'd pranced around the house enjoying it without him. Why else would he have designed such a renovation, why else would he have carried her picture along with the children in her father's locket? They might have been a family again when the war ended. And he hadn't given up hope even though she'd done nothing to encourage him.

When her tears subsided, she placed the items back into the box, but not her father's locket, not Granny's handkerchief. They went into her pocket. She placed the stack of photographs inside last and saw on top Norman's photograph of the Arno during his year in Florence. How sentimental to keep these photos, so unlike the Norman she'd slept beside all those years. She untied the stack.

She recognized sites from Florence—the Piazza della Republica, the Boboli Gardens, the Ponte Vecchio, Michelangelo's statue of *David*. She saw others, Victoria and Cornelius, Norman's confirmation at St. Mark's, his brother, his nephews, their St. Patrick's Day wedding, Grace and Harold as infants. And then she came to it—Cristina, her hair longer than Agnes had ever seen, smiling with a seductive twist of her lips, like a heroine from a Renaissance masterwork.

She became dizzy. There was Cristina, sitting on a fountain above cobblestone steps in a city square. A European city, one with the exact same kind of cobblestones as in the Piazza della Republica. Cristina had been in Florence with Norman. Agnes turned the picture over. It read, in Norman's rectangular handwriting, *October 1929, the fall we discovered Mary Alden.*

She dropped the photograph on the floor and released a terrible howl. The fiendish puzzle fell into place. Their furtive looks at one another, the way they kept their distance, how Cristina avoided being alone with Norman, little remarks Cristina made.

I can picture him, standing on the platform, blinking his blue eyes at you, waving good-bye.

There aren't many people who'd take on a Goliath of a man like he did, his gold watch smashed into a million pieces, being stabbed in the abdomen.

I suppose he wore your father's locket every day.

And when Agnes had said that she missed him, Cristina had said, *Yes, I know exactly what you mean.*

She couldn't deny the truth that assaulted her from every angle, and even if she did try, the photograph told the whole story. But Mary Alden, what did she have to do with their Florentine rendez-vous?

She lay there sobbing in the corner of her dining room. The empty house screamed a black void into her heart and beyond. She hated her house now, she hated the life they'd built inside these walls, she hated the lies at its foundation. She longed to be free of it and to escape from the infernal pressure cooker.

She rose from her bedraggled state and made up her mind without hesitating for the first time in her life. She bounded up the stairs to her bedroom.

How clean and orderly her green bedroom was, so unlike her life! She opened the closet and pulled on flats for walking, grabbed her purse from the bureau, stomped back down the stairs and out of the house, slammed the door behind her—but turned around to go back inside. She grabbed the photograph of Cristina and stuffed it into her purse.

The sun's heat punched her in the face when she emerged onto Rittenhouse Square from tree-lined 19th Street. But she took no time to notice the beauty of the square, the magnolias and jasmines, the oaks and elms. She turned east onto Locust Street, focused on her destination like a tiger on an impala. The sun pounded her head. She'd forgotten her hat and gloves, but she didn't care if she got as freckled as Fanny Brice playing Baby Snooks.

She passed the Warwick Hotel and St. Mark's so quickly, she developed sharp pains in her shins before reaching the Bellevue-Stratford. She began to limp and had no choice but to slow down. Saturday shoppers filled Broad and Locust Streets, people scurrying to finish errands before the afternoon. Agnes ignored their stares, their offers of assistance as she limped by. She noticed a group of young cadets at ease at 13th and Locust—Navy men. She practically spat. No music played in her head while she raced across town. She didn't even glance at Washington Square, then turned down 6th Street.

She couldn't bear to look at the square where she'd spent so many of her days, reading books, playing with Racer, enjoying picnics with Mama and Uncle Collin. In two blocks, she'd pass her parents' red-bricked mansion. Granny had encouraged her there, against the odds, to marry Norman. She wanted none of it.

She continued her walk down 6th Street past the Pine Street intersection with her eyes on the sidewalk. But she couldn't escape the red-bricked house on the opposite corner. Anger seethed out of every pore. She stared the house down.

"So what if you've been right all along?" she screamed— no one to hear.

"So what if I made all the wrong decisions. I'll live my life as I please."

Her body cried out in agony. She pushed her limits with no regard for the pain in her shins and abdomen, the brutal sun scorching her white skin, out of breath, her heart racing. Would she collapse in the street? She wanted to reach Cristina's house while her courage soared.

She passed Lombard and South Streets, just one more block to Christian Street. And when Agnes reached Christian, she looked down the empty street and there it stood, the small row house with dark-yellow bricks and black trim. When Agnes arrived, she didn't loop around the side of the house to the back kitchen and the stove's usual scents of garlic and rosemary. She walked to the front porch and banged on the door.

Time stretched into a vacant eternity before it finally opened. There was Cristina in a white sleeveless sundress and hair net. An ordinary day at home.

"Agnes, look at you! You look like a wilted daisy. What's happened? Has Germany surrendered?"

Agnes walked in and looked down at herself. Her ponytail had unraveled, and she'd perspired all over her dress. It was hot as hell in this room, and Cristina had no fans. She dropped her purse on a side table and stepped in front of Cristina. She heard the boys clattering in the kitchen and then Mrs. Cassata's voice. They were having lunch.

"I have a question for you, the first of many. Who was Mary Alden?"

"What are you talking about, Mary Alden? Have you taken leave of your senses?" Cristina stiffened before she looked in the mirror near the front door, took off her hair net, and fluffed her hair. Agnes wasn't fooled by the gesture any more than she was fooled by the false words.

"When I met Norman, you told me he'd been seeing a friend of yours named Mary Alden. She was the woman Norman had the affair with back in '40, or so he said. I'd like to know how to find her."

Cristina leaned into Agnes and put a hand on her shoulder. "Keep your voice down. I don't know what you're talking about. If you're going to come here looking like that and asking crazy questions ... well, I don't know what."

Agnes stepped back from Cristina's touch. "Please just tell me how I can find her." She'd give Cristina some time before shifting tactics. She waited, and stared at Cristina.

Cristina turned away and sat on the sofa. A portrait of Jesus and crucifix hung behind her. Gracie Honeywalker's words came into her head. *He'll look over you, Miz Agnes.*

"Sit down and let's make sense out of this. Why do you want to find Mary?"

"I opened Norman's box from the Navy. I found some interesting surprises inside." A jumble of memories, happy and sad. She squelched them.

Cristina lowered her eyes from Agnes's stare and pointed her mouth downward. "What did you find?"

"Enough that I need to speak with Mary Alden," she said, fastening a sharp look on Cristina. "The woman my husband bedded four years ago."

Cristina played the librarian and tapped her index finger to her chin as if a lost reader had come to inquire about a rare edition. "I don't know how to find her. Mary left Pottstown. She moved to Doylestown after her husband died."

"I think you do." Agnes began to pace. Would she make a scene, say something that would draw Mrs. Cassata from the kitchen? Perhaps she should let Cristina's mother judge what her daughter had done.

Cristina squirmed on the sofa. "Agnes, please sit down. You're pacing about like a madwoman."

"I'm tired of lies," she said, slowing her words down, not just to intimidate Cristina, but also to calm her racing heartbeat and jumpy nerves. "Mary Alden never existed. She was a figment of your imagination, or some idiotic joke at my expense between you and Norman."

Cristina walked to the staircase. She stepped on the landing and placed a hand on the banister. Her hand was shaking. Beads of sweat had started to form on her forehead.

"Cristina, enough of the dramatic gestures. I should've known years ago that you and Norman had a past. How long did you and he have an affair?"

"That's preposterous," Cristina said, breathing so deeply into her chest, her bosom expanded, and she groaned like a horse when she exhaled. "We could barely stand each other. I would never do a thing like that to a friend as important as you."

"There's no way you'd know everything you do without it being so. You knew about the gold watch. You knew about my father's locket. I gave that locket to Norman when he boarded the train for Washington, a parting gift." Agnes stared her down, but Cristina looked away.

"You told me, of course," Cristina said, then whispered, "And let me remind you, keep your voice down. Do you want my mother to hear?"

"I never told anyone, not even my own mother," Agnes said, lowering her voice. "That locket was the most important thing I ever gave him. I gave it to him for good luck. Now how did you know about all of those things?"

"Please listen, Agnes." Cristina began to cry. "It wasn't like that at all."

The dull prodding from the bottom of Agnes's stomach reminded her that she hadn't eaten since breakfast. "We've known each other for thirteen years, and you stand there and deny it?"

"I don't know what's happening, Agnes, what's gotten into you."

"Just the truth! I was a fool not to figure it out, but I should've seen the sparks between you and him were more than just contempt."

She looked at her friend shaking at the foot of her stairs. For the first time, she noticed how heavy Cristina had become. Too bad, youth and innocence could last only so long. She reached for her purse.

"Good, I think you should leave. You're too upset to talk rationally. We can talk about this another time."

But instead of reaching for the door, Agnes pulled the photograph out of her purse and shoved it at Cristina. Her eyes widened and her cheeks slackened, but then she tightened her lips. She finally looked away and leaned into the staircase railing, as if about to fall.

"Now will you stop lying, Cristina? The gold watch, the locket. You're the woman he was with when he rescued Woodrow Wilson's granddaughter. You were in contact with Norman while he was in England. And the photograph from Florence. You were having an affair with him back in '29."

Cristina faced her and took the photograph. Her face began to quiver, and wrinkles formed on her forehead, on her cheeks, around her lips, then above her eyes.

"All right, you have it!" Cristina shouted. "It's all true!"

"What's all the fuss about?" a distant voice asked. They whipped their heads around to see Cristina's mother standing in the doorway, hands on her hips, a scowl on her face. Donnie and Ronnie stood behind her. "The very idea, arguing like that with children in the house."

"Agnes and I are having a discussion. Ma, you're done with lunch. Take my boys to Washington Square." Cristina walked over to her mother and kissed her on the cheek. "For me, Ma, please."

Mrs. Cassata sighed but agreed. Once the door closed, Cristina continued. "Yes, it's true, but what does it matter? You had your husband and children. He loved you right up to the end, even after he went to England. He wrote me a letter I've still got. He wanted to reconcile when he came back from England. He wanted to be the kind of husband you deserved. His words."

Cristina began climbing the stairs. "Where are you going?" Agnes asked.

"To get the letter, to prove it."

Agnes didn't want to read any letter from Norman to Cristina. "You don't need to do that, but I do want to hear the whole story, beginning to end."

They sat on the sofa. Cristina quietly told Agnes how it began. Norman, a student at the Philadelphia School of Design, flirted with Cristina who worked in the library. She followed him to Florence on her grandparents' inheritance and returned home with no money but with an expectation of marriage. But Norman dropped her not long after they started at Smith and Weisskopf, and then came Angelo, Agnes, and separate lives. She wrote to Norman when her family grew desperate for money, and he helped secure the librarian job for her.

"Do you remember that evening he disappeared from Rittenhouse Square?" Cristina said. "The day you and I saw each other after so many years apart."

Yes, Agnes nodded, remembering the mystery of that evening. The pieces began fitting together. She listened to every syllable of every word.

"You'd mentioned your evening plans, and I was curious to see the two of you together. Angelo was playing poker that evening, and the boys were with Ma and Pop, so I walked to the park. And when you left Norman alone, I confronted him about ending our friendship. I knew he'd done it. He told me it was too risky, for us to be friends. When I refused to comply, he ran off, fuming. And except for that one day in your kitchen, we didn't see each other until meeting at 16th and Walnut, one afternoon in the fall of '40."

That terrible day, Cristina continued, Norman harried over work, a weak moment, something exciting that had them forgetting their responsibilities. And when it was over, they regretted it and met one night to end it, only to be exposed by Norman's stabbing. And finally a letter from England, Norman asking her to help him win over Agnes when he came home.

A disconnected air of unreality permeated the room. "I'm overwhelmed," Agnes finally said. "Most of all, I don't understand why you never said anything. You could've told me. I would've understood, even the secrecy about that insane evening in Rittenhouse Square. But not the adultery, Cristina. Marriage is a sacrament, an oath before God. That I don't understand."

Cristina shook her head. "There was no point. You were infatuated with Norman and wouldn't have believed me. I'd also gotten married and wanted to put the whole unpleasantness behind me—"

"Does Angelo know?"

"Yes, he knows everything."

Agnes had been the only one left in the dark. A part of her still couldn't believe it. She'd wake up and call Cristina. *You wouldn't believe the nightmare I had.*

But Agnes had to persist and get all of her questions answered. "There's a point that still bothers me, Cristina. How did you know I gave Norman my father's locket? Did he write about it in the letter?"

Cristina hesitated. "I don't want you to read more into it than what it was. When Norman left, I went to the train station and watched from the distance. I saw you hand the locket to him just before he boarded."

Cristina was there, spying, watching her, Norman, and all of them say good-bye. She'd intruded even on that final moment. She felt as violated as if Cristina had exposed every intimate secret she'd shared for all the world to hear. Had she told Norman anything Agnes had confided over the years? She couldn't bear any more. She stood up and picked up her purse and the picture of Cristina in Florence.

"Here, this is yours," she said, putting the photograph on the table. "I'm leaving. I have to prepare the house for my daughter's birthday party. But one final question, Cristina. What does it mean on the back of this photograph, *the fall we discovered Mary Alden?*"

Cristina stifled a throaty sob. "You might as well know. Mary Alden was a cranky widow from Manchester on holiday at Norman's *pensione*. She stayed in the room next to him. The first time Norman and I were together, she knocked on the door and complained about the noise. Mary Alden was our code for sex."

Agnes moaned, opened the door, and walked onto the porch. Cristina followed, her voice falling to a whisper.

"Don't leave like this. Norman's in the past," Cristina said, her words quick and staccato sharp. Her face became equally urgent, her mouth quivering, the nostrils pulsing, and her eyes drilling into Agnes. "Yes, we lied to you about Italy and the incident in '40. Please don't let this end our friendship. I'm sorry, honey, I'm so sorry. You have no idea how many times I agonized over this, what it was like at confession, how awful it felt to hear the bitter pain in your voice, knowing I caused it."

The heavy pulsing that had been pressing against Agnes's temples seemed to dissipate at least a little, replaced by something like a low wave of sadness emanating from her heart. She thought about her years of laughter and joy with Cristina, the friend who'd been there since before she met Norman—all gone in just a short two hours. And the thought drained her of energy.

"One day I'll forgive you, but I can never forget. I don't think we can be friends again, not like we were. Right now I don't ever want to see you."

She left Cristina and walked down the street, Cristina's whimpering extinguished before she turned back up 6th Street. She needed to get home. Preparations for Grace's party could wait no longer. Agnes detected a breeze from the north. The air might still be as hot as coal, but the breeze felt good on her wet dress.

No turning back now, no hesitating about her future. She hated her city now, this sticky heat and her terrible problems. She didn't need the September 22 deadline and couldn't wait to give Dr. Friedman her answer. She'd request starting before the first of November. She'd be rid of Philadelphia, Cristina, even Norman, whose body lay in a cemetery only a few miles away. They'd have a new start. Victoria and Brian would visit. There'd be financial security. And Mama would be in Washington. So would Patrick. Perhaps she might finally get to know her only sibling.

She walked slowly now. Every fiber of her body ached. Her temples pounded with a headache from the sky's diffuse glare. Why hadn't she brought a hat? Her green eyes were far too sensitive. Though she had a lot of work to do for Grace's surprise party, she needed to settle her thoughts before heading home. The children would be gone until late afternoon, and she could whip up the party in just a few hours after the children went to sleep.

Too tired to cross the street and avoid Mama's old house, she walked by it. Odd, but in the handful of times she'd passed by this house since leaving it in '32, she'd stayed on the opposite side of the street. This was the first time in years she walked close enough to touch it. And so she did.

Her heart ached at the touch, the rough texture of the bricks she knew so well, the earthy smell, its back gardens. The bricks scalded Agnes's hand, but she ignored the heat. So many years gone to her now. Virtually nothing remained from her life at this house. Daddy gone twenty-five years, Granny a dozen, Mama in Washington almost ten.

She clutched the walls, mourning what she'd lost. Maybe you had to lose everything before you could really grow up. Had she ever grown up, had she ever really made a hard decision on her own? Others had made decisions for her. There'd been Granny, Mama and Daddy, Norman, and especially Uncle Collin. But now she alone had to do it.

She felt Daddy's locket and Granny's handkerchief in her pocket. She'd forgotten they were there. But she pulled out the locket and looked at the pictures of her and the children. Norman's children. Her heart contracted again. No, if she were to leave Philadelphia, she needed to reconcile with her past — with Norman, Cristina, and even Brian — and mistakes she'd made along the way. The cruelty of leaving Mama without saying good-bye, her false accusations against Uncle Collin, deceiving Norman in their marriage. If she didn't reconcile all of this, doubt would nag her forever, wondering if she'd made the right choice to leave Philadelphia. If she failed at this, she'd never truly be free and independent.

She deliberated. Urgent questions popped into her head, questions about her parents, growing up here, being on her own, why she left this stately house, what had drawn her to Norman Balmoral, the Church, her faith in God. Did she believe? Did she understand anything anymore? Could she forgive and be forgiven? If she didn't seek forgiveness, the uncertainty would bind her to an intolerable tyranny.

Uncle Collin, her only remaining family in Philadelphia. A wave of love bubbled up from her heart and into her mind. He was the one person whose forgiveness she really wanted to seek. Finally, after procrastinating four years, she resolved to see him not in a month, not tomorrow, but today. No matter what words had passed between them, what pain he'd endured at her hands, she knew he'd help. It was two o'clock. Uncle Collin would be at St. Patrick's, in the church, the parish, or the rectory, preparing for late-afternoon prayers.

She kissed the bricks of her old house, breathed in its history, and said good-bye. From now on, only forward. The wind swooped up as she hurried past Independence Hall, and the sky began to darken in the west. She didn't care that ominous weather threatened from that side of town. The answers to her questions lay in that direction.

24

A GNES WALKED UP THE STEPS and entered the narthex of St. Patrick's. The doors were unlocked for afternoon prayers. Her achy feet throbbed, but she ignored them. She'd be facing Uncle Collin in mere seconds. She reached for the holy water and crossed herself, an instinctive ritual even after so many years away. She opened the door to the nave.

Uncle Collin stood at the altar facing her, his head bowed and eyes closed, making some customary prayer for guidance before preparing the altar. Her heart contracted as she got closer. She marveled at his tenacity, his white hair and black-framed glasses a constant presence in this parish. But he was aging like anyone else, his black robe and tunic wrapped a bit too tight around his waist.

The nave seemed smaller than she remembered. She'd never counted the pews, but surely there'd been more? Hadn't the pulpit stood higher from the nave? Eight stained-glass windows hugged the roofline, Christ on the cross, Mary and the infant Jesus, Lazarus rising from the dead, Jesus ascending the mount. An equal number of marble columns supported the building, the pulpit built into the front left column, the hymn calendar posted to the right. She recognized No. 168, "Amazing Grace."

She wondered why Uncle Collin didn't hear her but then remembered from one of Mama's letters that Uncle Collin's hearing had declined. Third pew left, she curtsied and kneeled to pray. In her scramble for a prayer, she grasped at three words — honesty, compassion, forgiveness. Let her be honest with Uncle Collin, she asked God, have compassion for those who'd wronged her and understanding for those she'd hurt.

"Agnes Mary, you surprise me." She looked up. Uncle Collin faced her from the altar. "Though I have prayed daily that you would come."

His bass, the same as always, melted her. She sat back in her pew and wept into her hands. Where did the sobs come from, now that she faced her uncle, the mentor who'd watched over her since Daddy died, the man she'd disappointed? Sitting here brought back a swirl of memories she couldn't cast away — Mama and Daddy sitting together in a pew, Granny Limerick's white lace and funeral, Norman sitting by her side at Gracie Honeywalker's, lunch with Cristina at the Reading Terminal, laughing with Brian at the piano, and sex with Norman. How she missed his body near hers, the touch of his soft, milky skin.

Uncle Collin stepped down from the altar, his face twisted and uncomfortable. "Child, please stop. We have much to talk about, and I've only got an hour."

She wiped her nose on her dress. "Uncle Collin, I'm so lost. And I'm so sorry for everything I've done. I alienated Mama years ago, I've lost my best friend, I made a wreck of my marriage, I've said cruel things to you—"

"Slow down, my dear. You must calm yourself before we speak. May I get you a glass of water?"

Uncle Collin returned a minute later and she gulped down the water. He sat beside her, his arms on the pew in front. "I've wanted to see you for a long time but I waited. You had to come here of your own free will."

"I've felt the same, Uncle Collin, but I didn't have the courage until today."

"Tell me how you've adjusted to being a widow. It is a year since your husband died?"

It'd be a year in another two weeks. She told Uncle Collin about her children, the offer to work in Washington, their trip to New York, Brian moving into the house —

"No, those are bare facts your mother already has mentioned. I want to know about you, on the inside," he said, pointing to his heart. "We know each other far too well to dance around banalities."

Agnes looked at him next to her in the pew. Older, a little slower in his movements, his fingers arthritic, his glasses thicker than she remembered. He leaned forward, caring in a way she hadn't thought possible after their hateful words. He'd obviously recovered from his anger, and a nine-year wall of silence certainly meant a lot of anger. But she'd also stayed on her side of that wall, though her anger had dissipated only weeks after that terrible Mother's Day.

"For the first time since Norman died, I realized that he's gone forever," Agnes said, determined to calm her shaky voice. "Something happened today, and I really felt his death. For the rest of my life, I have to live with the mistakes ..."

Did she want to make Uncle Collin privy to the battles behind the scenes? And she thought about her terrible sin, enjoying Norman's absence before he died, even smiling and laughing since. But she continued, "... mistakes we made in our marriage. And we never apologized to each other."

"Tell me about this."

Agnes felt a lump rise in her throat, but she stifled it. She spoke very slowly, nearly enunciating every syllable. "I'd rather not go into details, but Norman wanted us to live one way, and I wanted us to live another."

"I'm not surprised. Norman Balmoral—he was assertive, even demanding? The head of the household, his word was not to be disobeyed?"

She thought about Norman's edicts. Windows open at night, cold air throughout the house, no piano competition. And when she thought about the past twelve years, she never thought about lost opportunities that she'd sacrificed except where he was concerned. She said as much to Uncle Collin.

"Having an assertive husband would've been a blessing for you," he said, "but also a curse. It was always so eager to please you were, yet you had this rebellious streak that was impossible to tame. Your mother and I could never understand why you needed to rebel against those who loved you."

His words hurt, but as upset as she felt, it was her penance to listen.

"I'm going to say something very harsh, Agnes, before I say something kind. You must listen nonetheless. There was a reason your fornication with

Norman Balmoral constituted such a great sin. I'm not talking so much about the act. The real sin was that you obligated yourself to marry him without knowing him. Knowing if the two of you could accept your differences, if you even knew what they were at the time. The sacrament of marriage deserved better from you."

She thought back to that signal moment when Norman had taken her and her body shuddered. The fault lay just as much with her as it had with him. He'd resisted, at least at first, but she'd made the first move. No, it could not be that the responsibility lay at her feet, but yes, she had to be honest with herself.

Agnes felt her brain squeeze against her temples. "I'm overwhelmed. I need to excuse myself."

"I have more to say, niece—" but Agnes didn't wait. She ran out through the sacristy into the parish and down the hall to the office bathroom.

She began to hyperventilate. The black-and-white checkered tile frightened her, stark and simple, so unlike her life. She ran to the toilet, preparing to vomit. Her heart raced, her body shook, and she felt her stomach heavy with acid, but she didn't throw up. She paced and ended up in front of the mirror. Her heart still raced, and she still felt vomit symptoms, but nothing except painful memories arose in that frozen eternity.

It began with Norman when she saw him that first day so long ago, running in Independence Park, admiring his legs, his muscular physique—so odd, yet so appealing. Norman took great pride in his appearance, but only because he believed in perfection, in discipline, in being responsible. She tried to slow her heart rate for several minutes, but memories of Norman—their first day working together, that blue suit—kept her in a fever.

She'd been standing in front of a bathroom mirror like this one when he walked in on her and started telling her how to behave. Agnes replayed the scene word by word, gesture by gesture, as if it were occurring in front of her this very instant. And at the end of the scene, she recalled his quick strides away from her. Back to the work he loved better than anything, Norman the architect. In his last gift, he'd redesigned their house—their home together—for her.

And their life together as husband and wife ... she could admit now that he didn't know how to manage a headstrong, independent wife. And that's exactly what she was, headstrong and independent. But Norman had loved her enough to want to try again. She thought about what her response might've been had he come home and asked her, all the possibilities. Finally, as her heart rate began to fall and her tears dried on her face, she prayed that she'd have agreed to try.

Oh, how she missed this impossible man. She'd never feel his coarse warmth in bed again, walk by his side, play with their children together. Her eyes began to melt, but she squelched a second round of tears. She had a family and a new job in Washington waiting for her. She stared in the mirror, wondering how the little girl in pigtails who played Mozart minuets for Daddy had become a middle-aged widow with a splotchy house dress, smudged face, and wild red hair. Yes, she was sad that Norman had died, but somehow life would have to go on without him.

What a bedraggled appearance she made. She'd go home and finish preparing for Grace's party. Grace and Harold, at least she had that left from Norman. So she washed her face in the basin, straightened her hair and dress, and headed out to say good-bye to Uncle Collin.

He sat on the sofa in the front office. He'd taken off his robe and sat there in street clothes, not even a tie around his neck. She couldn't recall the last time she'd seen him without a clerical collar. Perhaps before she'd married Norman?

"I've asked Father Ryan to say prayers," he said. "I'll do two Masses tomorrow morning instead. Priests as old as I are allowed to have the occasional family crisis. Come sit by your uncle, Agnes."

She obeyed, but for the longest time, they said nothing. Agnes felt an odd sense of comfort in this placid moment. After all that had happened between them, how could she feel so contented? He had damned her the last time they'd spoken and even now he reiterated his belief that she'd sinned. Nothing had really changed, so why did she feel such peace in his presence?

Agnes began to squirm. "I want to tell you about Washington, Uncle Collin."

"All in good time. I apologize for upsetting you, but I warned you I would say something harsh before I—"

"Uncle Collin, there's no need. It's water under the bridge."

"—before I say something kind. What I have to say is that despite the risks you and Norman took, you were blessed with two very godly children. They are loved by many people—you, Norman, his family, your mother, even the ubiquitous Mr. Larney."

This was it, this was why she could feel secure with Uncle Collin even when he emitted the thunder of God. As fierce as his wrath could be, no other person on Earth could match the healing power of his blessings.

"It is clear to me that you and Norman did well as parents. And I'm certain you'll continue that by yourself until you marry another man—"

"I couldn't possibly marry again," she said, her body almost retching at the ghastly thought. "I'm sorry. I didn't mean to interrupt you."

"It is very much unlike you, so I will overlook it," he said and laughed. "It is also clear to me that you and Norman had a difficult time accepting each other's differences. Is that correct?"

"Yes, we never made peace with each other, and it's too late now."

"That's untrue, at least for you. It's never too late to achieve the state of grace that is essential for all who deliver themselves freely to God. You can forgive your husband truly and pray that he forgives you from heaven above."

His preaching on occasion had bored Agnes, but today it warmed her heart.

"Agnes, I'm going to tell you a story I think will resonate with you. And you know the participants. It involves your father and your piano teacher."

She cocked her head at the mention of Brian and Daddy.

"Did you know that Mr. Larney has a long history with our family?"

"Of course. He's been my piano teacher since I was six."

"No, it goes back several years before you were born. He was a young man, barely twenty, when your father treated him at the Pennsylvania Hospital. He'd been attacked at Broad Street Station on his way back from New York City. Witnesses said three young men followed him off the train, hurled vicious insults at him, and clubbed him just outside the depot. They ran off and left him for dead. But Martin treated him at the hospital and saved his life."

Agnes winced—Brian, as a young man, viciously attacked. She'd never known, nor had she known her father saved Brian's life. So that's what youth was like for Brian—because he was different, because he was attracted to men. For so many years, Brian had been alone in the world except for his students and the pedantic Mrs. O'Toole. It enraged her to think about the brutality.

"Martin did much more than simply treat Mr. Larney's wounds. He visited him daily for months. When Mr. Larney recovered, he invited him to the house, introduced him to your mother and grandmother, and brought him here to St. Patrick's. They became very good friends, enough so that a few parishioners became alarmed and asked me to intervene. But I refused."

His words enthralled her. Not since Granny died had anyone spoken anything so real to her about Daddy. Brian certainly had never said anything.

"Your father didn't judge Mr. Larney. He cared for people exactly as they were, and he especially valued Mr. Larney. Through the years, I often have reflected on the meaning of their friendship . . ."

His words trailed off, as if unsure of how to proceed. "I concluded that Martin and Mr. Larney had a friendship that embodied the best of all Christian values, the grace to love another human being exactly as God created him, without judgment, with full acceptance.

"Martin arranged for a reconciliation between Mr. Larney and his mother. He found him a home with Mrs. O'Toole where your grandparents had lived. He persuaded parishioners to send their children to him for piano lessons—and sent you too. That decision gave you the greatest happiness of your life."

Tears edged their way out of her eyes' corners, but they were happy ones. Her father had loved Brian just as she did—as a friend who valued his unique qualities. A friendship that transcended sex and romance, and yes, a friendship that could be expressed now and then with a kiss as soft as a profiterole.

"Grace without judgment, grace with full acceptance. I urge you, Agnes, to reconsider your husband's life. Celebrate him as he was, cherish his qualities as your father did with Mr. Larney. In the final analysis, what matters most of all is our journey to grace. Trust in that journey, my dear."

Had she judged Norman, had she failed to accept him?

Daddy wouldn't have done this.

My father never would have treated Mama like this, Norman.

Why can't you be more generous to your family like Daddy was?

These bitter words had made their mark. She said a silent prayer of contrition and asked Norman to forgive her. He had sinned — as had Cristina — but so had she. What right had she to judge them?

"To err is human, to forgive divine," she quoted, tears of understanding trickling down her face. "Bless you, Uncle Collin. It's to my dying day I'll be remembering this."

"I'm relieved to hear this tone in your voice. I worried for years that your marriage would bring you endless heartache. You're too imaginative to obey anyone, let alone a husband. But you must live your own life. My only hope has been that whatever you do, you do the thing you love best."

Who'd said that? She felt a breath of nervous air in her throat. Ah, yes, Granny. *Do the thing you love best, and all good things shall follow.*

"Thank you." She reached over and kissed him on the cheek, just as she'd done as a little girl. The time had come. "Uncle Collin, I said some terrible things the last time we spoke. I've regretted it ever since. Will you forgive me —"

He raised his hand. "Child, you were always my favorite niece — yes, even if you were my only niece. Those remarks caused me great pain. But I do forgive you. You might've borne false witness against me, but I did the same with you. So I ask you to forgive me too."

❧

She emerged from the rectory to dark clouds clashing. The wind had died down, the air still, as if waiting for something to happen. When she turned onto 19th Street, the sky opened up and a maelstrom poured into the streets of Philadelphia. The downpour soaked Agnes. Her shoes squished in the pools of water on the sidewalk, and her hair clung to the sides of her head. The rain poured down her face. It cleansed her of the dust, grime, and perspiration she'd collected during the day. Late-afternoon shoppers scrambling for cover stared at her. She didn't care.

And then a thunderclap frightened her, so she ran for cover at her reliable favorite, Longacre's Instruments and Music.

Mr. Longacre and two pointy-glassed assistants Agnes didn't recognize were making a cackle with stacks of papers. She'd always felt at home here, never more so than now. It'd be the best of all possible places to wait out the storm.

"Good afternoon, Agnes. A little wet outside, wouldn't you say?" Mr. Longacre said, a little more disheveled than usual. His shirttails fell over his slacks, and he didn't wear a tie. He seemed distracted, even harangued.

"May I use the ladies' room? I've been outside most of the afternoon."

"In this weather?"

"I had errands," she lied, but knew he'd see through it. After all, she had no shopping bags. "May I?"

"Of course, you know where it is."

Ten minutes later Agnes emerged from the bathroom. She looked into the back office as she walked by. No organization, stacks of papers and music scattered all over Mr. Longacre's desk, surrounded by pens, notepads, folders, even napkins and empty bottles of Coca-Cola. Good Lord, if this were her office, she'd whip it into shape in an hour.

"We're doing inventory in advance of the sale," Mr. Longacre said as he squeezed by her with another stack. "So it's a bit cluttered right now."

"Are you having a sale?" She made a mental note to stock up on Schumann and Debussy before they moved to Washington.

"Not as you think." He plopped the papers on his desk and sat down. "I'm selling the store. Mrs. Longacre's had enough of cold Philadelphia winters and insists we move to Florida."

Nothing sounded more revolting. Leave Philadelphia for Florida, a state with wild alligators, mosquitoes, and humidity that made this afternoon feel like a spring breeze? Why would anyone do such a thing?

"We'll be moving to Miami Beach some time before Christmas. We'd like to sell the music, instruments, and the store before we go."

"Oh, no! I cannot imagine Rittenhouse Square without this store."

"I'm not thrilled by the notion, but it's the best decision for us. We're tired, and we want to stop working, especially since Normandy."

She looked into his eyes, fatigued and sad, and knew the true reason for their leaving. Their only son had been killed on D-Day.

"Everyone's so busy and has something to do these days," he said. "I don't expect to find a buyer, so we'll probably close down. Even if we don't sell, we're moving away."

The thought sickened her — a whole lifetime of memories for hundreds of Philadelphians, anyone who loved music, anyone who sang or played, all gone in a flash. She sat down in the chair opposite him. "But the store's a Philadelphia institution. What would we ever do without it? It's far too valuable to let it go so quickly."

"The store's of limited value, I'm afraid."

"How can you possibly put a price on your life's work?"

While she waited for him to answer, she noticed the change in him since those happy years before depression or war. His chin sagged almost onto his chest, his eyelids drooped, and he'd lost nearly all his hair. "These days, very easily. The piano music and inventory are quite valuable — the pianos well over $8,000, the music almost as much, another $10,000 for the site itself."

They exchanged small talk a few minutes longer, but Agnes had lost her appetite for conversation. Longacre's Music and Instruments would be closing. It made no sense, as if the William Penn statue had gotten tired of City Hall and decided to sit on a lounge chair under a palm tree in Miami Beach. She peeked out the office door and looked out the window. The rain had stopped.

"Thank you, Mr. Longacre," she said. "I'll make sure Brian's students come to buy music before you close."

She walked outside to the smell of wet grass, leaves, and trees coming from the square. Two thoughts jumped at each other in her head — the sale of Longacre's Music and Instruments and her widow's pension. Could she buy the store herself?

❧

A tantalizing mist swam through the air. Her shoes might squeak and slosh on the sidewalks, but her mind was abuzz with the refrain, *I could do it.* She sat down on a wet bench in the middle of Rittenhouse Square. The park's trees and bushes drooped from the weight of the sudden storm, casting a vibrant dark green all the way across the square as only an afternoon summer storm could do. It was the loveliest sight she'd ever seen.

Her mind raced on ahead. She'd already decided to move to Washington, but why? Of course, security for the children. But she had all the security she needed right here, her family and her home. And that included Brian, her father's best friend—her own, really—as well as Victoria, the other merry widow of Balmoral. Brian Larney and Victoria Balmoral, opposite sides of the same coin.

If she weren't leaving Philadelphia for security, then why would she leave? Oh yes, Cristina and her affair with Norman. "Why in the hell should I leave my home because of Cristina and Norman?" she said, no one to hear.

If she left home because Norman had lied about his relationship with Cristina, she'd be allowing someone else—yet again—to chart her life's path. No.

She enjoyed her job at the War Department and her friendship with Dr. Friedman. And she certainly did well at it, enough to catch President Roosevelt's eye. But she imagined doing it for the rest of her life, all day, six days every week, and cringed. She liked what she did there, but she didn't love it.

Her mind went back to Macy's, Grace and Harold turning the store upside down trying to find piano music because what they most wanted for Christmas was to see their mother smiling again. She and Norman certainly had created two little geniuses. They knew what she loved best, better than she did herself.

Her heart danced as the certainty filled her. "Music has always been my life."

Life offered no guarantees and owed her nothing. She knew very well that nearly everyone she loved had moved on—Norman, Daddy, and Granny to the grave, Mama to Washington, Uncle Collin and Cristina with their own lives—and she'd moved on. Sadness might have shaken her to the core that day like the mournful slow movement from Mozart's 23rd piano concerto, but now happiness surrounded her with a cool glow.

She stood up and straightened her posture. She would buy Longacre's Music and Instruments. She had no idea how they'd manage, but do it she would. Her mind was made up. And she'd made the decision all by herself.

Agnes burst into the house only a few minutes later to the smell of roast chicken, carrots, onions, and potatoes, the hallmarks of one of Victoria's special meals. She heard Brian's lyrical playing of the Chopin *Fantasie* float in from the music room. Taking off her shoes as Keaton plodded down the hallway to greet her, his tail wagging and tongue lapping at her, she looked about her, the house all ordered, boxes put away. Victoria and Brian must've finished the job she'd abandoned. She walked into the parlor. Grace sprawled herself on the sofa reading *Little Women,* and Harold sat on the floor building a Lincoln Logs house. Her chipmunks.

Her daughter, how beautiful Grace was, her hair long and flowing onto her face with Norman's cheeks and dimple, her newly spectacled eyes sparkling and intent on the book, her knees up in front of her. Agnes could see her as an adult. She would have a career, something with words, sentences, and paragraphs, and excel at it. But for the few years she had before surrendering to adulthood, Grace could be a child, the girl who cocked her head at the world, scrunched up her eyebrows, and said *why not?*

And her son with his blond cowlicks, his fine hands with thin fingers, and his utter concentration on buildings and love for machines, how could he be anything other than a great architect like his father? But no, she couldn't plan their lives. If anyone knew a mother had no business orchestrating a child's life, she did. But how could she not want the best for her darling chipmunks?

Grace looked up first. "Mama, you're soaking wet. Where've you been?"

"Mama, Elliott Johnston has a new puppy dog who's the best ever," Harold said. "Please, can we get our own puppy for Keaton?"

She patted their dog's head and kissed him on the nose. "Let's ask Keaton himself. Keaton, what do you think of another dog?"

Victoria walked in, her apron wearing the evidence of dinner preparations.

"Where have you been? Brian and I worried ourselves to death this afternoon. And look at you. Caught in the storm, I see. Serves you right." Though Victoria scolded her, her eyes laughed.

Agnes smiled back. "I've had quite an afternoon. I want to tell you all about it, but it can wait until I've cleaned up."

"Dinner will be ready in twenty minutes."

"Would you tell Brian? I'm going upstairs to change."

She heard Victoria's footsteps lead to the music room, where Brian had launched into Chopin's *Grande Valse Brillante*, but she didn't hurry up the stairs.

She kneeled to the floor and started helping Harold with his house. Her dress might soil the Oriental rug, but that didn't matter. She wanted to remember this moment for the rest of her life.

Grace buried her head back into *Little Women*. Perhaps one day her daughter might become a writer just like Jo March, for Grace imagined all sorts of creative things and loved anything artistic, be it music or ballet. Harold absorbed himself in his house, just like Norman would've done. After a minute, she stood and opened the windows. A cool breeze flowed in.

Good Lord! Grace's birthday party and she hadn't done a thing except a little dusting. Well, she'd check with her miracle workers and see what needed to be done. If she had to stay up until four to finish, she'd do it.

She went upstairs to change for dinner. Agnes wondered how the future might unfold as she looked about her bedroom. She'd rename the store Limerick's Music. She'd walk her dogs every morning, greet customers, balance the books, order music, sell instruments. Victoria and Brian would be there too. It might be rough in the beginning, but they'd survive, her family of five. How could it be otherwise if she did the thing she loved best?

She could see herself at Brian's recitals, playing alongside children decades younger. They'd visit Mama in Washington, and she'd finally make an effort with her brother, whoever he might be. She'd invite Uncle Collin for Victoria's Friday fish dinners. And Cristina—perhaps she might forgive her one day.

After the children grew up, she'd travel. She'd walk the pebbled streets of Europe—yes, she'd even visit Florence. She'd wind through the jungle paths of Southeast Asia and the craggy hills above the Golden Gate Bridge. But she'd never lose sight of home. Yes, life would turn out differently than she planned—but she'd always have Philadelphia and this house.

Agnes undressed and washed her face, arms, and hands in the basin. She surveyed the closet and almost chose the white dress she'd worn to Norman's funeral, but no, too depressing. She needed to pack that dress away, forever. So she put on a pale-blue frock and headed down to the dining room.

Victoria sat at the far end of the table in what had been Norman's place. The children sat opposite each other, Brian next to Grace. They were talking ballet but stopped when she took her seat at the head of the table.

Victoria met her eye. "Here's the cat who ate the canary. You have a decision, that's plain as day."

"Family, we're staying in Philadelphia. This is our home."

Sighs of relief and clapping hands broke out around the table.

"Thanks be to God!" Brian made a sign of the cross.

Victoria clutched Brian's hand. "Yes, Brian, thanks be to God."

Grace sprouted the widest smile and most dancing eyes Agnes ever had seen, and her voice danced a happy minuet. "Does this mean we'll stay at Friends? What about Saturday ballet?"

"All that stays the same, Grace, but some other things will be changing around here." She looked at Brian and his sixty-year-old hands, veiny and muscular from a life at the piano. Such caring hands, so like Daddy's — Brian, a connection to Martin Limerick, right here at home. His home too.

"I'm resigning from the War Department on Monday. We're buying Longacre's Music and Instruments."

They looked at each other, mouths and eyes wide open. No one said a word.

"The Longacres are retiring to Florida, and I'm buying their store. They don't know it, but I'm marching in there Monday morning and offering to buy it at full price, because it's worth every penny. Brian, I'll need your help with the music and the instruments. Victoria, you'll help me run the business — that is, if you would like to."

Victoria spoke first. "How exciting, my dear! I'm thrilled. But will we have enough money? We'll spend a small fortune for a store."

"That's where your good head for business will come in, Victoria. It might be difficult at the beginning, but we'll do just fine. How can it be otherwise when you do the thing you love best?"

"What an adventure for Miss Killer Thumbs and her family," Brian chimed in, clapping his hands, leaning down to Grace, and playing nosies. "Center City's only music store. Think of the recitals, the concerts, the lectures from visiting musicians. We can bring music to every corner of our city if we like."

Agnes clasped her hands and looked around the table, the one she and Norman had brought into this house, now hers. She looked at her daughter, happy again with her books and dolls, growing up faster than Agnes could've imagined. She peered across the table at Harold, her little gentleman, just as smart and passionate as his father. Her eyes met Victoria's, and she felt the spark of life that had returned to them. And finally she rested her gaze on Brian—the last, essential link who made this family whole again.

"We do like, but first let's eat this wonderful meal. You've outdone yourself again, Victoria. It's going to be an enchanting life, the five of us. Brian, would you say grace?"

MUSICAL REPERTOIRE

Johann Sebastian Bach
Cantata in G Major, B.W.V. 147, "Jesu, Joy of Man's Desiring"
Invention in B Minor, B.W.V. 786

Samuel Barber
Piano Suite in C Minor, Opus 20, the *Excursions*

Ludwig van Beethoven
Piano Sonata No. 8 in C Minor, Opus 13, the *Pathetique*
Piano Sonata No. 14 in C-sharp Minor, Opus 27 No. 2, the *Moonlight*
Piano Sonata No. 21 in C Major, Opus 53, the *Waldstein*
Piano Sonata No. 23 in F Minor, Opus 57, the *Appassionata*
Piano Sonata No. 26 in E-flat Major, Opus 81 No. I, *Les Adieux*
Piano Sonata No. 30 in E Major, Opus 109, the *Brentano*
Piano Sonata No. 31 in A-flat Major, Opus 110
Piano Sonata No. 32 in C Minor, Opus 111
Symphony No. 3 in E-flat Major, Opus 55, the *Eroica*
Symphony No. 5 in C Minor, Opus 67

Johannes Brahms
Piano Sonata No. 3 in F Minor, Opus 5

Frédéric Chopin
Fantasie in F Minor, Opus 49
Grande Valse Brillante in E-flat Major, Opus 18
Nocturne in B-flat Minor, Opus 9 No. I
Piano Sonata No. 2 in B-flat Minor, Opus 35, the *Funeral March*

Claude Debussy
Arabesque No. I in A Major, L. 66
L'isle Joyeuse in A Major, L. 106
Suite Bergamasque in D-flat Major, third movement, "Claire de Lune"

Edward Elgar
Variations on an Original Theme in E-flat Major, Opus 36, the *Enigma Variations*

George Gershwin
Concerto in F Major
"I Got Rhythm"
Rhapsody in Blue

Felix Mendelssohn
Symphony No. 4 in A Major, Opus 90, the *Italian Symphony*

Wolfgang Amadeus Mozart
Piano Concerto No. 23 in A Major, K. 488
Piano Concerto No. 24 in C Minor, K. 491
Piano Sonata No. 11 in A Major, K. 331
Serenade No. 13 for Strings in G Major, K. 525, *Eine Kleine Nachtmusik*
Symphony No. 40 in G Minor, K. 550
Twelve Variations in C Major, K. 265, *Ah, vous dirai-je, Maman*

Sergei Prokofiev
Piano Sonata No. 4 in C Minor, Opus 29

Franz Schubert
Impromptu in E-flat Major, Opus 90 No. 2
Piano Sonata in B-flat Major, Opus Posthumous, D. 960 No. 3

Pyotr Tschaikovsky
The Nutcracker Suite, Opus 71

Frederic Weatherly
"Danny Boy," after the "Londonderry Air" by Jane Ross

ACKNOWLEDGMENTS

It all started at The Writing Salon in San Francisco, headed by the estimable Jane Underwood with creative writing teachers such as Karen Bjorneby, Chris de Lorenzo, and Pamela Weymouth. Without their nurturing support, I never would have gotten so far as a first chapter, let alone a completed manuscript.

Karen Bjorneby, in particular, served as the project's mentor from its inception all the way to its conclusion. She provided guidance, wisdom, and her own experiences as an accomplished writer to point my novice pen in the right direction. Ultimately, she also performed a comprehensive editing of this novel. The imprint of her literary critique can be found on every page of this book.

Peers on both coasts workshopped the novel, and I'm thankful for their critiques and camaraderie: Brian Crawford, Emily Dreyfuss, Mera Granberg, Carol Jauch, Ellen LaPointe, Dave Lenoe, Linda Lucero, Kat Meltzer, Cheryl Ossola, Hillary Read, Robin Silverman, and Thaai Walker in San Francisco; Anne Doten, Sabin Hinton, Adam Jacobson, Kate Newton, and Stephen Sears in South Florida.

I am grateful for the diligent work of Peter Atherton, who edited the final draft, allowing me to publish a gaffe-free novel. I'd like to thank Judy and Bruce Borich of Middle River Press, as well as their proofreader, Susan Bryant, who brought the first edition's publication to life, and Dean Trantalis, Esq., who represented the novel's interests.

Several close friends, including Jim Slagle, Ralph Zitterbart, and the late Mark Havers, read the novel in full and provided valuable feedback. Mark, who reached adulthood only a decade after Agnes, said that once having read the novel, he'd never look at a kitchen table in quite the same way.

Finally, I want to thank my spouse, Mike Girard, for putting up with my impossible ways during the endless hours I worked on this project. I have time for you and the pets now, sweetheart.

Photographic Acknowledgments

Cover. Independence Hall, 5th and Chestnut, 1921
1. Rittenhouse Square, 18th and Walnut, 1935
2. The Reading Terminal Market, 13th and Market, 1912, by the Free Library of Philadelphia, Print and Picture Collection
3. The P.S.F.S. Building, 12th and Market, 1962
4. Society Hill mansion, 4th and Locust, 1938
5. Home at 36th and Hamilton, 1963
6. The Stanley Theatre, 19th and Market, 1935
7. St. Mark's Church, 17th and Locust, 1931
8. University of Pennsylvania campus, 36th and Woodland, 1939
9. The Italian Market, 9th and Montrose, 1954
10. Scullers on the Schuylkill River, Kelly Drive, 1984
11. Nathaniel White farmhouse, Goshen, New York, 2011, by Tim Murray *(piggyfork)*
12. The Pennsylvania Hospital, 8th and Spruce, 1960
13. Spruce Street brownstones, 19th and Spruce, 1950
14. The Bellevue-Stratford Hotel, Broad and Walnut, 1966
15. University of Pennsylvania Hospital, 39th and Woodland, 1952
16. The Academy of Music, Broad and Locust, 1916
17. City Hall, Broad and Market, 1936
18. Juniper and Locust mansions, 13th and Locust, 1917
19. 30th Street Station and Chestnut Street Bridge, 30th and Chestnut, 1956
20. Pennsylvania Lumberman's Building, Broad and Walnut, 1917
21. Pennsylvania Railroad Bridge over Kelly Drive, 1914
22. F.D.R. at wartime, The White House, 1943, by the U.S. Library of Congress
23. Rittenhouse Square East, 18th and Locust, 1959
24. Rittenhouse Square, 18th and Walnut, 1934

Except as noted above, the photographs were provided by PhillyHistory.org, a project of the Philadelphia Department of Records.

Thank You

ABOUT THE AUTHOR

James McKean Wood is a software engineer who received his Bachelor of Science in Applied Mathematics and Computer Science from Carnegie-Mellon University in 1984 and his Master of Science in Computer Science from the University of Pennsylvania in 1988. He has previously worked for Siemens Corporation and Google, Inc. and is presently employed by the Ultimate Software Group, Inc. in Weston, Florida. He was trained as a classical pianist by Margaret Groninger and Ralph Zitterbart of Pittsburgh, Pennsylvania, and in creative writing by Ms. Karen Bjorneby of San Francisco, California.

He lives in east Fort Lauderdale, Florida, with his spouse, Mike Girard, and their pet dog Chester, cats Agnes and Patrick, and parrot Dudley.

www.jamesmckeanwood.com